# A SINGLE OBSESSION

Books by Rachel Knowles

Available from Sandsfoot Publishing:

The Merry Romances
*A Perfect Match* (Book 1)
*A Reason for Romance* (Book 2)
*A Single Obsession* (Book 3)
*A Misguided Devotion* (Book 4)

Women of Weymouth
*Miss Harding's Hope: A Christmas Regency Romance*
*Miss Vincent's Vow* (Book 1)

Multi-author Series
*Engaging Miss Shaw* (Hearts of the Hall)
*The Disappointed Daughter* (Cousins of Cavendish Square)

Available from Pen & Sword History
*What Regency Women Did For Us*

# A SINGLE OBSESSION

THE MERRY ROMANCES 3

## RACHEL KNOWLES

Sandsfoot Publishing

ISBN (eBook): 978-1-910883-09-9

ISBN (Print): 978-1-910883-10-5

Cover design by Miblart

Published by Sandsfoot Publishing, an imprint of Writecombination Ltd, 28, Sunnyside Road, Weymouth, Dorset. DT4 9BL

For Andrew, the love of my life

*The truth hit me with the force of
a mail coach...*

*I* wanted *to marry Andrew.*

# Eliza Merry's Family Tree

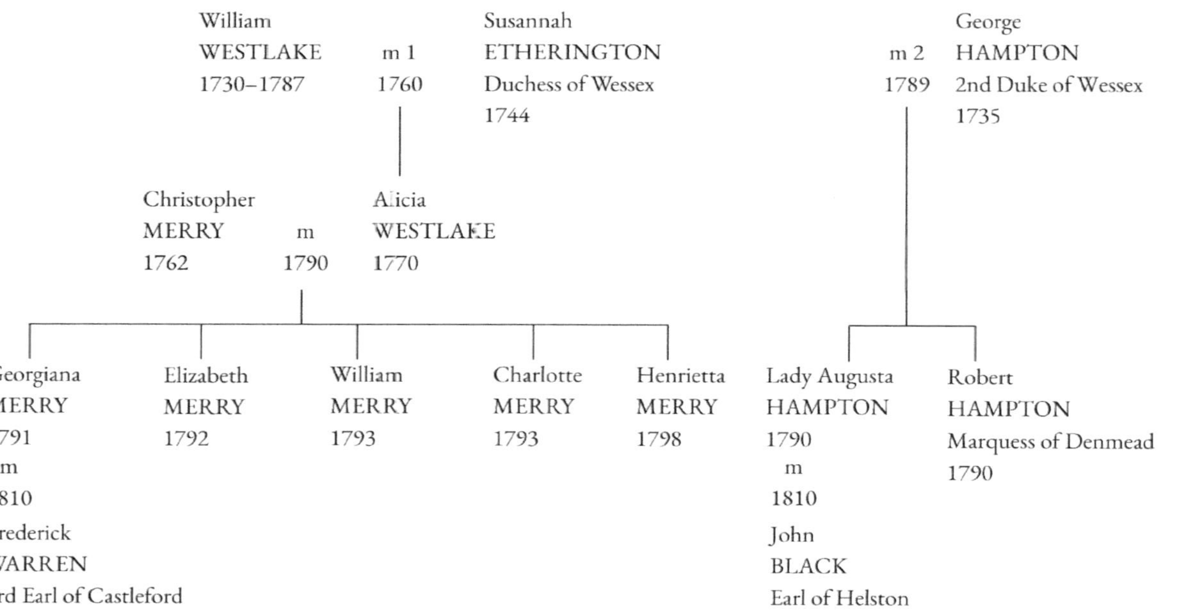

# Beau's Family Tree

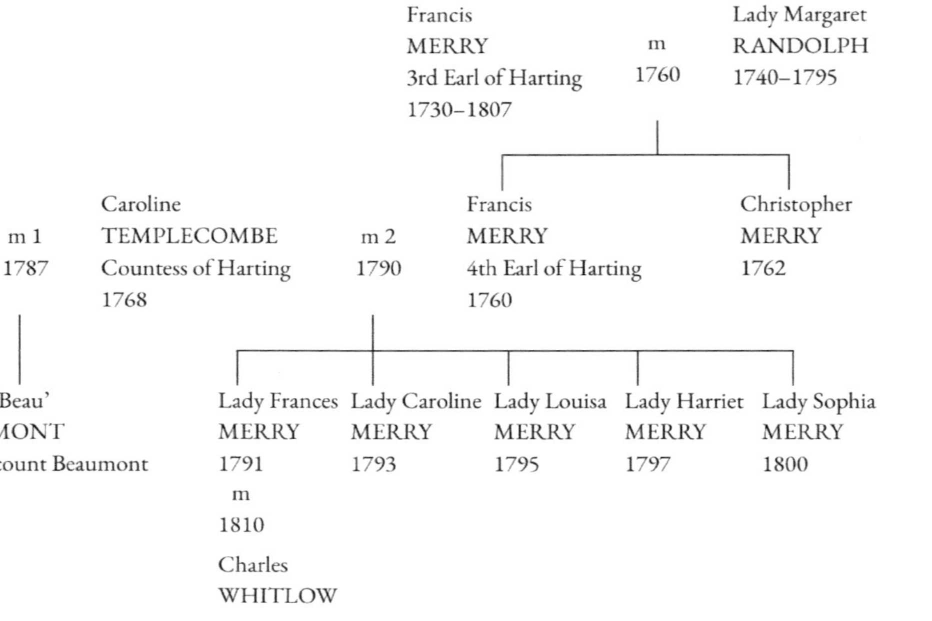


Key: m = married

# Chapter 1

## WEST MEON, HAMPSHIRE,
## JANUARY 1811

ELIZA MERRY'S EYES GLOWED with excitement as she put her foot in the stirrup and swung herself into the saddle. Finch glowered at her, but she paid no heed.

Why should she change her mind because her groom disapproved of her joining the hunt dressed like a man? This was her last chance to escape from her skirts before the trials of the London season, and she intended to make the most of it.

Finch let out a frustrated huff as he made ready to accompany her. "There's still time to go home, Miss Eliza."

"Feel free," she said, throwing him a saucy smile before urging her mount into a trot.

She soon caught up with her brother, who brought up the rear of the hunt. William gave her a welcoming grin, and they rode on side by side. The hunting party was too used to her brother's friend Robson to question her presence. As long as she did nothing to draw attention to herself, no one would recognise her.

Eliza inhaled deeply, and a contented smile spread across her face. She refused to let Finch's disapproval dampen her mood. He might be her most trusted servant, but that didn't give him the right to dictate her actions.

Though it was a barren time of year, being outdoors, whatever the weather, always made her feel more alive. The air was crisp, and the last remnants of the frost glistened on the grass that wouldn't resume growing for several more weeks. The trees were bare of leaves, but small clumps of evergreens provided bursts of colour, as did the occasional daffodil, poking its head up through the hard earth with the promise that winter would not last forever.

It was impossible not to feel cheerful, surrounded by such beauty, as she rode across the fields on the back of a splendid horse without having to worry about being reprimanded for not behaving in a ladylike manner.

After they had been riding for some time, the hunt led them through a field edged by a boundary wall, which Eliza judged to be about five feet high. Most of the hunting party were taking a long detour up the field to where a groom held open a gate.

All except two. Two men had not altered their path and were advancing toward the wall.

Eliza was too far behind to make out who they were, but even from this distance, she could tell their mounts were magnificent beasts.

She watched in admiration as the first rider chivvied his black hunter into a canter and headed straight for the wall. As he approached it, he shortened his horse's stride and with little effort, he cleared the brick barricade with room to spare.

The second rider followed suit, taking the wall at the same place, though with less clearance.

Dare she copy them or was it too great a risk? She knew the ground was even on the far side, having ridden over this land many times before, but she was not as confident of her mount. Although the grey hunter she rode would have no problem navigating the obstacle, he was a more powerful animal than she was used to. All would be well—provided she could control him, so he didn't rush the jump.

If she had been riding her own mare, she would not have hesitated. However, she rarely had the chance to ride Whisper astride, and never in the hunt, because her horse would give away her identity, no matter how well she was disguised.

Excitement bubbled up inside her at the thought of flying through the air, even for a moment. The idea was too tempting. She glanced around for Finch. Good. Her groom was too far away to stop her. No doubt he would give her a lecture afterward, but she had made up her mind. She was going to jump.

She was about to break into a canter before Finch guessed what she planned to do when William came racing past her. Eliza tensed. He was going too fast. Sure enough, his horse struggled to get his strides right, and her breath hitched as his mount's rear legs clipped the top of the wall.

With a shake of her head, she muttered to herself. How could her brother be so careless as to rush the jump? He was fortunate to have made it over at all. She would show him how it should be done.

Eliza urged her horse to increase his pace and headed for the boundary. Steady now. She needed to keep him in check, so he didn't approach the barricade too fast. Using all her strength, she controlled the animal's excitement, and they flew over the wall with ease. They landed safely on the other side, and with a sigh of relief, she brought her mount to a standstill.

Feeling rather pleased with herself, Eliza bent low over the horse's neck, stroking his mane and whispering words of praise. As she turned to her brother, ready to gloat about how superior her jump was to his, she realised William was not the only huntsman waiting for her.

The riders who had cleared the wall in front of them were beside him, and they were looking straight at her. The sight of them made her heart stand still, because she was no longer in any doubt who they were.

Two gentlemen she knew.

And not just any gentlemen. One was her sister Georgiana's brother-in-law, Anthony Warren. The other was his best friend Beau—the Viscount Beaumont—the man she had been in love with for the past three years.

What was he doing here? He was supposed to be in Newmarket. She had not seen him for months—not since her sister's wedding—and this was not how she had pictured meeting him again. Dressed as a man.

Would he recognise her? Experience had taught her that people saw what they expected to see. No one expected to see the rector's daughter masquerading as a man—and so they didn't. However, she did not trust her disguise to hold up under scrutiny. Although she had pulled this rig many times, she had always avoided being singled out before. It had been a mistake to jump the wall and draw attention to herself.

Eliza panicked. How could she have been so foolish? What if Beau recognised her and was scandalised by her behaviour? Despite harbouring a hope that he would be amused rather than shocked, she wasn't ready to put it to the test. Not before she'd had a chance to win his heart.

Whatever was she going to do? Ride away as fast as she could or brave it out?

Before she could choose, Beau rode forward, taking the decision out of her hands.

"That was magnificent. He's a big horse for such a whipper-snapper like yourself to manage, but you did it with style."

Eliza leaned forward to ruffle her horse's mane as heat flooded her face. "Thank you, my lord."

She inhaled deeply and let out the breath slowly. Then again. And again. If she did not stay calm, she would give herself away, and her reputation would be ruined.

As the warmth in her cheeks faded, Eliza risked sitting up in the saddle. It was a relief to find Beau was no longer looking at her. His gaze was fixed on two riders who had veered off from the rest of the hunting party and were heading toward them.

One was Finch, coming to reprimand her for taking the jump. The other sat in his saddle with the elegance of a sack of potatoes. How on earth could the man hunt with such a bad seat? As he drew closer, she recognised Mr Whitlow, her cousin Frances's husband.

Before Mr Whitlow could reach them, Beau chivvied his horse into a canter, calling over his shoulder to Anthony to follow. Eliza let out a huge sigh of relief as Beau rode away. It was gratifying to hear him praise her horsemanship, but it was far too dangerous.

She withdrew her gaze from Beau's retreating form and realised Anthony had not moved. He was staring right at her. She dared not breathe. Had he penetrated her disguise?

After a long moment, he nodded, and sped away after Beau, and Mr Whitlow altered his path to follow them.

Eliza released the breath she had been holding and braced herself for Finch's displeasure. What made it worse was she knew it was justified. How could she have guessed that Beau and Anthony were riding with the hunt today? If she had known, she would not have risked the masquerade, let alone the jump.

Finch rode straight up to her brother, his eyes blazing with anger.

"Of all the cork-brained things to do. I suppose it never occurred to you that you might not make it over the wall in one piece. As for you," he snarled, looking her in the eye, "words fail me."

Eliza tossed her head in defiance and rode off. She refused to admit that, on this occasion, he was correct.

She had not gone far before Finch and William caught up with her. Her groom took up a position on her left flank whilst her brother drew his horse alongside her on the right.

"Sorry. Finch's orders. For your protection."

Eliza pursed her lips and refused to answer, but inside, she screamed with vexation. Even in male garb, her freedom was curtailed.

Unbidden, some of her mother's favourite words floated into her mind. *Be thankful, Eliza Merry. That is God's will for you.*

Why should Finch's protectiveness stop her from enjoying what remained of the hunt? She wouldn't let it. Biting back her irritation at her almost military escort, she determined to be thankful and make the best of the situation.

It wasn't that hard. The sun shone, and she sat astride a fine horse, unencumbered by her skirts. And despite the unnerving nature of her encounter with Beau, he had praised her riding.

As long as no one penetrated her disguise, all would be well.

The light was fading by the time the wily fox went to ground, and the hunt drew to a close. Eliza was wearier than she cared to admit and had to resist the temptation to slump in her saddle. When Beau rode up to join them, she had reason to be thankful for her groom's highhandedness. Neither Finch nor her brother made room for him, so he had to fall back alongside Mr Whitlow.

Eliza could not help overhearing their conversation.

"You would not think such a young fellow would risk his neck going over that wall," Mr Whitlow said, presumably nodding in her direction. "But no. You would lead them on."

Her hackles rose in Beau's defence.

"I didn't ask anyone to copy me," the Viscount said in a measured tone that suggested he was trying to restrain his irritation.

"All the same, you could not resist the wall, despite what befell your father."

"What do you know of that? It occurred when we were both still in leading-strings."

"My wife has told me all about it. Given what happened to him, I thought you, of all people, would be more cautious. You were reckless to take such a risk. Absolutely reckless. You should follow my example and marry and produce an heir. It is the responsibility..."

"Time to go," said William, as Beau's prosy brother-in-law continued to deliver his diatribe.

Without waiting for a response, her brother veered off to the left and increased his speed as he headed for a track through the trees. Eliza set off behind him, with Finch at her side. She was not sorry the day's adventure was over, and was surprised to find herself longing for the protection of her petticoats.

They followed the trail through the woods until they reached a clearing near the end of the parsonage garden. After drawing her horse to a stop, she slipped to the ground and passed the reins to Finch, urging her brother to hurry and fetch Charlotte to bring her clothes.

She stood fidgeting for what seemed like an age before William's twin appeared, carrying a large cloak bag, which she dropped at Eliza's feet.

Charlotte's brow was creased with worry. "I'm so glad to see you're still in one piece. You were gone so long, I was certain your horse must have thrown you. Please hurry."

"I'm sorry, but the fox just ran and ran."

"If I have to listen to you speak about foxes—"

Eliza unbuttoned her jacket and tore it off, followed by her neckcloth, waistcoat, and shirt. "No more talk of foxes, I promise." She yanked a rather creased gown from the cloak bag and slipped it over her head, pulling it down to cover her breeches and hide William's old boots from sight.

"I don't know why I agreed to do this," Charlotte muttered as she did up Eliza's buttons. "I should have told Father."

Eliza twisted around to face her sister. "You wouldn't?"

After a long moment, Charlotte spoke. "No, I would not, though maybe I should. I was so scared you would be discovered, and if you were, your reputation would be in tatters. I wish you wouldn't take risks like this. You can imagine how horrified I was when I learned Anthony and Beau were in Hampshire and were joining the hunt. Did you see them?"

Eliza dared not admit how close she had come to being found out today. It would only make Charlotte worry. "Yes—but I'm sure Beau didn't recognise me."

"That's a relief. What about Anthony? Not that I would fret over him. If he saw through your disguise, he would laugh it off as a joke. Everything's amusing to him. But Beau was surprised you missed seeing the hunt off, so he's bound to ask you at dinner—"

"Dinner?"

"Beau was moaning about Mr Whitlow's tedious company, so Hetta invited him and Anthony to eat with us. That's why you must hurry."

Eliza's mouth went dry. Much as she wanted to see Beau again, her youngest sister's invitation was not well timed. She would barely have enough time to dress for dinner. "Oh my goodness. You're right. I must hurry."

She yanked off her wig much more quickly than she should have done, causing her to wince. Her long blond hair was in danger of falling all over her face, but she had no time to fix it. She retrieved a rather squashed bonnet from the bag and pushed it down onto her head with considerable force before tying the ribbons.

After slipping her arms into her pelisse, she buttoned it up to the top, and then grabbed the clothes she had discarded. She stuffed them into the cloak bag, trying not to sniff them in the process as they reeked of the day's exertions. If she smelled half as bad as the clothes...

A bath. She needed a bath. Eliza hurried back to the house with that one thought in her mind. Because if she didn't bathe, she wouldn't be able to hide where she'd been all day.

And she certainly wouldn't be able to face Beau at dinner.

# Chapter 2

B Y THE TIME HE and Anthony arrived at the parsonage, Beau regretted accepting Hetta's invitation to dinner. As he stood on the step, waiting for the front door to open, he longed to be somewhere else. He had not been near the house in over three years, and it was bound to be awkward, given how his last visit had ended.

Beau pulled at his neckcloth. He shouldn't have come. Mr Merry would be obliged to receive him, whether or not he wished to, or risk offending his brother—Beau's stepfather, the Earl of Harting. That did not, however, mean he'd be welcome.

It was therefore a pleasant surprise when Mr and Mrs Merry greeted him warmly, as if they had forgotten about the past, or at the least, didn't hold it against him.

But Beau could not forget. It still brought him out in a cold sweat as he recalled how Mr Merry had ripped his character to shreds for trying to elope with his eldest daughter, Georgiana.

He shuddered at the memory, but was thankful Georgie's father had forbidden the match. The humiliation he had suffered was insignificant when compared to the alternative—of being saddled with a wife who never listened to anything he said.

The genuine warmth in the welcome he received did much to soothe his nerves. Perhaps the visit would not be so bad after all.

The first part of the evening passed smoothly. Discussion of the hunt lasted throughout dinner and continued when the gentlemen were left to their port. All too soon, however, it was time to join the ladies in the drawing room, and Beau felt his stomach churn the moment he walked through the doorway.

It was the same every time he had to make polite conversation. He felt a touch of envy as he watched Ant walk across the room and start talking to Mrs Merry with ease. His friend was as much at home in the drawing room as he was in the saddle—but Beau wasn't.

Not even his mother could have found fault with his coat of dark blue superfine that fit across his shoulders to perfection. Or with his tight black pantaloons or snowy white cravat, though it lacked the modish perfection of Anthony's Mathematical style. He looked the part of an elegant gentleman of fashion, but on the inside, he was still wearing his buckskin breeches and boots.

Beau felt as awkward as if he were a groom dressed up as a gentleman, always fearing he would say something wrong and reveal he spent more time in the stables than in polite society. If only he could escape there now.

As his gaze passed over each occupant of the room, he felt increasingly out of place. Hetta and her father were embarking on a game of chess. William had taken up his sketchbook and was busy with his pencil, no doubt drawing a portrait of one of them. Maybe even him. Charlotte had joined in the conversation with Anthony and her mother.

He was about to give into the temptation to flee when his eyes rested on Eliza—the only one of the Merry girls interested in horses. During dinner she had sat beside him, paying close attention to the discussion about the hunt, though hardly saying a word.

She shot him an encouraging smile, and Beau felt the knots in his stomach unwind a little. Perhaps she would engage in some undemanding conversation about his favourite subject.

He took the seat next to her on the sofa. "I was surprised not to see you this morning, Eliza. What was so pressing that you missed seeing the hunt off?"

She shot him a startled glance. Had he said something wrong?

"Darn it. Should I address you as Miss Merry now that Georgie's married?" He gave her a pleading look. "Please say I can still call you Eliza. We're almost family, after all. It would be so much easier if you gave me permission to use your name as I'll probably forget and keep calling you Eliza regardless."

"I'd like that."

"So, did you have a pleasant day?"

To his surprise, two spots of colour appeared on her cheeks. Why had such an innocuous question made her blush?

"Yes, thank you. I did."

When Beau realised she wasn't going to expand on her answer, he tried again.

"It was a marvellous day for a hunt. There's nothing quite like riding through the countryside on the back of a horse."

"No, there's not."

Beau wondered whether he had made a mistake trying to talk to her. It was hard work conversing with someone who said so little. He was sure she had been livelier in the past, when he had visited the parsonage as a youth.

Could she be shy? Surely not. Why would she be shy with him when she had known him all her life?

"How is Romeo doing?" she asked, breaking the silence.

Beau's lips broke into a wide smile. He had not expected her to remember their conversation at her sister's wedding. Most people didn't really listen when he enthused about his seedling stud, but Eliza had recalled the name of his prized bay colt.

His eyes glistened as he pictured his darling. "Romeo is doing well, thank you. My head groom, Jem, says he's a real chip off the old block. Looks just like his father, complete to the white stocking on his back right leg. If you recall, he's sired by Waxy, and that cost me a pretty penny, I can tell you. But you have to pay to get a good sire and Waxy's a champion. I plan to race him in October. Who knows? Maybe one day he'll win the Epsom Derby for me like his father did."

Once talking about his preferred subject, he needed scant encouragement to continue. Eliza smiled and nodded from time to time, and seemed content to listen. To find someone who was prepared to indulge him in going on about his passion was a rare thing, and he took full advantage of his willing listener. She said little, but he could tell she was interested in what he was saying by the way her eyes shined up at him.

When he had exhausted his plans for expanding his stud, he returned to the subject of the hunt. Although she must have heard all the details over dinner, she encouraged him to give her a full account.

"I just can't get over how lily-livered the other riders were, not jumping the wall. As for Whitlow—ugh!—he couldn't stop going on about the risk I'd taken. You'd think the man was fifty, not twenty-five. So chicken-hearted—"

Beau stopped short and dropped his eyes, aware he had allowed himself to rattle on as if he had been talking to Ant. He could hear his mother's voice in his head. *You are a viscount, not a stable hand. If you cannot speak as befits your rank, do not speak at all.*

"You are too harsh," Eliza said. "Not everyone rides as well as you. Would you risk such a jump if you rode like Mr Whitlow?"

Beau glanced up at her words. When he saw the gleam in her eyes, his nose twitched with amusement. "No. I suppose you're right. It's a miracle he got through the day without falling off. But to lecture me as if he were my father—it was the outside of enough. He had the nerve to accuse me of setting a poor example for your brother and that young man riding with him."

"I doubt Will needed any encouragement."

"Your brother's a fine rider, but it was his friend who caught my attention. You should have seen him—it was impressive that so slim a youth could control such a powerful mount. I think he would make a fabulous jockey. Do you know him? Would he be interested in such a career?"

"I'm afraid not," Eliza said. "I believe his parents have other plans for him."

Beau let out a heartfelt sigh. "Isn't that always the way..."

Their conversation was interrupted by a request for music. At her mother's bidding, Eliza got up from her seat, a resigned expression on her face. Moved by her obvious reluctance, Beau rose beside her, tucked her arm into his own, and walked her across the room to the pianoforte.

That, however, was as far as his gallantry extended. If music was on the menu, he couldn't get away fast enough. After waiting while Eliza sat and selected a piece to play, he withdrew to the furthest end of the room. As soon as the opportunity arose, he intended to escape to the stables.

Whilst he had enjoyed their conversation, he would leave Anthony to admire her performance.

Eliza fixed her eyes on her music, willing her hands to produce the notes on the page. It would have been preferable to sing as well as play to distract her audience from her lack of expertise on the pianoforte, but her throat became parched at the prospect of singing in front of anyone outside of her family. Especially Beau.

Not that he was listening. She had thought she was making a little headway with him. He had sat talking with her for long enough. Did he like her? Admire her? If so, his admiration did not stretch to pretending to enjoy her performance. He had moved so far down the room she could not see him anymore.

Anthony, on the other hand, was lounging over the end of the instrument as if enraptured by every note she played. Even the wrong ones.

At last, the ordeal was over. As expected, no one requested another, and she had no intention of playing a second piece unasked.

Eliza returned to her seat on the sofa, but Beau did not resume his place at her side. Where was he? She longed to glance down the room to find out, but restrained herself, fixing her eyes on the pianoforte instead. Charlotte played a complicated sonata by Beethoven which Eliza wouldn't attempt, even in private. The notes took on a magical quality with a depth of expression she knew she would never exhibit.

When her sister had finished, Anthony encouraged her to play another. He chose a piece of music and held it in front of her, asking for her approval with a look. Charlotte gave him a quick nod and shifted along her seat, and—to Eliza's amazement—he sat down beside her, and they played a duet together.

Eliza was taken aback. Anthony was full of surprises. Apart from at concerts, she had never seen a gentleman play in public before.

Finally succumbing to temptation, she glanced up to the far end of the room to see how Beau was reacting to his friend's performance, but he wasn't there. He must have slipped away from the drawing room during Charlotte's first piece—or maybe earlier, while she herself was playing.

Whilst disappointed to think he had not stayed to hear her, she could not blame him. She would escape too, if given the chance.

When the pair finished their performance, Anthony made a great show of offering his hand to her sister and raising her to her feet so they could take their bows. Eliza applauded as much for the novelty as for any enjoyment of the music. It was a rare circumstance to see Charlotte look so gratified.

Anthony walked away from the pianoforte and before Eliza was aware of it, he had sat down on the sofa next to her.

"I know your secret," he said in an undertone, with no preamble whatsoever.

Eliza gulped hard, forcing herself to stay calm. Keeping her head down, she refused to meet Anthony's gaze, afraid she could not hide her guilt. Did he truly mean what she feared? Had he seen through her disguise?

Before she could gather her wits and feign ignorance, Anthony spoke again.

"Don't worry. Your secret's safe with me."

Eliza cast him an anxious glance.

A mischievous grin spread across his face. "You've got a lot of spunk for a girl."

Anthony's smile was infectious. Despite his horrifying revelation, the corners of her mouth crept upward.

"You make a good-looking youth," he whispered, "but you make a beautiful lady."

Eliza felt the colour rushing to her cheeks. She supposed she should be grateful she was back in known territory, but when gentlemen started flirting with her, it deprived her of all ability to form sentences in her mind.

"I see I've discomposed you. You don't appear to enjoy my compliments. Most ladies thrive on them."

"I guess I'm not like *most ladies*. I never know what to say. 'Thank you. You look beautiful too'?"

Anthony laughed. "You are supposed to blush—which you've done admirably—and utter a demure thank you or rap my knuckles with a fan or simply flutter your eyelids and wait in eager expectation for the next compliment."

"So, it means nothing?"

"Flirting is a silly game we play in society to keep us amused."

While Eliza digested his words, a noise distracted her. Beau had slipped back into the room and was taking his leave of her parents.

"Is it a game everyone plays?" she asked, casting a covert glance in Beau's direction.

"Of course. It is an unspoken rule that gentlemen must flirt with pretty ladies."

"If that is so, perhaps I should learn the rules."

"That would be a shame. You are perfection itself as you are."

She rapped his hand with her fan with rather more force than she intended. "Stop it."

He shot her a wicked grin. "You're learning fast."

Eliza was not so sure. It was easy to treat Anthony's compliments lightly, but what if it was Beau who said those things? She would find it hard not to take such words seriously if her heart was involved.

But the situation had not arisen.

It was a lowering thought that—despite Anthony's assurance that everyone played this game—Beau had not made the slightest attempt to flirt with her.

# Chapter 3

AFTER THE HUNT, BEAU returned to his stepfather's estate in Alton. The ride should have been pleasant, but it was spoiled by his half-sister's wretched husband, who insisted on accompanying him. By the time he arrived at Holybourne House, he was counting the minutes until he could escape from Whitlow's moralising talk.

As the house came into view, Beau's heart sank. A carriage sat on the gravel outside the front, and there was no doubting Lord Whitlow's crest on the door panel. Frances must have come to visit her mother and was bound to be staying for dinner. Darn it. Was he never to be rid of Whitlow's irksome company?

For a moment, he considered riding into Alton, and eating at The Swan. Dare he? No. It wasn't worth It. The relief would be short-lived. It would be preferable to endure a few more hours of Whitlow's company rather than face his mother's recriminations if he failed to appear at her dinner table.

While his valet helped him dress for dinner, Beau wondered if he would survive the evening without losing his temper.

He delayed as long as he dared before making his way to the drawing room, where his mother was entertaining her guests. One glance around the room was all he needed to see that the evening would be even worse than he had feared. Frances had brought Whitlow's parents and sister with her as well.

"At last," Lady Frances exclaimed as he walked into the room and the visitors rose to greet him.

With an awkward smile, Beau bowed to Lord and Lady Whitlow and then to the others. He intended to take a seat as far away from them as possible, but Frances was not having it. Pressing her lips together in displeasure, clearly unimpressed with his lukewarm greeting toward her new family, she grasped his arm and led him to where her sister-in-law stood.

Her eyes flashed with challenge, as if daring him to pull away. Beau was helpless to resist, and he found himself face to face with Miss Whitlow. She had jet black hair, a porcelain complexion, and a curvaceous figure that many men would find alluring. He might have found her attractive if it was not for the predatory gleam in her eye.

Panic threatened to overwhelm him as he realised he faced a greater challenge this evening than holding onto his temper. He had witnessed the manoeuvres of too many matchmakers not to guess what Frances was up to.

He would have given anything to throw off her grip and run from the room, but he did not dare. Everyone was looking at him—including his mother.

"You met my new sister at the wedding, Beaumont, but I don't think you had the chance to get acquainted," Frances said, drawing Miss Whitlow forward. "I'm sure you would love to hear about my brother's young racehorse, wouldn't you, Harriet?"

Miss Whitlow peaked up at Beau from under her eyelashes. "Yes, I would, if it is not too much trouble."

Beau struggled to repress the shudder that coursed through his body as a result of that flirtatious look. Though offered a blank canvas to talk about Romeo, he'd never felt less inclined to do so.

Not for a moment had he doubted that Eliza's interest in his horses was genuine, but Miss Whitlow? That was another matter.

Unable to remain silent without appearing rude, he described Romeo to an apparently appreciative audience, but he suspected her interest was manufactured to curry his favour.

Beau was relieved when dinner was announced, and they proceeded to the dining room. He held back, hoping to avoid sitting next to Miss Whitlow, but it was a forlorn hope. His mother made sure of that.

However, by dint of asking a few questions about her family, Miss Whitlow provided all the necessary conversation, and he applied himself to eating with more than usual diligence.

After brushing through dinner tolerably well, Beau sat with the other gentlemen over his port for as long as he dared. Here, at least, he had an ally in his stepfather. Lord Harting would have been content to sit with him all evening, but Lord Whitlow and his son had been promised a game of whist and lingering was not an option.

Beau foresaw an evening of purgatory. He was not a card player. Counting cards and tricks was beyond him, making his play erratic. On this occasion, however, there was an advantage to playing, as he would not be expected to make much conversation during the game.

Having expressed his willingness to play, he sat down at the table, only to find Miss Whitlow taking the chair opposite.

Frances snickered. "Oh, I shouldn't do that, Harriet. You would do far better to be my partner. Playing cards is not Beaumont's strong point."

"You shall not dissuade me," Miss Whitlow replied, flashing a look at Frances that made Beau feel uneasy. "My mind is made up. I am determined to partner Lord Beaumont."

As the game progressed, Beau's sense of uneasiness increased. Though she must have regretted her willingness to play with him when they lost every hand, the smile did not depart from Miss Whitlow's lips. With a sinking heart, Beau realised she was bent on being pleased.

At last, the tedious game was over, and a maid brought in the coffee and tea. Beau rose from the card table and hovered with a semblance of politeness while he waited for Miss Whitlow to sit. Once she was seated, he found an excuse to talk to his stepfather and took a place next to him, as far away from her as possible.

Frances, however, was not to be deterred from forcing her new sister's company on him.

"Harriet, please would you be so kind as to take some coffee to Beaumont? He takes cream, but no sugar."

Beau tried not to feel hunted. Frances was telling Miss Whitlow how he liked his coffee as if it were a matter of great import. It was tempting to change his habits just to foil her.

"Your coffee," said Miss Whitlow, holding out a cup to him with a flash of her thin smile, and a flutter of her eyelashes.

Beau took the cup with a murmured word of thanks and breathed a sigh of relief as she walked away.

The relief was premature. Once she had procured herself a cup of tea, Miss Whitlow returned and, as there was no seat for her, Beau rose to his feet, feeling obliged to offer her his own.

He would have made his escape, but Miss Whitlow did not give him a chance.

"So kind," she said with a simper. "But why don't we move to the sofa, where we can both sit?"

"I think...perhaps..."

"Yes?" Miss Whitlow fluttered her eyelashes again.

Unable to think of a polite excuse not to do as she suggested, Beau followed her to the sofa. He forced a smile onto his lips, which he hoped would pass for the appearance of pleasure, and took his seat next to her.

Inwardly, he groaned. How had he let this happen? Not only would he be forced to make polite conversation with Miss Whitlow, but he was also in danger of being overheard by his mother and Frances and the irritating man she had married.

"Now, do tell me about Tuesday's hunt," said Miss Whitlow, staring up at him with wide eyes. "I am quite certain you rode magnificently."

"Recklessly, more like," said Whitlow with a sneer before Beau could think of a reply.

All his irritation at the man's disapproving comments came back with full force, and Beau struggled to repress a desire to thump him. Why did he have to bring it up again?

Lady Harting gave him one of those cold, penetrating looks he dreaded. "Recklessly?"

"Rode full pelt at a six-foot wall and jumped it," Whitlow said, his voice dripping with disdain. "And such a needless risk as well as there was a gate just a little further up the field."

Beau was eager to justify himself before his mother started lecturing him. "You exaggerate, Whitlow. The wall was not more than five feet tall, and I cleared it with room to spare. To ride within your capabilities is not reckless, and I knew *I* was more than capable."

Whitlow grew red in the face at the implication that he could not have jumped the wall if he had tried, but it did not shut him up as Beau had hoped.

"What is more," he continued, "three other riders followed his reckless example, including young Merry, the rector's son."

"I see," said Lady Harting in a voice devoid of emotion.

Beau waited with bated breath, expecting his mother to say more, but instead, she changed the topic of conversation and nothing more was said of the hunt that evening.

Not for a minute did Beau suppose that would be the end of it. He knew his mother too well to hope he could escape a reprimand.

And if she had been unwilling to scold him in front of an audience, it meant she was more than ordinarily displeased with him.

Beau was tempted to hazard his mother's displeasure and flee from Holybourne House before she could deliver her lecture, but he knew better than to risk it. He needed to let her vent her spleen, because if he left her temper to brew, the outcome would prove even more unpleasant.

Determined not to exacerbate his mother's mood further by appearing at breakfast in a bedraggled state, Beau sacrificed his early morning ride and arrived at the table neat, well-groomed and on time.

He need not have bothered. His mother ate in her bedchamber, leaving him to eat in restful silence with Lord Harting.

As he left the parlour, a footman stepped forward. "Her ladyship asked if you would be so good as to step up to her sitting room when convenient."

Beau let out a frustrated huff under his breath at the hypocrisy. The politeness of the message did not fool him. This was not a request. It was a summons.

On his way to the stairs, he stopped to check his appearance in the huge, gold-rimmed mirror that hung in the entrance hall, opposite the Harting coat of arms. A quick glance at his reflection showed he hadn't yet upset his valet's handiwork.

Carrick had persuaded him to have his cravat tied in a more complicated style than normal. Whilst Beau agreed it made him look a tad more modish, and therefore more likely to appeal to his fashion-conscious parent, he wished it did not make him feel as if he were being throttled.

Though he suspected that was not because of the tightness of his cravat, but his nerves at having to face his mother.

After tugging at his neckcloth to give himself a little more room to breathe, he practised a variety of expressions, wondering which one was most likely to win her approval. With a look of contrite submission on his face, he climbed the staircase and walked across the corridor to her ladyship's rooms.

He took a deep breath, knocked on the door, and waited.

A few moments later, it opened, and his mother's maid ushered him into the sitting room, where her mistress sat at her desk, writing.

"That will be all, Reed," Lady Harting said, dismissing her woman without raising her head. She kept scratching away with her quill for another minute or two, while Beau stood there, tugging at his neckcloth, which now felt even tighter than before.

It was not until after she had folded her letter with unrushed precision and sealed it with wax that his mother rose from her chair and faced him. The pained expression on her face did nothing to ease Beau's anxiety, and he braced himself for the torrent of criticism he knew was coming.

"I've tolerated your recklessness for long enough, Beaumont. No more. I won't stand by and watch you throw your life away. Do you wish to follow your father to an early grave? What were you thinking of, jumping that wall? Certainly not your responsibilities. I've tried to instil in you what is expected of a man in your position, but you refuse to listen. Your father would have been grieved indeed if a distant cousin inherited his title because you had died without an heir."

Beau heard the underlying message only too well. His crime was not that he had endangered his life, but that he'd threatened the succession.

With more than a little resentment bubbling under the surface, he repeated what he had said the night before. "There was no risk, Mother. I knew I could clear that wall."

"What of young Merry who will inherit this estate one day? You must know I'm hoping he will choose one of your sisters as his bride, realising as he does that they would have inherited if they had been boys. Besides, how would I ever have looked my dear Alicia in the face again if her only son was killed following your example?"

Beau tried not to choke on his mother's words. *Dear Alicia* indeed. Her studied politeness toward Mrs Merry contained not an ounce of affection. There was no love lost between the two women, on her side, at least. And he failed to see why it was his fault Merry had copied him.

"He cleared the wall safely," he said, a touch of sulkiness in his voice.

"You are missing the point. Though you both came away unscathed, it could have been a different story."

She moved to the window and stood in silence, looking out. Beau waited, wriggling uncomfortably, wishing he had not missed his ride. That would have worked off some of his restless energy.

At length, his mother turned round, walked back across the room, and looked him straight in the eye.

"If you are going to risk your life in this foolish manner, it is high time you took a wife and set up your nursery."

Beau's heart sank. He might have known she would use this episode to renew her efforts to coerce him into marriage. It was something she'd done before.

He opened his mouth to utter a light-hearted reply, but his mother must have guessed he was not taking her words seriously, because she glowered at him in such a way he shut it again.

"I thought the matter settled to my satisfaction last season, but your reluctance to come to the point left Georgiana open to other offers. I assumed you could win the hand of a mere rector's daughter, but perhaps I overestimated your advantages. It is a mother's weakness, to be prejudiced in favour of her own offspring."

Beau tried not to let her words get to him. His mother had never shown him any such natural affection. Her so-called partiality stemmed from an unerring belief in his rank and fortune, nothing more. She must believe they outweighed the deficiencies she saw in his person.

As for calling Georgie *a mere rector's daughter*, it was laughable. If she hadn't been an heiress, connected to the Duke of Wessex by her grandmother's second marriage, his mother would not have countenanced the match for a moment.

It was fortunate he and Georgie had agreed they would not suit. Now she was wed to Lord Castleford, and not even his ambitious parent could expect him to court a married woman.

Which begged the question—who would be his chosen bride this season? He ardently hoped it wouldn't be Miss Whitlow.

"By your father's will, I control your fortune until you are twenty-five or married. If you continue this wildness, I will have no choice but to cut off your allowance. I trust I make myself clear?"

Beau heard right enough. It was the tactic she always adopted. He had no income of his own. Without access to his inheritance, he could not afford to feed his horses or pay his staff. For that, he was reliant on his mother—and she knew it.

He would have to lie low for a while and avoid provoking her. Was that even possible? His uncertainty must have shown on his face.

"I see you sense the urgency of the situation. I doubt you can control your rash behaviour. You are too like your father. Obsessed with horses with no care for the future. At least he had the wisdom to provide himself with an heir before he threw his life away on the hunting field. I expect you to do the same."

Beau pondered her words. Was he like his father? Had he inherited his reckless nature, along with his love of horses? His mother seemed to think so—and she hated him for it.

"Do I make myself clear?" Lady Harting repeated, spitting out every word like a well-aimed dart.

"Yes, madam."

He would attend a few balls and look as though he were making headway with some poor lady or other in order to keep the money flowing. And if he could not avoid it, he would marry.

For the sake of his horses.

# Chapter 4

FOR THE NEXT FEW weeks, Beau hid away at his hunting lodge in Newmarket—the only property his father had left him outright. Devoting his days to Romeo, he was as close to contentment as he'd ever been. The only cloud on the horizon was his mother's threat, and the fear of losing everything he'd worked for if he did not do as she asked.

In his more optimistic moments, he fooled himself into thinking she would soon forget he had risked his life by his reckless riding, and leave him alone.

She did not. After one blissful month, his mother requested his presence in London. She made it clear she did not believe he could mend his ways, and as he was more than half inclined to agree with her, he submitted to the inevitable.

After delaying as long as he dared, he left for the metropolis, hoping to convince her he was looking for a wife, so she would have no cause to stop his income.

Beau arrived at his lodgings in London on the first day of March. This season, he was not living under his stepfather's roof. It had been a battle to secure this privilege, but the fear of seeming to keep her son at her beck and call had won his mother over. She cared enough about appearances to grant him this little freedom.

His mother would know he'd arrived as soon as he sent his carriage round to the Harting House mews. That he had, yet again, come when she summoned. How he hated yielding to the power she had over him.

He tamped down the wave of humiliation threatening to overwhelm him, and, in a minor act of rebellion, strode toward White's rather than going to pay his respects to his mother. There he was certain to discover congenial company while he dined, and if he were fortunate, he would find Anthony without having to track down his whereabouts.

He *was* fortunate. Ant was the first person he saw as he walked through the door. Jumping up from his seat, he slapped Beau on the back in welcome and invited him to join him over a bottle of wine. As neither man was much of a letter writer, there was plenty of talking to do.

"How is your soon-to-be prizewinning colt?" Anthony asked.

"Romeo is incredible. You should see him run, Ant. It's as if he were powered by steam. He'll be ready to race at Newmarket in October as planned and, as long as Jem can control him, I'm certain he'll be as magnificent a champion as his sire."

"I'm surprised you can bear to leave him."

Beau let out a deep sigh. "I had no choice."

"Ah. Your mother?"

"How did you guess?"

"Bad, is it?"

Beau gave a resigned nod. "Whitlow told her about the wall we jumped in the Hampshire hunt. Of course, he exaggerated the risk we took, but Mother latched onto it like a limpet. It was excuse enough for her to demand that if I cannot curb my reckless behaviour, I should marry and provide myself with an heir before I put an end to my existence."

"Your mother can nag, but she can't force you to tie the knot."

"Oh yes, she can. She's threatening to stop my allowance if I don't do as she asks."

"Not that again."

"Indeed, and unless I keep her happy, I'll have no income to pay for my horses."

"There must be another way. What a shame you weren't in town in time to enter the lottery. Twenty thousand pounds would have set you up for a few years."

Beau rolled his eyes. "Stop winding me up. You know what I think of lotteries. Such a waste. The chances of winning are so slim you might as well throw the money out the window."

"What about Romeo? If he becomes the winner you think he is, there'll be prize money, and in time, he could be worth a fortune as a stud horse."

"That's the problem. Time—or lack of it. It will take months, even years, for Romeo to produce a return, and I can't wait that long."

"Not if you bet on his success. As an unknown, you'd be bound to get good odds on him. I know you're not much of a gamester, but you're a dab hand at assessing the horses, and if you think Romeo will win, you'd be betting on a certainty."

It was a tempting idea, and for a moment Beau caught Anthony's excitement, but then his spirits sank again. "To solve my problems, the bet would have to be huge, and a huge bet means a colossal risk—a risk I'm not willing to take. Even if it worked, it will be some months before Romeo is ready to race, and in the meantime, there would be ongoing costs I can't meet."

He banged his fist down on the table. "It's not fair. Why don't I have control of my fortune yet? It makes me sympathise with the Prince Regent. To have waited all these years to rule, and yet, even now, to have restrictions placed upon him—at his age! It must be galling for him to know the government doesn't trust him."

"With good reason. He hasn't exactly proved himself the most reliable of characters. As for his spending habits—"

"I'll have to marry," Beau cut in, his voice full of despair.

Anthony put his arm around his friend's shoulders. "Cheer up. It hasn't come to that yet. You need to be seen in the right places and appear to be doing what your mother wants. Impress her by taking the initiative. You can start tomorrow at Georgie's ball. Dance and flirt with two or three well-dowered beauties and her ladyship will soon leave you alone. It'll be just like last year."

"Maybe. But if she keeps pushing me, I'll have to court someone, and you know what it's like. If you pay a lady too much attention, she gets expectations, and before you're aware of it, you're obliged to offer for her."

"What if you spread yourself about a bit? Share your smiles with more than one lady. That seems to work for me. Prevents any of them from getting ideas."

"It sounds exhausting, but it might work—if I can escape being labelled a rake. Will it satisfy my mother, though? I need to keep her happy, and if it comes to it, I guess I shall be obliged to marry to save my horses."

Anthony raised his glass. "In that case, to your bride, whoever she may be."

·♥·♥·♥·♥·♥·

Eliza stared in the mirror and allowed a smile to creep onto her lips. It was not a big smile, but enough to bring out the dimple in her chin. Though pleased with her appearance, it was not her reflection that made her grin. Today was the day of her sister's ball—and Beau would be there.

For that reason, she wanted to look her best. Sarah had worked wonders with her hair, lacing strands of pearls into her long blond tresses, which were piled high on top of her head with just a few select tendrils falling down by the side of her face. The pearl and diamond drops in her ears were a gift from her grandmother, the Duchess of Wessex.

They had arrived with a letter wishing her well for the season and urging her not to forget herself and embarrass her relations by making a foolish match. Eliza trusted her grandmother would not consider marrying Viscount Beaumont to be throwing herself away, for that was the only match that interested her.

With a deftness learned by years of practice, Sarah slipped Eliza's white ballgown over her head without disturbing a hair. Eliza twirled this way and that, watching the light catching the pearls sewn onto the skirt until bid to stand still. Her maid was fastening the back of her dress when Georgiana entered the room.

"I see Madame Giselle has excelled herself," she said, looking over Eliza's appearance with approval. "You look beautiful."

Once Sarah had left, Eliza looked to her sister for reassurance. "You are sure he'll come, aren't you?"

Georgiana's face clouded over. "Can't you forget about him for one moment? I should hate to feel that my efforts on your behalf have been wasted should the wretched boy not deign to turn up."

"He is *not* wretched!"

"Oh well, maybe that was uncharitable of me, but he *is* hopelessly unreliable. Remember, he spent last season dancing attendance on me, so I should know."

"Then you don't think he'll come?"

"How am I supposed to know? He said he would come, but short of telling Anthony you're in love with his best friend and making him bring Beau with him, I'm not sure what else you expect me to do."

Eliza paled at the thought of Anthony discovering how she felt about Beau. It was bad enough that he teased her about her masquerade in the hunt.

"Don't you dare say a word to him."

"As if I would," Georgiana said, taking her sister's hand. She paused for a moment. "How do you feel?"

"Nervous. I wish I had your confidence. You're aware of how hard I find it to converse with strangers. I shall blush constantly, be horribly tongue-tied and appear like every other insipid young lady making her come-out in society."

"Is that such a bad thing?"

Eliza shrugged. "Not if it will make you happy, but to me, it feels more of a masquerade than dressing up as a boy."

Georgiana squeezed her hand, saying with a lightness that did not quite match the sternness of her expression, "I would be obliged if you would keep the *boy* locked up tonight. No doubt our aunt will be watching, and I should so hate to give her any reason to criticise either of us."

"Thank you so much for reminding me," Eliza said with a groan. There was little chance of the livelier side of her nature coming out this evening. "I already feel nauseous with anxiety, and you've made it worse. It makes me quake to think of performing in front of Lady Harting when it is so important I make a good impression on her. Your words have just set my heart into a fresh flutter of nerves. I wish I were more like you, then I wouldn't tremble at the thought of her noticing me."

Charlotte interrupted them by barging into the room, dressed for the ball, with a forbidding expression on her face. Georgiana shot Eliza a look of desperation before going downstairs to make a last check on the preparations.

"Why do I have to attend Georgie's ball when I don't want to get married?" Charlotte said, scowling at Eliza.

"You might change your mind."

"I won't."

"I'm not much different from you."

Charlotte rolled her eyes. "You're completely different. You *want* to get married."

"But I'm only interested in one man. Dressing up in your finest and parading around on your best behaviour to attract a husband like some animal up for auction is wasted on me."

"Humph. Then I'll make sure I'm not on my best behaviour, and then maybe I can scare any potential suitors away."

"You wouldn't dare."

"If anyone flirts with me, I'll scream."

"You mustn't," Eliza said, fixing Charlotte with a fierce stare. "Georgie would be so mortified."

"No, I suppose you're right, but it will be hard to restrain myself."

Eliza gurgled with laughter. "What a pair we are. Georgie has warned me to keep myself in check and now I'm urging you to do the same—for the sake of family honour!"

# Chapter 5

As THEY ENTERED THE ballroom, Eliza plastered a smile on her lips, and tried to quell the fluttering in her stomach. For Georgiana's sake, she was determined to play her part. She was relieved to see Charlotte followed her lead, though she could tell her smile was as forced as her own. As long as she saw Beau, Eliza knew it would be worth it.

However, her excitement at the prospect of seeing him dissipated when she found herself surrounded by a sea of unknown faces. She cast an envious glance at Georgiana, who seemed to revel in all the attention. What an admirable countess her sister made.

Georgie was taking her role as their chaperon seriously and selected two young gentlemen out of the throng to introduce to her sisters and lead them into the first dance.

"What a waste of time," Charlotte said as they met again at Georgiana's side when the set ended. "My partner had no conversation whatsoever."

"I think that would be preferable to mine," Eliza said. "The gentleman I danced with paid me a string of compliments that made my cheeks burn with embarrassment, leaving me with very little to say."

"My partner tried that," Charlotte admitted, "but I just ignored it and asked him who his favourite composer was. He seemed surprised, and lapsed into silence."

Eliza sympathised with the man. It was the sort of question she would have struggled to answer.

She found her second partner no better than her first. He paid her such outrageous compliments that it would have been laughable if she were not so embarrassed. She hoped her lack of conversation would discourage him, but the gentleman did not seem to notice anything amiss with her inability to find a suitable response.

When she returned to Georgiana's side, Eliza found her sister talking to Anthony. He stopped his conversation, turned to her, and bowed.

It was a relief to see a face she recognised, but she had become a little wary of his company since that humiliating day when he had uncovered her masquerade at the hunt. As far as she could tell, he had kept his word, and not told anyone of his discovery, but he delighted in reminding her that he was the keeper of her secret.

Eliza hoped he was not in a teasing mood tonight. She was not sure her nerves could cope with it.

Before she had figured out what to say to him, she was distracted by the sight of Charlotte, striding across the ballroom without her partner, a fiery expression in her eyes.

"Oh no," she murmured.

Georgiana jerked her head around and took a deep breath as their sister joined them.

"If that horrid man ever touches me again, I will slap him," said Charlotte.

"What did he do?" Anthony asked, his face alight with amusement. "Should I call him out?"

Charlotte glared at him. "It is no laughing matter. He pressed my hand in a familiar way."

Anthony struggled to stifle his laughter. "Don't be too harsh on him. He's a younger son and needs a rich wife."

"Well, I wish he would pester some other lady. I have no intention of marrying him or anyone else. It is not as if he has an ounce of intelligence either. A man who can't tell the difference between German and Italian has clearly got no brain."

Anthony smirked. "Don't tell me you tried to talk about the opera with him."

"He said he liked opera."

"Everyone says that. It's fashionable to like opera—but there are only a few of us who truly love it," Anthony said.

"Humph."

"You need not dance with him again," said Georgiana in a soothing voice.

"There is no fear of that. I already told him so."

Georgiana stared at their sister in horror. "What did you say to him?"

"That I would sooner dance with Don Alfonso."

Anthony burst out laughing, drawing undue attention to them, but Eliza didn't know why. Who was Don Alfonso anyway?

Georgiana saw her confusion and hastened to explain. "He's a character from *Così fan tutte*—an old man. Not a flattering comparison."

"How did he reply to that?" Anthony asked Charlotte, struggling to get his words out, because he was laughing so much.

"Nothing."

"Was there anything else you wished to say to him but didn't?"

"Plenty."

"Then dance the next with me and let me hear your acerbic tongue at its best."

Anthony cast a wicked look at Eliza and her elder sister. "This should be fun."

Georgie glowered at him. "Don't encourage her."

But it was too late. Charlotte's eyes sparkled dangerously as she accepted Anthony's offer and allowed him to take her arm.

With a sigh of relief, Georgie turned her attention back to Eliza. "Now, who shall we choose this time..." she said, half to herself.

Another gentleman was introduced to Eliza, and once again, she was swept into the dance.

The routine was just the same. Her partner paid her compliments, and she blushed and sent him the occasional shy smile. Fortunately, that was all that was required of her.

By the time their dances were over, Eliza was struggling to keep her emotions in check. She was weary of smiling at gentlemen whose names she could not remember, and who made her feel so uncomfortable with their silly compliments. Why couldn't they just dance?

But that wasn't the real problem. The real problem was that Beau hadn't come.

She had depended on dancing with him tonight, and if he wasn't coming, she would have spent all this nervous energy for nothing.

Was he as unreliable as Georgie claimed? No. She refused to believe it. He must have a good reason for his non-appearance.

But even if he didn't, could she blame him for choosing to spend the evening in a more convivial manner?

·♥ · ♥ · ♥ · ♥ · ♥·

Beau had spent the day with his cousin, Charles Templecombe. After riding in Hyde Park, they had repaired to Tattersall's, where he had dissuaded his relative from buying a showy animal he would have been embarrassed to have in his stables.

Over dinner at White's, they commiserated with each other about being pushed into marriages they didn't want, and then moved onto Beau's favourite subject. Horses.

As he enlarged upon his hopes for Romeo, his fears about the future melted away. Even the threat his mother held over his head seemed distant. It was always that way when he got talking about horses. Nothing else mattered.

When they had exhausted the topic of Beau's prize colt, his cousin plied him for tips for the upcoming races at Newmarket. Beau had plenty to say about the matter, and he was in the middle of a detailed account of the most likely winners when the clock struck eleven.

"Aren't we supposed to be going somewhere tonight?" Templecombe asked.

"Darn it. I forgot. Lady Castleford's ball. And we were having such a pleasant evening."

Reluctantly, the cousins left their club and went their separate ways. Beau walked up the hill and along the road to his lodgings, trying to ignore the sinking feeling inside.

He could imagine the scathing words on his mother's lips when they met. Not only had he failed to call on her, but now he was late to Georgie's ball. Anthony had encouraged him to keep her ladyship happy, and he had fallen at the first hurdle.

Carrick was waiting for him. His evening clothes were already laid out—black pantaloons, a dark blue jacket of Bath coating, and a spotless white shirt, waistcoat and neckcloth.

"I'm late."

"Yes, my lord."

The only point of dispute was his cravat. Again.

"I suggest the Cascade, your lordship."

"No. I'm nervous enough without you making me feel as if I'm being choked."

"As you wish, my lord, though I believe her ladyship would approve of the style I've perfected."

Beau's face heated as he foresaw his mother's disapproval should he present himself with his neckcloth indifferently tied, and submitted to his valet without another word.

It was almost midnight when Beau arrived at the Castlefords' townhouse. As expected at this late hour, neither Lady Castleford nor her husband were still at the door, which he thought was just as well, as Georgie would only scold him for being so late.

Beau entered the ballroom while a dance was in progress, giving him plenty of time to observe who was there. As his gaze drifted around the room, he spotted his half-sister, Lady Caroline, going down the set. Beside her was the Whitlow girl.

Beau repressed a shudder and looked away, keen not to meet her eye. The last thing he wanted to do was give her any encouragement. She had made it abundantly clear she was on the catch for a husband, and he was her intended victim.

As the dance drew to a close and ladies returned to their chaperons, he was aware of hopeful glances being sent in his direction. The speculative looks on their faces were almost enough to make him turn tail and run.

To his relief, he spotted Anthony on the far side of the ballroom, talking to Georgiana and her sisters. At least he would have a comrade-in-arms in his battle against matchmaking mothers, his own included. With that thought in mind, he made his way toward his best friend.

He'd only taken a few steps when he caught a flash of purple out of the corner of his eye. Without thinking, he turned his head to see what it was.

At once, he realised his mistake. Darn it. He recognised that purple turban.

It belonged to his mother.

# Chapter 6

ELIZA HAD GIVEN UP any hope of Beau attending the ball when she spotted him coming across the room toward her. Her heart beat faster in anticipation, and she eagerly turned to Georgiana to tell her the good news, only to discover her sister was making another introduction.

"Eliza, Charlotte, may I present Lord Beaumont's cousin, Mr Templecombe," she said.

"Delighted to meet you," the man stammered. "May I have the honour of the next, Miss Merry?"

Eliza felt pushed into a corner. If she accepted, as she knew was expected of her, she would have to refuse Beau if he asked. She could not risk it. This might be her only chance to dance with him tonight.

"Forgive me," she said, smiling sweetly up at Mr Templecombe, "but I am engaged for the next. Perhaps the one after?"

The bewildered man bowed and invited Charlotte to stand up with him instead.

Georgiana scowled at her. "Engaged?"

"He's here," Eliza whispered as she nodded her head in the direction she had seen Beau.

But when she looked back, he had disappeared from view. "I thought he was coming over to talk to you...that he would be bound to ask me to dance..." Eliza said, swallowing her disappointment.

"Whatever you thought, it was no reason to claim to be engaged for the next. You have put me in an awkward situation. I can't introduce you to a different partner without slighting Mr Templecombe."

As Eliza wondered what she could do to set things right, her gaze fell on Anthony, who was standing nearby, talking to his brother. As soon as he finished speaking, she beckoned him with a look.

He obediently took a step toward her.

"Mr Warren, have you come to claim your dance?" she said with a confidence she was far from feeling. She beseeched him with her eyes to play along and stand up with her for the next.

"Could I forget?" he said, taking her hand and raising it to his lips, placing a lingering kiss on her gloved hand.

"How could you remember?" she said under her breath, biting back a smile.

"You know it is usual for the man to do the asking," he said as they moved toward the set that was forming.

"You need not have accepted if you did not care to dance with me."

"And give you a set-down in front of such an audience? I am far too gentlemanlike to pursue such a course of action."

"What a blow to my vanity. You act to preserve your own character and happen to save mine in the process."

Anthony's nose twitched with amusement. "Rogue! And how is my little rebel enjoying her first London ball? Done any more dressing up recently?"

Eliza's smile vanished. She refused to answer.

"You look magnificent when you try to ignore me."

"Stop it. You promised."

"I vowed not to tell, not to keep quiet about it."

"That's not kind. Quit teasing me or I'll never dance with you again."

Anthony pouted, but his eyes were still laughing. "That would be a shame. You're an excellent dancer. Georgiana moves well, but you seem to float around the ballroom floor."

"Next you will say I dance like an angel," Eliza said, with a note of mock despair.

"Oh no. Who uttered such a commonplace compliment as that?"

"I don't know," she said with a shrug. "I haven't danced with a single gentleman I know, apart from you. My head is swimming with the names of all the people I've met. How am I supposed to remember who anyone is?"

"You mean you didn't learn who all the eligible gentlemen were beforehand? You shock me. I thought that was required learning for every young lady making her debut. But I don't think you need to worry. Remembering who people are is overrated. Just continue looking beautiful and keep that sweet smile on your lips and you'll do fine."

"You really think so?"

"Forgetting their names—as long as you forget *all* their names—and asking to be reminded with a tender apology will make them eager to become the one you remember in the future."

Eliza bit her lower lip as she considered his response. She half thought he was jesting, but it was not a bad idea to admit her inability to distinguish one gentleman from another. She had no desire to be courted by any of them, and it might dissuade them from trying.

When the dancing drew to a close, Anthony accompanied her into the supper room, filled her plate, and then sat beside her recounting amusing stories of his exploits while they ate.

As most of his tales included Beau, Eliza was content to listen, but she could not stop herself wondering what had become of him.

Beau wished he hadn't spotted that purple turban, but it was too late now. He cast a wistful glance across the ballroom to where Anthony stood before resigning himself to the inevitable. Sure enough, as he turned back, he met his mother's glare full on.

As was her habit, she summoned him to her side with just a look, and in the interests of self-preservation, Beau changed direction to obey the parental summons.

He stopped in front of his mother, who was standing with Lady Whitlow, and bowed. "Good evening," he said with a nonchalance he was far from feeling.

Lady Harting looked him up and down and gave a nod of approval. It was the tiniest of movements, but he saw it because he was looking for it. He let out the breath he had not realised he was holding, glad to know he had passed muster—for now, at least.

Her eyes narrowed. "What a pleasant surprise to see you, Beaumont."

She motioned toward Miss Whitlow, who had appeared at her mother's side. "You remember Mr Whitlow's sister Harriet, don't you?"

Beau saw the trap too late. He could not avoid asking her to dance without being rude. "Miss Whitlow, would you be so good as to honour me with the next?" he said, trying to keep the reluctance out of his voice.

As he had expected, she was quick to accept, peeking up at him from under her eyelashes in a way that might have been provocative if he had liked her. The look gave him a queasy feeling at the bottom of his stomach. He offered her his arm, and they walked across the room to join the dance that was forming.

He supposed he should make some conversation with his partner. "Are you enjoying the ball, Miss Whitlow?"

She puckered her lips. "Now I am."

Beau was unprepared for such a direct attack and floundered as he sought a response that was neither rude nor encouraging.

"We had quite given up on you, Beaumont. It is too bad of you to hold us in suspense by arriving so late."

Beau felt sure she would have rapped his knuckles with her fan if they weren't in the middle of a dance. He supposed he should say something in reply.

"I was delayed." It was a lame excuse, even in his own ears, but at least it was true, in a manner of speaking. He would not admit he was late because he'd been having such a pleasant evening with Templecombe they'd forgotten the time.

"We missed you."

"I...um...it's warm in here tonight," he said, ignoring her words.

"And you would prefer to be outside, riding in the park, instead of dancing with me."

How was he supposed to answer that? Of course, he would rather be out riding, but if he admitted as much, it would hardly be complimentary to his partner.

"It is always a pleasure—"

"Forgive me," she said. "What an impossible position I put you in. I know you'd choose riding over dancing, even if your partner was the most charming lady in the world."

Beau did not care to have Miss Whitlow claim she knew him well enough to speak for him, however accurate her assessment. He gave a weak smile, hoping that was a sufficient compliment to satisfy her. The woman didn't need any encouragement.

"Your mother told us you have taken lodgings this year. It must be strange not to live at Harting House, but I suppose you will buy a place of your own once you are married. Whitlow and your sister are staying with us this season, but they're looking to acquire a suitable townhouse. Somewhere large enough for a family."

The thought of Whitlow setting up his nursery sent shivers down Beau's spine. Doing his best to ignore Miss Whitlow's comments, he talked about the weather. Then the dance. And then the journey to London until the set was over.

It was at that point he realised with an inner groan that he had inadvertently asked Miss Whitlow for the supper dance, and rather than returning her to her mother, he would be obliged to spend the next half an hour waiting on her at the supper table and trying to find something to say to her which stayed well away from such topics as marriage and family.

A sudden burst of laughter shattered the well-bred chatter across the room. All eyes were drawn to Anthony, who laughed at something Eliza had said. After a moment, everyone went back to their conversations, and the gentle hubbub resumed.

But Beau was only giving half an ear to what Miss Whitlow was saying. He still had Anthony and Eliza in his view, over his companion's shoulder.

To judge by the look on her face, Eliza was enjoying Anthony's company. He hoped Georgiana had warned her sister that her husband's brother was an arrant flirt. It would be too bad of Ant to break her heart.

From all he had seen of Eliza, she was a shy little thing and probably wouldn't know how to deal with unwanted attentions. Though if her smiles were anything to go by, Ant's attentions were not unwanted.

At last the interminable supper was over and Beau could return Miss Whitlow to her mother, to await her next partner when the dancing resumed.

After relinquishing her with considerable relief, he walked away, planning to search for Anthony, but he was halted in his tracks by a woman standing in his way.

His mother.

He stifled a sigh. What did she want now?

# Chapter 7

LADY HARTING FLARED HER nostrils, the ends of her lips curled down in disapproval as she addressed her son.

"It was a pity you could not arrange your schedule to arrive on time tonight, Beaumont. Have you paid your respects to Lady Castleford yet? She is looking very well. Most fortunate in her choice of husband."

Beau wriggled uncomfortably under the piercing look that accompanied his mother's words—words that did nothing to hide her disappointment that he had not married Georgiana himself.

"No, madam. I have not had the chance. When I arrived, I came straight to your side, and have only just now returned Miss Whitlow to her mother."

"Then pray do so, Beaumont. It is the height of bad manners not to wait on your hostess. She may not even know you are here, as I doubt very much whether you deigned to send a reply to her invitation."

Beau could feel the heat creeping up his neck. Embarrassment and what? A kind of resignation to his own uselessness. He had replied—but only because his valet had reminded him. How was it his mother could crush him with just a few well-chosen words?

"I will remedy my negligence at once." With a quick bow of his head, he escaped.

He spied Georgiana across the room and made his way to her side.

"Lord Beaumont," she said with a mischievous smile.

"Lady Castleford," he said, returning her grin as they exchanged bows. "You're looking very beautiful this evening. Marriage evidently suits you."

"Indeed, it does. Perhaps you should try it one day."

Beau pulled a face. "Maybe I will—*one* day."

"So kind of you to grace us with your presence. I supposed I had misread your reply…"

"You thought nothing of the sort. I forgot. And I was late. But if you're going to make me feel bad about it, you needn't bother. My mother has already scolded me. Please accept my apologies for my disgraceful behaviour."

"Very well. Seeing as you asked me so nicely."

Just then, Anthony joined them with Eliza on his arm.

Beau nodded carelessly to Ant, but his eyes lingered rather longer on his companion. When had Georgie's little sister turned into such a beauty?

She was several inches taller than her sister, her figure slender. Whereas Georgie's eyes were a deep blue, Eliza's were like pale sapphires, and a few tresses of her blond hair framed her elfin face, which was almost devoid of colour. With the white of her dress, she looked like an ice maiden—the only contrast being the red of her generous mouth.

"Miss Merry, how delightful to see you again," he said with a dignified bow.

Eliza acknowledged his greeting with the slightest upturn of her lips, her eyes glowing with something he could not quite put his finger on.

Was she pleased to see him? He wasn't sure. It niggled Beau that her reception of him was so reserved. She'd been laughing with Anthony, but *he* had barely warranted a smile.

He decided to see if he could provoke a more enthusiastic response.

"Would you dance the next with me?" he asked with the most dazzling smile he could muster.

The reaction to his words was not what he expected. Eliza pursed her lips together as if she were dealing with something unpleasant. Was dancing with him so distasteful that it provoked such a negative effect?

"I can't," she said. "It's promised to Mr Templecombe."

Anthony clapped him on the back. "Should have turned up earlier if you wanted to dance with the most beautiful woman in the room."

Beau tamped down his annoyance. How had Templecombe secured a set when he could not? And what was Georgie doing, letting her sister partner him? Didn't she know his impoverished relative was on the lookout for a rich wife?

Somewhat deflated, Beau scowled at his cousin as he claimed his partner and then stood, leaning against a pillar, feeling unreasonably irritated. He knew he should ask someone else to dance, but perhaps they, too, would find a reason for refusing him.

Georgiana did not let him linger there. She was taking her role as hostess seriously and hastened to introduce him to a rather plain-looking girl who looked so pleased to be asked to stand up with him it soothed his ruffled feathers.

It was just as well. If he made a spectacle of himself, his mother would have shown her displeasure. Or worse. She might have insisted he dance a second time with Miss Whitlow.

In his efforts to stay well away from his mother, Beau gravitated back to Georgiana's side after returning the wallflower to her chaperon. Charlotte was deep in conversation with Anthony. He overheard enough to deduce that she was ranting about her last partner's lack of musical knowledge. Certain he would be chastised in a similar manner, Beau made a mental note never to ask Charlotte to stand up with him.

He kept an eye open for Eliza, who had not yet returned. No doubt Templecombe was making the most of having stolen her from under his nose, and would gloat, if Beau gave him half a chance. He was still annoyed his cousin had secured a dance with Eliza, whereas he had failed, and he was of a mind to try again.

In the meantime, he dropped a word in Georgie's ear. "Don't encourage Templecombe to dangle after your sisters. He's only interested in their dowry. His father has threatened to send him into the army unless he finds a rich wife, so the fellow's desperate."

"That is hardly loyal to your cousin, but you need not worry. Neither of my sisters is in any danger of succumbing to his charm."

Beau sniggered. "That's cruel—but it's as well to be aware."

"Thank you for your concern," Georgiana said, giving him a penetrating look, as if trying to uncover the true motive for his warning.

Dash it. Why shouldn't he show an interest in the welfare of her sisters?

He prolonged the conversation, asking after the rest of her family, until he saw Eliza approaching on Templecombe's arm. To judge by the number of gentlemen moving in their direction, Beau guessed he was not the only one trying to secure a dance.

Taking advantage of the fact that Eliza was with his cousin, he stepped forward and greeted them both before they reached Georgiana, cutting out the competition.

"Miss Merry," he said, with what he hoped was a charming smile, "will you dance the next with me?"

"I should be delighted," she said, returning his smile somewhat timidly.

He took her arm, feeling as if he had captured a prize as he paraded her past the line of disappointed gentlemen, all casting envious looks in his direction.

They joined the set that was forming, and Beau waited in silence for Eliza to raise her eyes before addressing her. She did not so much as glance up at him.

At first he thought she was uncertain of the dance and needed to concentrate on her steps, but it soon became clear this was not the case. She was light on her feet, and he deemed it unlikely she would step on his toes. She glided through each figure with a lightness and elegance that a novice would not possess.

When she had still not looked at him after several minutes, he wondered whether he'd mistaken her pleasure in being asked to dance. Did she find him so objectionable she could not bear to look at him?

He was fast talking himself into a state of dejection when he caught his partner's eye. Eliza blushed without him saying a word.

The truth hit him, followed swiftly by a wave of relief. She was shy. How unlike Georgie!

A memory flitted across his brain of reaching a similar conclusion when they had talked after the hunt. He remembered that on that occasion, they'd soon fallen into relaxed conversation, and applied himself to putting her at her ease.

"How do you like London, Eliza?"

"I'm happy to be here."

"More to do in town, I guess. Such as the theatre. Are you as fond of seeing plays as Georgie?"

"No."

Different again from her sister.

"What about music? I know you play the pianoforte. Do you enjoy concerts?"

"Not really."

"What about the opera?" he said, naming his least favourite entertainment.

"I've never grasped even the basics of Italian," she said, "and attending the opera makes me feel inadequate—as if I'm missing something. I just don't seem able to appreciate it the way others do."

"Unlike Charlotte."

"Yes," she said in a gush of feeling. "Very different from Charlotte."

Beau gave her a conspiratorial grin. "My feelings exactly. I'm sure you've learned by now that Castleford's brother Anthony is a huge fan of the opera. That is one thing we can't agree on. How he can endure that caterwauling beats me. But you do like dancing?"

"Yes, I do. Very much. And you?"

"That depends. It's a pleasure to dance with you, but it's a penance to partner someone like my sister, Caroline. Just look at her. She dances as she rides—with some skill, but no energy, no feeling, and no sense of rhythm. It's probably why she has such a dreadful seat on the back of a horse. She always makes riding appear a chore and her dancing is much the same."

Eliza followed his glance up the set. She bit her lip, her eyes twinkling with amusement, though she was not so ill-mannered as to agree with him.

"I don't think I've ever seen you ride. At least, not since you were a girl. I expect you ride like you dance," he added with a lopsided grin. "With grace."

It gratified him to note that Eliza glowed with pleasure at his compliment.

Encouraged by her reaction, he spoke what was uppermost in his thoughts. "Truth is, much as I'm enjoying dancing with you, I would rather be riding across the countryside. There's something about being outdoors that gives me energy, whereas this"—his eyes swept over the room—"does not."

"I know what you mean."

Beau gazed at his partner, puzzling over her words. Did she? Did she understand? There was no hint of deception in her face—no suggestion that she was just saying what he thought he wanted to hear. She was so different from Georgie, it was...surprising.

Every comment he made met with the same encouraging responses. A cheerful look, a few words, and sometimes a fuller reply.

There was no fluttering of her eyelids. No provocative pouts. No requirement to make clever conversation. Just a genuine appearance of pleasure, reflecting her enjoyment of the dance and, he thought, of his company.

It was most refreshing.

"I hope we'll have many opportunities to stand up together again," he said as they walked back to Georgiana.

Eliza's lips curled into a full smile. "As do I."

Beau's eyes were drawn to the dimple which appeared in her chin. Was it always there when she smiled? He hadn't noticed it before and found it disconcertingly alluring. There was something oddly satisfying about making Eliza smile like that.

"Perhaps you could save the last dance for me?"

"Perhaps I could," Eliza said, with another dazzling smile.

He returned Eliza to Georgiana's side, feeling like a king, but his buoyant mood was short-lived.

As he moved away to find his next partner, Beau came face to face with his mother. Again. Her eyes gleamed, and a thin smile was pasted on her lips.

"I am glad to see you secured a dance with Elizabeth. It is well you are taking your duty seriously at last. There is a gracefulness in her deportment and a meekness in her manner which is most pleasing. I trust you made sure your partner enjoyed standing up with you?"

*Duty.* Beau's stomach clenched. His enjoyment of the dance fled at the implications of her words. She wanted him to court Eliza and by standing up with her, he had unwittingly fallen in with a plan of his parent's making, not his own.

"I believe so," he said in a colourless voice.

"Excellent. I count on you to ensure she keeps enjoying your company."

The sick feeling in Beau's stomach grew. He should have guessed his beloved parent still hankered after a connection with the Duke of Wessex. If not one of the Duchess's granddaughters, why not another? He'd failed to gain Georgie's hand, so his mother expected him to win her sister instead.

How could he face Eliza again, knowing she was his mother's choice? He wasn't such a cad as to raise expectations he was not willing to fulfil, and despite his mother's ambition, he had no intention of getting married this year if he could help it.

Out of the corner of his eye, Beau saw Lady Whitlow approaching with her daughter in tow, and his spirits sank even further. His mother might favour Eliza, but she encouraged Miss Whitlow too, and *that* woman had set her sights on him.

Beau didn't think he could cope with another attack tonight. Just thinking about her flirtatious behaviour brought him out in a cold sweat.

"Good evening, madam," he said, with a quick bow to his mother, taking his leave before the Whitlows could reach them.

He needed to escape before he was forced to dance with Miss Whitlow again.

With that single thought in mind, he headed for the door.

# Chapter 8

THAT NIGHT, BEAU DREAMED of dancing with Eliza. It was a pleasant, floaty sort of dream in which she glowed up at him with her captivating dimple showing, and he awoke with the ghost of a smile on his face.

It quickly faded as he remembered what had happened. His mother had made the mistake of approving of Eliza. Instead of encouraging him, it had made him wary, reluctant to fall in with any plan of his parent's making.

But it was the fear of being forced into dancing with Miss Whitlow again that had sent him running to find more congenial company. Undemanding male company and sporting talk. In his hurry to escape, he had forgotten he had as good as promised to partner Eliza for the last dance.

He rested his head in his hands and chided himself for being as useless as his mother thought he was. Eliza was not to blame that her ladyship approved of her. It was childish of him to act contrary to his own inclination just to thwart his parent's plans. And if the alternative were Miss Whitlow, he would only spite himself.

He was sorry to have let Eliza down and was determined to make it up to her. Perhaps she would care to go for a drive. That was much more to his liking than a ball or the dreaded Almack's assemblies. Maybe Georgie could put in a good word for him and persuade her sister to forgive him.

When he arrived at Warren House, he was fortunate to find the ladies at home and without visitors.

As Beau entered the drawing room, Eliza's face lit up, giving him high hopes he would be forgiven.

"I can't tell you how sorry I am that I wasn't able to claim another dance with you last night, Eliza. I was unavoidably detained."

"You mean you forgot."

Her words threw him off balance. He had expected her to accept his pathetic apology at face value as any other young lady of his acquaintance would have done, not to challenge him as to the real reason for his failure to claim the dance.

All was not lost, however, because there was no rancour or upset in her voice.

He looked at her sheepishly from under his lowered brows. "Yes, I forgot. Please, forgive me."

And he really hoped she would.

"I already have."

A tentative smile spread across his face. He had not expected to get over that ground so lightly. "Would you like to come for a drive around the park this afternoon?"

"Will you be driving your bays?"

"Of course."

"All four of them?"

Beau's eyes opened wide, a curious expression on his face. "How do you know I have two pairs of bays?"

"I don't know exactly. It is more an assumption that you must have bought a second pair when you were elected to the Four Horse Club."

"I'm impressed. I've a good mind to drive both pairs for you, though it will cause some stares. It will be tempting not to rattle around the park at high speed, but I think I can handle it."

If he wanted any reward for his decision, it was the glow of happiness on Eliza's face and another glimpse of the charming dimple in her chin.

Eliza was in a state of rapture. Beau had called for her as promised that afternoon, and now she sat beside him on the seat of his high-perch phaeton behind four of the most beautiful horses she had ever seen. To judge by the smoothness of their movement, Beau had done an excellent job of matching the second pair.

She itched to get her hands on the reins, but dared not ask. Perhaps it was as well. Four horses would be a lot to handle, and she would rather try it in a less crowded environment than Hyde Park on a sunny afternoon in the season.

Half-way around the circuit, Eliza caught sight of two ladies strolling along the path together. Her heart sank as she recognised them—Lady Frances Whitlow and her sister-in-law, Harriet.

She glanced at Beau's face. He looked about as pleased as she was to see his sister and her companion, and Eliza hoped he would drive past without stopping.

It was too much to hope for. Frances hailed him and, with a resigned look on his face, he drew his horses to a standstill.

"Elizabeth," her cousin said, smiling up at her. "What a delight to see you. I don't believe we have had the chance to talk since I was married."

Eliza murmured some words of congratulation, but almost before she finished, Frances spoke again.

"Harriet, this is my cousin, Miss Merry. You may have seen her at Lady Castleford's ball. Elizabeth, this is my new sister, Miss Whitlow."

The two ladies bowed their heads in acknowledgement.

It warmed Eliza to note that Beau greeted his half-sister and her companion in the briefest way and focused his eyes back on his reins immediately. When she glanced at the two ladies, she realised why.

Harriet Whitlow had stepped forward, so she was almost touching the carriage and was casting a most provocative look up at Beau.

"Aren't you going to invite me to take a turn around the park, Beaumont?" she said, purring like a cat. "I should so love to feel the paces of your beautiful horses."

Before Beau could utter a word, Frances addressed Eliza. "I'm sure you won't mind giving up your seat to Harriet for a short while, will you?"

Eliza's face clouded over with disappointment. She looked beseechingly at Beau, who shot her an apologetic grimace. Eliza wanted very much to say no, but without Beau's support, she felt unable to refuse the combined forces of the other two women.

Beau's groom jumped down from his perch and helped Eliza exchange places with Harriet. A self-satisfied smile spread across Miss Whitlow's face, and she shot Frances a triumphant glance as Beau gave a light touch of his whip and sent his bays trotting off around the circuit.

Eliza watched wistfully after them before reluctantly turning to her cousin.

"Such a charming girl, my sister. Very popular with the gentlemen. Beaumont will be lucky if he can get her."

Eliza stared after the disappearing phaeton and said nothing as she absorbed her cousin's words. Should she be concerned? Did Frances have any reason to suppose Beau *wanted* to get Harriet? She would have liked to ask, but somehow, she could not find the words.

"I confess I was a trifle jealous of Harriet's ensemble today. How I wish I could wear that shade of green to such effect. You must admit, she looked ravishing. Beaumont couldn't keep his eyes off her."

After walking only a short distance, Frances declared she needed to rest. They found a bench and sat down to await the carriage's return. "I tire so easily in my delicate condition."

Eliza was aware her cousin was in the family way, but she had no wish to listen to her talk about her approaching confinement, and refused to give her any encouragement.

Frances seemed disappointed by Eliza's lack of curiosity, but was determined to tell her about her *delicate condition,* whether or not she wanted to hear it.

"Mama says I have a robust constitution and there is no reason I cannot enjoy the season now the nausea has passed. How is your sister? No nasty sickness to stop her from enjoying herself?"

Eliza's temper rose at her relative's poorly concealed nosiness. It hadn't even crossed her mind that Georgie might be in the family way. Her sister had certainly not said anything to her, but she was determined not to let Frances know that.

"She is in perfect health, thank you. Not everyone is susceptible to sickness."

Her cousin made some non-committal sound and reverted to the subject of her own condition.

"Whitlow is delighted, of course, as are his parents. So vital to secure the succession of the barony. I hope Georgiana will provide Castleford with an heir. Such an important duty of a wife."

"A duty? Children are a gift from God."

"Yes, yes. I know," Frances said, dismissing Eliza's words as an irritation, "but it would be a shame if she failed Castleford in this."

With difficulty, Eliza bit back some of the inappropriate responses that came to mind.

"Castleford is perfectly happy with his choice of wife, whether they have ten sons or none. You only have to see them together to know that."

Frances tittered in a way that grated on Eliza's ears. "Yes, indeed. So quaint that Castleford dances attendance on his wife everywhere she goes."

The battle was on. Eliza's eyes sparkled with indignation. Georgiana would quake, knowing her sister was in danger of saying something outrageous.

"It must be so comforting for her to know Castleford's love does not depend on her ability to produce an heir." She made a show of looking about her. "I don't see Mr Whitlow. Is he tired of accompanying you out already?"

Frances curled up her nose disdainfully, her lips down-turned in scorn. "How unfashionable that would be. Whitlow is at his club. Gentlemen do not care to squire ladies around unless they are on the lookout for a wife."

Eliza could stomach no more of Frances's arrogance. She jumped up from the bench. "Let's walk."

Despite her cousin's protests, Eliza strode away from her along the path. She soon recollected herself and walked back to her companion, but she refused to engage in any further conversation.

At last, the Viscount's phaeton came bowling down the track and stopped beside them.

Miss Whitlow had a smug expression on her face and shot Frances a knowing look before turning back to Beau. After gazing into his eyes for what Eliza thought was an excessive length of time, Harriet favoured him with another of her provocative smiles before allowing his man to hand her down from the phaeton.

Eliza fidgeted with her reticule, embarrassed to observe Harriet's behaviour. Such brazen confidence produced a lowering sensation in the pit of her stomach. How could she compete with such a woman?

Her spirits lifted when she caught Beau's groom raising his eyebrows in his master's direction behind Harriet's back before turning a politely disinterested face toward her as he helped her climb back into the phaeton.

As she took her seat, she glanced across at Beau, and her spirits rose even more. He did not look smitten by the very obvious charms of Harriet Whitlow—he looked harassed.

They bid their farewells to the two ladies, and Beau turned his attention to his horses, letting out an audible sigh of relief as they drove away.

Eliza could not suppress a grin. In that moment, she was quite content. Seated beside Beau, she felt no need to talk as she enjoyed the breeze blowing on her face, cooling the annoyance from her heated conversation with Frances and Harriet's flirtatious behaviour.

Beau seemed to appreciate the quiet and when they arrived back at her sister's house, he gave her a definite smile of approval before handing the reins to his groom so he could help her down from the phaeton himself.

On balance, Eliza thought it was no bad thing that she had been forced to give up her seat to Harriet for a time. The contrast between them was so great that the comparison must benefit her. Beau had seemed so relieved to be rid of Miss Whitlow there could only be one interpretation.

A whisper of hope settled in Eliza's heart. He preferred her to Harriet.

# Chapter 9

BY THE TIME EASTER Sunday arrived, Eliza's confidence was waning. She had seen Beau often, and danced with him at every ball, but it was hard to keep believing he preferred her when he danced as much with Miss Whitlow.

Horrible Harriet pursued Beau relentlessly, and he seemed unable—or unwilling—to resist her. Eliza feared her rival would stop at nothing to catch him, even to the point of trapping Beau into marriage if the opportunity presented itself.

Eliza knelt in the pew of St George's Hanover Square and prayed for forgiveness for the wicked thoughts she harboured toward her rival. She knew the Bible said she should love her enemies, but it was hard—so hard—to love Harriet Whitlow.

As she rose from her kneeling stance and retook her seat, she glanced across at the Harting pew. She could not seem to stop herself, although she'd already noticed Beau wasn't there. She was disappointed he was missing church on Easter Sunday.

After the service had finished, Harriet approached her. She seemed to delight in mocking Eliza whenever the opportunity arose.

"Such a waste of a new bonnet," she said, looking at Eliza's hat.

"Why? I like to wear my best for church, especially as it's Easter."

"Because Lord Beaumont is not here," she said, as if stating the obvious. "I saw you glance at the pew. Didn't he tell you he would be absent?"

Eliza stiffened at Harriet's mocking words. No, Beau had forgotten to mention he would not be in church today. Had he told Harriet? The possibility upset her, and she did not trust herself to reply.

"Frances says Beaumont only attends service because his mother requires it. I do not suppose he would take kindly to being obliged to attend church every week."

"No, indeed. I don't care to be *obliged* to attend church every week either," said Eliza.

Harriet's brow puckered. "And yet you must. Because of your father. And now, because you are staying with your highly religious brother-in-law. I daresay the habit is so ingrained, you would find it hard to stop."

"But I have no wish to stop. I said I don't care to be *obliged* to attend. I come because I want to."

Harriet gave a muffled laugh, as if such a notion had never crossed her mind. "If we only came because we wanted to, the church would not be half this full, and Beaumont would probably never attend church at all, but spend the time with his precious horses instead."

Eliza could hear the contempt in her voice and thought what a dreadful wife Harriet would make Beau. She despised what he loved. Horses. Racehorses.

Her lips spread into a wide smile as realisation dawned. She knew why Beau wasn't here—he was at Newmarket for the races. No one would insist on his driving back from Suffolk to attend a service in London. How foolish of her to forget.

"But then, Beau's absence today does not reflect a reluctance to be in church. It is unavoidable. Not even my father would expect it of him under the circumstances."

She watched a look of disbelief descend onto Harriet's face, followed swiftly by one of chagrin as it occurred to her that Eliza knew why Beau was not here. And she was sure Harriet did not, though she did her best to hide it.

"No, of course not. It would be quite unreasonable."

"Indeed." Eliza bowed her head toward Harriet before moving away to join her sister, unable to quell the distinct feeling of triumph she felt in having bested her rival.

She would pray for forgiveness for her uncharitable feelings later.

The following Tuesday, Eliza was obliged to visit the British Gallery with her aunt—and Harriet. She stared up at a painting, wishing for the tenth time that morning she had realised Beau was out of town before accepting the invitation. To spend hours staring at pictures without the balm of his presence was purgatory.

It was small consolation that her aunt also bemoaned his absence. Eliza feared it did not augur well for Beau when he returned from Newmarket.

At least she had persuaded Charlotte to come too. To face Lady Harting and Miss Whitlow devoid of moral support would have been unbearable.

Harriet had something intelligent to say about every piece of artwork they looked at, earning her approving smiles, whereas Eliza was totally out of her depth, and struggled to find anything to say at all.

"What vigorous pencil work," Harriet said. "Wouldn't you agree, your ladyship?"

"Indeed. A dramatic representation of Christ's burial. What's your opinion, Elizabeth?"

Eliza thought Jesus looked too old, but she didn't think her aunt would approve of such a flippant comment. She shot a desperate glance at Charlotte for inspiration, but her sister shrugged her shoulders, showing she was just as clueless.

Eliza knew she had to say something. "I...I..."

The more she floundered, the hotter her cheeks became, and the superior look on Harriet's face grew. "I...agree," she said, as nothing else came to mind.

Her aunt looked down her nose at her niece with a pinched expression on her face, but after a moment, she moved onto the next picture.

Eliza let out a sigh of relief. She hooked her arm in Charlotte's and they trailed as far behind her aunt and Harriet as they dared.

"I'm sorry," Eliza whispered. "This exhibition is—"

"Over there." Charlotte nodded toward a middle-aged lady with an intelligent-looking face. "Isn't that Miss Austen?"

"Yes. I believe you're right."

"We should pay our respects," her sister said with an eagerness that made Eliza suspicious. "Father would want us to. Please, Eliza."

"What's the urgency? What aren't you telling me?"

Charlotte had the grace to blush. "The Austens are hosting a concert that Georgie's been invited to…"

Eliza's heart sank. Music was even worse than art. If Miss Austen extended the invitation to Charlotte, she would be bound to include her as well. Another evening of purgatory—and one she would avoid, if she could.

Drawing their conversation to an abrupt close, Eliza hurried to catch up with Lady Harting. Charlotte scowled at her, but she was unmoved and gave her full attention to the next painting.

"Good morning," said a deep voice from behind them.

The whole party turned, and there was William with a broad grin on his face, delighted with himself for surprising them.

Lady Harting acknowledged her nephew, and he bowed to Miss Whitlow before offering each of his sisters an arm.

"What are you doing here?" Charlotte asked him as they lagged behind again so their conversation could not be overheard. "You aren't in any trouble, are you?"

"No, you goose. A friend was driving into town, so I hitched a lift to come and see how you were doing. Georgie told me where you were, and I couldn't wait for you to get back, so I thought I'd surprise you."

"Humph. I don't believe you for a minute. You wouldn't have been in such a rush to find us if we were out shopping."

William grinned at his twin. "You know me so well. I've been craving a chance to cast my eye over this year's exhibition, and this seemed the perfect opportunity. But why on earth are you here? Since when did either of you enjoy looking at paintings?"

"We don't," Eliza said with feeling.

"Then why did you come?"

Charlotte put her hands on her hips and glared at him. "I thought that was obvious. Lady Harting invited us."

William's face lit up with amusement. "Never tell me Beau is here, too?"

"No. Lucky for him, he's at the races," said Eliza, "but I thought he was going to be here, otherwise I would never have agreed to come."

"Beau's out of town? Bother. I wanted his advice."

Eliza gave her brother a penetrating look.

After a few moments, he succumbed to her silent interrogation. "If you must know, I'm thinking of setting up my carriage."

"Can you afford it?" asked Charlotte.

He dropped his gaze, refusing to meet his sisters' eyes. "I must have a way of getting myself about. I may have let it slip out in Grandmama's hearing—"

Eliza was not impressed by his underhand tactics. "You wretch! Do you mean she's paying?"

He looked sheepish. "Maybe…"

"You'd better make sure you spend Grandmama's money well," Eliza said, poking him in the chest.

"That's why I wanted Beau's advice, but I'm at a standstill if he's out of town. I've only got a few days and so I'll probably have to leave before he's back."

Eliza's eyes sparkled with excitement. "I could help you choose a pair."

"No."

"Don't you trust me?"

"Of course I trust you, but how can it be done? I can't take you to Tattersall's with me."

Eliza pouted, feeling the weight of her skirts dragging her down. "Why not?"

"I don't think ladies go there. I'd take you if I could."

"What if I dressed up as your friend Robson, like I do for the hunt?"

"Absolutely not," said Charlotte, reminding them of her presence. "You're mad even to think of it."

"She's right this time. If Georgie found out, she'd be furious."

"Please, Will." Eliza could see his resolve weakening. "If you take me, I promise to sit for my portrait without complaining."

Her brother's eyes lit up. She knew she had him then.

To persuade Charlotte to agree would be trickier, but not impossible, as her sister had unwittingly shown how to win her over. It would be a sacrifice, but it would be worth it.

"I'll come with you to speak to Miss Austen," Eliza said, "and I'll even attend the concert with you if I must."

Charlotte sniffed. "Very well, but I still advise against it."

"Tomorrow morning?" asked Eliza, barely able to contain her excitement.

William nodded. "And now, perhaps you'll let me look at the artwork."

"Please do. See if you can keep up with Horrible Harriet," said Eliza. "She can spout as much rubbish about the paintings as you can, and her superiority is becoming intolerable."

William's nose twitched. "Horrible Harriet, is it? I'm certain I can relieve you of her company for a while."

He walked across toward Harriet. Charlotte and Eliza exchanged glances and followed. If William was out to make mischief, they wanted to see him in action.

"How are you enjoying the exhibition, Miss Whitlow?"

"Very much, Mr Merry. An excellent display of art."

"As one connoisseur to another, I am eager to know what you think of Hall's *Haemon and Antigone*."

Harriet glowed at his attentions, but hesitated to offer her opinion. "It is a very fine piece."

"Hmm. I confess I'm not keen on the way he has painted the lights. They're like scattered grapes—but perhaps you have a different perspective. I would be delighted if you would give me your point of view."

William offered Harriet his arm, and after a moment's hesitation, she took it. Though not wishing to appear inconstant to the absent Beau, she could not resist the lure of walking around the gallery on the arm of a handsome gentleman. And even his sisters admitted their brother was a very good-looking young man.

"Would you join us?" he asked, offering his other arm to Lady Harting. She took it, and the three of them moved away, leaving Eliza and Charlotte to lag behind.

With her eyes set on the prize of a visit to Tattersall's, Eliza seized the opportunity to approach their neighbour from Hampshire. "How do you do, Miss Austen?"

The two girls dipped into a curtsey and the lady acknowledged them with a graceful nod.

"We did not expect to see you in London," Eliza said. "How are your mother and sister?"

"In good health, when last I heard. I'm staying with my brother Henry in Sloane Street. Your father and mother, are they well? And all your family?"

"Yes, thank you. We're residing with our sister in Berkeley Square."

"Ah, yes. Lady Castleford. I must congratulate you on her marriage. It was a love match, was it not?"

"It was."

"I am delighted for her. I believe everyone should have the chance to marry for love if they can. And what say you, Miss Charlotte? Do you approve of your sister's marriage?"

"I am happy for her, but I say there is no shame in remaining unmarried."

"No," said Miss Austen, her eyes shining. "Provided she is rich, there is no need for a lady to marry, but spinsters have the deplorable habit of becoming poor. To always have to depend on others is not pleasant. It is best to marry for love, however, so my advice to you both is to be prudent about where you bestow your affection, and if at all possible, make sure you fall in love with rich men. To be poor is not...comfortable."

She paused for a moment, lost in her thoughts, but then continued in a brighter tone. "But I have no cause for complaint. I'm blessed with a large family and a dear sister and plenty to occupy my time. Which puts me in mind of something. My brother's wife is holding a party next week and has hired some excellent players. I believe she has already invited Lady Castleford, but knowing how much you love music, Miss Charlotte, I shall ask her to send a note, including you both in the invitation. I do hope you'll be able to come."

"You are most kind," said Charlotte, "but I trust it's not too presumptuous of me to ask you to invite Lord Castleford's brother rather than my sister? I assure you, Mr Warren would appreciate the music a great deal more."

Miss Austen's eyes sparkled with amusement as she agreed to Charlotte's suggestion, and Eliza wondered if she believed she was forwarding a romance. Eliza wasn't about to disillusion her. She was too grateful to Charlotte for saving her from the concert, and did not want to jeopardise her narrow escape.

They took their leave and returned to their aunt's side. It was doubtful whether Lady Harting had even noticed their absence, as William had kept his audience enthralled with an endless supply of comments about the artwork they were viewing.

Eliza found the rest of their visit to the British Gallery more pleasurable. Time passed much faster now their brother was with them. And although she still did not appreciate the paintings, she could savour the delicious prospect of the next day, when—for a few hours—she could escape from her skirts, and all the restrictions that went with them.

# Chapter 10

THE FOLLOWING MORNING, ELIZA escaped from the house undetected. She was glad she had invested in one of the robe pelisses that were currently in fashion. If she kept the loose-fitting coat pulled close, it covered her jacket and breeches, whilst her wide-brimmed hat hid her wig. She hoped no one would notice the rather mannish boots poking out underneath.

When Eliza arrived at the mews, Finch was already saddling up her horse.

He turned to greet her, but his brow puckered as he met her gaze. "I know that look. What mischief are you brewing now?"

"Can't you guess?" she asked, moving to the back of the stall and whisking off her coat and bonnet. "Let's just say that I shan't be needing the side-saddle today."

"Mr Robson," her groom said in a voice so full of disapproval that Eliza could almost taste it. "I did not expect to see you in London."

Finch tutted as William appeared at her side, and handed her the top hat she'd been unable to put on earlier. "I might have guessed."

"We're going to Tattersall's," she said, with a defiant lift of her chin.

Her groom grunted. "I suppose there's no point trying to dissuade you?"

"None at all."

With a disapproving sniff, Finch resumed his work, muttering under his breath as he prepared the horses. Not until she and William were mounted did he address her again. "Be careful."

Eliza nodded and rode out of the yard.

"Happy?" asked William, riding alongside her.

"Yes—though I'd rather be in the country. I long for a good gallop. Here, all I can do is trot around the park at a sedate pace—not what

I call a proper ride. I couldn't gallop on this horse if I tried. I doubt she's capable of it. Which is probably why Georgie put this mount at my disposal—to make sure I didn't forget myself."

"Oh dear. What a trial. How unfortunate our sister knows you so well."

"I appreciate she's only trying to protect me from myself, but it makes me reluctant to ride at all. Particularly not with Beau when he's always so magnificently mounted."

"I suppose he's driven you around the park with his bays."

"Several times."

"Has he let you take the reins?"

"I haven't liked to ask. He has such beautiful horses, and I wouldn't care to be responsible for—"

"Don't be ridiculous. You drive better than I do, and if Beau won't trust you with his team, I don't know why you're wasting your time with him. Ask."

"I'm not sure I dare. I'd be tempted to spring them—"

William chuckled. "Perhaps you're right to wait until you're away from London. You'd be sure to set tongues wagging if you tore around Hyde Park at high speed."

When they arrived at Tattersall's, some of Eliza's confidence deserted her, but it was more than outweighed by the excitement of seeing the interior of the famous repository. Once inside the stables, they were lost in the crowd of fashionable gentlemen examining the horses on offer. Remembering her male character, she swaggered along beside William and started looking over the animals up for sale.

They passed by a few stalls until they came to the first pair. Eliza looked at the pedigree and shook her head. "Anything that's come from Mr Burton's stable is not worth considering. He can't judge horseflesh to save his life."

Her brother snorted. "How did you learn that?"

"I keep my ears open. I've heard Beau moaning about him."

They moved to the next pair, and Eliza stepped forward to examine them. "Too long in the back."

"What about these?" he asked, pointing to some bays.

She looked them over. "Hmm. A nice pair by the look of it, but no way of telling if they'll pull well together. Do you recognise the name of the seller?"

William shook his head, and as he did so, he must have seen something. He twisted back round to face her, his eyes wide with alarm. "We need to go. Now."

Eliza followed his gaze, and her breath hitched as she caught sight of Anthony and Beau, who had just walked through the door of the stables.

She gave a quick nod, realising her danger. Anthony would recognise her at once.

"They must have returned from Newmarket and come to settle their debts," William said.

An acquaintance hollered Anthony, and he veered off in the opposite direction from where they stood, but Beau hovered just inside the entrance, making it impossible to escape.

William kept his back to the door, trying to block them from his line of vision, but it was too late. Beau had seen them and was heading straight for their position.

"Merry!" he cried. "And your friend—Robson, wasn't it?"

Eliza knew she had to brave it out. To run away would attract too much notice. If she could just keep up the bravado, no one would suspect.

William did his best to draw Beau's attention. "You're the very man I wanted to see. I'm looking to set up my carriage and brought Robson along with me to inspect what was on offer. He's got a pretty good eye for a horse. Better than me. I fancied the greys, but he said they were too long in the back."

Beau glanced at the horses Eliza had criticised and nodded. "He's right. But these"—turning to the pair of bays they had been considering—"might be just what you're looking for."

"That's what Robson said, but neither of us has heard of Mr Cunningham."

Beau's face clouded over, and Eliza wondered what kind of man he was. "You haven't been around the race track, Merry, or you'd be familiar with the name. He owns a large stud in Sussex, including Majesty who's unbeaten this year."

"Is he likely to be trading a broken-down pair?"

"No. Cunningham wouldn't allow anything second-rate to be associated with his name."

"Then why's he selling? Does he need the money?"

"Far from it. He's a very wealthy man. These two are from his stables. I've seen them in action, and they're a sweet-stepping pair. You won't do better for the price."

Eliza saw Anthony moving toward them and judged it was time to go. "I'm glad to see my advice was not amiss. Please excuse me," she said, nodding at Beau and then at her brother. "I have another engagement."

She spotted a clear path to the entrance and, her heart pounding, she slipped past Anthony while his back was turned. She hoped Beau wouldn't mention Robson's presence to him, or she would be bound to face a fresh round of teasing.

Once mounted and riding back to the mews alone, Eliza breathed freely again. She revelled in her narrow escape, but it had been far too close for comfort. With reluctance, she had to admit Georgiana was right, and it was time to lay Robson to rest.

Eventually, Beau would see through her disguise, and she could not predict his reaction. Anthony thought it was a good joke, but his opinion was unimportant.

How would Beau react if he discovered she had been masquerading as a man?

# Chapter 11

THE NEXT MORNING, AFTER dressing with extra care, Beau presented himself at Harting House in answer to a parental summons. No doubt, the visit would be even more unpleasant than usual as his mother would be peeved with him for escaping to the Newmarket Craven race meeting without taking his leave of her.

He had known there would be consequences, but he didn't regret his decision. He had feared she would discover some way to prevent him from going, and he'd needed to get away.

From her. And from the pressure she was putting on him to find a wife.

Beau pulled at his intricately tied cravat, took a deep breath and entered the drawing room. His mother sat in a chair by the fire, her back straight and her fingers intertwined in her lap with her thumbs pressed together.

"How kind of you to take the time to visit me, Beaumont."

"I came as soon as I received your message."

"How strange. I thought I sent it round to your lodgings three days ago."

"I'm sorry, madam, but unfortunately I was out of town and my man did not give me the note until this morning."

She flared her nostrils as she glared at him. "As you say, how unfortunate. I had no notion you had left London."

Heat coursed up Beau's neck and into his cheeks. On this occasion, he deserved her recriminations. It had been rude of him to go out of town without taking leave of her.

"I apologise for not informing you of my intentions."

His mother said nothing, and Beau felt the tension in his body mounting.

After a long pause, she spoke again. "You were missed at Lady Helston's ball on Tuesday."

Drat. He'd forgotten about that.

"I'm sorry. I was otherwise engaged."

She sucked in her cheeks in displeasure. "I am taking a party to the opera at the King's Theatre tomorrow evening, and I wish you and Elizabeth to accompany me."

Beau's spirit of contrition evaporated. Was this her way of punishing him for daring to leave town without her permission? To attend the opera with his mother would be agony. He would have to listen to the infernal squawking, unable to understand a word, and pretend to be enjoying it to satisfy his parent.

At least she wanted him to bring her niece rather than the Whitlow girl. He much preferred Eliza's company, even though she was his mother's current favourite. She understood horses—and she didn't expect him to appreciate opera.

Beau frowned. Eliza disliked opera as much as he did, and she would not thank him for inviting her to endure such an evening's entertainment. It would be torture for both of them.

He had to make a push to get out of it, for both their sakes. "You'll have to excuse me, Mother. I have other plans." He hoped she would not enquire what those other plans might be.

She drew her eyebrows together. "I am sure you can change them."

Darn it. It wasn't going to be that easy to fob her off.

An idea popped into his head. "I'm afraid that won't be possible, because I'm taking Elizabeth to Astley's."

"Astley's?"

"Elizabeth likes horses."

She pursed her lips and glared at him. After holding his gaze for what seemed like an age, she turned away. "Very well. Another time."

With a nod, she dismissed him.

Beau did not need to be told twice. He made a hasty exit and headed straight for Lord Castleford's residence in Berkeley Square.

To his relief, when he arrived at Warren House, he found the ladies at home.

He took a seat next to Eliza, but before he could speak, Charlotte addressed him. "I hope you're here to beg forgiveness."

He stared blankly at her. Why must he ask for forgiveness?

"There was no need for you to say anything," Eliza said, scowling at her sister. "I told you I didn't look for him."

"Did you forget something?" Charlotte continued. "Lady Helston's ball?"

Darn it. Had he asked Eliza to stand up with him for the first two dances?

"I'm sorry. Did I leave you standing?"

"It's nothing. I realised you wouldn't be there and gave the set to someone else."

He wrinkled his nose in confusion. "You knew? But I never said...I confess, I forgot about the ball..."

"How was Romeo?"

Beau blinked. How did she know where he'd been?

"Your colt—he's still doing well, isn't he?"

He nodded, amazed at Eliza's acceptance of his failure, brushing it aside as if it were nothing. She seemed more concerned about his horse than the fact he had not made good on the dances he'd promised. Without further encouragement, he launched into a full account of Romeo's progress.

"And the races?" Eliza asked in a tight voice, a look on her face that failed to hide her disapproval. "Did you win?"

Her expression unsettled him, and his chest tightened in response. He was keen to make her understand. "I won, but only a few hundred pounds. I don't gamble what I can't afford to lose, so I won't wager large amounts of money, even when I'm almost certain they'll come good. It's not worth the risk of being wrong."

As fast as it had appeared, the sternness melted away. "I see."

The sudden pressure in his chest subsided, and it startled Beau to discover how relieved he felt to have wiped that disapproving look from her face.

It was at this point he remembered why he'd come. "Eliza, would you care to accompany me to Astley's Royal Amphitheatre tomorrow night?"

"I'm afraid I am already engaged to go to the King's Theatre with Lord Castleford and my sisters."

Beau's heart sank. That was the worst possible answer. His mother would see her there and know he'd lied.

"However, Georgie knows I'm not fond of the opera, and I'm certain she will release me from the engagement." Eliza turned to her sister. "You don't mind if I go to Astley's with Beau instead, do you?"

He held his breath as he waited for Georgiana to answer.

"Of course not."

Beau could breathe again, and he beamed at Eliza in gratitude. "I'll call for you a little after six. I'm so pleased you can come."

And relieved.

How fortunate Eliza hated the opera as much as he did. She had saved him from another scold from his mother.

# Chapter 12

Eliza sat in the drawing room after dinner the next day, waiting for Beau to call for her. She watched the clock as the hands edged their way toward the appointed time, twiddling her fingers in nervous anticipation.

"Stop fidgeting," Georgiana said. "You're only going to Astley's. I still can't believe you would rather watch a children's entertainment than come to the opera."

"It is not a children's entertainment," snapped Eliza. "And I cannot see why my preference should surprise you. It might not be as sophisticated, but I've heard the performers are well worth watching."

"You always preferred horses to humans."

"Who said I was talking about the horses?" Eliza said with a wicked smile, her eyes twinkling. "I believe some of the riders are decidedly good-looking."

"Elizabeth Merry!" Georgiana exclaimed, turning a deep shade of pink. She picked up a cushion and catapulted it across the room at her sister.

Eliza laughed and threw the cushion back. "Glad to know I can still make you blush, Lady Castleford, even if you are an old married woman. Are you sure you wouldn't rather come to Astley's with me?"

"Quite sure. I have no need of other good-looking men. I am perfectly satisfied with my own."

The door opened, and a footman entered carrying a silver salver. He came up to Eliza and bowed.

She picked up the note, which was addressed to her in scrawly, almost illegible, handwriting. Although she had never seen it, she guessed it was Beau's hand, and she bit her lip as she broke open the seal.

It only took her a moment to digest the contents. Her disappointment must have shown.

"Has he cried off?" Georgiana asked.

Eliza shook her head. "No. He warns me he's had to enlarge his party to include his sister Frances and, worse still, Harriet Whitlow."

"I never thought Frances would condescend to visit Astley's."

"I'm sure she would go anywhere that suited her purpose. It is clear she wants Beau to marry her sister-in-law and is doing everything she can to throw Harriet in his way. I'm certain Frances will feel at home at Astley's. After all, her manners are only fit for the stables."

"Don't you dare say that to Frances's face," Georgiana said. "We would never hear the end of it from our aunt."

"You said yourself she's vulgar—and she is."

"I hope she doesn't ruin your evening. It's not too late to change your mind and come with us to the opera instead."

Eliza stuck out her tongue in response.

"There's no need to be rude. I get the message, but I can't help wishing for your sake that Beau could learn to say no."

"I expect he did it to please Lady Harting," said Eliza, bristling in his defence.

"You mean he was too scared to refuse."

Eliza closed her eyes, trying to calm her growing frustration. It disappointed her that Georgie had such a low opinion of Beau. He would stand up to his mother when he needed to. After all, he had not allowed her to force him into marrying Georgie last year. Not that Castleford would have let him.

"You know Beau depends on his mother's goodwill to keep him in funds," she said, reopening her eyes. "He has to do what she says, or she will stop his allowance and he won't be able to pay for the upkeep of his stables."

She saw Georgie was unconvinced by her words, but it was no more than she expected. Her sister would never appreciate how important Beau's horses were to him in the same way she did.

At last the carriage arrived and Eliza hurried outside, wearing a dark blue pelisse and clutching her reticule in her hand. She tried not to let the unwelcome addition to their party bother her and urged her lips into a smile for Beau's benefit. It was the first evening she had spent in his company for over a week, and she was determined to make the most of it.

A footman helped her mount the steps, but as she climbed inside, she discovered her forced smile was unnecessary. The carriage was empty apart from a single passenger. Anthony.

"Beau thought you wouldn't care to be squashed up beside the Whitlows, so I offered to bring you instead. Templecombe begged to be included and Beau gave in, thinking his cousin might be of some use to entertain the other ladies."

"How thoughtful of him," she said, stifling a chuckle. Beau might value his cousin's friendship, but why he thought any woman would pay his relative the slightest attention when he and Anthony were there was beyond her.

Her companion raised his eyebrows, obviously seeing more of her amusement than she meant to show.

"Don't look at me like that," Eliza said, rapping her fan on his shoulder. "I'm certain Mr Templecombe will be a welcome addition to our party, and from what I have seen of him so far, he is unlikely to expose my lack of book learning."

Anthony let out a guffaw. "You could say that. Poor Templecombe. He learned even less at Cambridge than Beau did. Can't figure out why Beau let him come, as he knows his cousin is on the lookout for a rich wife. I suppose he must have been the only person available at short notice."

At this, Eliza's ears perked up. "Just when did Beau ask you to join him?"

"Last night, at White's. If he hadn't sounded so desperate for male support, I wouldn't have given up an evening at the opera to come. Daresay he would have had to accompany his mother to the King's Theatre if he wasn't already engaged to attend Astley's with you."

Eliza pursed her lips in disapproval. That explained why Beau was so relieved she had changed her plans to go with him. He had fabricated an alternative engagement to avoid a trip to the opera. Whilst she sympathised with his motivation, she disapproved of him lying—even though it had extricated her from the same evening of torture.

An unwelcome thought occurred to her. Was she any better masquerading as Mr Robson? Was she as guilty of lying as Beau? When had deception become second nature to her?

She brushed away the unpleasant feelings, unwilling to discuss them, and changed the subject.

"Thank you for the warning about Mr Templecombe's matrimonial aspirations, but I doubt he'll overstep the line. And if he does, I'm certain Beau will put him in his place."

Anthony rolled his eyes, but Eliza ignored him.

Why did everyone have such little faith in Beau?

He would take care of her. She was sure of it.

"Where are they?" Beau muttered under his breath as he waited for Ant's carriage to arrive at Astley's. "What could be taking them so long?"

He hovered at the entrance to the box he had secured, keeping his distance from the rest of the party—especially Miss Whitlow. She had spent the brief journey sending flirtatious comments in his direction, and he refused to subject himself to more of the same until he had his friend's support.

For all the help Templecombe gave him, Beau could have been alone with the ladies. He'd regret allowing him to come if he discovered his cousin had wheedled an invitation out of him to pursue Eliza.

When Ant and Eliza arrived, Beau welcomed them like a man on a desert island welcomes a ship.

"Good evening, Miss Merry," he said, keeping his tone formal whilst the others were listening. "I hope you approve of this box. It's in an excellent position to watch the performance. I considered getting seats in the pit, so we could be nearer the action, but you get a better view from up here, though you're not so close to the horses."

Lady Frances screwed up her nose. "The pit? You must be joking. Even from this distance, the stench makes me feel nauseous."

Beau felt tempted to ask his sister why she had forced her company on him if she disliked the odour so much, but kept his mouth shut. He glanced at Eliza and, from the exasperated expression on her face, he guessed she was thinking the same thing. As their eyes met, she bit her lip, and they shared a covert grin before she looked away.

"I like the smell of horses," Beau said after a lengthy pause.

Miss Whitlow kept silent, but the way she wrinkled up her nose expressed her feelings.

After Beau had shown Eliza to her seat, Miss Whitlow claimed his attention by asking him a question about his matched bays, trying to regain the ground she had lost.

But she'd already revealed her true opinion, and he would not forget it.

He did not believe for one minute she was interested in his horses and offered only a brief answer. The start of the performance saved him from further conversation.

Perched on the front of his chair, he leaned over the edge of the box, his eyes fixed on the arena. As he glanced to his side, he noted Eliza sat in the same position, and his nose twitched with amusement. She must have felt his gaze on her, because she glimpsed at him for a few seconds and smiled before returning her attention to the performance of *The Tyrant Saracen and the Noble Moor*.

When it was over, Eliza turned to him, her eyes wide with wonder.

"What magnificent animals—and so intelligent."

He was about to agree when Frances sniggered. "Intelligent? They are dumb beasts, Elizabeth. Well-trained, but dumb. Next, you will tell me they have feelings."

A spark appeared in Eliza's eyes. "But they do. I believe God made animals with the ability to think and feel. If a donkey could express its feelings when God opened its mouth, then I'm sure a horse could do the same."

Frances and Miss Whitlow looked at each other as if they thought Eliza was mad, but Beau knew what she was talking about. He struggled to remember many Bible stories, but he recalled the tale of Balaam's donkey, because it had stuck in his mind because of its oddity—that a donkey should see an angel before a man.

Beau grinned. "Balaam was the foolish one, not the donkey."

Eliza turned toward him, her face wreathed in smiles, delighted he was familiar with the story. "Yes, indeed. It pays to listen to animals."

Her eyes flitted over the arena. "Is that how they perform such marvels? By talking and listening to the horses and creating some kind of bond? To stand on the back of a horse without holding on is one thing, but to stay on whilst it gallops around and then jump to another, going at the correct speed, is nothing short of incredible."

Beau's eyes shone in response. "Getting the horses to move at the same speed is the straightforward part. I reckon I could achieve that. If you know your horses, and they know you, it would be possible. My bays are so used to pulling together, I think they would run in time with each other for me. The tricky bit is the stability. I believe there is some magic in riding around the ring that helps. I think I could do it—if I could keep my balance."

"Don't be ridiculous," said Frances. "You couldn't possibly perform like that. Why would you even want to?"

Beau scowled at his sister. "I bet I could." He pressed his mouth into a firm line that dared her to contradict him.

"You're on."

Templecombe's words drew all eyes to him. "I bet you ten guineas you can't do it."

Beau stared at his cousin. His first thought was that it was madness, but then the idea took root. Could he do it? Did he trust his horses enough? Did he have faith in his own sense of balance?

He glanced at Anthony, who shrugged his shoulders.

If Ant wasn't sure he could do it, perhaps he should laugh it off. His mother would certainly expect him to.

But before he could say another word, Miss Whitlow laid her hand on his arm. "Do not do it, Beaumont," she said in a husky voice. "Mr Templecombe is not serious. Don't risk breaking your neck for a wager."

Beau threw off her hold and glared at her, his temperature rising with his temper. "Don't you think I could do it?"

Miss Whitlow coloured.

"Of course you could," said Eliza with quiet confidence.

Frances scowled at her, turning her mouth down in disdain. "Don't encourage him," she said in a dangerously low voice, before turning her scowl on him. "You're being ridiculous to give Templecombe's foolish words even a moment's consideration. Mama would not approve."

It was an unfortunate phrase for Frances to use if she wished to dissuade him. Anger bubbled up inside Beau until he thought he would explode. He refused to let his mother dictate his life. Not this time. This was something he could control.

He stretched out his arm toward Templecombe and they shook hands. "Done," he said, with a smug look at Frances.

"I wouldn't be so sure of that. I'll tell Mama and she will put a stop to your stupidity."

Beau did not take her words lightly. No doubt she would report the whole to their mother, but he refused to be cowed by her threats.

However, if he wanted to win his bet, he needed to arrange it fast. Perhaps Astley would loan him his riding school for an hour or two.

He raised his chin in defiance at Frances and turned back to Eliza with an affectionate smile on his face. To know she believed in his ability with horses touched the very depths of his being. She had shown faith in him. It was a novel experience, and he liked it.

Eliza blushed at the warmth in his expression and lowered her eyes—but she was smiling.

And he could not help noticing the enchanting little dimple had reappeared on her chin.

# Chapter 13

TWO DAYS LATER, AT Eliza's insistence, Anthony took her to watch Beau carry out his bet. She told Georgiana they were going to Astley's riding school and left her sister to assume she was having a lesson with the great Mr Astley.

A prick of guilt stabbed at her conscience for concealing the true purpose of their outing, but she brushed it aside. What was the point in distressing Georgie by telling her? It would only lead to an unpleasant argument, and the outcome would be just the same. Nothing was going to stop her from viewing the Viscount's performance.

Eliza sat in silence, twisting her hands round and round in her lap, all the way to Astley's. Although excited at the prospect of seeing Beau ride, she feared for him if something went wrong. She didn't doubt his ability where horses were concerned, but he was attempting an extraordinary feat, and animals were unpredictable. She'd taken a tumble or two from a horse over the years with little harm, but not everyone was so fortunate. People died in riding accidents. Perhaps she'd been foolish to encourage him.

However, she was wise enough to know he could not draw back now. It was not the money, but his pride at stake. She took confidence in the fact that Mr Astley had agreed to give Beau exclusive use of his riding school. The man must have faith in his ability to succeed, because he would not care to have a dead nobleman on his hands.

When they arrived at Astley's, Eliza was taken aback to discover the audience for Beau's equestrian performance had grown. A crowd had gathered, and a glance informed her she was the only lady present.

"I thought this was to be a private affair," she said to Anthony, feeling conspicuous and out of place.

"Sorry."

Eliza shrugged. "It would not have made any difference. I had no intention of missing this."

"Maybe not, but I should have warned you. Templecombe never could hold his tongue. As might have been expected, he could not keep the wager to himself. Word spread around the sporting fraternity, and a sizeable number have laid bets on whether Beau will succeed."

"Do they think he will?"

Anthony hesitated and then shook his head. "He wasn't born to it like Astley, who's been performing tricks since he was five. I'm afraid they've come to watch Beau fail."

"Doesn't anyone believe he'll do it?" Eliza asked indignantly.

"Me. I trust his judgement with horses. If he thinks he can do it, I believe him. Besides, someone had to take the bets, didn't they? If he succeeds, I'll do very nicely out of it. Stick with me, and no one will bother you."

"I would have fitted in better in breeches," she said under her breath as she followed Anthony toward an empty area of seating.

He stopped in his tracks and frowned at her. "Thank goodness you didn't think of it. If you had done so and someone recognised you..."

His words hung in the air, his expression so stern that Eliza was relieved he hadn't seen her dressed as Mr Robson at Tattersall's.

They sat down toward the back, at some distance from where the other gentlemen had gathered around Mr Templecombe, but still with an excellent view.

Eliza tried to ignore the crowd and focused all her attention on Beau, who was walking into the arena to a tumultuous round of applause and cheering. He had one of his pairs of matched bays with him. Eliza suspected it was the duo he had owned longest—the pair he had been driving together for several years.

He mounted a horse and rode around the ring. The second followed, keeping pace with the first with little effort from Beau. His mouth was working, encouraging his horses, but she was too far away to hear what he said.

As she watched, Beau slipped his feet out of his stirrups and climbed onto the back of the left-hand horse, just behind the saddle, as it continued to move around the ring. She held her breath, saying a silent prayer for his safety, as he stood up and wavered for a moment before finding his balance.

Without realising what she was doing, she reached out and grabbed Anthony's hand, but then snatched it away as heat flooded her face. He gave her a quick reassuring smile and then both pairs of eyes fixed on Beau.

A sudden movement, and Beau jumped onto the back of the other horse, and slipped down into the saddle, letting out a whoop and pumping the air with his fist to the cheers of the audience. After a couple more circuits, he drew both horses to a standstill.

Mr Templecombe leapt out of his seat, vaulted over the barrier and landed in the ring.

He hurried over to where Beau stood and slapped him on the back. "Well, blow me down. You did it."

The other gentlemen crowded into the arena, offering their congratulations.

Eliza and Anthony made their way to the front of the seating area.

"I'll be fine," she said, urging him to go to his friend's side, as he was clearly impatient to do.

He needed no further encouragement and sprang over the balustrade to join the crowd of gentlemen.

Eliza stared at Beau, her heart glowing with admiration. She revelled in the praise his sporting colleagues heaped on him, content simply to be there.

Just for a moment, he glanced over their heads toward her. As their eyes met, she mimicked a round of applause with her hands. He bowed his head, acknowledging her congratulations, before his face disappeared into the throng of men around him.

Beau basked in the praise coming at him from every direction. He'd done it. It was a feat of horsemanship he'd never attempted before, and he had succeeded—first time. It was just as well, given the number of spectators, as it would have taken years to live down the embarrassment if he'd failed.

They'd all bet against him, but he had proved them wrong. No one had expected him to succeed, except Ant.

And Eliza.

He remembered the lone woman in the crowd and was glad she'd witnessed his victory. She had believed he could win his wager and come to see him do it. Few women would have chosen to watch such a performance and fewer still would have applauded it—but Eliza had.

What a relief he hadn't failed and let her down when she'd shown such faith in his skill.

The crowd parted as the riding school owner approached him.

"Very good, Lord Beaumont," Mr Astley said, striding over to the Viscount on his long legs. "If you ever hit on hard times, come to me for a job."

Beau shook his hand heartily. "Thank you, but I think I'll stick to riding one horse at a time. It is most kind of you to accommodate me. I don't expect it would have been so easy on the flat."

"No, indeed," said Mr Astley. "That's the beauty of the ring. Helps one's balance wonderfully."

Anthony drew near and patted Beau on the back. "Well done, old friend. You've won against the odds, and they will all pay for their lack of faith in you. We'll make a nice little profit out of this."

Templecombe linked arms with his cousin. "Time to celebrate. To the Admiral Nelson!"

"A moment, gentlemen," Beau said, withdrawing his arm. "I must see to my horses."

A general groan went up from the crowd, but no one tried to stop him as he headed out the rear of the arena to where Jem was waiting with the bays.

Beau nuzzled each horse, whispering his thanks in their ears, before leaving them to his groom, and walking back into the ring.

At once, his sporting cronies swarmed around him, sweeping him away to celebrate. As they propelled him along, Beau glanced over the seating area. He wanted to say goodbye to Eliza, to thank her for supporting him, but there was no sign of her.

Where had she disappeared to? Had one of his exuberant companions upset her?

A second glance showed him Anthony was missing. He must be returning Eliza to Georgie's house.

That was a relief—or was it?

Eliza had demonstrated remarkable loyalty by showing up to watch him win his wager, but she had come with Ant, and when he remembered the way his friend flirted with her, he felt...unsettled.

His brow furrowed. Why should Ant's behaviour bother him?

He didn't know. It never had before. But it niggled him now.

# Chapter 14

WHEN ELIZA ARRIVED AT Harting House for her aunt's ball the following evening, she was still glowing with satisfaction over Beau's successful bet. She wondered whether Frances had carried through on her threat and told her mother of the wager. If so, she suspected Beau would need to tread extra carefully around Lady Harting for a while. Not for a moment did she believe her aunt would take any pride in such a feat of horsemanship.

Eliza glanced about her, looking for Beau. She spotted one of his half-sisters, Lady Caroline, on the arm of a mature gentleman, a smug and rather superior expression on her face. He must be her betrothed, Lord Felbridge. To judge by appearances, her cousin was proud of catching an earl, even though he was a widower some twenty years older than her, desirous of a young bride to give him the heir he craved. She hoped Caroline actually liked the man.

At last, she caught sight of Beau, and her heart skipped a beat. Would he ask her for the first dance? No. It was unreasonable of her to hope for such a thing. As the son of the hostess, he would be required to open the ball with someone much more important than her.

"Miss Merry, may I have the honour of the opening set?" asked a peer whose name she couldn't recall, drawing her attention away from Beau to the gentleman in front of her.

"I would be honoured, my lord." That at least was true. She could feel honoured whilst wishing she danced with someone else.

His lordship proceeded in his normal fashion, paying her excessive compliments and putting her to the blush. It occurred to her that, although they had encountered each other frequently, she knew him no better than the day they first met, and she still stumbled over her words in his company.

Eliza wondered whether Caroline was better acquainted with her betrothed than she herself was with her dance partner. Probably not. The Earl was making a match based on her family and dowry, and it had little to do with love.

He had admired her beauty and the way she behaved in public, but the proposal had come so fast he'd had no time to discover where Caroline's interests lay, or if they held similar views on matters of faith and family. It seemed a slim basis on which to build a marriage.

What a depressing thought. But was she any better? She loved Beau and knew they shared the same passion for horses and the outdoors, but she was willing to marry him without ever having talked about things that mattered. Was it enough that she cared for him, or was she being foolish?

Back at her sister's side, Eliza tamped down her uncertainty and focused on Beau as he made his way toward her to claim her hand for the next set.

To her dismay, Miss Whitlow waylaid him before he reached her. Eliza's spirits plummeted as her rival took his arm in a possessive manner. He must have asked Horrible Harriet to stand up with him.

She swallowed her disappointment and, in her efforts to appear cheerful, she greeted Anthony's arrival with such a dazzling smile that an onlooker might have suspected this was where her heart lay.

His customary grin spread until his entire face beamed back at her. "Dance?"

Eliza nodded and took his arm, relieved to have a break from warding off unwanted attentions.

She kept her gaze lowered as they moved across the ballroom to take their place in the set, resisting the temptation to discover Beau's whereabouts.

"You're not responding to any of my compliments."

Eliza's head jerked up. "I'm sorry. Did you say something?"

Anthony sighed, a teasing look in his eyes.

"Don't you know the rules? Everyone flirts with Lord Castleford's good-for-nothing brother."

"I've told you before, I'm not *everyone*. Why would I want to flirt with you? You're like an honorary brother to me."

"Ouch! You certainly know how to take the wind out of a man's sails."

Though his words were playful enough, his tone was uncharacteristically hollow, and the mirth had gone from his eyes.

Eliza gulped hard and looked away. Was he saying he wished he were something more to her?

No. She must be mistaken. He had declared his determination never to marry more times than she could remember. It was just as well. She would hate to come between Beau and his best friend.

A few moments later, Anthony resumed his teasing, with no hint of awkwardness in his voice.

"Is there no one you feel tempted to flirt with? You can confide in me as your honorary brother."

Without thinking, Eliza looked around the room until her gaze settled on Harriet, who still clung to Beau's arm. Too late, she realised she was in danger of giving herself away, and snapped her attention back to Anthony's face, trying to look nonchalant.

Had he seen the direction of her eyes? And if he guessed who she was looking at, would he taunt her about it the way he teased her for masquerading as a man in the hunt? She did not think she could bear it.

"Who is he? I'll make him come and pay homage to you to bring the smile back to your cheeks."

But Eliza was not fooled. His lips might declare his ignorance, but the brightness in his eyes said otherwise.

Anthony had seen. He knew.

Her gaze unconsciously strayed once more to Harriet, who cast Beau such a provocative look that Eliza turned away in embarrassment. She felt so naïve. How could she attempt to rival that?

"No."

No? What did he mean? Was he saying she had no chance of winning his friend?

"Don't try to compete with that," he whispered in her ear. "Trust me. Don't change a thing."

"I couldn't compete with *that* if I tried," she said, peeping up at Anthony from under her eyelashes, making him bark with laughter.

His laugh drew several pairs of eyes, and Eliza had to suppress her amusement at the warmth of the look Anthony gave her in response, as a single word accompanied it. "Minx."

Eliza shot him an impish smile and hung on his arm as he led her into the dance.

Beau was not enjoying the evening. He had opened the ball as required, dancing with Augusta as he had done so many times before her marriage to Lord Helston. After this, he had hoped he would be free to choose his own partners.

But no. His mother had drawn Lady Whitlow and her offspring into his path and openly praised the baroness's daughter in front of him, making it impossible for him to avoid asking her for the next dance.

Not without being abominably rude and incurring his mother's displeasure, and he couldn't afford to do that.

To say he felt uneasy was an understatement. His mother must have heard about the wager by now. Why hadn't she confronted him about it? What game was she playing? She was always cross and disappointed with him, so it was hard to judge if she was more displeased with him than usual.

One thing was certain. She was more determined than ever to throw eligible females in his direction.

Every woman he danced with smirked and tittered, saying things that would have gratified his vanity if he believed them.

Miss Whitlow was the worst. She hung on his arm as if they had some sort of understanding and flaunted her substantial charms in his face. It felt like a mousetrap. If he let his guard down for one moment, he would be caught, and the ensuing pain would be excruciating.

Did she hope to tempt him to overstep the boundaries of propriety and compromise her, to force him into marriage? Such a thought sent a tremor down his body, and he wished he could run from the ballroom.

But of course, he could not.

There was only one lady who hadn't set her cap at him. Eliza Merry.

His gaze drifted around the room until he spied her dancing with his best friend. Again.

Just at that moment, she glanced at Anthony in such a way that Beau was taken aback. It was no surprise to see Ant flirt with Eliza, because he acted like that with everyone, but if he was not mistaken, Eliza was responding in kind.

His chest tightened and his hackles rose. A surge of protectiveness swept over him, making him feel exasperated with his friend. What was

Ant playing at? He shouldn't encourage Eliza to fall in love with him. He would never marry her.

Beau refused to stand by and watch him break Eliza's heart. Why was Georgie allowing such unsuitable gentlemen to focus their attentions on her sister? First Templecombe, and now Ant. He'd have to have another word with her.

At the end of the set, Beau promptly returned Miss Whitlow to her mother and headed straight for Georgiana.

"You shouldn't encourage your sister to dance with Ant," he said without preamble. "She knows he's sworn not to get married, doesn't she? Aren't you worried she will fall in love with him and break her heart?"

Beau did not appreciate the amused smile that hovered over Georgie's lips. She was not taking his words seriously.

"I can hardly stop her dancing with my brother-in-law."

"I suppose not, but don't let her lose her heart to him. He'll never marry her."

"And you will?"

Beau felt as if he'd been knocked sideways. Would he?

If his mother insisted he take a wife, he would rather marry Eliza than anyone else. Especially Miss Whitlow.

Eliza didn't have to pretend to like horses, and she had shown a lot of spunk, coming to watch him win his bet.

But he wasn't ready to lay his cards down yet. He had no wish to fall in with his mother's plans if he could help it, and he still hoped to avoid getting married at all.

"I'm just looking out for your sister," he said, refusing to meet Georgie's eyes.

When Ant and Eliza joined them, they seemed to be sharing some private joke and all Beau's irritation with his friend came flooding back. If Eliza wanted to flirt, she could jolly well do so with him.

"Would you dance the next with me, Miss Merry?" he asked her in his most formal voice, his smile somewhat forced and in danger of resembling a scowl.

Eliza's cheeks turned pink, but whether with pleasure or embarrassment, he couldn't tell. "I would love to."

Without a word to Anthony, Beau took Eliza's arm and walked off, though the dance was not yet forming. He needed to get away from his friend before he said something he would later regret.

Beau's confidence wavered when Eliza kept her eyes fixed on the ground. Would she refuse to flirt with him? Maybe her smiles were only for Ant. The thought was somewhat irritating.

"You're looking very beautiful tonight."

Beau gave a silent groan. How had he come out with such a well-used line? Couldn't he produce something more original than that?

Eliza blushed furiously at his unimaginative compliment, but said nothing and didn't so much as glance up at him.

He tried again. "Has anyone ever told you that you dance like an angel?"

This evoked a better response. She stared up at him, an impish grin on her face. "Often."

For a moment, their gaze held, and he was struck by the colour of her eyes. Such a pale blue and yet not wishy-washy, but sparkling with intensity.

"Your eyes are like sapphires," he said, staring into them and seeing his own reflected there.

"Oh!" she exclaimed, biting her bottom lip as her shy smile spread. "What a pretty thing to say."

Her response encouraged him, but he wanted more. He still hadn't persuaded her to peek up at him from under her lashes like she'd done with Ant. He did not know flirting could be such hard work.

Eliza dropped her gaze, but he continued to stare into her heart-shaped face, wishing she would look up at him again.

He could no longer see into her eyes, but he was aware of the charming dimple that appeared in her chin when she smiled and, just above it, her mouth.

Hardly realising what he was doing, he focused on her mouth. He found it...mesmerising.

What would it be like to kiss those full, red lips?

<h1 style="text-align:center">Chapter 15</h1>

ELIZA FELT THE INTENSITY of Beau's gaze before she saw it. It lit a beacon of hope in her heart. He liked her. She was sure of it.

Probably not as much as his horses, but more than Harriet. She had not seen him looking at her rival that way. And right now, that was the most important thing. That he preferred her to Miss Whitlow.

All her instincts told her Beau needed help. She could not fathom what had brought him to her side in such a strange mood. What had made him act like that? He had never tried to flirt with her before.

The fire in his eyes looked dangerous. If she was not mistaken, he had been focusing on her mouth before he met her gaze, and that meant only one thing.

He wanted to kiss her.

Her heart quickened at the thought, but this was neither the time nor the place. She wouldn't trap him into marriage by encouraging him to embrace her in the middle of his mother's ballroom.

His gaze was doing strange things to her insides. It would be safer if he stopped staring at her like that. She needed to do something. Fast.

If she could get him talking about horses, maybe that unsettling light in his eyes would disappear.

She took a big gulp. "Tell me about the Four Horse Club."

A bewildered expression passed over Beau's face, as though he had forgotten where he was, but then he seemed to come to his senses. The fire in his eyes flickered and died, and he launched into a detailed account of his driving club.

"We meet several times every year, when we all rig out in the same style. Can't say I care about clothes that much, but it gave me a genuine sense of pride when I put on my blue and yellow striped waistcoat for the first time. Some of the others have made a thing of trying to mimic a coach driver and—"

"You won't break your teeth, will you? Anthony says he knows of one member who had them knocked out so he could whistle like a coachman."

Beau's face hardened at the mention of his friend's name. Eliza could barely stop herself from grinning. Was he jealous?

"I would not go to that extreme." He paused and stared into her eyes. "Would you care if I did?"

Eliza's colour deepened. She could not find her tongue in response to the directness of his question. A brief nod was the best she could muster.

Beau seemed satisfied, and his face softened. "It's the driving skill required that attracts me, not the need to mimic a coachman."

By this time, the set was forming, and they took their places. They exchanged a few words during their dances, but the conversation was light, and he did not flirt with her again.

Eliza could not decide whether or not she was sorry.

Beau returned Eliza to her sister and headed for the door of the ballroom. He needed to escape—from what, he wasn't sure.

What had just happened to him? Had he been about to kiss Eliza? His nerves must have addled his brain.

Half-way across the room, his mother interrupted his path—accompanied by Lady Whitlow and her dreaded daughter. Drat. He had been so wrapped up in his thoughts he had not seen the ambush waiting for him. There seemed no alternative to asking Miss Whitlow to stand up with him again.

During the dance, he tried not to watch Eliza, but found his eyes repeatedly drawn in her direction. Her partner gazed at her, as if he was moonstruck, and Beau fought against the desire to stop him forcibly from focusing on her lips.

Alarmed by the strength of his reaction, he gave his partner his full attention. It was as well she did not require him to make much conversation, or he might have said something unfortunate.

As their dances drew to a close, Beau hastened to return Miss Whitlow to her mother.

"Oh, I feel a little light-headed," she said, leaning on his arm so heavily he was almost knocked off balance.

He cast her a sideways glance. She didn't look faint. In fact, she appeared rather red in the face. Perhaps she had overexerted herself in the dance.

Beau stifled a sigh as he realised he could not take that risk. The last thing he needed was to have Miss Whitlow fainting in his arms in the middle of the ballroom.

"Let me help you to a chair," he said, urging her toward the side of the room, but she dragged on his arm and didn't move.

"Air. I need air," she said in a weak voice, accompanied by a pathetic look. "I would hate to make a scene at your mother's ball."

Beau could not have agreed more. Regardless of fault, he would get the blame for it, and it would give his parent more ammunition to fire at him about how useless he was.

He knew better than to open the doors that faced the garden and expose the company to a chill, so he led Miss Whitlow into a side chamber which wasn't being used for the entertainment. He pushed open the window onto the balcony.

"Let me fetch your maid." He made to leave the room, but Harriet grasped his arm as he went past her.

"Don't leave me." Her voice sounded hysterical as tears coursed down her face, not marring her beauty in the slightest.

It was a talent that might have fooled a man without five half-sisters—but he was not that man. He had seen his sisters pull the same stunt to get what they wanted.

Beau was unmoved by a sense of pity, or a need to comfort a woman in distress. His heart beat faster as he saw his danger. He wanted to rip his arm away, but if Miss Whitlow went into hysterics, his mother would be sure to make the most of it. She might even use the incident to push him into marriage.

He shuddered. If he had been in any doubt before, now he was certain. The faintness was a convenient ruse to catch him. It was a trap, and fear of his mother's displeasure had sent him running straight into it.

How could he have been so gullible? More to the point, how on earth was he going to get out of this unscathed should someone find them alone like this? Particularly if that someone was his mother.

As if in answer to his question, the door—which he had been careful to leave ajar—opened a little further. His stomach clenched in anticipation, but it was Eliza, not his mother, who walked into the room.

Any relief he felt was short-lived.

Her eyes narrowed as they fell on Miss Whitlow, who had not relinquished her grasp on his arm. "I beg your pardon, am I interrupting something?"

"Not at all," Beau said, trying to keep the panic out of his voice. "Miss Whitlow feared she was going to faint and asked for some air."

Eliza stared hard at him, as if assessing the situation, before turning to face his erstwhile partner.

"How unfortunate. What an impossible dilemma for such a chivalrous gentleman as Lord Beaumont—whether to fetch your maid or stay with you, when you might faint at any moment. What a happy chance I arrived when I did, or you could have been stuck here alone for hours, fearing to send his lordship for help lest you swoon while he is gone. But do not worry. I am your salvation. I'll remain with you whilst his lordship fetches your maid."

Beau repressed a grin. Eliza had presented Miss Whitlow with a dilemma as impossible as the one the wretched woman had forced on him. She must submit to Eliza's aid, or be exposed as a liar.

"I would not want to put you to the trouble, Miss Merry. A little air was all I needed. I'm feeling better already."

Miss Whitlow rose from her chair without relinquishing her hold on Beau's arm, but he pointedly offered the other to Eliza, flashing her a warm look of gratitude as he did so.

He regretted it almost at once. To judge by the tight expression on the other woman's face, she had caught the warmth in his look, and he feared it did not bode well for his rescuer.

Eliza had made a formidable enemy by saving him from Miss Whitlow.

Beau hoped she thought he was worth it.

# Chapter 16

It was almost a week later that the dreaded summons arrived. Beau had been to watch young Belcher fight in a boxing benefit at the Fives Court and returned to his lodgings after an evening of revelry with his sporting cronies to find the letter waiting for him.

In some ways, it was a relief. His mother had kept him on tenterhooks for days, not knowing when he would have to face the full force of her disapproval over his equestrian antics at Astley's.

He knew what the missive said without opening it. And he could predict equally well how the interview would proceed. His parent would express her shock and displeasure at his behaviour, reminding him how useless he was, though not exactly saying it, and insist he make more of an effort to find a wife.

He tossed the letter aside, wishing he could throw off his mother's requests so easily. Like an obedient pup, he would go running. But not tonight. He could not deal with her demands tonight.

The next morning, he awoke with a headache and a horrible sense of foreboding. Why did he feel so low? Then he remembered. The letter.

He rang for some coffee and reluctantly allowed his valet to shave him, not trusting the steadiness of his own hand, and not daring to delay before presenting himself to his mother. He needed her in the best possible mood if he were to brush through this with the least damage.

Fortified by the coffee and a substantial breakfast, he broke open the seal on his mother's letter.

Darn it. They had returned to Alton for Frances's lying in. Didn't his sister have a home of her own? Why must she go back to the family house to give birth to her brat? Instead of a short walk across town, it would take him most of the day to reach his mother. It was too bad of her.

Carrick betrayed not the slightest emotion when told to prepare an overnight bag, as his master needed to visit Holybourne House.

Beau scribbled a note to Ant, telling him he had to leave London, and sent word to the Harting stables for his curricle to be brought round. There was no way he was going to be cooped up in a travelling carriage all day. If he must make the trip into Hampshire, he would at least drive himself.

It was a pleasant journey he had done many times before, and Beau was rather sorry when he reached the end. He watched Jem take his curricle around the side of the house to the stables, wishing he were going with it.

Experience had taught him it was unwise to delay interviews with his mother, and so he headed straight for the house, determined to get over the rough ground as lightly as possible.

"Afternoon, Dawson," he said to the elderly butler holding the door open for him. "Came to visit my mother. Is she at home?"

"It is a pleasure to see you as always, Lord Beaumont," the man replied in the long-suffering tone of one who had known his lordship all his life. A footman stepped forward to relieve Beau of his greatcoat and hat whilst Dawson continued.

"Lady Harting is in the drawing room."

"Alone?"

"No, my lord. Lady Harting is with Lady Whitlow, Lady Frances Whitlow, Miss Whitlow, and Miss Sophia Whitlow. Would you care to go up?"

Beau screwed up his face in disgust at the thought of seeing Frances, whom he blamed for this summons, and what sounded like her husband's entire family—the female side at least.

"No. Think I'll take a wander outside until my mother's visitors have gone."

There was never any question where he would walk. His feet drew him to the only place in Holybourne House where he had ever felt truly at home—the stables.

Quincey greeted him with genuine warmth. Lord Harting's head groom had always found time for him. Though his mother deplored the fact that her only son was on such familiar terms with the grooms, she had failed to keep him away from the stables and had given up trying.

"Has my stepfather bought anything decent since last I was here?"

Quincey snorted. "Nothing that could compare to your bays, that's for sure. His lordship bought a hunter that will do well enough if he takes the trouble to rid the beast of his foul temper, but I'm not holding my breath. He hasn't got the same knack with horses you have."

Once in the stables, Beau lost all sense of time, and it was over an hour later when he remembered why he had come.

Reluctantly, he made his way back up to the house, hoping he didn't smell too much of horse. His lighter mood vanished when Dawson informed him Lord and Lady Harting were awaiting him in the drawing room.

That was ominous. His mother's custom was to rake him down in private. To criticise him was her unique privilege, and she rarely required an audience. He couldn't remember her bringing in his lordship before to witness.

Taking a deep breath, he followed behind Dawson, who announced his arrival. Beau greeted his mother and stepfather with a cheerfulness he was far from feeling.

"How kind of you to find the time to wait upon us," she said in clipped tones.

He tried to brush it off, answering with more diplomacy than truth. "Always a pleasure to see you. I didn't realise you had gone out of town."

The last part, at least, was true.

His mother cleared her throat and flashed her husband a pointed look.

He seemed to recollect his duty. "You must be perfectly aware of the anguish you have caused your mother, Beaumont."

Beau tried, unsuccessfully, to look as though he did not know what his stepfather was talking about. "I have?"

"It has come to our attention," the older man continued in a painfully slow voice, "that you have been foolish enough to wager that you can perform on horseback like one of Astley's troupe. Is that true?"

"Yes."

"Your mother feels"—he gave a brief cough—"as do I, that you treat your life with contempt to risk it so readily and demands that you forego the bet."

Beau's expression hardened. There were some things that were a point of honour. He would no more renege on a bet than he would cheat at cards. "I regret to say that is impossible."

"I insist," said Lady Harting, a steely look in her eyes that reminded Beau forcibly of the time he had been caught fighting with the gardener's lad when he was a boy. He felt twelve years old again under that glare.

"I would not if I could, but I can't. The wager has already taken place."

Lord Harting's face lit up. "Did you win?"

"I did."

"Well, I never..." His stepfather sounded as if he were about to congratulate him, but his words hung in the air.

Beau turned back to his mother in time to catch the piercing look that had subdued her husband. He also noticed something else. His mother's face had gone white, and it was wracked with pain.

What could it mean? Was she suffering from visions of him lying dead on the ground at Astley's? Did she love him more than he'd always believed?

His eyes clouded over, and he was overcome with remorse, but before he could muster an apology, his mother dispelled the short-lived illusion.

"How dare you?" she hissed as her eyes bore into him, her chin quivering with rage.

His remorse vanished in an instant. She was more distressed he had flouted her wishes than that he might have killed himself. How stupid of him to think she cared.

Deep down, he wondered whether he acted recklessly to provoke her—to evoke some kind of reaction, to prove to himself he was wrong to believe she didn't love him. Had she shown just a little genuine affection toward him...but as it was, he was on the defensive—again.

"I knew I could trust in my horses."

She flared her nostrils in disgust. "You are missing the point, Beaumont. I thought I had impressed upon you the need to curb your recklessness, but it appears you have not taken my words seriously. Instead of finding a wife, you have risked your life fulfilling a ridiculous bet."

Beau suppressed a sigh. As he had expected, it was the same old story, with his mother harping on again about her desire for him to get married.

He pursed his lips, struggling to spit out the words he felt she required. "I will try harder to find myself a wife."

"That is no longer enough. I am tired of your half-hearted promises. You *will* marry before the season is out. I have given notice to your tenants, and on Midsummer's Day, you take possession of Langcroft

Park, with or without a bride. If you wed, you will have all the wealth of the estate at your disposal. If you refuse, I will reduce your allowance to such a level you will be forced to retire there and learn how to manage your property."

She snorted with amusement. "No more racing. No more hunting. Nothing that could bring about your premature death. You will spend your days at a desk, poring over ledgers with Harris, learning all that your estate manager can teach you. I expect your progress will be slow, if indeed you are capable of learning anything at all."

As his mother talked, Beau's bottom jaw fell lower and lower, leaving his mouth wide open in shock. He was stunned. Lost for words. She had threatened him before, but he had never imagined it would come to this. It was nothing short of blackmail.

She had placed a noose around his neck, and he knew she would not hesitate to pull it tight if he did not do as she asked. If he did not marry, he would be cut off from everything that mattered to him. Banished.

The picture she had painted of that banishment was bleak indeed. He was not averse to learning more about his estates, but his mother was right. He had no head for figures and the thought of being stuck inside an office all day, trying to grasp what was beyond him, made him feel sick.

It was some consolation he would get to live in his own house at last, but if he did not marry, he would have no funds to maintain his current stables, let alone develop his stud.

He would have to marry for money. It was humiliating and hardly a compliment to his future wife, but what choice did he have? He could see no other way. He felt like a small boy being promised sweetmeats once he had received his smallpox inoculation. Once the pain was over, he would get the reward.

That thought disturbed him, twisting his gut. Marriage should not be like an inoculation. His mother had poisoned his view of it, but he knew it wasn't always that way. Georgie had shown him that. There was a harmony between her and Castleford that declared their marital happiness to the world without them saying a word. But then, they married for love, not money.

He felt a pang of envy, but dismissed it from his mind. It was hopeless to hold out for something more. Castleford was a much better person than he was. Not even his own mother loved him, so how could he expect anyone else to? He didn't deserve it.

"You leave me no choice. I will find myself a wife before the season is out."

"Oh no. That won't be necessary. My patience has run out. You have had two months to find yourself a wife, and you have failed."

Beau paled at her words. What did his mother mean? Had she chosen his bride as well? He prayed she would not expect him to marry Miss Whitlow.

"I will hold a select house party here, ostensibly to entertain Frances while she is in seclusion. You will attend. I am inviting Miss Whitlow"—Beau's chest tightened—"and my niece, Elizabeth. Harriet has already accepted. By the end of it, I require you to be engaged to one of them. If you wish to have a choice of wife, take my invitation to Elizabeth in person and ensure she accepts."

A sense of relief swept over him. His mother was giving him a choice, and one of his options was Eliza.

Eliza, who shared his love for horses, didn't like opera, and had believed he could win his bet. To say nothing of his gratitude to her for rescuing him from Miss Whitlow's scheming at the ball.

What a rare occasion, that his own preference should coincide with his mother's.

Now all he had to do was persuade Eliza to accept the invitation, because the alternative was too horrible to contemplate.

# Chapter 17

IN THE DAYS THAT followed Lady Harting's ball, Eliza had every hope that her relationship with Beau would be different.

She was sure something had changed that night. Twice she had saved him. Once from himself, from kissing her in the middle of the ballroom. The other from the clutches of Harriet—who had poked at her with undisguised spite ever since.

But rather than build on the intimacy of that evening, he had kept his distance, and now he had left town without so much as a word.

Which was why Eliza had gone for a drive with Anthony, rather than Beau, in a somewhat melancholy mood.

She feared he would tease her about her attachment to his best friend, but he didn't even mention it. Instead, he cheered her up by regaling her with stories of their antics at Cambridge.

At the end of their outing, she invited Anthony to step inside with her, as he was half-way through a diverting account of the time Beau had ridden a horse into one of their college buildings.

"Didn't he get into trouble?" Eliza said as she entered the drawing room. "I can't imagine—"

The words froze on her lips as she realised her sisters were not alone. Beau was there. He leapt to his feet and bowed, sending her a tentative smile as he met her gaze.

Eliza's pulse raced as she acknowledged his greeting, even more so as she examined his face. Though his mouth smiled, his eyes were clouded with uncertainty. There was a tightness in his expression and creases on his forehead that a regular visit could not explain.

No. She was sure he was bothered about something more than whether she would go for a drive with him.

Eliza perched on the edge of the chair nearest to where Beau had been sitting and waited to find out if she was right.

"I thought you were out of town," Anthony said to his friend, as he entered the room behind her. He nodded casually to Georgiana and Charlotte, sprawling his long limbs in front of him as he sat down.

"As you can see, I'm not."

Beau retrieved a letter from his jacket pocket and handed it to Eliza. "I've brought an invitation from my mother."

She took it, broke open the wax seal and spread out the single sheet of paper. As she read the contents, she didn't know whether to laugh or cry.

Out of the corner of her eye, she was aware of Beau, still stood in front of her, shifting his weight from one foot to the other as he waited for her to finish reading.

"Lady Harting invites me to stay at Holybourne House for a few weeks, to help support Frances's spirits in the days running up to her confinement."

"I beg your pardon?" Georgiana said. "Our aunt wants you to go to Alton in the middle of the season to keep Frances company? I don't believe it."

"It's true," Beau said.

Georgiana glared up at him. "Oh, do sit down. I shall get a neck ache trying to converse with you up there."

He muttered a word of apology and perched on the edge of his chair in the same uncomfortable manner Eliza had adopted.

"Your mother is asking a lot," her elder sister said with a frown. "Are there to be many other guests?"

"No—just family."

"Including you?"

"Yes."

"Am I invited?" Anthony asked.

He scowled at his friend. "No. I told you—just family."

"Very intimate," Georgiana said.

Beau coloured under her penetrating gaze. "You know what my mother's like once she has an idea in her head. I'm sure you can spare Eliza for a couple of weeks. Please, Georgie."

"Well?" she said, transferring her gaze to her sister. "It's your choice."

Eliza's heart beat uncommonly fast. To spend such a long time under her aunt's critical gaze was an intimidating proposition. But the nature of the invitation—so intimate. It could not be turned down.

"My mother is depending on you. As am I. Please say you'll come," Beau said, pleading her with his eyes.

"Yes."

He let out an audible sigh of relief. "Thank you. I'm sure my mother will be delighted. I'll let her know at once."

With that, the two gentlemen took their leave.

As the door shut behind them, Eliza flew across the room and gave Georgiana an enormous hug.

"Thank you for letting me go," she said, grinning from ear to ear as she flopped onto the sofa beside her in a most unladylike manner.

"As if I could stop you. I'm your sister, not your guardian. It's perfectly respectable for you to stay under your aunt's roof, even if it's a poorly disguised attempt at throwing the two of you together. Don't be fooled into reading too much into the invitation, though it was Beau who brought it to you."

Eliza's face clouded over. "What do you mean?"

"This isn't Beau's idea, but some plan of his mother's. She has obviously decided you would make a suitable wife for him and is keen to forward the match."

Eliza acknowledged the possibility—the strong possibility—that this was true. Beau would not choose to spend time with his mother and sister of his own free will. She imagined he was as appalled at the prospect as she was.

Even now, the thought of facing her aunt made her quake. But then she remembered the pleading look on his face, begging her to accept an invitation she had never considered refusing.

"I'm convinced Beau wanted me to accept."

"To please his mother."

Eliza jumped up from her seat and started pacing around the room. "Why do you always think the worst of him? Why can't you believe he wishes me to go because he likes me?"

Georgiana rose and walked toward her, grasping both her hands.

"Even if he prefers you to the other women of his acquaintance, that does not mean he loves you, Eliza. Be careful. I want you to be as happy as I am with Cas. If Beau doesn't love you..."

Eliza ripped her hands away from her sister's hold. "You don't know that."

"Does Beau even know what love is?"

"Well, if he doesn't, we know who is to blame. But I love him. I'll show him what love looks like."

"I'm afraid you'll marry him, and he'll break your heart. He might not be faithful..."

It hurt that her sister had so little confidence in Beau. She wished she could make her understand.

"Don't despair, Georgie. He is as different from Castleford as cheese is from cake, but they are both good to eat. Just because he doesn't look like the solid Christian man your husband is, that does not mean he's not. If you'd observed the way he cares for his horses, you would not doubt he would be kind to his wife. I do not believe he would make me unhappy. And even if he does not love me now, that doesn't mean he never will. Our story is still being written."

Eliza prayed her words were prophetic, and not just wishful thinking.

# Chapter 18

After securing Eliza's consent to his mother's invitation, Beau made a hasty escape from town. He was blowed if he was going to miss the first spring meeting at Newmarket. If Eliza refused to marry him and his mother carried out her threat, it could be his last dash to the races for years.

Once on the racecourse, he put all thought of the house party behind him and concentrated on the subject at hand. Horses.

He laid his bets on the races over the next few days in his usual conservative style. Funny to think how reckless he was in other matters, but so cautious with money. It probably came from having been kept on a tight leash all his life.

It was the one thing he could thank his mother for. He could make his allowance go a long way, and by careful betting on horses with short odds, he had built up his capital. That was how he'd been able to start breeding horses, and that was how he would continue.

"If I'm as successful as usual, I should be able to afford a horse or two from the Duke of Grafton's stud when it goes under the hammer."

"I sincerely hope your tips are up to standard," Anthony said, "otherwise I'll be obliged to call on my brother to bail me out."

"If you moderated your stakes, you wouldn't have to worry."

"Where's the fun in that?"

Beau huffed at Ant in despair.

He just laughed and turned away. "Oh no. Here comes trouble."

Beau swivelled around to see what had prompted his friend's words and an unwelcome sight met his eyes. Mr Cunningham was swaggering toward them. The wealthy stud owner had a habit of addressing him in a patronising fashion, and Beau's stomach clenched in anticipation.

"Playing it safe again, Lord Beaumont?"

Beau sucked in his cheeks in irritation. The fellow delighted in taunting him, flaunting that he had money to burn at every opportunity. Cunningham could afford to lose. He could not.

"Of course. It's always safe to follow my instincts."

The other man sniggered unpleasantly. "Ah yes, your famous instincts. Yet you refuse to put your faith in them by betting more than paltry amounts."

"Moderate sums on reliable bets. That's my approach. I won't stake over ten pounds on a long shot, no matter how tempting."

Cunningham flicked an imaginary speck from the front of his coat. "You'll never get rich that way."

"You're mistaken," Beau said, struggling to hide his growing annoyance. "I come away from the races richer every time. Are you able to say the same?"

The older man acknowledged the hit with a slight tilt of his head, but the superior smirk did not leave his lips. "No—but I can afford not to."

He breathed out a deep, satisfied sigh, as if dwelling on the delights of his own fortune. When he spoke again, there was a note of pity in his voice that made Beau grind his teeth together. "If you're looking for safe bets, you must back Majesty."

"I already have. I don't doubt he'll win, barring an act of God."

To hear Beau's unfeigned praise of his horse seemed to soften Cunningham a little, and he gave a genuine smile. "Majesty won't let me down. He's unbeatable."

"In this field," Beau muttered under his breath.

Cunningham's smile vanished as quickly as it had come. "What did you say?"

Anthony had kept quiet during this conversation, but now he shot his friend a pointed look. They both knew Beau's words would rile his adversary.

"I agreed with you. Majesty is unbeatable *in this field*," Beau said, pretending not to see Ant's warning glance. "I don't foresee any of the other contenders rivalling him. There is always the chance of a freak mishap, like your jockey having a stroke half-way round the course, but barring that, he'll win."

Cunningham was not to be put off. "If there is a horse to rival him, why isn't he racing?"

"Too early. I won't race Romeo until he's ready."

"Your treasured colt?"

Beau stiffened at the contempt in the man's voice. "He's fast."

"Is he?" said Cunningham, stroking his chin. "I'd like to see him run."

"And so you shall—in October."

"There must be some way I can persuade you to race him sooner. There has been so little competition of late. Bring him to the Epsom meeting next month and I'll stake my Majesty to win against your Romeo."

Beau looked at the man as if he were mad. "You want me to risk my colt against a known winner? I don't even know what he's capable of yet."

Cunningham's gambling instincts were fully aroused. "Come on, your lordship. Surely you believe in your own horse."

Anthony put a restraining hand on his friend's arm, but Beau needed no encouragement to refuse the challenge. "I won't risk losing Romeo by racing him too early."

"Hmm. What if I made my offer a little more inviting?" Cunningham said, his growing excitement making his eyes shine. "I contend Majesty is unbeatable now. In October, who knows? I can't wait for your colt to be ready. Race him in May, and if he's victorious, I'll give you Majesty *and* five thousand pounds. If you lose, I get your horse. That would be prize enough for me, as I feel I would be cheating you out of your animal, because I'm so certain I'll win."

Beau's jaw dropped, his eyes growing wide as saucers. Had the man gone insane? "You haven't even seen Romeo run."

"That's irrelevant. It is *you* who needs to have faith in the speed at which he can go. I *know* how fast Majesty is."

Beau paled at the possibility of losing his colt, but his heart beat faster at what Cunningham was offering. This was a chance he could not pass up.

It was a cry for independence. If Romeo won, he could finance his stables until he turned twenty-five and inherited his fortune. He would no longer need to do his mother's bidding. And he would not have to wed Eliza.

The thought was not as pleasing as he'd expected, but he shook it off. Though he doubted he would find another lady who suited him so well, he wasn't ready to marry anyone.

Cunningham was getting impatient, waiting for an answer. He'd taken hold of the idea and was desperate for Beau to accept.

Templecombe strolled up and joined the group as Cunningham offered an even greater prize.

"Tell you what, let's open it up a bit. A subscription race with stakes of, say, two hundred guineas each. The Cunningham Stakes—I like the sound of that. The five-thousand-pound bet stands between us, irrespective of the other runners. If Majesty is placed higher than Romeo, I win. If Romeo beats Majesty, you triumph, and I'll pay up, even if by some freak occurrence some other horse storms in and steals the victory.

"I'll be really generous and even put up the stake for you and offer two hundred guineas for second place. That way, if Romeo comes in second to Majesty, you'll have the money to repay me for the stake, and all you'll lose is your colt. If you cry off and don't show, you'll owe me the two hundred guineas. You can't expect more from me. Come on, act like a man."

Templecombe, with more enthusiasm than understanding, slapped his cousin on the back. "Go for it. You're always boasting about how fast Romeo is."

Beau was conscious of Anthony glaring at him, but he kept his eyes down, refusing to meet his friend's gaze.

"Think what you're doing," Ant urged him in an undertone. "Why risk Romeo on a whim when you said you wouldn't race him until the autumn?"

Beau was sorry to ignore his friend's words, knowing they made sense, but he had already made up his mind. This was his chance to take control of his life.

He held out his hand to Cunningham. "You're on."

Anthony exclaimed in disgust and walked off without a word.

Beau felt the loss of his support, but this was something he had to do. It was a risk, but he would never forgive himself if he did not make a push to break free.

He might never get another opportunity.

Later that evening, over dinner, Beau tried to explain his actions to Ant.

"You must understand what a chance this is."

"A chance for you to lose everything you've worked so hard for."

"Romeo is fast. He'll win for me, you'll see."

"You said he wasn't ready. How can you have changed your mind so quickly?"

Beau thumped his fist on the table. "Because it's the only way to escape marriage. If I'm not engaged by the end of this house party that my mother's organised, I'll be banished to Langcroft Park with nothing to live on."

"Ouch!"

"Exactly."

"Who does she want you to wed?" Ant asked, not meeting his eyes.

"Eliza. She's invited that dreadful Whitlow girl too, but I suspect that's more to ensure I come up to scratch."

"I don't understand. You like Eliza. Why don't you wish to marry her?"

Beau's eyes narrowed. "What is it to you?"

Anthony held his hand up, a tight expression around his mouth. "Woah! I know I've always said I'm not in the market for a wife, but Eliza tempted me to reconsider—until I realised she viewed me as an honorary brother. It's just as well. However perfect I find her now, I'm sure she'd bore me within six months, and I'd hate to break her heart. But we were talking of you, not me. Why don't you want to marry her?"

A wave of relief passed over Beau. The thought of Ant pursuing Eliza did not sit well with him. He told himself it was because he was concerned for her, but he had the niggling suspicion it was more than that.

Ant repeated his question, and Beau ran his fingers through his hair, as he tried to word an answer. "It's hard to explain. I'm fond of Eliza, but I detest being told what to do. You don't know what it's like. My mother is slowly suffocating me, taking away even the most important choices of my life."

Ant laid a hand on his shoulder. "Then we'll have to hope Romeo comes up trumps and wins your freedom."

"Thanks. I've instructed Jem to bring him to Alton in gentle stages. I wish he could go straight to my place at Beddington, which is much nearer Epsom, but I don't take possession of Langcroft Park until Midsummer's Day, which is too late. Jem's father will find room for Romeo in the stables for me. I expect he'd throw all Harting's horses out to house one of mine. You can't buy loyalty like that.

"When Romeo arrives, I'll try him out, and if he's not ready, I won't race him. Though it would be humiliating to have to withdraw, I'll do it if need be. But I'd much prefer not to pull out unless I must, and I doubt it will come to that. Trust me. I won't have to part with Romeo. Instead, I'll gain a magnificent racehorse and a tidy sum besides."

"Have you considered what you'll do if by some mischance you lose?"

Beau let out a long puff of air. "I'll marry Eliza."

"Don't make it sound as if she's a consolation prize. She's an absolute treasure."

"That's a warm compliment for your honorary sister," Beau said, fighting off a scowl.

"Anyone would think you were jealous."

Was he? Maybe. He was certainly a tad suspicious of Ant's true intentions, despite his previous assurances.

Beau didn't care to hear him speak of Eliza in that way, even if his friend's words were nothing less than the truth. She *was* an absolute treasure. A real sweetheart of a girl.

His breathing hitched for a moment as he considered the warmth of his own feelings for Eliza—the girl he was trying *not* to marry.

He would only wed her if this failed, and his mother forced him to—wouldn't he?

# Chapter 19

ELIZA DID NOT ENJOY the journey to Alton. Although she had counted down the days, now that the house party had arrived, she half-wished she wasn't going.

She didn't cherish the thought of exchanging the precious company of her sisters for that of her cousin, whilst the dreadful prospect of living under her aunt's roof for several weeks threatened to stifle her pleasurable anticipation of spending time with Beau.

If he even wanted her there. Despite her bold declarations in his defence, she could not dismiss Georgie's fears from her mind. Perhaps it was true he had only invited her because his mother told him to and not because he cared for her.

Beau's behaviour since delivering the invitation had done nothing to reassure her. He had forgotten he'd agreed to take her for a drive the Tuesday after, and he had been markedly absent from the two balls she had attended in the week that followed. She would have felt neglected if she hadn't been well-acquainted with the racing calendar and knew he was in Newmarket.

The only time she had seen him was when the Four in Hand Club met. Lord Castleford had driven her and her sisters to watch the members lining up their carriages before they set out. It had been a proud moment, seeing Beau sat on the box of his barouche behind both pairs of matched bays, dressed in the colours of the club, with Anthony alongside him.

But there had been no chance for conversation, and she hadn't seen him since.

By the time the carriage was half-way to Alton, Eliza felt sick with anticipation. She looked so pale that her maid fussed and insisted on her using the smelling salts, which she always had on hand when travelling.

Sarah pinched her mistress's cheeks. "Can't have you arriving to see his lordship looking like a ghost."

"I am here to entertain Lady Frances."

"Of course you are. Quite natural for you to come away when the season is in full swing just to please your aunt."

Eliza glared at her. How was it that a lady's maid was always familiar with her mistress's business? She'd said nothing to the woman to reveal the state of her heart, but somehow, she knew.

It was reassuring to know she had an ally in Sarah. With the ordeal ahead of her, she might need one.

When the travelling chariot pulled up outside Holybourne House, it was a very weary Eliza who stepped down. Thank goodness the journey was over. She hated travelling in a closed carriage, and would have liked to have ridden part of the way.

At least Finch had gone to fetch Whisper from her parents' home, so she could ride her own horse tomorrow.

Eliza looked around, expecting to see Beau waiting to greet her, but he wasn't. She bit back her disappointment, reasoning that she could not have expected him to remain inside on such a fine day.

The butler greeted her with all due state, but there was the slightest hint of a smile in his eyes when they rested on her, recognising her from her previous visits.

"Lady Harting apologises for not being here to greet you in person," he said. "She is visiting Lady Whitlow. Her ladyship thought you would want to rest before dinner. Ash will show you to your room."

Eliza was surprised but pleased she did not have to face her aunt until later. She muttered a weary word of thanks, but her smile was genuine, and the butler so far forgot himself as to give her a reassuring smile back.

The footman led her upstairs to a suite of rooms overlooking the gardens at the rear of the house. She lay down on the bed, not expecting to sleep, but the weariness of a day spent in a closed carriage was too much for her, and within a few minutes, she dozed off.

She awoke feeling refreshed and hungry. Fortunately, it was almost the dinner hour. She washed her face and Sarah helped her into her evening dress—a new one she hoped Beau would like. Her maid re-pinned her hair and then Eliza picked up the matching reticule and, taking a deep breath, she opened the door.

To her surprise, Ash was hovering outside. Had he been waiting there the whole time she'd been resting?

A footman hardly seemed necessary. Did her aunt suppose she would get lost? She had stayed overnight before, when attending balls at the Winchester Assembly Rooms, the year she turned sixteen. Unlike her sister Georgiana, who had no sense of direction at all, she could have navigated her way around the house with no difficulty whatsoever.

Ash led her to the drawing room where Eliza supposed she would find her elusive aunt and cousin, and maybe Beau as well. The door opened and the first person she saw was not Lady Harting or Frances, but the abominable Harriet Whitlow.

Her aunt greeted her with an effusive show of affection, which Eliza found most disconcerting.

"My poor child, you look worn out from your journey. What a mercy it is that the gentlemen are not dining with us tonight, so there is no need to concern yourself that you are not looking your best."

Eliza's heart sank. No gentlemen. That meant no Beau. Just Lady Harting and Frances and Horrible Harriet.

Her aunt pinched her cheek in what should have been an affectionate gesture, but Eliza had to steel herself not to pull away. Sarah had tweaked her cheeks with tenderness. Lady Harting's pinch seemed to confirm she was lacking in some way. She wondered whether her aunt revelled in making her feel about two inches tall.

The dinner was as painful as she had foreseen. Four ladies eating in state was rather overwhelming. Never at her best under Lady Harting's watchful gaze, she found it hard to contribute anything to the conversation. The strange thing was, the less she spoke, the happier she thought her ladyship looked, and the self-satisfied smile on her aunt's face deepened as the meal progressed.

After dinner, they moved into the drawing room, and Lady Harting requested some music.

"Why don't you play for us, Elizabeth?"

All eyes turned toward her, and heat burned her cheeks as she tried to decline, but her aunt insisted.

"A little reluctance is becoming, but do not overdo it. Take your place at the pianoforte and delight us."

Eliza had no choice but to move to the instrument, feeling as if she were on the way to the gallows. Her performance would delight no one. If she could overcome her nerves to sing, it would distract her audience from her indifferent playing, but as she felt her throat go dry at the prospect, she dared not try.

She sat down, closed her eyes, and drew a deep breath, wishing she were as talented as Charlotte. Eliza might despair of her younger sister's fears and foibles, but even she, with no appreciation of music, could tell that when Charlotte played, the keys sang.

After rifling through the printed sheets for what seemed like hours, she found a sonata she was familiar with, which she hoped would not reveal her lack of talent. She bashed out the piece as best she could, missing out the sections that were too difficult, and with a huge sigh of relief, she reached the end without disgracing herself.

The other ladies gave a weak round of applause, and Harriet moved to take her place.

Lady Whitlow must have invested a lot of money in music masters, and her daughter must have spent many hours practising, because her performance put Eliza to shame. Lady Frances applauded her sister-in-law loudly and begged for another piece.

Eliza decided it would be better for her not to play in public if she could help it, and certainly not directly before or after Harriet, as it would be bound to reflect badly on herself.

The evening dragged. When her rival tired of performing, Lady Harting called for the card table to be set up and invited them to join her for a game of whist.

It was an invitation that could not be refused. Eliza's heart sank further. She was even worse at cards than she was at playing the pianoforte. She had never considered herself ill-equipped for going into society, but tonight had forced her to realise how inadequately she was prepared.

Her throat seized up in panic and she could not find the words to excuse herself from the ordeal. She had not thought the situation could get any worse when Lady Harting chose to partner her.

Eliza knew she would embarrass herself and hurried to warn her aunt she was a very indifferent card player.

Harriet sneered. "Didn't you play cards at home? I was practically born to it."

Eliza did not think that was anything to boast about.

"I expect it was banned," said Frances with a snicker. "You will recall her father is a rector—and an enthusiast at that."

Harriet raised her eyebrows and stared at Eliza as if she had two heads. "An enthusiast? I didn't realise your family took their religion so seriously. I'm surprised you did not give us a rendition of a hymn earlier rather than a sonata."

Eliza said nothing, unable to find the words to counter Harriet's barbed comments. It was some slight consolation that her aunt did not look pleased. Her mouth grew firm, and she glared at Frances before turning to her niece.

"It is fortunate I am an excellent player. Watch and learn. I am certain I can make up for your inexperience."

Lady Harting had been overoptimistic. Her aunt's eyes became dark with displeasure, her smile rather forced. Eliza guessed she was making a mental note never to partner her at whist again, and certainly not for money. It was as well that they were playing for points and not pounds this evening.

Her aunt did not prolong Eliza's agony. After two games, she rose from the card table and rang for the tea tray. With one look at her niece's furrowed brow, Lady Harting announced she must be tired from travelling, and gave her no option but to retire.

Eliza submitted, though she would much rather have waited for the gentlemen's return. It was the prospect of seeing Beau that had kept her going all evening.

And it was the only thing that supplied her with enough courage to face the next day.

# Chapter 20

The next morning, Eliza woke to the sound of birds singing outside her window. She lay back on her pillows, listening to their song, enjoying the moment. How strange to hear the sounds of the country after so many weeks of town clatter and noise. Despite the trauma of the previous evening, it was the most peaceful she'd felt since leaving home.

She slipped out of bed, walked to the window, and opened the shutters so she could see into the gardens. She feasted her eyes on the greenery laid out before her. Nearest to the house, the neatly mowed lawns were bordered on each side with flowerbeds bursting with bright colours, with a walkway covered with trailing roses along the far edge with an arch in the centre.

Beyond the rose walk, there was another stretch of grass, which sloped away into the distance where she could make out the lake, reflecting the sunlight on its waters. Not a single cloud marred the blue of the sky and the day beckoned to her.

Dressed in a green riding habit with a matching shako hat, Eliza headed for the stables. As she reached the bottom stair, a footman appeared out of nowhere. Like a wooden soldier, he stood in silence against the wall, eyes straight ahead, ready to leap into action if, and only if, she spoke to him.

"Good morning, Ash."

He bowed his head toward her. "Good morning, madam," he said, as if it were perfectly normal for a guest to address him by name.

Eliza was never tongue-tied with servants. "As you've probably guessed," she said, her eyes twinkling as she glanced down at her habit, "I'm going for a ride."

"Very good, madam. Do you require any assistance?"

She shook her head. "I know my way, thank you. Wait—what time is breakfast served?"

"At ten o'clock, madam."

Eliza uttered a word of thanks and headed down the corridor and out the back of the house. She strode across the lawn with a rather mannish gait, her long legs in a hurry to reunite her with her horse.

Finch had guessed she would want an early ride and Whisper was standing waiting for her, saddled up and ready to go.

"You read my mind," she said, giving her groom a warm smile before he helped her into the saddle.

With a gentle word, Eliza spurred her mount into action and rode out of the stables, followed at an appropriate distance by Finch.

She took the track that led down the hill to the river and, as soon as they were away from the house, she urged Whisper into a trot. Beyond the lake there was an open stretch of ground and, with a slight touch from her whip, Eliza encouraged the mare to lengthen her stride into a canter.

At length, she turned back toward the glistening water and drew Whisper to a standstill at the lake's edge. She dismounted without help, sliding to the ground with ease. Reins in hand, she stood on the bank to admire the view across the lake and up the hill to the house.

As she breathed in the fresh country air, drinking in the peace, a family of ducks swam out from under the arch of the bridge to her right, making ripples over the surface as they went. Eliza closed her eyes. All she could hear was the gentle quacking from her feathered friends, swimming off into the distance, and a myriad of birds chirping their early morning greetings.

Then there was another sound—the sound of horse's hooves—coming from the far side of the bridge. Unwilling to interrupt her peaceful reverie, she kept her eyes shut, supposing it to be an estate worker going about their business.

Eliza expected the horse to pass right by her, but instead of hearing the hoofbeats fading into the distance, they came to an abrupt halt, and a hearty male voice hailed her. She did not need to open her eyes to recognise who it belonged to.

"Morning, Eliza," said Beau, dismounting. "I'm glad to know you arrived safely. I didn't expect to see you up and about so early. Do you usually rise with the sun?"

"Hardly up with the sun, but I love to ride before breakfast when I can. But you—I've been completely taken in. I thought you were a gentleman of fashion, and yet here you are, coming back from a ride with hours still to go until midday."

Beau shrugged. "I can't stay inside when there is a fine morning like this beckoning, whatever time I've gone to bed the night before."

"Nor I."

"Sorry I wasn't here when you arrived," he said casually. "Friend of mine was selling a horse and if I didn't look at it yesterday, he couldn't guarantee holding it for me to see. We all decided to go as Whitlow thought it might suit him if I didn't want it and besides, he was ready to jump at any chance to escape baby talk. As for Harting, I think the prospect of being the only man at the table was too much for him. Probably comes from having all daughters. I suppose my mother looked after you all right?"

Eliza gave a weak smile, but said nothing, refusing to lie and yet unwilling to tell the truth. She brushed away the realisation that she had endured a torturous evening without Beau there to protect her because of a horse. What had she expected? It was unreasonable to have hoped he might have altered his plans for her. And he could not have known how difficult she would find the evening without him.

"Did you buy the horse?" Eliza asked, directing her thoughts into a more positive channel.

"No. A lively stallion with lots of good points, but not quite what I was looking for. Harting bought it instead. I'll show it to you later, if you want."

A dreamy look came into Beau's eyes as he glanced around him.

"I played here in the woods and on the lake when I was a child. Used to come with Jem Quincey, the man who's now my head groom. He was the closest thing to a brother I had growing up. We often escaped from the house in the middle of the night to watch the badgers. It took us weeks to work out where their set was, but it was worth it.

"We would take up position in the undergrowth and wait for them to come out and hunt. If we stayed awake long enough, that is. Once we both fell asleep and if Jem's father hadn't found us, I would have got into no end of trouble. I crept into the house by the servants' door and up the backstairs and no one was any the wiser, though I am surprised my stepfather didn't suspect something when I couldn't stay awake that evening."

He pondered for a moment. "Come to think of it, I believe Harting *did* know about it. He chose not to notice to keep the peace. Don't blame him. It was my mother who made a fuss about things like that. She's always hated me mixing with the stable hands. I would have been subject to one of those *it is not the sort of behaviour we expect from a peer of the realm* talks."

Beau shuddered, as if shaking off such an unpleasant memory.

"I should like to see the badgers," Eliza said. "Are they still here?"

"I don't know. It was years ago, and I can't say I spend a lot of time roaming the woods at night these days. I'll ask Quincey."

Whisper decided, at that moment, to make her presence known, nuzzling into Eliza's hand.

"I suppose we should get back for breakfast," she said, with a note of reluctance, unwilling to trade her present company for a household of people who made her feel unaccomplished and uneasy.

Finch stepped forward to help her into the saddle, but Beau got there first.

"Allow me." He cupped his right hand, and Eliza felt the colour rushing to her face as she placed her left foot firmly in it, resting her gloved hand on his shoulder while he raised her up. It was an action she had performed hundreds of times with Finch, and it had never caused her the slightest embarrassment.

Yet, because it was Beau, she was acutely aware of how close she was to his body.

He took her boot and placed it in the stirrup, and she turned, trying not to think of his hand on her foot, concentrating hard on sorting her reins out until the heat in her cheeks died down. Only when he stepped away and was mounting his own horse did she lean over and straighten her skirts.

They rode back to the house in silence, but as they approached the stables, Beau turned in his saddle to face her. "Would you care to join me tomorrow? I ride out every morning before breakfast."

"I'd like that," said Eliza, a gentle smile hovering over her mouth.

Perhaps staying at Holybourne House wouldn't be so bad.

# Chapter 21

BEAU STOOD AT THE foot of the stairs, smiling to himself as he waited for Eliza to change out of her habit. It had been a pleasant surprise to come across her by the lake. She was more at ease than he'd ever seen her before, as if being in the countryside had the same beneficial effect on her as it had on him.

The thought of taking long rides together, away from his mother's watchful eye, appealed to him more than he cared to admit.

Eliza didn't keep him waiting long. After only fifteen minutes, she hurried downstairs again, her eyes still glowing from the morning's exercise. He was impressed by how fast she'd changed, but it was still not quick enough. They had lingered overlong by the lake, and they were behind time for breakfast.

"Thought my mother might not scowl at me so much if we went in late together," he said without meeting Eliza's eyes, feeling the need to explain why he was waiting for her.

When Beau looked up, she flashed him a grateful smile as she took his arm. He led the way to the breakfast parlour, hoping his mother would not cut up too stiff at their tardiness. He grimaced briefly at the footman on duty, who by the slightest flicker of his eyebrows expressed his empathy for Beau's plight before showing them into the room where the rest of the household waited.

A quick glance around the parlour confirmed his fear that they had not started without them. He saw with dismay that his mother was glowering at him, her eyes sending fiery darts in his direction. "How kind of you to join us, Beaumont."

Ignoring her displeasure, he turned to Eliza, who had stayed behind him, as if for protection, and invited her to sit.

When his parent's eyes lighted on his companion, all at once, her expression changed. The frown melted away and was replaced by a sickly sweet smile. Poor Eliza. Did she realise she was the chosen one?

"I hope you slept well," his mother said, encouraging her niece to take the seat next to her.

"Yes, thank you," Eliza replied in little more than a whisper, casting him a desperate glance as she took the offered chair.

Beau looked at her curiously. His mother was not angry with her and yet, if he was not mistaken, Eliza quaked at the attention just the same. Perhaps his mother's favour was as hard to take as her displeasure.

He responded to Eliza's cry for help by obediently taking the adjacent chair, but his mind soon wandered from the rather one-sided conversation his mother was having with her, distracted by the much more interesting debate going on between Harting and Whitlow. They were discussing the rival merits of the horse his stepfather had bought the day before and Whitlow's favourite stallion.

Beau always had something to say about horses and entered the conversation with gusto. A visit to the stables seemed like the only way to resolve their argument about which horse was superior.

He was on the point of rising from the table when he realised he had not said a word to Eliza since they had sat down. The cheery smile he had seen on her face earlier had disappeared, worn away by his parent's interrogations.

He had so often suffered that drain of confidence when facing his mother that he felt a ready sympathy for Eliza's plight and told the others to go on without him.

Eliza had already pulled on her gloves, and was about to leave the table, but she couldn't seem to get away from his mother's questioning.

"I daresay Chanctonbury Hall can accommodate at least fifty guests overnight."

"I'm afraid I don't know," said Eliza.

"Come, come. You must know how many bedrooms your sister's home has."

"No. I don't."

"Beaumont's residence has twenty bedchambers. Not as grand as Holybourne House, but a beautiful, Neoclassical mansion built by the renowned architect Robert Adam. My first husband commissioned the house when he inherited the estate. I am sure my son would love to show it to you one day."

Eliza dropped her eyes in confusion, as if unsure how to respond. His mother certainly wasn't leaving her in any doubt regarding how she felt about her as a prospective daughter-in-law.

"I am driving into Alton this morning with Frances and Miss Whitlow," she said with what Beau deemed a condescending smile. "There is room in the landau for a fourth. I expect you will be glad of the opportunity to purchase some new gloves."

His mother cast a significant look at Eliza's hands, where the tiniest hole was visible at the end of one finger. The ready colour flooded Eliza's cheeks as she hid the damaged glove under her other hand. With an inner sigh, Beau realised even his mother's current favourite was not immune from her criticism.

He pitied Eliza, feeling in some measure responsible, as he had made them late, keeping her talking by the lake. She had probably grabbed the damaged pair in her haste to change for breakfast, but if he admitted as much, he would be sure to draw his mother's fire. Beau decided it was time to make his escape before he became her next target.

As he rose from his seat, Eliza turned and stared up at him. Two pale blue eyes pleaded with him to rescue her before dropping their gaze to examine her hands.

Beau saw the desperation in her unspoken plea, and something inside him stirred. Eliza was looking to him for help, because she believed he would come to her aid.

What a strange sensation to have someone relying on him. No one relied on him. It was an unfamiliar feeling—and not unpleasant.

"I'm sorry to deprive you of Eliza's company," he said to his mother, "but I volunteered to show her the new horse."

Lady Harting smiled sweetly, but the steely look had not disappeared from her eyes. "I am sure Elizabeth would prefer a visit to the shops to a morning in the stables."

Beau winced as his mother enunciated every syllable of Eliza's full name, expressing her disapproval of his use of the shortened form.

Did she believe she was offering Eliza a treat? He thought otherwise and determined to rescue her from his mother's company.

His mind made up, he had to think fast.

"Maybe, but we won't spend the entire morning in the stables," he said, though that had been his intention. "When we've looked over the horse, we're going to take my curricle out so that Elizabeth can have a go at taking the reins. She's never driven my bays, and I know she is itching to try."

Eliza's entire face lit up, her eyes shining gratefully up at him, making his chest swell with pride. "Yes, indeed."

One glance at his mother told him that, though not best pleased, she had noted Eliza's response and would not prevent them from spending the morning together.

"As you wish. I trust the driving lesson will prove amusing." She nodded gracefully and then turned to address Frances.

Beau recognised the sign of his dismissal and, pulling Eliza's chair back, he offered her his arm and they left the room together.

Once in the hallway, out of his mother's earshot, he heaved a sigh of relief at the same moment as Eliza did.

They turned to look at each other, and as their eyes met, they chuckled.

Still grinning, they headed for the stables.

By the time Eliza entered her bedchamber to change for dinner, her cup of contentment was brimming. It had been a wonderful day. She had enjoyed every minute—apart from the awkward conversation with Lady Harting at breakfast, when Beau had seemed to forget her very existence. After that, he had focused his attention on her. She had not had to share him with Harriet Whitlow—only with the horses.

They had spent several hours in the stables. He had examined Whisper and approved of her mare. The same could not be said for all of Lord Harting's horses. Those bought under Beau's recommendation were sound, but her uncle had added others, which Beau dismissed as showy beasts that had cost his stepfather too much.

When they had exhausted the contents of the stable, he fulfilled his promise and took her out in his curricle with the two bays he had owned longer. Eliza was an experienced driver, but she had never handled such a powerful pair before. Her bosom swelled with pride that Beau trusted her to take the reins. True, at first he had remained poised, ready to seize control if needed, but after that, he seemed content that she could handle them and sat back in his seat to enjoy the drive.

Sarah interrupted Eliza's pleasant reflections with unwelcome news.

"You've got company tonight, miss. Lord and Lady Whitlow arrived not half an hour since."

Eliza's shoulders drooped at her words. "Oh no. Why did they have to visit and spoil my lovely day?"

"Tush. They've come to see Lady Frances, not you."

"But I'll be on display again. My mouth will clam up and I won't be able to counter Harriet's spite. I feel a headache coming on. Perhaps I should plead sick and eat my dinner in my room and retire early."

"I'm sure Miss Whitlow would be heartbroken."

"Hmm."

Sarah's sarcastic response was not lost on her. Her maid had a point. Harriet would gloat at having the field to herself, and if Lord and Lady Whitlow wanted the Viscount for a son-in-law, they would not grieve over her absence either.

What about Beau? It wouldn't be kind of her to leave him to their joint attack. She would rally to his defence, though every fibre of her being rebelled at the prospect of facing the Whitlows.

"You win. I'll go down to dinner, even if it kills me."

# Chapter 22

ELIZA'S COURAGE FADED AS dinner progressed. Seated between Beau and Lord Whitlow at the table, she was ignored by both. Harriet claimed all the Viscount's attention with her lively chatter, whilst her father seemed more interested in his food than conversation.

When they had finished eating, the ladies went ahead into the drawing room, leaving the gentlemen to enjoy their wine. Harriet made a point of inviting Eliza to sit with her, including her in the conversation with the others. Eliza wondered what mischief her rival was brewing.

"What is your opinion, Miss Merry?" Harriet asked, showing her an open sketch book. "Is it like or not?"

Eliza gazed down at the page in front of her. It was a pencil drawing of Beau's face. She was familiar with every inch of his countenance and was forced to admit it was a fair depiction. Not as accurate a portrait as her brother William would have drawn, but far better than anything she could create.

Before Eliza could answer, Frances snatched the book from her lap and gave it to her mother. "What do you think, Mama? Isn't it an excellent likeness? Harriet is so skilled."

Lady Harting held it so Lady Whitlow could see. She looked down at the drawing of her son. "Very talented indeed," she said. "It is a handsome sketch."

"But not, perhaps, as handsome as the original," Harriet's mother said with a little laugh, as though saying something witty.

Eliza cringed, but her aunt gave a thin smile, accepting the compliment on her son's good looks with a slight bow of her head.

Harriet turned to her, her eyes gleaming with malice. "Do you draw?"

It was a simple enough question, but Eliza guessed her rival knew the answer already and sought to throw her into a poor light. Her cheeks grew warm as they all watched her.

"No."

"You prefer to paint?"

"No," she said, her face growing warmer under the continued scrutiny.

"Then what do you favour? Embroidery?"

Eliza thought of her clumsy stitches and would have laughed if it were not so embarrassing. She never could sit still long enough to master any of the regular female accomplishments.

"No."

"How unusual. Mama insisted we all learn to draw, paint and embroider, as well as play and sing."

"Hush, Harriet. Not everyone has the same advantages," Lady Whitlow said.

The arrival of the gentlemen saved Eliza from further embarrassment. It did not surprise her they had not lingered long over their wine as she had caught a significant look passing between Lady Harting and her husband as they left the dining room.

Harriet wasted no time in abandoning her. After drawing their conversation to an abrupt close, she gravitated straight to Beau's side.

Mr Whitlow sat down next to Eliza on the sofa with a cup of coffee in his hand and, with no encouragement, told her a long and complicated story relating to his father's estates that could not evoke the slightest interest in anyone else.

However, she saw it as the lesser of two evils. A lengthy, boring tale was preferable to being forced to play the pianoforte, so she faked her absorption and listened until her cousin's husband ran out of words.

"Let us have some music," her aunt said.

"Pray excuse me, Mama," said Frances, resting a hand on her swollen stomach with a titter, "but I cannot get close enough to the keys."

Lady Harting gave her daughter an indulgent smile and turned her gaze on Harriet. "Miss Whitlow, perhaps you would be so kind as to perform for us?"

"I would love to." Harriet rose from her seat and looked expectantly up at Beau, who stood near her, where she had cornered him, the moment he entered the room.

He offered her his arm and hovered next to her as she took her time to select her music and sit down at the instrument. As she played a long and complicated piece, he sidled away from the pianoforte until he reached the sofa where Eliza was sitting. He sat down on the opposite side of her to Mr Whitlow, and they listened in silence until Harriet finished playing.

Eliza joined in the applause and dared to hope the company had heard enough music. Lady Harting instructed a servant to set up the card tables and suggested a game of whist. Although the prospect of more cards filled her with dread, Eliza thought it would be a relief to escape the torture of playing the pianoforte.

Harriet had other ideas.

"But Miss Merry has not played for us yet. She must have the chance to exhibit as well."

Eliza tried to refuse, but when everyone turned to stare at her, the words stuck in her throat, and all she managed was a little shake of her head as she stared down at her lap, hoping to be excused.

"I believe Miss Merry is shy," said Harriet. "Beaumont, encourage her to perform for us."

Eliza gazed up at him in despair. His eyes met hers and he saw her reluctance, but there was nothing he could do to help. Harriet had forced him into an impossible position. He must beg her to play or appear rude, though he knew she did not want to, and he did not care for her performance, good or bad.

"Do play for us, Miss Merry," he said, rising from his seat and offering her his hand.

Eliza rose and let him lead her over to the instrument. She chose the same piece of music she had performed the previous evening, hoping the familiarity would quell her nerves. But she had reckoned without the enlarged audience, and conscious of Lady Whitlow's sneering expression at the end of the first movement, she played the rest even worse than the day before.

Eliza retired to the sofa, her cheeks glowing red with embarrassment. She clenched her hands together in her lap, willing the colour in her face to fade. The only person who seemed pleased with her poor performance was Harriet, who applauded herself for showing her rival in such a poor light.

A glance toward her aunt showed Eliza that Lady Harting looked far from delighted. But whether her look of contempt was directed at Harriet or herself, Eliza could not tell.

Mr Whitlow got up and moved to the card tables, eager for a game of whist, leaving Eliza alone with Beau on the sofa.

"She rides like you play," Beau whispered without looking up.

Eliza didn't know how to take his words. The reference to her poor playing did nothing to boost her confidence, but it was a minor triumph that he thought so little of Harriet's skill on horseback.

"But you ride like she plays," he said, glancing sideways at her so their eyes met. "We can't be good at everything—and I don't give a fig how well you play."

Eliza felt the heat of embarrassment melt away under his approving gaze, and her mouth spread into a wide smile. She could cope with any amount of criticism of her playing if Beau praised her riding.

If she hadn't been in her aunt's drawing room surrounded by people, she would have been tempted to reach out and squeeze his hand, because the compliment delighted her so much.

An unwelcome voice intruded upon Eliza's pleasant thoughts.

"Join us, Beaumont." Harriet sat at one of the card tables with her brother opposite. "Frances is tired and retiring for the night, so you and Miss Merry must play together."

Eliza was not fooled by her friendly tone. The horrid woman was trying to embarrass her again, by forcing Beau to partner her when she was bound to lose.

He didn't respond immediately. Instead, he glanced sideways at Eliza, raising his eyebrows slightly as if asking her opinion.

She gave a tiny shake of her head. "I play cards worse than I play the pianoforte," she muttered under her breath.

"Please excuse us, Miss Whitlow," Beau said, not rising from his seat. "We are indifferent whist players and have no desire to display our incompetence in the face of your undoubted talent."

Eliza felt a bubble of joy welling up inside her. *We are indifferent.* He spoke as if they were a team. A couple. She liked the way it sounded. And he was standing up for her against Harriet's scheming.

Her rival abandoned the card table with apparent grace, but her eyes sparkled with annoyance. She walked over to the sofa where they sat and loomed over Beau, gazing down at him with a possessive gleam in her eyes. "Perhaps you would prefer a game of piquet or backgammon?"

He leapt to his feet as if he'd been scalded, but said nothing.

Eliza twisted her hands in her lap, waiting for his response. He wouldn't succumb to such underhand tactics, would he? If they embarked on a two-player game, Harriet would have gained the advantage and have Beau all to herself.

She couldn't believe it was what he wanted, but his hesitation suggested he was struggling to find a way to decline the wretched woman's pointed invitation without being rude.

Eliza's spirits sank. If Miss Whitlow was determined to monopolise Beau, perhaps she should retire early and leave them to it. She had endured enough already without having to observe Horrible Harriet fawning over him for the rest of the evening.

She rose to her feet beside Beau, sending him a forlorn glance before making her retreat. Their eyes met, and she could see the haunted look in them—a look she blamed on Harriet.

As he held her gaze, his expression changed. His eyes sparkled, as though coming to a sudden decision. "Do you play spillikins?"

Eliza nodded, and a smile crept onto her lips. That was a game she could play well.

"Excellent." He turned to Miss Whitlow and her brother. "I'll pit my skill against anyone who thinks they can beat me."

Harriet sniggered. "You cannot be serious. Spillikins is a children's game."

Mr Whitlow's face, however, grew animated. "I used to be rather good at that. I'm happy to accept your challenge, Beaumont."

"So am I," said Eliza.

Ignoring Harriet's lack of enthusiasm, Beau sent a servant to fetch the spillikins from the schoolroom. They were soon seated around the card table with a tangled pile of wooden sticks in front of them.

Beau insisted Eliza should go first. She leaned forward, examining the pile before successfully capturing a stick without jogging any others. With a gleeful smile, she removed a second and a third, before causing a slight movement when she sought to capture a fourth.

"Your turn," she said, looking at Harriet, who had reluctantly agreed to join in the game.

After spending a long time examining the pile before settling on the stick she was going to remove, Harriet knocked another spillikin on her first attempt.

Eliza glanced at Beau and, by the smallest rise of her eyebrows, she communicated what she thought of her clumsiness. Only by the slightest twitch of his nose did Beau show he had seen and understood.

Mr Whitlow proved to be a skilled player. More dexterous than his sister, he won two sticks before making a mistake.

Then it was Beau's turn. He lifted the first stick easily, causing him to flash a triumphant look in her direction, but it made him over confident, and Eliza bit back a smile when he failed to extract a second without nudging the stick next to it.

He let out a groan as play passed once again to Eliza, but on his second turn, he fared much better. Eliza's pile of sticks grew fast, but Beau's grew even faster. Mr Whitlow played a creditable third, but Harriet captured only two sticks and became increasingly impatient for the game to finish.

Her competitive instincts aroused, Eliza played close attention to Beau's moves and as the game progressed, she gained on him. At the last count, she was the winner by a single stick.

"Beaten at the last fence," Beau said. "I'll get you next time. See if I don't!"

"Not if I can help it," Eliza retorted.

"You are to be congratulated on your excellence in this children's game, Miss Merry," said Harriet, failing to keep the sneer out of her voice. "Your dexterity is admirable. I believe I am better suited to whist, where winning depends on playing a skilful hand rather than having a steady one. More thinking and less deftness required."

"Yes, indeed," said Eliza, not knowing what else to say.

Her rival gave her a long, disdainful look and moved away.

Eliza glanced up at Beau, who still stood by the card table. His eyes were alight with laughter, and she grinned in response.

Miss Whitlow had embarrassed her earlier, but the tables had turned, and Harriet's spitefulness had sent him to her rescue.

And to be rescued by Beau made all the embarrassment worth it.

# Chapter 23

ELIZA WOKE EARLY AGAIN the next morning, looking forward to her ride with Beau. The corners of her mouth curled up in a satisfied smile as she thought about how he'd come to her rescue the evening before.

Her maid was already laying out her riding dress.

"No, Sarah," Eliza said, dismissing the outfit she was preparing. "My new habit today, please. The scarlet one that was finished just before we left London."

"Yes, miss. I'm certain Lady Frances will appreciate it."

"I doubt it, but you must know she won't be going out with me this morning in her condition."

"You don't fool me," Sarah said, shaking her head and tutting as she helped her mistress into the red habit.

Eliza acted as though she had not heard, but a traitorous warmth spread over her cheeks.

"Going riding with his lordship, are we?"

"What if I am?"

"Well, you be careful, miss, and don't start on one of your freaks to impress him. He's a top horseman, and you would be bound to come unstuck if you tried to best him."

"Thank you for the warning," she called behind her as she left the room, with her matching scarlet riding hat already pinned onto her head.

She walked downstairs and out into the garden with a light step, almost colliding with Lady Harting's woman as she went out the back door. Reed dipped into a curtsey and hurried inside. Eliza was wondering what could have enticed the maid outside so early when she caught sight of a black-haired man striding away from the house.

He glanced behind him, and as he did so, she realised she'd never seen him before.

Oh my. Did Reed have an admirer? What would Lady Harting say to that?

As she approached the stables, Eliza forgot all about him. She heard voices ahead, and her heart sank as she recognised the sharp tone of Harriet's voice.

To her dismay, she discovered both Beau and her rival were already mounted.

Harriet's smile didn't deceive Eliza. Her cheeks glowed, her nostrils flared, and her eyes—her eyes flashed with malice, mingled with triumph and something like pity.

"When I discovered you had been riding before breakfast together yesterday, the temptation was too much, and I knew I *had* to join you. You won't mind if we go on ahead. My horse is becoming rather restless."

Eliza huffed under her breath. In her opinion, Harriet's mare was a sluggish beast, and if she really considered her hard to control, she must be as poor a rider as Beau had suggested.

With a flick of her whip, Harriet urged her mount into a walk. When she reached the entrance to the yard, she turned and called over her shoulder. "Come, Beaumont."

Eliza stared at Beau, willing him to contradict her rival, but the resolution with which he had acted the night before seemed to have deserted him. With a shrug of his shoulders and an apologetic smile, he urged his mount forward and followed Harriet out of the stables.

As Eliza stood, staring after them, her eyes glazed over.

Yesterday, Harriet had humiliated her in front of everybody, and now she had stolen her ride.

And Beau had let her.

Her shoulders slumped as she processed her disappointment. Why had he left her standing? Was she fooling herself to think he preferred her to Harriet? The beautiful, accomplished Harriet. Would he be better off marrying her?

Eliza gave herself a little shake. What was she saying? Beau might have succumbed to the horrid woman's sly tactics in the same way she had the previous evening, but he *did* prefer her. She was sure of it.

Harriet would not make him a comfortable wife. She did not understand him. She didn't even *want* to understand him. All she desired was what he could give her in terms of wealth and position.

Beau deserved more than that.

Eliza pressed her lips together in renewed determination. She would not let her have him. He might not love her, but she loved him, and she knew she was much better suited to be his wife.

Finch frowned when he saw the resolve on her face. "No playing off your old tricks."

"What makes you think I'm planning any?" she said, flashing him a bold glance before mounting her horse.

He shook his head. "Don't forget you're a lady now."

"Yes—and what a bore it is, always having to conform."

Not waiting to hear what other words of wisdom her groom wished to impart, Eliza urged her mount forward and Whisper trotted out of the stables.

It was some time before she caught up with the others. They had abandoned their horses and were walking alongside the stream which fed into the lake. Stepping stones enabled a person to cross to the other side without having to walk up to the bridge, which was some distance away.

Beau had tethered Jet and was hopping from one stone to the next with ease, perhaps hoping to put some space between himself and Harriet, who stood by the stream, begging him to stop.

Eliza's spirits rose. All was not lost. He was putting up a fight.

She pulled up her horse and slid gracefully to the ground. After handing the reins to Finch, she joined her rival at the water's edge.

"Do tell Beaumont to come back, Miss Merry. I feel sure he will take a tumble."

Eliza tried not to scoff. "I doubt it, but if he does, he'll only get wet."

Harriet stared at her as if she had said something unbelievable. "But he might ruin his clothes, as well as losing his dignity."

Eliza was not impressed that this was Harriet's chief fear—that Beau might look ridiculous. Her eyes danced with laughter. "Surely you don't believe he's afraid of cold water?"

Harriet must have observed the derision in her expression and hastily altered her concerns. "He might twist his ankle or bang his head."

"Have you such a low opinion of Beau's sense of balance? If you had watched him jump from one moving horse to another, you would not think it likely he would fall crossing a stream."

The other woman reddened, sorry to have voiced her fears.

"Look," said Eliza, hoisting her skirts a little, wishing she were wearing breeches instead, and stepping onto the first stone. "I'll show you how easy it is."

Harriet squealed.

That was all the encouragement Eliza needed. She had not intended to follow Beau all the way across the stream, but it was too tempting, especially with him watching her, his eyes full of admiration.

Without difficulty, she skipped from one stone to the other until she reached the other side.

Beau offered her his hand for support as she stepped onto dry land again and grinned. "Impressive balance. Is Miss Whitlow coming too?"

Eliza's eyes gleamed wickedly. "I doubt it. She's too scared. If she feared you would fall in, I don't suppose she'll risk the journey herself."

"Good," Beau muttered under his breath.

Eliza pursed her lips, trying not to laugh. She didn't think he'd meant her to hear that.

"Shall we explore the wood?"

"I'd like that," she said, taking his arm.

They had not gone far before they heard a cry for help. They turned back toward the way they'd come and saw that Harriet, not to be outdone, had overcome her fears, and was crossing the stream. She had taken a few steps but seemed to have frozen on the middle stepping stone, unable to go forward or backward.

Eliza rolled her eyes and, with a little shake of her head, returned to the water's edge, with Beau right behind her.

"I suppose we'd better rescue her," he said, sounding as reluctant as she felt.

He was about to cross to where she was stranded when Eliza caught a look on Miss Whitlow's face that suggested she was not as helpless as she appeared. It made her suspect Harriet had manufactured her plight in order to draw Beau's attention back to herself and would probably throw herself into his arms in the process.

Determined to thwart her scheme, Eliza laid a restraining hand on his arm. "Let me go."

With ease, she crossed to the middle of the stream, where Harriet stood unmoving. "Give me your hand," she said, stretching out her right arm toward her.

Her rival scowled at her, but was forced to accept the proffered help or admit she was not stuck after all. She grabbed her hand, pulling on it with such force that Eliza almost lost her balance.

"Easy now," she said as she regained her footing, a warning look in her eyes.

As Harriet stepped toward her, Eliza moved back to the previous stone and then repeated the process, stretching out her arm again to offer support.

This time, as Harriet trod on the new stone, she jerked her rescuer's hand.

Eliza caught the malicious gleam in her rival's eye before losing her balance and toppling into the stream.

She gasped as her body hit the cold water with a tremendous splash, splattering Harriet, who let out a high-pitched squeal. The stream was less than two feet deep, and she landed, rather inelegantly, on her rear.

If she had fallen of her own doing, she would have laughed—but this was no accident. She had been knocked off balance on purpose, and she was fuming.

Though tempted to yank the ungrateful woman in after her, Eliza managed, with some difficulty, to control her temper. It soothed her somewhat when she saw, from her undignified position, that she had doused her rival with enough cold water to wipe the smile off her face.

Finch left the horses with Harriet's groom and darted across the stream to Eliza's rescue, whilst Beau headed toward her from the opposite direction.

Beau reached her first. Without thinking of his boots or his clothes, he jumped down into the cold water, splashing Harriet all over again. She squealed, but he ignored her, giving Eliza all his attention.

"Are you hurt?" he asked, holding out his hand toward her.

She heard the concern in his voice and grinned as she allowed him to pull her to her feet. "No, just wet."

"No point in using the stones now," he said with a chuckle.

"None at all."

They waded back across the stream to where the horses were tethered.

Eliza gazed down at her sodden riding habit. She thought wistfully that it was a shame its first outing had been so eventful. It would probably never look the same again.

Although the soaking had not been her fault, she knew she was not blameless. She had crowed to herself about Beau's preference for her and taken unholy pleasure in leaving Harriet behind on the far side of the stream.

And she had put on the new habit out of vanity, hoping Beau would admire her.

If her father saw her now, he would give her one of his *you should have known better* looks and remind her that pride comes before a fall.

Words Eliza knew she would do well to remember.

# Chapter 24

Beau's thoughts were not so profound. He was struggling to think of anything except how attractive Eliza looked. He studied her face. Despite her recent wetting, her pale blue eyes hadn't lost their sparkle. Then his gaze dropped to her riding habit, and he gulped hard. The damp scarlet material clung to her slim figure, making it difficult to concentrate on anything else.

Conscious he was staring at her, he glanced away. Eliza's groom was doing his best to help a semi-hysterical Miss Whitlow to use the stepping stones to return to dry land.

Beau closed his eyes to regain his composure. He abhorred over-emotional females.

When he reopened them, they fell on Eliza again, who stood, peacefully dripping by her horse, waiting for her groom to finish his rescue.

Beau frowned. She would catch cold if she remained any longer. Could Miss Whitlow think of no one but herself?

Stooping, he cupped his hand, ready to assist Eliza mount.

"I'm afraid it will be a soggy lift. Wouldn't you rather leave it to Finch?"

"I'm so wet already, it won't make any difference."

She eyed his damp garments and chuckled. "I think you may be right."

Without further argument, Eliza placed her foot in his hand and with the slightest pressure on his shoulder, despite her sodden state, she let him raise her until she was seated on her saddle.

Miss Whitlow coughed loudly. Now she had been rescued, she stood by her horse, looking, he had to admit, rather magnificent, with her nostrils flaring and her eyes ablaze.

But Beau was not attracted to her in the least. He could not forget her scheming or the hysterics he had just witnessed. He needed to distance himself from this woman as much as possible and refused to respond to the implicit summons. Instead, he nodded to her groom to help his mistress.

Without waiting for Miss Whitlow, Beau mounted Jet and with a nod to Eliza, they headed back the way they'd come. As his stallion broke into a canter, her mare did likewise, and they rode back to the house together.

He suspected that awful woman had pushed Eliza into the stream on purpose, out of spite because she was jealous. Yet another reason he wanted nothing to do with her.

If he had gone to her rescue as he had intended before Eliza forestalled him, would she have pushed him in too? Probably.

And then she would have fallen in on top of him. He shuddered at the thought.

When they reached the stables, they abandoned the horses to the grooms and the soggy pair made their way back to the house. Beau guided Eliza to the conservatory entrance, thinking it might be preferable to drip in there while he sent for help.

Fortunately, his mother's efficient servants had been on the lookout for their return, and a footman waited to open the door for them as they approached. He grimaced apologetically at the man who was trying, unsuccessfully, to hide his surprise at the picture they presented.

"I'm afraid we're a little wet. Please bring some towels and fetch Miss Merry's maid."

"Yes, my lord," Ash said, scurrying off on his errand.

"And arrange a bath for Miss Merry," he called after him.

Beau was left alone with Eliza, who was wearing a damp and enticingly clingy scarlet habit.

He had to distract himself. Think about something practical. She was wet. Getting cold.

"You must get out of those clothes as soon as possible," he said, and straightaway wished he hadn't. The picture his words painted didn't distract him at all.

Eliza flushed deep red, but launched into speech with a lightness that was at odds with her obvious embarrassment. "I hope my hat survives the wetting," she said, unpinning it from her head. "It's the first time I've worn it and I know it sounds vain, but I was rather pleased with the way it looked."

"If it doesn't survive, I'll buy you another. Now, we must get your boots off. Can't have you treading water through my mother's home."

He bid her sit down on one of the stone benches that littered the conservatory, raised her right foot and undid the laces. As he pulled the boot off, he brushed her heel with his hand.

Beau had not considered that such an everyday task could prove so intimate. Perhaps he should have left a servant to do it after all.

Trying to forget the intimacy of the action, he tipped her boot up and a trickle of water came out, making Eliza chuckle.

He then lifted her other leg and removed the second boot. The same tingling sensation occurred when his fingers brushed her ankle. As he was about to tip it up and empty it on the floor, Eliza leaned forward and grabbed the boot from him, pouring the contents over the nearest plant.

She was pressing her lips together, trying not to giggle, but it was too much for her, and a little gurgle of amusement escaped. Beau found the sound infectious, and soon they were both roaring with laughter at the ridiculousness of the situation.

"Now, no messing about. When you get upstairs, take your wet clothes off, and warm yourself up in a nice hot bath."

Eliza fired up red again, and he realised that, in his concern for her well-being, he had embarrassed her for the second time. Yet her eyes glowed with the exhilaration of a shared adventure and laughing together, and something more he didn't understand.

Whatever it was, it was captivating, and Beau couldn't take his gaze off her.

She peeked up at him shyly. Her charming dimple showed on her chin and her lips—her full red lips—beckoned to him.

"Eliza," he said huskily, bending his head toward her.

But before he could claim a kiss, they were interrupted. Her maid bustled into the room, and after wrapping her mistress in a towel, she hurried her away, tutting as she went.

Beau stood, dripping, staring after Eliza, feeling bereft, wondering what had come over him.

Back in his bedchamber, changing out of his wet clothes, he pondered what had just happened. The scene in the conservatory had shaken him more than he was prepared to admit—even to himself. He had come so close to kissing Eliza, and from that point, there would be no turning back.

Although he would rather marry her than any other lady of his acquaintance, he wasn't ready to commit himself.

Not yet. Not while there was still a chance of avoiding marriage altogether if Romeo won at Epsom.

He needed to pull away—for both their sakes. The last thing he wanted was to injure Eliza by raising expectations he hoped to avoid having to fulfil.

He had already singled her out more than he ought, and laid her open to Miss Whitlow's spitefulness, which seemed to increase the more attention he paid her.

After arranging for a tray to be sent up to Eliza's room, Beau entered the parlour, a little on the late side, to join the rest of the household for breakfast.

"Are you recovered from your wetting?" Miss Whitlow asked as he took his place at the table.

"Yes, thank you."

"I expect Miss Merry regrets the impulse to jump in the stream so you would be obliged to rescue her," she said, daring Beau to contradict her.

"Are you saying it wasn't an accident?" Frances said. "I did not think my cousin was so brazen. How despicable."

Beau's mouth firmed. He glared at his half-sister as he tried to put the record straight. "You are mistaken. It was a mishap, and it's a mercy she didn't pull Miss Whitlow in with her."

"That's kind of you to say, Beau, but I see how it was," said Frances with a patronising smile.

"I'm thinking of taking a rod down to the lake," Whitlow said, cutting across their conversation. "Want to come?"

"Splendid idea," Beau said, grasping at the chance to escape. If he didn't get some respite from Miss Whitlow before long, he might lose his temper with her—and that would not be pretty.

If he was honest, that wasn't the only reason. He needed some breathing space from his growing attraction to Eliza.

He was not ready to face her yet. If he did, he might not be able to stifle the impulse to kiss her.

And that would change everything.

·♥·♥·♥·♥·♥·

After spending the day down at the lake with Whitlow, Beau had been reminded of two things. How much he disliked fishing and how tedious he found his brother-in-law.

By dinnertime, he longed for Eliza's straightforward conversation and was tempted to abandon his previous decision to keep his distance. However, despite being seated next to her at the table, Miss Whitlow sat on his other side and once more monopolised his attention, preventing him from saying more than a few words to Eliza.

Perhaps it was just as well. He needed to stop showing her such a distinct preference while he still could.

Beau lingered over his wine with the other gentlemen for as long as he dared and held back as they entered the drawing room to join the ladies. He stood in the doorway, trying not to look in Eliza's direction, and yet found his eyes drawn to where she sat, with her head bent, looking nothing like the lively girl he had rescued from the stream.

The card tables were already set up. Was that why she seemed so downcast? He wished he could save her from the ordeal of playing, but to do so would draw just the sort of attention he was trying to avoid.

"Do you play, Beaumont?" Miss Whitlow asked, directing him with a pointed look.

He knew he must. He couldn't risk anyone accusing him of coming to Eliza's rescue again. It was for the best.

"Yes. Dare you play with me?"

Miss Whitlow cast a smug look at Eliza and beamed at him. "Oh yes. I dare."

"Miss Merry? Do you play with us?"

"Pray excuse me. I have a headache."

Straightaway, his mother fussed around her, ordering her to retire to bed at once. Eliza accepted her dismissal without a fight, as if sleep was all she longed for.

As she bade goodnight, Beau glanced up at her and their gazes locked. There was no doubting the sadness in her eyes. He was a fool to think she wouldn't notice the change in his behaviour.

Last time they'd met, they had laughed together—and he'd almost kissed her.

Now, he was putting her at a distance, and she knew it, but she didn't stop him.

Miss Whitlow would not have let him retreat. If he had given her half as much encouragement, she would have ordered her wedding dress.

Beau hated Eliza looking at him like that. Not accusing him of anything, but so forlorn.

It did something to his insides that was most unpleasant.

He would make it up to her tomorrow. No matter what the cost.

# Chapter 25

THE NEXT MORNING, ELIZA rode before breakfast as usual. Alone. It was no surprise Beau didn't join her, but she wasn't certain if he stayed away for fear of another close encounter with Harriet, or if he was continuing to avoid her.

She still couldn't believe how fast the previous day had gone downhill. After that blissful moment in the conservatory, when Beau had been about to kiss her, she had been full of hope. But then he had ignored her for the rest of the day, leading her to the disappointing conclusion that almost kissing her was a mistake.

How would she ever grow closer to him if he backed away at the slightest sign of intimacy?

At breakfast, Eliza said little, wondering what the day would hold. Would Beau absent himself again? Would he seem as remote as he had the previous evening?

At the end of the meal, Lady Harting rose. "I will leave you young people to occupy yourselves. There are duties I must attend to as the lady of the house. Beaumont will take care of you." She flashed a piercing look at her son. It was clear his behaviour the day before had displeased her, and she was giving him no chance to repeat it.

Beau ducked his eyes, but Eliza knew he had seen his mother's displeasure and dared not disobey her.

"I understand you are an expert at archery, Beaumont," Harriet said. "I doubt I can compete with your mastery, but I would love to match my aim with yours."

Eliza shuffled in her seat, willing her cheeks not to burn with embarrassment at the innuendo in Harriet's words. She glanced up at Beau, but he seemed oblivious. Hadn't he noticed, or was he too used to such talk to care? It made her feel very young and naïve.

"What an excellent suggestion," said Frances. "I would love to watch you compete."

Beau sniggered. "We wouldn't want you taking part—baby or no baby. Your aim is way off. You'd be endangering us all."

She glowered at him, but he just pulled a face and glared back.

"I say it is a jolly fine idea," Mr Whitlow said, though no one had solicited his opinion.

His wife smiled at him as if placating a small child. "I knew you would, my dear."

Eliza cringed at the condescension in her voice. It was lowering to see Frances treat her husband like that after less than a year of marriage.

"Then we're all agreed," said her cousin.

"Not all," said Beau. "Eliza has not given us her view."

Harriet's eyes glinted with malice. "Perhaps Miss Merry does not know how to use a bow. Is archery permissible at the rectory?"

The mocking insult ruffled Eliza's temper. She remained silent, balling her hands into fists underneath the table rather than unleash her tongue until she'd calmed herself. It didn't help that she couldn't give a satisfactory retort to the attack. Though not forbidden, no one at home had ever shown the slightest interest in the sport, and so she'd never had the chance to try.

"Well, Elizabeth. What do you say?" Frances said. "Do you know how to use a bow?"

Forcing her hands to relax, Eliza regained control of her temper. "No, but I'd like to learn."

Harriet smiled with satisfaction, anticipating another opportunity to expose her in front of Beau.

Eliza hoped she could prove her wrong. She was not bookish, but her balance and dexterity were excellent, and she usually shone at such activities. Provided she could pick it up as easily as she expected, she had every hope of performing well.

They moved outside to the lawn, on the opposite side of the house to the lake. Servants bustled around, settling Frances into a chair and setting up the targets on a clear, flat stretch of grass.

Eliza was encouraged to see Beau embrace the challenge of teaching her to shoot. If he had been keeping his distance from her on purpose, he had changed his mind, showing no reluctance to get close to her again today.

He handed her a brace and a shooting glove to protect her hand and, taking a bow, he deftly strung it and showed Eliza how to hold it. She took the bow and tried to copy what he had done.

He shook his head.

Eliza frowned. What had she done wrong?

With raised eyebrows and a lopsided grin, he reached for the bow and turned it up the other way. "Always make sure you hold it the right way up or you'll break it."

Out of the corner of her eye, Eliza caught Harriet and Frances stifling a giggle as they exchanged a disparaging glance, but she refused to be cowed by their amusement and laughed at herself.

"How silly of me," she said, casting Beau a roguish look that drew an answering smile. "I'll be sure not to repeat that mistake."

"Now, stand sideways to the target and turn your head to face it. That's right. Good girl." He stood behind her and showed her how to take an arrow from her pouch and fit it in her bow. Eliza was eager not to make a fool of herself again, but it was hard to concentrate with Beau standing so close to her. She could feel the warmth of his breath on her neck. It was most distracting.

"Hold the bow with your left hand and draw the string back with just two or three fingers of your right hand. Don't pull the arrow toward your eye—more to your ear," he said, adjusting the direction she was pulling in.

"Bend your neck a little, like this." Eliza gulped hard as he touched her neck, sending tingles all down her spine.

"When you've drawn the string back most of the way, aim for the target. Once you know where you're aiming, pull it back the rest of the distance and release. You're trying to land your arrow as close as you can to the middle. Hit gold and you earn nine points. Go on. Have a try."

Still distracted by Beau's proximity, Eliza's first attempt only carried half-way to the target.

"Oh dear," Harriet said, laughing in mock sympathy. "It seems you are not as adept at shooting as you are at riding. Perhaps you should sit and watch."

"No, thank you," Eliza replied with a false smile.

With Beau's encouragement, she tried again. The spurt of anger left her feeling more in control of herself. She was determined not to be beaten.

She pulled back the string, took aim, and released the arrow. This time was better. It went three quarters of the way to the target.

She shot another, and another, but each one fell short.

Eliza frowned. She knew her aim was true, but she couldn't seem to get the length right.

"Watch me," Beau said. Eliza observed as he set his arrow, aimed, and sent it sailing toward the gold area in the centre of the target.

She thought she could see what she was doing wrong and took Beau's place and shot another arrow. It flew through the air and landed in the outer white circle.

"Bravo!" Beau said.

Eliza glowed under his praise, but she knew she could improve. She realised she had pulled slightly to the left that time and made a note to compensate for it with her next arrow.

Harriet grew restless, waiting for her to finish her archery lesson. She seemed determined to divert Beau's attention to herself. "I can see I shall have my work cut out to beat you, Beaumont."

Eliza could hear the unspoken words. Harriet assumed she would be no competition. Her next speech confirmed it.

"Perhaps we should play in teams to give Miss Merry a chance. She is, after all, a mere beginner and we have been practising for years. How about you and me against my brother and Miss Merry? I am sure we would make a fine team."

Beau's face clouded over. Eliza was relieved to see he was aware of Harriet's machinations, but it was Mr Whitlow who came to his rescue.

"Don't see how that would give Miss Merry a chance, Harriet. You're a far more accurate shot than I am. You and Beaumont would be bound to win. Besides, I thought you wanted to pit your skill against him. Better to play as individuals."

His sister reluctantly conceded.

They agreed to shoot two dozen arrows to determine the winner.

Eliza watched as Harriet took her stance and fired four shots at the first target, one after the other, each landing in the gold centre.

"Well done," Beau said. "Capital shooting."

She looked smug, preening her feathers like a peacock, and giving Eliza a very condescending smile as she passed her. "Don't be too dismayed if you can't match my performance. I've been hitting gold for years."

Mr Whitlow went next, notching up a reasonable tally, but nothing to compete with his sister. Beau matched Harriet's score with ease, and then it was Eliza's turn. She prayed she would not embarrass herself.

Beau gave her lots of encouragement, and she was relieved to find she improved with every shot.

Harriet's face grew more contorted as the match progressed, annoyed with her rival for improving so fast. No doubt, she was even more bothered by the way Eliza dominated Beau's attention, asking for help and advice, which he was more than happy to give. He helped her gauge the wind and adjust her aim accordingly.

Harriet allowed herself to become so ruffled that during her next turn, three of her shots hit red rather than gold. She yanked her arrows out of the target and one of them broke in her hand, obliging her to get another out of her quiver for the following round.

As the match progressed, Beau's aim remained steady, only missing the centre a few times.

Harriet failed to recover her poise, and her accuracy continued to deteriorate. The more Eliza improved, the worse Harriet's aim became. At the third end, Eliza overtook Mr Whitlow and her rival exclaimed at her brother's mediocre performance.

"How could you be overtaken by a beginner, Whitlow?" Harriet said in a loud voice, so everyone could hear. "But then, Miss Merry has advanced with such speed you would not think she was a novice now. Are you positive you haven't shot with a bow before today?"

Eliza's eyes flashed with anger. How dare Harriet question her word? She might not always be as truthful as she meant to be, but it was unthinkable to fabricate such a story just to get close to Beau. What was more, she could not bear the other woman's hypocrisy. She did not doubt her rival would have pretended to be a beginner if she had thought it would serve her cause.

Harriet gave her a disdainful look. "I admit it would be tempting to be taught by such a master, but to improve so rapidly…"

Eliza closed her eyes and took several deep breaths to calm herself. If she wanted to triumph over her opponent, she needed to regain her composure.

Her efforts to overcome her anger paid off. On the last end, she hit the centre of the target with all four arrows, beating Harriet, and taking second place behind Beau.

"I'll have to watch you in the future," he said to her, his eyes glistening with praise. "If you shoot like that as a beginner, I can see you'll give me a run for my money once you've had a bit more practice."

"Congratulations," said Harriet. "I am clearly missing my mark today."

Eliza wondered whether she was talking about her archery or her flirting. She smiled to herself. This time, she had won on both scores.

# Chapter 26

Miss Whitlow did not take her defeat well. She continued to poke at Eliza, questioning if she was the archery novice she claimed to be, until Beau spoke up in her defence.

Too late, he saw his mistake. Miss Whitlow praised him for wanting to see the best in people and increased her veiled spitefulness toward Eliza whilst flirting all the more with him.

Beau found it hard to concentrate on any of the conversation at breakfast the next morning. He'd foregone his early ride, because Miss Whitlow had threatened to join him, and by avoiding the stables, he'd missed Romeo's arrival.

His only thought was to finish the meal as quickly as possible so he could see his young racehorse.

"I would love to go for a tour around the estate," Miss Whitlow said, staring at him.

Beau dipped his eyes, hoping that her wish wouldn't turn into a demand for his time.

"A drive would be perfect, would you not agree, Frances?" Lady Harting said. "We could make the circuit in the landau."

Miss Whitlow pursed her lips, looking less than pleased it was his mother who had taken up her request rather than him, but her disappointment was gone in a moment. She was not easily deterred. With a slight change of tactics, she fluttered her eyelashes in his direction. "Perhaps the gentlemen would care to ride with us?"

Beau saw his morning in the stables disappearing fast. He ground his teeth as he tried to think of a way to get out of accompanying the ladies. His gaze drifted to Eliza's face to be met with a sympathetic look.

Miss Whitlow must have seen this exchange and directed her next comment at her. "You'll join us, won't you, Miss Merry?"

Beau frowned at Eliza, a question in his eyes. She cast him an imploring glance, as if she depended on him to rescue her from the drive she clearly didn't want to go on.

It was becoming a habit to respond to that look. Perhaps he could save them both from the ordeal, for a time at least.

"What a tempting idea, Miss Whitlow," Beau said, flashing her a dazzling smile, "but my colt has just arrived from Newmarket, and I promised to show him to Miss Merry at the earliest opportunity. We're heading for the stables after breakfast, but no doubt will catch you up shortly."

Beau was vaguely aware of Miss Whitlow responding with a very thin smile, but he was not really paying attention.

His eyes were fixed on Eliza, who gave him such a look of gratitude he felt like a hero.

Beau paced up and down the hall while he waited for Eliza to change into her habit. She had told him to go ahead, but he was too gentlemanlike for that. However, when she hurried downstairs, just fifteen minutes later, dressed for riding, he shot her a smile of genuine appreciation for having kept him waiting for so little time.

They left by the rear door and made their way to the stables. He strode so fast Eliza had to scurry to keep up, but she didn't complain or ask him to slow down. She seemed to understand his eagerness.

As they entered the building, Romeo whickered in welcome. Eliza held back as Beau hurried over to the colt's stall and nuzzled his head up against him, whispering words of affection.

"I'll give you some time alone together," his groom said with a chuckle.

Beau twisted round, ready to chide the man for teasing him, but he caught Jem looking at Eliza, not his horse. He suddenly felt unsure of himself. Was his groom talking about Romeo or Miss Merry?

Jem grinned, his eyes alight with laughter, and strolled off to another part of the stables.

Beau turned again to Romeo, running his fingers through his mane and feeling the warmth of his face against his own, both horse and man lost in the joyful reunion.

When he finally pulled away, he was surprised to see Eliza standing there, watching him share those precious moments with his colt. With a twinge of guilt, he realised he'd forgotten all about her.

Beau drew her forward. "Meet Romeo," he said, with a father's proud smile.

"He's beautiful," she whispered, apparently seeing nothing amiss with his behaviour. They stood together, side by side, as she reached up her hand and ran it through his mane. Romeo nuzzled his head toward her, recognising a friend, and she put up her face next to his in much the same way he'd done a few moments before.

Quincey interrupted their private reverie. He untethered the colt and led him out into the yard so they could have a proper look at him.

"All well?" Beau asked.

Lord Harting's head groom nodded. "Aye. I've given him a once over. Your people have taken good care of him, and Jem's made sure not to fatigue him on the journey here. Best bit of horseflesh I've seen in a long while, if your bays will pardon me."

Beau was not offended, his heart swelling with pride to hear such praise of his darling. He enthused for some time about Romeo's finer points to a ready audience. He did not miss the fact that he had rattled on about his colt for over ten minutes without the slightest complaint from Eliza. She stood there in silence, lapping it all up, her eyes shining, as proud of Romeo as if he were hers.

He smiled to himself. It was rare to encounter someone who loved horses as much as he did and—in his experience—rarer still to find a lady who could keep her mouth shut for so long when standing next to an eligible bachelor.

"Very good, Quincey. I won't take him out today. Give him time to rest."

The man gave a brief nod and led Romeo back inside. A few moments later, the stable door opened again, and Jem came out, leading his master's black stallion.

Beau sighed and shot Eliza a wistful glance. "I suppose we should go, unless we want to be raked down by the ladies—present company excepted."

Finch had already saddled her horse, and Beau stepped forward to help her mount, but then paused, embarrassed, feeling conspicuous under Jem's watchful eyes.

While he hesitated, her man assisted her into the saddle, and after arranging her skirts, Eliza rode out of the yard.

Beau mounted Jet and trotted after her, followed at a modest distance by both grooms.

"Seems a pity to waste such a beautiful morning dawdling after a carriage," he said as he drew alongside. "If I know my mother, they'll be going at a snail's pace."

She darted him a wicked look. "Much too great a waste."

He watched in surprise as she touched her horse's flank with her whip and cantered off in the opposite direction from that which the carriage had taken.

He urged Jet forward and sped after her. "You've gone the wrong way."

She neither slowed her pace nor changed course. Hadn't she heard him?

It was some quarter of an hour later that Eliza finally drew rein.

"You're headed in the wrong direction, and I bet you know it."

"The wrong direction?" Eliza asked, a picture of innocence.

"The landau went the other way."

Her eyes danced with amusement. "Sounds to me, then, that this is the right way to go. Wouldn't you agree?"

Beau grinned. "Most definitely."

"It was the least I could do to thank you for saving me. The thought of a dull morning's drive was more than I could stomach."

"Why didn't you just say no?"

The light went out of her eyes in an instant. "I...didn't know how. I struggle to find the words when everyone's staring at me."

Eliza's vulnerability pulled on Beau's heartstrings, drawing his deepest sympathy. How well he knew that feeling of inadequacy. "I'm glad I could rescue you."

"I'm glad I could rescue you back."

# Chapter 27

T HEY RODE ON TOGETHER in companionable silence until Eliza halted on the summit of a hill from which they could see most of the estate.

"Ridiculous, isn't it?" Beau said, as he drew alongside her, spitting out his words in frustration as he looked around. "I know this land better than my own. Hardly surprising, of course, as I haven't seen Langcroft Park since I was a boy. However, my mother has decreed that the situation is about to change. The tenants have been given notice and in June, I take possession."

"That's a good thing, isn't it? The sooner you learn about your property and the people who depend on you, the better."

"But how will I cope, Eliza?" he said, trying not to sound as desperate as he felt. "I've never even ridden over my lands as an adult. I'm ignorant about estate management and fear I'm not cut out for it."

"How do you know if you've never tried? You should always assume you can do something until it's proved otherwise. Besides, managing your estates well does not mean doing it all yourself. There is no shame in relying on a competent steward. Father says it's wiser to focus on what we do best and find those we trust to do the rest."

"And what do I do best? Sometimes I think I'm no good at anything."

"Nonsense. God has blessed you with a rare talent for horses."

Beau admired the confidence with which Eliza spoke and allowed her words to sink in. He'd never thought of his ability with animals as a gift from God before, and he rather liked the idea.

"We can't pick what talents we're given, but we can choose what we do with them. You should concentrate on what you're good at—horses. You'll have space to grow your stud at Langcroft Park, won't you?"

He let out a loud huff. "In theory, yes, but I'll only have the funds to do so if I marry."

As Eliza's face turned red with embarrassment, he realised what he'd said. He stammered out an apology. "I'm sorry. I shouldn't have said that...I..."

She gave him a reassuring smile, though her cheeks still glowed. "It's no matter. The terms of your inheritance aren't a secret in the family. I know how hard it is for you."

Pricked with guilt, he dropped his eyes, unable to meet her gaze. He didn't deserve her compassion.

Beau knew he wasn't being fair to her. He'd tried to draw back and stop the intimacy growing between them, but when the alternative was Miss Whitlow, it was no surprise he kept returning to Eliza's side.

What would she think of him if she realised he still hoped to avoid matrimony? Would she be so understanding?

Desperate to escape from such uncomfortable thoughts, he steered the conversation into a different channel.

"This will all be your father's one day, won't it?" he said, surveying the landscape.

"I don't suppose he'll want it."

Beau blinked in surprise. "He won't?"

"Father doesn't put much store on worldly wealth. He says money does not make you happy and we should be more interested in storing up treasures in heaven than on earth."

"I'm no good at either," Beau muttered.

Eliza acted as though she hadn't heard him. "Father's content being a rector. I don't think he wants the responsibility of the earldom and all this. He never expected to succeed, being the younger son."

Beau nodded. "Ant would understand. He doesn't want to inherit. As long as his funds don't run out, he's perfectly happy being the carefree younger brother. And now Castleford is married to Georgie, he no longer needs to fear his duties falling on him."

"Unless they have no sons," Eliza said in a small voice.

He let out a bark of laughter. "What are the chances of that? They'll have a nursery full of little brats before we know it and some of them have got to be boys."

"Yes, of course."

Beau's eyes flew to her face. He'd heard those clipped tones before, and instinct told him something was wrong. Her pinched expression confirmed it.

He wished he could wipe away the concern clouding her features. "What is it?"

Eliza gave him a wistful smile. "I was thinking how unbearable it would be if Frances had a boy and then another...and Georgiana had...none."

Her words trailed off, spoken so softly that Beau only just caught the last word.

His chest tightened, and he gazed into the distance, not knowing how to respond. To talk about babies made him feel uncomfortable. He knew he'd have to face up to having children someday, but he hoped that day was a long way off.

The trouble was, he didn't know how to be a parent—and the thought terrified him.

He'd not known his own father, and Harting was invariably distant. The dominant figure in his life had always been his mother—and he didn't want to be like her.

At length, he turned back to Eliza and met her eyes, which were full of tenderness and something more he couldn't identify that seemed to pull him in. Perhaps having children with this woman was not such a dreadful prospect...

Beau shifted uncomfortably in the saddle. What was he thinking? It was his mother's idea that he should get married, not his. It was his duty to wed and produce an heir at some point, but he was not ready to take a bride yet—or was he? Would he ever find another woman who suited him as well?

He doubted it. Perhaps he should stop trying to escape marriage and wed Eliza.

The notion was not as dreadful as he'd imagined. Quite the opposite. Warmth flooded his being as he allowed the idea to settle.

Until a much less pleasant thought came to him. If he proposed to Eliza now, his mother would have dictated his future—and he would not marry at her command if he could avoid it.

What was the hurry anyway? If he won the bet and gained his independence, he would be free to make his own choice—and he would choose Eliza.

He must not give in now, or his mother would win.

"Frances will probably have a hideous baby girl who looks just like her," he said, trying to break the tension with a joke, "and who could be jealous of that?"

Eliza gave a tight smile. "No one."

Beau saw the tears glistening in her eyes and knew he'd said the wrong thing, but it was too late to take his words back.

The moment had passed, and it was just as well. He wasn't used to thinking so deeply about such things and was shocked to find how much he cared. He was concerned Eliza was upset—and it grieved him.

Beau tried to think of something that would bring a smile to her face again.

"Do you know if the badger set we watched as boys is still there?" he said, calling back to Jem, who had drawn up some distance away. "I was telling Eliza about it the other day and wondered."

His groom shrugged. "I don't know, but I can find out. I'll ask my pa."

Beau acknowledged his words with a nod and turned back to Eliza, but she didn't look up.

He urged Jet forward, eager to be on the move again, as if he could ride away from the heaviness weighing on him because he'd let her down.

It was only to be expected. He always disappointed his mother. He was bound to disappoint Eliza, too.

It exacerbated his feelings of inadequacy when Finch drew alongside her and talked to her in an easy manner. It galled him to think of her groom consoling her where he had failed.

With a flick of his whip, he chivvied his horse into a canter and left them to it.

Beau was some distance ahead of them when he met the landau coming the other way. His mother gave him a disapproving stare, but then, what was new about that?

"Where is Elizabeth, Beaumont? You were supposed to be taking care of her."

A fresh wave of guilt coursed over him. "She's not far behind."

Miss Whitlow grinned like a Cheshire cat, revelling in the fact he had arrived alone.

"That was not very gentlemanlike of you to desert her, but I suppose a Corinthian like yourself could not resist the lure of a good gallop," she said, pouting her lips in a way some men might have found attractive.

He had to admit such looks had enticed him in the past—but not now.

The thought no longer surprised him, but when had he changed?
When had he decided the only smiles he was interested in were those
of Eliza Merry?

# Chapter 28

That night, Eliza could not sleep. She had shared another moment of intimacy with Beau—a connection that went beyond friendship—and again he had pulled away. She did not know whether to be encouraged by his preference for her company or not. Perhaps she was fooling herself and he only preferred her to Harriet, because she was less likely to trap him into marriage.

After tossing and turning for a while, as if in a fever, she cast the covers aside and walked across to the window. She opened the shutters a little and looked wistfully out into the darkness. It was a still night. The sky was cloudless, the moon almost full, and the stars appeared especially bright.

If she had been at home, she might have risked a walk, but as a visitor in her uncle's house, she did not dare. It was a shame, for no doubt the cool air would have helped calm her thoughts and her fluttering heart and enable her to get some sleep.

A sound startled her. There it was again. Something was tapping against the wall on the far side of her bed. Oh no—did Lord Harting have rats? She had an aversion to rodents.

Aware of her bare feet and unable to gauge whether the noise was coming from inside or outside her room, she scurried back across the carpet and dived onto her mattress. She was about to pull the covers over her head to block out the tapping when she heard another sound—a voice at her door.

"Eliza? Are you awake?"

Beau? Why was he here? Was there bad news?

"Yes. What is it? Is someone ill?"

"Ill? No, of course not. Open the door."

She grabbed her dressing gown and slipped her arms into it, pulling the cord tight around her waist. Without a thought for the proprieties, she opened the door, bursting with curiosity. Why was Beau visiting her room in the middle of the night?

He was standing there, fully dressed.

"What are you doing here?"

Heat rushed to her cheeks as his eyes lingered on her form, imperfectly concealed beneath the flimsy wrapper, distracted by what she was—or rather wasn't—wearing. He seemed to forget temporarily why he had come.

"What is it, Beau?" she asked, all too aware of his masculinity, and feeling strangely vulnerable. "You said no one was ill, so why are you here?"

"Get dressed," he said in a somewhat husky voice.

"Why? It's the middle of the night?"

"Badgers!"

Eliza couldn't believe her ears. All thought of romance vanished. Her eyes shone with excitement of a different kind. He had remembered her wish, and they were going to find the badgers.

"Wait outside. I won't be long," she said, closing the door in his face.

She stood for a moment, contemplating what to wear. It was typical of a man not to realise getting dressed in the middle of the night was not straightforward. All her gowns fastened up the back, and she dared not send for her maid to help her.

Although she supposed she could ask Beau to do up her dress, she was not so lost to propriety as to consider asking him. It made her blush just thinking about it.

What was she to do?

In a flash, the solution came to her. Shirt and breeches!

She retrieved William's old clothes from where she'd hidden them at the bottom of her trunk and quickly put them on. After covering them with a full-length pelisse that buttoned up to the chin, she reckoned no one would guess what she wore underneath.

Eliza didn't scruple about abandoning the idea of putting on a bonnet over her hair, which had been plaited for the night. It seemed rather out of place to be wearing a hat for propriety when the adventure itself was highly improper. She added a sturdy pair of half-boots to finish her ensemble and hurried back to the door.

Beau gave her a look of approval, impressed at the speed at which she'd dressed. He put a finger to his lips, cautioning her not to say a word. Not that she needed any warning. She was as anxious as he was not to be discovered.

Eliza followed him along the corridor and down the servants' stair, and soon they were outside in the cool night air. Beau took her by the hand, leading the way down the hill to the woods by a footpath that was much more direct than the track they had taken on horseback. She had forgotten to pick up her gloves and warmed at the feel of his fingers entwined with her own.

Down the length of the path they hurried, Eliza scurrying to keep up with Beau's long strides. As they entered the trees, he slowed his pace and turned to her, a lopsided grin on his face.

"I still can't believe you got dressed in ten minutes," he said with a chuckle. "My sisters would have taken the best part of an hour."

Eliza glowed with pleasure at the compliment, but decided not to inform him just what she was wearing. "I doubt you could persuade Frances to get up and dress in the middle of the night at all. I can imagine the look on her face at the mere suggestion."

She could see Beau's answering smile in the moonlight, but then his expression grew more serious.

"I don't suppose there is any other lady who would have done," he said, looking down at her, his eyes strangely intense, "but fortunately, I wasn't tempted to ask anyone else to come with me."

With no warning, he cupped her face with his hands and brushed her lips with his own. "You're a girl in a million."

In silence, he retook her hand, and led her further into the woods.

Eliza walked beside him in a daze, raising her free arm and touching her fingers to her mouth, as if she could recapture the embrace that had caught her by surprise. Her heart was pounding so loudly she thought the whole wood must be able to hear it.

She'd often wondered how it would feel to be kissed by Beau, and now she knew. Even such a brief caress was magical, and she knew it was significant. He had overstepped that line at last, and the kiss was a seal—a promise of what was to come.

Or was it? There was nothing loverlike in Beau's behaviour now, dragging her unceremoniously through the wood. Had the kiss meant nothing to him?

It was painful to admit, but she knew Beau had kissed other women in the past. Not ladies of their class, but...*other* women. She recalled how he had stared at her just a short while before, when she had opened the door to him like a veritable hussy. Perhaps this was the inevitable response to her brazen behaviour.

Beau jerked to a stop, breaking in on her thoughts, and pulled her away from the path to crouch behind some bushes. She was about to object to such rough treatment, but before she could utter a word, he laid his finger across her lips, urging her to keep quiet.

With a great effort of will, she ignored the tingling sensation caused by him touching her mouth, and concentrated hard on where he was pointing. It must be the entrance to the set.

Her position was uncomfortable, but she didn't complain. She could feel Beau's warmth behind her as they waited, in silence, for something to happen.

They didn't have long to wait. She heard a noise and Beau stretched out his hand and pointed to one side where an adult badger was emerging, ruffling the undergrowth as it went.

Eliza was transfixed as she watched the striped animal move about, just a few feet in front of them, snuffling this way and that, presumably in search of food. Her eyes already glowed with pleasure when another badger came out of the set to join the first, with two babies in tow.

She could not drag her gaze away for a moment until, almost half an hour later, the badger family disappeared into their underground home.

"Happy?" Beau asked.

Eliza nodded fervently.

He helped her up, and stood looking down at her, his expression unreadable.

It was only now, when she no longer shared his warmth, that she realised how cold she was, and her teeth began to chatter.

Beau slipped off his greatcoat and draped it around her shoulders and drew her toward him. "We'd better return to the house," he said, somewhat wistfully, as though he, too, was reluctant to end their time together.

Eliza agreed and took his hand once more as they made their way back through the woods.

As they came to the edge of the trees, Beau stopped and turned to face her. He seemed to struggle to find the words he wanted to say.

"I meant it, Eliza," he said in a more serious tone than normal. "You really are a girl in a million. No one else would have been up for such an adventure. No lady, that is. Ant would have come with me, but ladies are always bound by propriety. But not you. You're different, and—"

"You don't need to remind me I'm totally lacking in principles," she interrupted with a groan. "My father would be furious if he knew."

"I didn't mean that. I meant you're game for anything. That I really..."

Beau stopped mid-sentence and, putting his arms around her, he drew her close.

Eliza tilted her face upward and waited, not daring to breathe, as he lowered his head and claimed her lips with his own.

This kiss was so unlike the first that it took her breath away. It was urgent, demanding a response, and sent tingles all down her spine and legs to her feet.

All her doubts about whether he cared for her fled in that moment.

She wrapped her arms around his neck, and kissed him back with fervour, revelling in the glorious sensation of knowing she was his at last.

# Chapter 29

BEAU HAD NOT RECKONED on how intoxicating he would find Eliza's kiss.

When he set out that night, his only thought was to bring the smile back to her face. After discovering there were still badgers in the woods, he'd wanted to take her to see them, without stopping for one moment to consider how improper it was.

And then she'd stood in the doorway, so scantily dressed, looking at him as if he were a hero and putting herself entirely in his power. He'd felt humbled by the realisation—and it had shaken him to the core.

In the woods, he'd stolen a kiss, but this was different. He'd tried to put his feelings into words, but his supply of flirtatious comments seemed totally inadequate.

So he had kissed her, and she'd melted beneath his embrace. And it was so intoxicating he was in danger of losing control.

A screech broke the silence, causing them to jump apart. Beau felt as if he'd been doused with a bucket of cold water. All his senses were on the alert as the echoes of a howl hung in the air.

They stood listening, not daring to move, as the noise faded away into an eerie silence.

Eliza grabbed his arm in fear. "What was that?"

Beau knew that sound. It was a human cry, and it had come from the direction of the stables. That could only mean one thing. Trouble.

His stomach clenched. Was someone trying to steal Romeo?

He had to get Eliza away from here. Fast. If there were horse thieves about, she was not safe. But if he took the time to see her inside, he might be too late.

Darn it. He would have to send her back alone. It was the only way to protect her and have a chance of saving his colt.

"Return to the house," he ordered, detaching her grip from his arm. "I need to check on the horses."

He turned on his heel and headed for the stables without a backward glance. If he looked behind him, his resolution would waver, and that might ruin everything.

He owed it to his horses to make sure they were unharmed, and he mustn't jeopardise Eliza's reputation by being found with her at night. He wouldn't want her to be forced to marry him.

How he hated to leave her like that. He wished he had a riding whip in his hand to slash away at the grass in his frustration. The anguished look on her face would be impressed upon his mind forever.

What must she think of him for deserting her? Perhaps she would stop believing in him like everyone else. He wouldn't blame her. He knew he'd behaved badly.

Beau half-ran, half-walked to the stables, eager to find out what had happened. There was a possibility it might be nothing more than a drunken stable hand stubbing his toe, but he doubted it. Fear gripped his stomach as he thought of more sinister possibilities.

As soon as he entered the yard, he knew something was wrong. In the moonlight, he could see the stable door stood wide open.

He went inside with a sinking heart, afraid of what he'd find there. As his eyes adjusted to the gloom, he made his way to where Romeo had been tethered, but he discovered no more than he'd expected. His young racehorse had gone.

As he entered the stall, he almost tripped over a figure lying motionless on the stable floor. He bent over the body, trying to see if the man was still breathing.

A second figure leapt out of the darkness and punched him in the stomach. Beau was winded, but reacted on instinct, lashing out with the punishing right that was well known amongst the amateur pugilistic community, sending his adversary staggering back.

While Beau was still reeling from the punch he'd landed, the man attacked again, knocking him off balance. They rolled on the floor together, arms and legs flying as each tried to overcome the other.

Though his assailant had winded him at the outset, Beau was much the larger man, and at last he broke free from his grip. He yanked his opponent's arm behind his back, pulling it up so hard that he forced a cry of pain.

There was something awfully familiar about that voice.

"Jem?"

"My lord?"

Beau released his hold with a heavy sigh. "What the blazes do you mean by attacking me like that?"

"I thought you were one of those men back again. They took Romeo, but not without a fight. He kicked one of them hard."

"It must have been his scream I heard."

Fortunately, Jem did not ask how Beau was close enough to hear the cry.

"Pa heard a noise and woke me. We were down here in a trice and went for the two men. They were taking Romeo out of his stall. One clouted me over the head with a pot or something. When I came to my senses, I saw someone leaning over my father. I thought it must be the man who'd milled me down."

His groom dropped his gaze. "I'm really sorry, my lord."

"And while we were busy fighting, they've got clean away."

Jem jerked his head up. "You don't know that. Take Jet and go after them. They can't have gone far."

"If you think I'm going to risk my stallion taking him out on a wild goose chase, think again. Despite the moonlight, it's too dangerous to ride across the fields. Even if we knew which direction they'd taken. Which we don't. The only thing we know is they won't have gone by road. Too easy to track."

Quincey stirred, and Beau stretched out his hand to help him up. He brushed himself down, but did not seem to have suffered any lasting damage.

Beau turned to Jem. "How's your arm? You're lucky I didn't break it. You fight like a mad dog."

"Actually, not so lucky. I think it *is* broken."

Beau's eyes had grown accustomed to the gloomy light, and he could see for himself that one of Jem's arms hung loosely at his side.

"Oh no. You poor fellow. Sorry. How typical of me to injure the wrong man."

"Don't blame yourself, my lord. It was my mistake."

Now the fight was over, the full horror of what had happened hit Beau, and he sunk down heavily on a bale of straw as if he had been shoved.

"Oh, Jem. What am I going to do? I've no horse and no jockey and a race in a fortnight's time that I desperately need to win."

He rested his head in his hands and sat, motionless, filled with despair, whilst Quincey and Jem stood, sheepishly looking on, not liking to leave him, but not wanting to interrupt the brooding silence.

He'd been so sure Romeo would win, but there would be no glittering success for his beauty. No prize money. Even if he got his colt back, his jockey was injured. Finding another with Jem's natural skill would be impossible at such short notice.

If he had won that race, Beau would not have needed to marry for the money.

Now he had lost everything. It had been a last cry for independence from his mother—and he had failed.

He cringed at the thought of Eliza's disapproval. He'd assured her that betting on someone's skill was not the same as gambling, but he was wrong. There was more to winning a horserace than he had assumed.

He'd taken a gamble and lost.

Beau let out a deep sigh. What in heaven's name was he going to do? The question went round and round inside his head, but no miraculous alternative presented itself. The answer was always the same.

To save his horses, he must fall in with his mother's plans. He would be obliged to offer for Eliza.

And if she ever found out about the bet, she would think he'd married her because he had no choice. She'd never believe he was marrying her because he wanted to.

The truth hit Beau with the force of a mail coach. He held his breath for a long moment and then let it out in a whoosh.

He *wanted* to marry Eliza. Sweet, trusting Eliza.

It was weeks since he'd decided he would rather wed her than anyone else. She was comfortable to be with. He liked how she dimpled when she smiled, and the manner in which her eyes twinkled at him when she was begging him to share a joke. That she shared his love of horses and rode more proficiently than any other woman of his acquaintance. How she relied on him to protect her from his mother. The way she believed in him.

The possibility of her refusing him made him feel sick. Not just for the sake of his horses. He could always marry someone else to save his stud. Miss Whitlow would certainly jump at the chance to become a viscountess.

But he didn't want anyone else. He wanted Eliza.

Even more than he yearned to get Romeo back—and that was saying something. He could start over with his stud, but if he lost her? It was too painful to contemplate.

From the moment he first touched his lips to hers, he knew he never wanted to kiss another woman. And when she had melted in his arms, such warmth flooded through his being that he thought he might ignite.

It pained him somewhere deep inside to think of her kissing anyone else. What if that someone was Ant? He could never face his friend again.

But he didn't just desire her kisses. He wanted more. Her smiles, her trust, her love.

Because he was in love with Eliza.

And it was unlike any love he had experienced before. He knew his life would be empty without her.

Why had it taken him so many months to realise?

Because of his mother. For as long as he could remember, she'd been trying to marry him off. It was like being prodded with a pointy stick so that he instinctively recoiled every time marriage was mentioned.

Would he have come round to the idea earlier if his mother had not pressed him so hard? Probably.

She'd invited Miss Whitlow to the house party to push him into Eliza's arms—and she'd succeeded. He hated to think Eliza was his mother's choice before she was his.

How would he ever convince Eliza he was not marrying her just to keep his horses? After all, he had more or less told her as much.

And now, what did it look like he cared about most? He'd raced over here to check on the stables, leaving her alone in the dark.

All at once, Beau roused himself. "Come down to the house with me, Jem, and I'll send for a surgeon. We must get that arm set before any lasting damage is done."

"What about Romeo?"

Beau sighed. "People are more important than horses."

"Are you feeling all right, my lord?"

Beau gave a wry laugh. "No, but I'm hoping I will be."

# Chapter 30

THE NEXT MORNING, ELIZA awoke at her usual hour feeling as tired as when she went to bed. But though her body was weary, her spirits were wearier.

After creeping into her room shortly after two o'clock in the morning in something of a daze, her feelings too jumbled to comprehend, Eliza had cried herself to sleep.

How could Beau leave her like that? Alone. In the dark.

The rejection she felt at his desertion was overwhelming.

She lifted a hand to her mouth and remembered the feel of his lips on hers. When they had kissed, she had dared to think he was falling in love with her—but she had been mistaken. If he had cared for her, he wouldn't have left her like that.

And for what? His horses.

They would always come first. She was simply the means to provide for the true love of his life—and she would have to get used to it or give him up.

Eliza yearned to be outside, but she refused to risk facing Beau before breakfast. Not while the pain was still so raw. Instead, she stayed in bed, delaying her morning ride in case he took it into his head to join her. It would do him no harm to be kept waiting. To taste what it felt like to be left alone.

Indeed, it was a shame she would not be there to witness his disappointment—if he was disappointed. She stifled a sob. If he even turned up to ride with her.

After sipping a cup of hot chocolate as slowly as she could, Eliza couldn't cope with being in bed any longer. She needed to be outdoors. To go for a ride and blow away these feelings of dejection.

She slipped out of her bed and pattered over to the window where the sunlight already streamed in through the open shutters. As she peered through the glass, she caught sight of Beau striding up the path toward the house from the direction of the stables.

To judge by the way he was thrashing the air with the whip in his hand, he was in a foul temper. It appeared he had gone to meet her for a ride and had given up waiting.

Beau's irritation transformed her own mood in a flash. He had got what he deserved. Disappointment. She gave herself a little shake, blinked back her tears and blew her nose. When had she become a watering pot? Staying indoors made her melancholy. She needed to get out into the fresh air.

Eliza hurried out of the house to the stables, making sure to avoid Beau. She had just enough time for a quick ride without being late for breakfast. She hoped Finch would not have put Whisper back in her stall already, thinking she was not coming.

Her groom had his hand on Whisper's bridle as Eliza walked into the yard.

He raised his eyebrows, not voicing the question that was clearly on his mind.

"Yes, I know it's not my usual time. Be quick and help me into the saddle or I'll be late back."

"You've missed his lordship," he said as he helped her mount.

"How very unfortunate."

"He waited a full half-hour. Seemed mighty eager to see you."

Eliza urged her horse forward. "I'm sure he'll get over it."

Out of the corner of her eye, she could tell Finch was taken aback at her ill-tempered response, but she ignored it, and as soon as she was clear of the stables, she increased her speed, cantering away from him, down the hill toward the lake.

Finch trailed behind her at a respectable distance, but when she paused at the bridge, he drew alongside her.

"What maggot's got into your head today, Miss Eliza?"

She pursed her lips. Finch had sat her on her first pony, and she was wont to give him more licence than others, but she was not inclined to take correction from him or anyone else this morning. She had just enough restraint not to utter the cutting reply that hovered on the tip of her tongue.

Finch took her silence as permission to continue. "I don't know what his lordship has done to upset you, but don't be too harsh on him—he's in mourning."

Eliza's eyes narrowed. "What do you mean *in mourning*? I don't understand."

"Romeo was stolen last night."

She gasped.

"Someone broke into the stables and attacked Quincey and his lordship's man. By the time Lord Beaumont arrived, his racehorse was gone."

That explained his bad mood. It wasn't about her at all. It was about Romeo.

Guilt pricked at her as she realised she'd been too harsh on Beau for deserting her last night. He must have guessed the noise they'd heard had meant trouble at the stables. He'd been right to race away from her, but he'd been too late to stop the thieves.

Poor Beau. She knew how much he cared for that colt.

Brushing aside the painful acknowledgement that his horses would always come first, Eliza let the ready well of sympathy rise to the surface.

Beau was hurting, and she needed to go to him. To comfort him in his loss.

Beau paced up and down outside the breakfast room, clenching and unclenching his fists, waiting for Eliza, but she didn't come. He'd raced to the stables that morning, longing to see her, but she hadn't turned up for her ride either.

Had she overslept or was she avoiding him?

His first thought on waking had been of Eliza, not of his stolen racehorse. He'd passed the remaining hours of the night dreaming of her woebegone face. What did she think of him, kissing her like that and then leaving her so abruptly?

But he would make things right. With Romeo's disappearance, he could no longer delay what his heart now desired. He was going to ask her to marry him.

With a sigh, he gave up waiting and went into breakfast without her. Everyone was still standing, talking about Romeo. His stepfather was most put out that anyone should break into his stables, and he could not seem to stop speaking about it.

"I spoke to the constable first thing, but he wasn't hopeful, I'm afraid. There's little these fellows can do. We must send for a Bow Street Runner."

"I appreciate that," said Beau, "but I'm not sure there's much they can do either. I suspect Romeo's well on the way to Ireland already. They couldn't race him over here. He's too recognisable."

"What puzzles me is why they only took the one horse."

"I expect they were disturbed before they could take any others," Lady Harting said calmly, as if the reason was obvious.

"Yes, but it is as if they knew the racehorse was here, and he's only just arrived. The thieves must have tracked him from Newmarket, though why they didn't make a grab for him on the road rather than attack my stables beats me."

Her ladyship screwed up her face in distaste, expressing her disapproval both of the subject and of her husband for pursuing it.

His stepfather seemed not to have noticed and was about to continue when the door opened, and Eliza entered.

To Beau's surprise, she came straight toward him, holding out her arms. He raised his own in response, and she took his hands and gave them a sympathetic squeeze before taking her seat.

"I'm so, so sorry to hear about Romeo."

"Thank you," he said, sitting down beside her.

Eliza spoke little during breakfast, but then, she rarely did. She always seemed to clam up in company, especially when his mother was present.

It was peaceful. He liked it that way. Now and then, their eyes met, and she shot him a small, reassuring smile.

Beau took this as a good sign. "I want to apologise—"

He broke off, unable to say more. Not here.

"Walk with me? In the rose garden, after breakfast."

She gave a brief nod of assent.

Now he had set things in motion, he wished breakfast would last forever, as all his old fears of inadequacy came tumbling in on him. His palms grew sweaty at the thought of what he was about to do.

Would he make a lousy husband? Would Eliza even want to marry him? How would she react if she ever found out about the bet and how he'd tried to escape marriage?

He feared that if she did, she would never believe he loved her and was marrying her because he *wanted* to, and not just to save his horses.

When he could delay no longer, he stood up from the table. As he exited the room, he caught a satisfied smile on his mother's face out of the corner of his eye. He found her approval unnerving, but he brushed it aside and headed for the garden with Eliza.

The roses were in full bloom, filling the air with a heady scent, but the effect was lost on Beau. He was almost choking with nervousness.

Away from the watchful eyes of the others, Eliza was a different person. "Your poor horse," she said, slipping her arm through his. "If only you had got there sooner, you might have been able to stop them. Is there nothing you can do to find him?"

Beau shrugged. "Harting is doing all he can. He's upset someone broke into his stables and can't understand why they stole none of his animals, but if the horse thieves knew what they were doing—as they must have done to nab Romeo—it's no great surprise. I wouldn't want any of his horses if you gave them to me. Strange they didn't pinch your mare, or Jet, though. Even stranger not to help themselves to my bays. They would have fetched a pretty penny and would be far harder to trace than Romeo."

Together, they walked along the rose-covered walkway.

"I'm sorry about last night," he said, staring at the ground.

Eliza didn't respond.

When he risked a look at her face, he saw she was biting her lip, gazing up at him with big, questioning eyes, a furrow upon her brow. He stared into the pale blue pools of mystery that seemed to see right into his soul.

She looked so sad, so vulnerable, that he wanted to sweep her into his arms and kiss her and tell her everything was going to be all right.

"Please say you forgive me."

"There's nothing to forgive," she said, looking away.

"Yes, there is. I left you alone in the dark, and I'm sorry."

Eliza's countenance lit up at his words. "You're apologising for leaving me?"

Beau screwed up his face in confusion. "What else would I be apologising for?"

"I thought you were sorry you..." Her colour deepened with every word.

As Beau stared at her rosy cheeks and the eyes that would not quite meet his, he realised what she meant. She assumed he was apologising for kissing her.

The corners of his mouth turned up and a wide grin spread across his face.

"No," he said. "I'm not sorry for that—and if you continue to look so adorable, I'm going to do it again."

Eliza finally met his gaze. Her eyes shone as a shy smile crept onto her lips.

He wanted to kiss her. Desperately.

He remembered how she'd trusted him to take her to see the badgers and the way she'd responded to his kiss before he'd deserted her, leaving her with desolation on her face.

But now the trusting look was back. It made him want to conquer the world for her. To cover her in kisses—but there was something he needed to do first.

He pressed his eyes closed and took a deep breath. When he reopened them, he tried to speak, but his mouth went dry, and no words came out.

Beau pulled at his neckcloth, which always felt too tight at such moments, and cleared his throat once, and then again.

"Eliza, will you do me the great honour of becoming my wife?"

He stared into her face, suddenly uncertain what her response would be. Afraid she would reject him and break his heart. It seemed like an eternity before she gave him her answer.

"Yes."

That was it. A simple yes. She had agreed to marry him.

The smile that had temporarily fled in his nervousness returned with full force. He couldn't help it.

Eliza wanted to marry him.

He opened his arms, and she walked into them, nestling up close to him. It felt so right. He lowered his head and, tipping up her chin with one finger, he pressed his lips to hers.

The kiss was tender and sweet, and he let it remain so, keeping his desire well under control in the cool light of day.

"I'll try to make you happy," he said, kissing her forehead. "I promise."

He placed her hand on his arm and gave it an affectionate pat, holding it there as they returned to the house together.

The first person they saw as they walked through the door was his mother. She stared at their linked arms and then at him.

For once, he didn't wilt under her gaze. "I'm delighted to tell you Eliza has agreed to become my wife."

"Has she, indeed? What a lovely surprise."

Beau shot his mother a curious look. She did not seem at all surprised that he'd finally done what she had been nagging him to do for so long. He had the distinct impression it was what she had expected, and that he had, once more, acted as a puppet, moving as she pulled his strings by proposing to *this* woman at *this* time.

He shook off the feeling that his mother had contrived his marriage and revelled in the pleasure that Eliza was his choice.

And she had said yes.

*Chapter 31*

Tʜᴇ ꜰᴏʟʟᴏᴡɪɴɢ ᴅᴀʏ, Bᴇᴀᴜ and Eliza travelled to West Meon so he could formally ask Mr Merry for permission to wed his daughter.

He only hoped Eliza's father would be as pleased with his proposal as his mother was.

There was no mistaking Lady Harting's delight at the match.

Within the hour, news of their betrothal had spread through the entire household. His mother had made sure of that. She would not risk him backing down, though he had no wish to do so.

He found it unnerving that his critical parent had so many smiles for him, but he had to confess it was a pleasant change from her perpetual disapproval.

Eliza looked as if she was in danger of suffocating from his mother's overwhelming kindness, but at least she no longer had to endure Miss Whitlow's spiteful tongue. As soon as that dreadful woman learned of their engagement, she formed an excuse to return home and left.

As the hour-long journey came to a close, Beau's stomach was still churning at the thought of facing Mr Merry. He couldn't forget the dreadful interview he had endured after trying to elope with Eliza's sister. Though humiliated, he'd been quick to agree he was not the right husband for Georgie.

But what if Mr Merry said no this time? Beau had already lost Romeo, but losing Eliza would be far worse. It still grieved him when he remembered his prized colt had gone, but his racehorse, though dear to him, could be replaced.

Eliza could not.

He kept telling himself that this time was different.

Their courtship had been conducted in public and he was now, very properly, coming to ask for her father's permission, not making a half-hearted offer for her hand because he had tried to elope with her.

Beau was sure Eliza was the right woman for him. He hoped her father would agree.

When they arrived at the parsonage, Mr and Mrs Merry were on the doorstep to greet them.

"I'd better get over the hard ground as soon as possible," he said to Eliza as the carriage drew up. "Pray your father will give his permission without a battle."

She squeezed his hand. "I'll pray, but I don't think divine intervention will be necessary. You're a good man. Why should he refuse?"

He shot her an uncertain look. Did she really believe he was a good man? He wasn't so sure, but he wanted to be. For her.

He helped Eliza out of the carriage, and she clutched his hand as they approached the house. With one last squeeze, she stepped forward to embrace her mother and then her father.

Beau hung back, observing the show of affection between Eliza and her parents, wondering what it would be like to grow up as loved as she was. A wistful sigh bubbled up inside him, but he subdued it before it escaped.

After hugging her father, Eliza turned to Beau and drew him forward. He bowed his head toward Mrs Merry, but she raised her eyebrows at the impersonal greeting. She threw him a mischievous grin so like Eliza's that his breath caught as she enfolded him in a hearty embrace.

Beau was taken aback, but responded to the warmth of her welcome, bestowing a kiss on her cheek before stepping away.

He turned to her father and hesitated, unsure of how to greet him. Before the pause grew awkward, Mr Merry held out his hand and Beau shook it, relieved he wasn't supposed to envelop his prospective father-in-law in a hug as well.

They retired to the drawing room for refreshment where Eliza's youngest sister Hetta joined them. She stared at him with such undisguised curiosity that he felt like an animal in a menagerie. It made him even more determined not to put off the dreaded interview any longer.

After gulping down a cup of tea, he cast a sideways glance at Eliza, who shot him an encouraging smile before he addressed her father.

"I would appreciate a little of your time, sir, if it's convenient."

"But of course. I've already written my sermon for Sunday, and as there are no pressing parish matters, I am quite at my leisure."

He led the way to his study and Beau followed, tamping down the sense of doom that lingered over him as he went on trial for the second time.

"I assume this isn't a social call," the older man said, sitting down behind his desk and encouraging him to take the chair opposite.

Beau gulped hard to clear his throat and began, not daring to meet Mr Merry's eyes. "Eliza has done me the honour of agreeing to become my wife. I've come to ask your blessing on our marriage."

"What makes you think I'll feel any differently about you marrying Eliza than I did about you marrying her elder sister?" he said with an expressionless face that gave Beau no clue what he was thinking.

"I was a mere stripling when I ran off with Georgie. It was foolish, and it was wrong, but I learned my lesson. There has been nothing improper about my courtship of Eliza."

Apart from the passionate kiss they had shared on the night Romeo had been stolen, but he hoped he would be forgiven for not mentioning that.

Mr Merry nodded and gave him a slight smile of approval.

"Do you love Eliza? Will you look after her and be faithful to her? When you marry, you are making promises—important promises—before God. They are not to be made lightly."

"Eliza is very dear to me," Beau said, growing red in the face as he struggled to get the words out. It seemed strange to acknowledge his feelings to her father when he had failed to express them to her. "You need not fear that I'll continue in my...bachelor ways."

"Does she hold you in affection?"

"I believe so, sir."

"As head of your household, will you lead Eliza and any children you're blessed with to follow the Lord by your own example?"

Beau hadn't expected that question. He wasn't sure he could lead anything, but with Eliza beside him, maybe he could. "I'll try."

Mr Merry gave him an encouraging nod. "A willing heart is all I ask of you. We are all learners in the school of life. How will you provide for your wife?"

This was the bit Beau had been dreading. "On my marriage, I come into my father's estate with an annual income of over five thousand pounds."

"Are you sure you don't wish to wed my daughter in order to get your inheritance?"

Beau closed his eyes briefly, gulped hard, and then opened them again. He looked Mr Merry in the face and admitted the truth.

"I won't lie to you, sir. I did not intend to marry this year, but my circumstances make it desirable. It did not take me long to realise that Eliza was the woman who suited me above all others. Please believe me when I say that even if it was no longer necessary for me to take a wife, I would still ask for permission to wed your daughter."

"You've surprised me. I had not expected such honesty, or such tact. I know well that your mother controls your fortune, and that it is she who is forcing your hand. You could have blamed her, but you did not. You did not have to admit your need for money, but you have. If you have been honest about this, then I am inclined to believe you when you say you care for my daughter. You have matured a good deal since my last interview with you in this room."

He stretched out his arm. "I trust we can leave it to the solicitors to draw up the settlements."

Until that moment, Beau had not realised how unsure he was about gaining Mr Merry's approval. He let out a tremendous sigh of relief and took the outstretched hand.

"Then you give your permission?"

"I do," he said, looking Beau in the eye. "Don't make me regret it."

Meanwhile, Eliza was being subjected to an interview of her own. After the gentlemen had left the room, her mother took her outside for a private talk, away from Hetta's ears. Eliza appreciated her thoughtfulness, as her youngest sister was prone to offer her opinion, whether or not it was asked for.

"Is this match what you truly want?" her mother asked, as they walked down the garden path, arm in arm.

"Yes. It's what I've always wanted—or at least, for as long as I can remember."

Her mother didn't reply, but the pinched look on her face suggested she wasn't convinced.

"You needn't fear I'm in love with a dream. I know Beau isn't perfect, but I see the man he can become with a woman who loves him and believes in him. You must see we are well-suited. Neither of us is bookish nor clever with words. We are active, outside people who both adore horses."

"Hmm. His passion for horses is no secret, and horses—especially racehorses—are expensive, but to be obsessed with the racecourse may prove even more costly. Gambling drains the deepest coffers. Are you certain he wants to marry you for the right reasons and not just to get money to fuel his obsession?"

Eliza swallowed the bile that rose in her throat at her mother's words. They were fears she had fought in her own mind, time and again.

"Beau does not gamble like other men," she said, focusing on the issue she could deal with most easily. "He knows horses and makes sound bets, and assures me he does not wager what he can't afford to lose."

"Very well. I'm not keen on wagers of any kind, but it is the way of the world. But what about his character and feelings? Does he share your faith? Does he love you? Do you trust him?"

Eliza avoided the first two questions, but answered the third without a moment's hesitation. "Yes, I trust him."

Her mother paused her walk and looked her in the eye. "Marriage is a monumental step. It is for life. You are promising not only to love, but to obey your husband. You must be sure of the character of the man to whom you make those promises. If you find you are mistaken—if anything shakes your belief in Beau before that moment when you vow to be faithful forever—do not push on regardless. Better a broken engagement than a lifetime of regret."

"I'll remember," said Eliza with a little laugh, wondering what had prompted her mother to say such a thing. It was absurd to imagine her ever changing her mind about Beau.

Her stomach tightened as she heard footsteps behind them. She recalled the insecurity in Beau's face as he had left the room with her father. Worry lines had creased his forehead and a nervous look had sat at the back of his eyes—the same look that often appeared when Lady Harting addressed him.

But her father was not like his mother. He was a reasonable man. He wouldn't refuse to give Beau his permission to wed her—would he?

If so, her happiness would be short-lived. Beau couldn't afford to wait for her to come of age, because he would lose his horses. He would have to marry someone else.

She murmured a desperate prayer under her breath and turned to greet him. Her stomach relaxed as she noted the wide smile on his face.

"Am I to welcome you as my future son-in-law?" her mother asked with a twinkle in her eye.

"Yes, madam, if you think I'll do."

Eliza leapt to his defence, taking his arm possessively. "Of course you'll do. No one else would."

He gave her arm an affectionate pat, and she found she couldn't stop smiling.

Her father had given his permission. Soon, she would be Beau's wife.

She listened in quiet enjoyment as her mother drew her beloved into conversation as they continued down the garden path together.

"How are your parents?"

"Very well, thank you. Mother eagerly awaits the arrival of her first grandchild."

"And your sisters? I understand Caroline has made an advantageous match. Do you approve of it?"

"I...I don't know. My parents haven't asked my opinion and I confess I've never given it much thought."

"And yet, she is your half-sister. You must have some views on the matter."

Beau hesitated before continuing.

"It seems unnatural to me that Caroline should wed a man old enough to be her father, but no one could doubt the match is to her liking. If you saw her face, wreathed in smiles as it is, I'm sure you would agree. She is as delighted as my mother that she received the earl's proposal within two weeks of arriving in London. But I don't think...I can't imagine she would marry him if he were *not* an earl. He is so many years her senior and not much of a society man. I hope she will not live to rue her choice."

Eliza nodded. "I agree. Nothing she has said to me suggests she has any affection for Lord Felbridge, but there is no doubt she is thrilled to be marrying someone of higher rank than her sister."

"A higher rank is not a recipe for happiness in marriage," her mother said with a frown.

She continued to chat about people in the parish until they were back at the house. "That's enough talk. I have a basket for old Mrs Jackson, who is suffering from her rheumatism. Please, would the two of you walk into the village to deliver it for me?"

Beau looked taken aback, as if surprised at the request, but Eliza agreed without a second thought, having helped care for her father's parishioners all her life.

And there was a bonus that came with this good deed—some time alone with her future husband. Perhaps they could plan their wedding trip. She wondered if he'd like to go down to the sea. They could stay in her parents' house in Weymouth. Ride along the beach together…

After fetching the promised basket from the kitchen, they set off for West Meon. Arm in arm, they strolled along the main street, drawing the eyes of everyone they passed.

To judge from the number of villagers who found an excuse to leave their houses, word of their arrival at the parsonage had spread. Eliza had known these people all her life and could not blame them for being curious about Beau.

Ever conscious of the man at her side, she glowed with pleasure as she returned their greetings, pausing occasionally to ask after an illness or whether a new baby had arrived.

These interruptions slowed their progress, but at length, they reached their destination and delivered the basket to Mrs Jackson, who showered them with her thanks. After making suitable enquiries into the old lady's rheumatism, Eliza bid farewell, retook Beau's arm and turned toward home.

As they left the village behind, she recalled her thoughts about the wedding trip, and was about to broach the subject, when it occurred to her that Beau had hardly said a word during the whole outing.

She glanced up at him, and her heart sank. His expression was unusually grim. Oh dear. This was a difficulty she hadn't foreseen. Going on errands of mercy was second nature to her. Didn't he approve?

"I'm sorry. Should I have asked Mother to send Hetta with the basket?"

Beau shook his head.

"You don't mind?"

"No."

"Then, what is it?"

"Strange. I wish I was as good as you."

"What do you mean?"

"This"—he pointed at the empty basket—"and this," he said, waving his hand in the air toward the village and everyone they'd met. "My mother gives to charity, but she would never demean herself by seeing to the needs of the poor in such a hands-on way. I suppose she might see it as the job of the rector or his wife—but not her. Not me. No one ever showed me how to care for people—to help them. I told your father I'd try, but I've got too much to learn. I'll never be good enough."

"Good enough for who?"

Beau shrugged. "For you. Your family. God."

Eliza bubbled with laughter. "Of course you're not good enough for God. None of us is. That's the beauty of God's grace—that we're saved by faith in Jesus and not by the things we do. Didn't you ever listen to what was preached in church?"

"Not much," Beau said, colouring up.

Eliza batted him with her hand. "It's not too late to change."

"I want to try. I'd like to take an interest in those who live on my estate. To give them reason to think I'm a good landlord, and a God-fearing man. You'll help me, won't you?"

Eliza's heart warmed at the seriousness in his tone. She had been right to believe in him. Already, he was proving himself to be a better person than Georgie had feared.

"I'd love to. We can work on it together."

She squeezed his arm as she revelled in that word.

Together.

# Chapter 32

OVER THE NEXT FEW days, Beau became increasingly convinced that asking Eliza to marry him was the best decision of his life. Once Mr Merry had given his permission, there had been no holding back, and Eliza's parents welcomed him into their home without reserve.

Although Beau had dined at the parsonage on many previous occasions, there was a distinct difference now. He hadn't been treated as part of the family in this way before. It was a novel experience, as his mother had never made him feel like this at Holybourne House. Perhaps that explained why his stepfather's house had never felt like home.

When there were no visitors, everyone ate together, though Eliza's sister was not yet out—an arrangement his mother would not have countenanced for a moment. At dinner, the conversation was informal, and even Hetta was free to express her opinion, which she often did.

He had never observed a couple who operated in such harmony as Mr and Mrs Merry. It was clear that raising their children was a joint effort, and Beau wondered why the thought had been abhorrent to him for so long. If this was what family life could be like, maybe having a child of his own was not such a terrifying prospect. And the prospect of creating a family with Eliza was...perhaps he should not think about that until after they were married.

They travelled back to Holybourne House in high spirits, arriving in plenty of time for dinner. After changing his apparel, Beau headed for the billiard room. He had promised to give Eliza a lesson in how to play and picked up a cue and idly potted a few balls while he waited for her to appear.

A few moments later, the door opened, and he looked up, with a ready smile on his lips for Eliza, when Anthony waltzed in.

"Ant! Where have you sprung from?"

"I was pining," he said with an audacious grin. "London seemed empty without you—and the incomparable Eliza. How is she? Better than you, I hope. You look weary."

Beau stiffened at the casual reference to his intended. Ant had no right to make flirtatious remarks about her.

"If I appear tired, it's because I've had a busy week. I have lost a racehorse and gained a wife. At least, she's not my wife yet, but she soon will be. And I've spent the past hour cooped up in a carriage."

Anthony closed his eyes and shook his head, as if trying to wake himself from a dream. "Can you run that by me again?"

"I have lost a racehorse," Beau repeated slowly, as if his friend possessed less than normal intelligence, "gained—"

"Woah. Stop right there. Romeo's missing? When? How?"

"Someone broke into the stables the night Jem arrived in Alton with him. By the time I got there, he was long gone."

"No! I don't believe it."

The familiar ache caused by his loss hit Beau again as Anthony put a comforting arm around his shoulders, shaking his head in sympathy as the entire story came flooding out. Well, not the entire story, as Beau kept Eliza's name out of it. He was relieved Ant didn't enquire how he was near enough to hear the thief's scream and was certain not to volunteer the information.

"So even if they find Romeo—which, in my opinion, seems unlikely—I've lost my jockey."

Anthony let out a long sigh. "I suppose this puts you in quite a spot. If your horse doesn't race, all our bets will be forfeit, as if he were a non-starter by choice. And you won't be the only one to suffer from it. You convinced me he couldn't lose and so I bet a substantial sum on him. I guess not even you can get it right all the time."

"Don't say that. I swear if he competed, he would win. I tell you, he's a born racer."

"Well, there goes your last cry for freedom. That explains why you're marrying Eliza. At least, I suppose it is Eliza you're planning to wed, and you didn't fall prey to Miss Whitlow. With Romeo gone, you had no choice. You were forced into it. Only way to keep your stables going."

"Yes, I was forced into it, but—"

Beau heard a gasp in the corridor and stopped mid-sentence. He ran to the half-open door and threw it wide.

No one was there. Whoever was listening had fled. He hurried out into the hallway with a sinking heart and was in time to see Eliza disappearing around the corner.

Beau froze where he stood. He feared he'd just made the gravest mistake of his life. Why on earth had he repeated Ant's words when they weren't true? Eliza had heard what he'd said and now she thought the worst of him. She had not stayed to hear any more.

He needed to explain he had not meant it. Without delay.

Pulling himself out of his stupor, he sped along the corridor, and caught sight of Eliza nearing the top of the stairs.

He called out, but she didn't stop, and he sped after her, only to be brought up short when she disappeared into the drawing room.

His shoulders slumped with disappointment. Eliza wouldn't let him talk to her. She didn't want to hear his excuses. Nothing else would have sent her running to his mother's side, where they couldn't converse without being overheard. He would have to wait until later.

Beau dragged his feet back downstairs and returned to the billiard room, where he slumped into the nearest chair.

"Who was it?" Anthony asked.

"Eliza. To judge by her gasp and her rapid departure, I assume she heard what I said, and now she thinks I've been forced into marrying her to save my horses."

"Haven't you?"

"Yes. No. I can't explain. I *want* to marry her, Ant. More than I would have believed possible a few weeks ago. She makes me believe I can be somebody—that I *am* somebody. What if she stops believing in me? Will she even wish to marry me still? How will I ever convince her? That I want her to be my wife because I love her?"

There. He had said it. Aloud. And he knew it was true. His affection for Eliza had grown into something so deep that if he lost her now, it would break his heart.

An expression flitted across Anthony's face that Beau could not quite make out. Was it regret, jealousy, or just a touch of sadness?

His friend let out a long puff of breath. "That changes things."

"If Romeo had won and I no longer needed to wed for money, I could have proved to her I wanted to marry her for the right reasons. How can I ever do that now?"

"You could try talking to her. Have you told her you love her?"

Beau winced.

Anthony closed his eyes and shook his head in despair. "You mean, you proposed to her, and you didn't even mention the word love?"

Beau's gaze roamed around the room, avoiding his friend's face.

"Why is it I—who have no intention of ever getting hitched—know all the right things to do, and yet those of you who are utterly smitten with a woman, don't seem to have a clue? Castleford was just the same. I despair. Talk to her. Tell her how you feel."

"I can't," Beau said, throwing his head back so hard that it hit the top of his chair. "She would never believe me now."

Eliza *had* heard Beau's words, and could not get away fast enough. Afraid that her involuntary gasp had revealed her presence, she hitched up her skirts and ran, not wanting to face him.

He had called after her as she sped up the stairs, but she didn't stop until she reached the drawing room. Schooling her face into an emotionless mask, she had opened the door and joined her aunt. It showed how much she wished to avoid Beau, that she would seek Lady Harting's company, but it was the safest place to be. There would be no opportunity for private conversation here.

The door to the billiard room had stood ajar and, hearing voices, she had hesitated on the threshold, suddenly shy of entering such a male domain. But then she had recognised Anthony's voice and had been about to join them when she overheard what he was saying.

*You were forced into it. Only way to keep your stables going.*

She had held her breath, waiting for Beau to deny it, but he hadn't. He had said those fateful words—words that could not be unsaid.

*Yes, I was forced into it.*

The last few days had been a lie. He didn't want to marry her at all. How could she have been so stupid? To think he liked her and might even be falling in love with her?

She had gone to meet Beau with a full heart, looking forward to the closeness she expected from him teaching her how to play billiards. He would have had to draw near to her, to show her how to hold the cue. His long arms would have stretched along hers to guide her aim. She would have felt his breath on her neck as he instructed her. Maybe he would have stolen a kiss.

She stifled a whimper. She had deluded herself. Her kisses meant nothing to him. She had indulged in a foolish hope that he was marrying her of his own free will, but she should have known better.

When he had kissed her that night in the woods, she had believed he felt something more. That at least he liked her, desired her. But even when he proposed, he had not kissed her like that again. It cannot have meant as much to him. How could it, when he had been so ready to leave her when his horses demanded his attention?

Eliza felt as if her heart was breaking into a thousand pieces as she accepted the painful truth she had not wanted to believe. He was only marrying her to pay for his stables. It had always been about his horses—not her.

A quarter of an hour later, Beau entered the room, and Eliza was somewhat appeased to see he looked ill at ease. A glimmer of hope arose within her that maybe he regretted his hasty words—words not meant for her ears.

But the hope drained away as quickly as it had come. It did not make the words less true, just because he hadn't intended her to hear them.

Beau made his way straight to her side. "Eliza, I—"

She gave him a curt nod and turned to welcome his friend, who had entered the room behind him. She was not ready to listen to his excuses. The pain of what she had overheard was still too fresh.

"Anthony! What a lovely surprise. Have you news of my sisters? Do tell." She patted the seat next to her in invitation. After shooting a sympathetic glance in Beau's direction, Ant sat down beside her. She maintained a lively dialogue with him until it was time for dinner, and then sunk into her customary silence.

Once the ladies had withdrawn from the dining room, Lady Harting bore down on her.

"You seem a little out of sorts, Elizabeth. You hardly ate anything. Are you well?"

Sensing a chance to escape, she raised a hand to her temple. "I confess, I'm feeling rather tired."

The older woman's eyes narrowed. "I think you should retire at once. You have a headache, and sleep is likely the best cure."

For the first and probably only time, Eliza was glad of her aunt's domineering ways. She had nothing to do but submit to her command. Besides, her head *was* aching, though not as much as her heart.

She dragged herself back to her bedchamber, where Sarah fussed over her, muttering all the while about her lack of animation and attributing it to tiredness.

Her maid tucked her up in bed and left her in peace, but Eliza's mind was not at rest, and she could not sleep.

She felt numb. All she could think of were those fateful words.

*I was forced into it.*

# Chapter 33

BEAU WOKE THE NEXT day with a single thought in his head. Eliza. He must talk to Eliza.

He headed for the stables, hoping she would not abandon their morning ride, but she left him waiting. Was she still suffering from the indisposition that had forced her to retire early the previous evening, or was she avoiding him?

When he walked into the breakfast parlour, she was the first person he saw. He let out a sigh, relieved to discover she was not keeping to her room. He'd be able to find an opportunity to talk to her, to put things right.

"Are you feeling better today, Eliza?" he asked, sitting down next to her.

She did not reply. He wondered if she'd even heard him.

He repeated his words, slightly louder, and she lifted her gaze from her plate, an emptiness in her eyes. Then, as if understanding dawned, she nodded.

"I'm sorry you missed our ride this morning. Would you care to take the horses out after breakfast instead?"

Her face was devoid of expression as she stared at him, assessing his words. The appraising look she gave him made him wriggle in his seat. Why was she looking at him like that? Was it so hard to believe he wanted to go riding with her?

"I don't think—"

"A ride? What a capital idea!" Anthony said, interrupting Eliza.

Beau scowled, but his friend continued regardless.

"I spent far too many hours cooped up in a carriage yesterday and I'm desperate for fresh air and exercise."

"I was suggesting a ride for two," Beau said with an irritated grunt.

"But I'm sure Eliza would want to come with us," Anthony said, turning to her, his eyes bright with mischief. "You'll join us, won't you? A ride in the sunshine will put the colour back in your cheeks."

A reluctant smile tugged at the sides of Eliza's mouth. Beau would have felt encouraged if she had directed it at him.

"Thank you," she said, addressing Ant. "I'd like that. I'll meet you in the stables when I'm ready."

Eliza did not keep them waiting long. Beau's eyes glistened with admiration when he saw her. She looked stunning in her red riding habit. As he hovered near her horse to help her mount, he remembered the last time she had worn that dress.

The day she fell into the stream. When they had laughed together in the conservatory. And he had almost kissed her...

Before he realised what was happening, Finch was helping Eliza into the saddle. Beau frowned, disappointed she had not let him assist her, as if signalling her desire to prevent any attempt at such intimacy today.

Stifling his frustration, Beau mounted his horse and rode out of the stables, breaking into a canter as he led them away from the house toward some fields, in a direction they hadn't ridden before.

The others followed, drawing rein when they caught him up. Beau ground his teeth in frustration. He had so much to say to Eliza, but Anthony's presence made it impossible for him to start. She wouldn't even look at him.

"Have you had any news about Romeo at all?" Ant asked, attempting to break the awkward silence.

"Nothing, but I'm not surprised. The constable enquired along the post roads, but I never held out much hope of him finding any information. If the thieves were canny enough to know my racehorse was here, they would not risk discovery by taking him on the main roads where any tollgate keeper could report their route. My stepfather's doing what he can. He's put an advertisement in the newspaper, and he offered to send for a Bow Street Runner, though my mother's not keen. But it's too late for that. I expect Romeo was miles away within a few days. I doubt I'll ever see him again."

"What a terrible business. You understand him being so upset, don't you?" Ant said, turning to Eliza, trying to draw her into the conversation.

"Of course, I'm upset," Beau snapped. "Losing Romeo is like losing a child, but it's not just that— "

"I know withdrawing from the race will take some living down, but you'll recover. You must put it behind you."

"If only it was that easy. I've let everyone down..."

"It's not your fault. You mustn't mind the money. Castleford will bail me out. He always does."

Eliza jerked her head toward Anthony, awoken from her indifference. "Money? You're going to lose money by Romeo not racing?"

He looked shamefaced. "I bet rather a large sum on Romeo winning. We all did. Beau said it was a sure thing, and he's so often right that—"

"And you?" she asked, looking into Beau's eyes for the first time that day. "Will you lose money?"

He felt the heat rushing up his neck under her accusing stare and tried to stammer out an explanation. "If I had won, it would have paid for my stables until I came of age. I would not have needed to get married, and I..."

Too late, he realised what he'd said. Eliza's face turned ashen, but her eyes were blazing with anger. With a light touch of her whip, she sent her chestnut mare cantering across the open grass toward a hill in the distance, refusing to listen to anything more.

"Race you," she called over her shoulder as her mare broke into a gallop.

Beau shouted after her in exasperation, but she was gone. He and Ant set off in pursuit, but the faster they galloped, the harder she pushed her horse.

When Eliza reached the crest of the hill, she momentarily slowed, but something must have frightened her mare, because she sped up again and disappeared out of view at an alarming pace.

Beau's exasperation turned to fear. He was familiar with the lie of the land and knew the danger she was in. On the other side was a steep slope ending in the wall that marked the edge of the estate. If she went over the top at that speed, she wouldn't be able to slow down in time. To jump the stone barricade would be nigh on impossible. The incline was too sharp.

He yelled after her to stop, but she didn't. Why wouldn't she listen to him?

Unless...

His breath hitched as he realised she wasn't being obstinate. Eliza had lost control of her mare.

Beau had never ridden so fast with such purpose in his life. All he was aware of was the thud of his horse's hooves racing in pursuit and the thump in his chest as his panic grew.

As he sped over the top of the hill, his heart almost stopped beating. Eliza was heading for the boundary at breakneck speed.

Not checking his pace, he swerved his mount to the right and urged Jet to ride down across the hillside at an angle. If he could get between Eliza and the wall, he might be able to steer her horse to safety.

Beau ignored the pounding in his ears and rode hard to cut across Whisper's path. For one horrible moment, he thought they would collide, but then, little by little, Whisper altered the angle of her descent to match Jet's, and both horses slowed as they reached the bottom of the hill.

Beau could see the relief on Eliza's face—her beautiful face that a moment before he had imagined lying crushed underneath her horse.

"What were you playing at?" he yelled as they drew to a halt. "You could have been killed!"

The look of relief vanished and Eliza's eyes once more blazed with anger. "Did you think I couldn't control my mount?"

"Yes. Do you make a habit of riding like a madwoman?"

"A madwoman! Is that how you see me? Did you plan on leading me on, thinking you were going to propose, only to leave me cold when Romeo won you a fortune on the racetrack? Were you really planning to jilt me so heartlessly?"

"I have no wish to jilt you at all."

"Of course not. Your horse has gone, and that has forced you to fall back on your insurance policy. Me. If I were cleverer, I would have made the connection earlier. You proposed to me the day *after* Romeo was stolen. If he had raced and won, you would not have had to marry me or anyone else. Now you must get married to keep your stables going. You lied to me. You said you did not gamble—that betting on your skill was different. But this? This is a wager you made and lost—and I am the loser."

Even while she tore his character to shreds, he thought how magnificent she looked, with her eyes burning and her chin sticking out obstinately, dimpling despite her anger.

"Eliza, it's not like that..."

But he spoke to the air. She had spurred her horse into a canter, and was riding back to the house without a backward glance.

Beau stared after her in dismay. The details of the race had emerged, and Eliza was furious.

Guilt weighed him down as he took himself to task. What a fool he'd been to keep the wager a secret. He should have told her. Trusted her with the truth.

He deserved her contempt. Every ounce of it. How he wished he could refute her accusations, but he couldn't. He had no defence. When he'd agreed to race Romeo against Mr Cunningham's Majesty, he *had* been looking for a way to escape marriage.

But now she thought he'd lied to her, pretending he cared in order to win her hand because he needed her.

And he *did* need her—but not just to save his horses.

# Chapter 34

*E*LIZA STRODE ALONG THE path back to the house with fists clenched so hard her nails bit into her palms.

"How could he treat me like that?" she muttered under her breath. "Do I mean so little to him? Why did he lie to me? Why did he make me think he cared?"

She stormed up the stairs and into her bedroom, slamming the door behind her, causing her maid to exclaim.

"What on earth has got into you, miss?" she said, putting her hands on her hips.

Sarah's scowling face had a sobering effect on Eliza. As she leaned against the closed door, her whole body shook. The shock of the near-accident and the subsequent argument finally caught up with her.

In an instant, her maid's demeanour changed. She fussed around her mistress, chattering away about trivialities, while she helped her out of her riding dress, and tucked her up in bed to rest.

Eliza's body had stopped shaking by the time Sarah had tidied up and crept out of the room. She no longer felt angry. She felt nothing at all.

The same thoughts tumbled through her mind in a never-ending cycle. Beau didn't love her. He was going to marry her because he must. Because Romeo was gone. For the sake of his horses. And she would always play second fiddle to them.

But after tasting what it felt like when she believed he loved her, could she settle for anything less? What was it her mother had said? *Better a broken engagement than a lifetime of regret.*

Would she regret it if she ignored her doubts and married Beau? She didn't know. She hugged her arms around herself and prayed for guidance. What was she going to do?

As the dinner hour approached, Sarah re-entered the room and laid out her evening dress. Eliza knew she either had to plead sick or get up and ready herself to face Beau and the others.

Delay would not improve the situation. No amount of time would put things right. She prayed God would give her strength for what lay ahead.

With fatalistic resolve, Eliza got out of bed and sat down at the dressing table so her maid could brush her hair out and pin it up again.

She went down to dinner dressed in a pale blue satin robe the colour of her eyes, worn over a white slip, with a matching shawl draped over her shoulders. Apart from her pallor, she was confident she looked her best. She wished she was as confident she had her emotions under control.

With a supreme effort, she plastered a smile onto her face and entered the dining room with the appearance of happiness, though she suspected her eyes said otherwise. That was the funny thing about smiling. You could put a false one on your lips, but your eyes only smiled if you were thinking happy thoughts. And her thoughts were most definitely not happy.

Beau tried several times to engage her in conversation during dinner, but Eliza would have none of it. She ignored him and directed all her remarks at Anthony, who sat on her other side.

It was not a wise course of action, and one Eliza soon had cause to regret. Lady Harting noticed her behaviour and when the ladies moved through to the drawing room, she drew her aside and started quizzing her.

"You seemed out of sorts at dinner. I trust all is well?"

Eliza gave a brief nod, but it was insufficient assurance for her aunt.

"Come, my child. What is troubling you? Are you overwhelmed at the prospect of becoming a viscountess? It is a heavy responsibility indeed to marry into the peerage. I was born to it, but you—you are a rector's daughter and I fear your training in these matters has not been what my girls have received. But you must not worry. You can rely on my support to learn about your duties. I will be at hand to help you deal with all the minutiae of your new role. To guide you and show you how things should be done. I am sure that, in time, you will become a viscountess that Beaumont will be proud of."

Eliza dared not look up in case Lady Harting saw the horror in her expression. To become a viscountess was an intimidating prospect, but not as daunting as dealing with her aunt every day. Did she plan to move into Langcroft Park with them to instruct her in her role? What a dreadful notion—but not as dreadful as the thought that Beau did not really want to marry her.

As the realisation hit her again, Eliza winced. It hurt so much she felt nauseous.

Lady Harting reached out a hand and lifted her chin, forcing her niece to meet her eyes. The older woman examined Eliza's face with a piercing gaze and then gave her cheek a gentle pinch.

"I fear my son has upset you. How doltish of him. You must forgive his thoughtlessness. Men can be so foolish sometimes. I'll have a word with him. I am sure it is merely a little misunderstanding, my dear. It will blow over. These things always do."

Eliza cringed to hear Lady Harting denigrate her son so readily, but she was too distressed by his behaviour to defend him. This was not some *little misunderstanding*. This was a betrayal—and she was not sure she would ever recover from it.

"I am uncertain it will. I fear Lord Beaumont does not *want* to marry me."

Lady Harting's face grew hard, her eyes narrowed and took on an icy expression that instinctively made Eliza shiver. "My son would never behave so dishonourably as to break off his engagement. Indeed, I assure you, he will not."

Though no doubt intended to reassure her, her aunt's words sent a chill down Eliza's spine. They were unnecessary too, because she knew Beau wouldn't back down from their betrothal. He needed her to save his horses. It was she who was deliberating whether or not she should marry him.

Strangely, the conversation with her aunt helped Eliza to decide.

How could she leave Beau to his mother's mercy or send him scurrying to Harriet in desperation? She couldn't. Despite everything, she still loved him. That would have to be enough. She would do her best to hide it and protect her heart by pretending their marriage was only a business arrangement to her as well.

At least she would know she had saved his horses.

And maybe, in time, she would learn to trust him again.

# Chapter 35

BEAU DIDN'T HOLD OUT much hope that Eliza would turn up for their ride the next morning, but he went to the stables before breakfast, just in case. His spirits lifted when he saw her mounting Whisper as he strode into the yard.

Eliza had hardly spoken a word to him since he had lost his temper. He wanted to kick himself for behaving in such an uncivilised manner. It did not matter how much she had scared him, riding like that. He should have been comforting her, not showering her with abuse.

But surely the fact she had turned up for their ride was a good omen.

"Good morning," he said with a tentative smile, daring to hope Eliza had forgiven him.

"Good morning," she said with the slightest upturn to her lips. It was a tight expression, but at least it was vaguely positive.

Beau was about to begin his apology when he realised she had raised her eyes and was looking at something—or someone—behind him.

"Are you ready, Anthony?"

Beau turned to see his best friend already mounted, and his smile faded. He had not been forgiven.

"You won't mind if we go ahead?" Eliza said over her shoulder as she urged Whisper forward.

Anthony shrugged in his direction and then followed her out of the yard.

Yes, Beau *did* mind. He minded very much. But there was nothing he could do about it. He was the one who had erred.

Perhaps he should let her go. He didn't deserve her. He deserved to be rejected. The thought of her marrying another man made him feel sick, but he had brought it on himself.

Is this what love felt like? No wonder Anthony avoided it.

Once mounted, Beau hurried to catch them up. He rode alongside Eliza and in response to his beseeching look, his friend rode on ahead to allow them a little private conversation.

"I'm sorry," he said, looking across at her, but she refused to meet his gaze and did not reply. "I did not mean—"

"It is of no consequence." She chivvied her horse into a canter and sped away from him.

He scowled after her fleeing form. Why wouldn't she give him a chance to explain? He had to make her understand.

Determined not to accept defeat, he tried again, but still Eliza refused to listen. As soon as he drew alongside, she fell silent. It was as if she had erected a barricade between them, which she would not let him cross.

After several further attempts to engage her in conversation, he gave up and rode on ahead.

Anthony did not help. He chattered away to Eliza and she, much to Beau's irritation, gazed up at his friend in the same manner he had been accustomed to her gazing up at him.

By the time they reached the stables, Beau was in a fair way to losing his temper again.

When Eliza dismounted and Ant offered her his arm to walk back to the house, his control broke.

"May I remind you Eliza is engaged to me?" he snapped, removing her hand from his friend's hold and taking it possessively in his own

Eliza didn't object, but cast Anthony a conspiratorial glance that lowered Beau's spirits even more.

They returned to the house in silence, Ant following behind with a wry smile on his face that did nothing to assuage his friend's temper.

Once inside, she disengaged her arm and hurried up the stairs to change for breakfast without saying a thing.

Beau stood at the bottom of the staircase, staring up at her retreating form, wondering how he was ever going to put things right.

Anthony came alongside him and opened his mouth to speak, but Beau gave him such a scowl that he raised his hand as if in self-defence.

"Don't say a word. You may be an expert in the art of dalliance, but you are *not* an expert on love."

Anthony's expression hardened, grimacing as Beau's words struck home, but in a moment the grim look passed, and he gave a mock smile in sympathy.

"To judge from the pain it is causing you, I am well out of it."

Beau did not stop trying to apologise. Over the next few days, he repeatedly sought to be alone with Eliza, but every time, he was thwarted. If he asked her for a ride, she invited Anthony to join them. If he talked to her in the drawing room, she drew his sister or mother into the conversation.

He lost hope she would ever relent. She was not unpleasant to him, nor disrespectful, but the friendship they had shared was gone. He had killed it—and he missed it so much that it hurt.

What irked him more was that Eliza seemed to have plenty of smiles for Anthony.

Beau had to face the fact that she had changed her mind and might regret her decision to marry him. He determined to force a frank conversation with her, even if it meant the end to all his hopes.

"Would you take a walk with me in the rose garden?" he asked Eliza as they finished breakfast on the third day.

"I believe my aunt wanted me to—"

"Nonsense," Lady Harting said, interrupting Eliza's excuse. "What kind of mother would I be to make you stay inside on such a beautiful day? Run along now and fetch your bonnet. Don't keep Beaumont waiting."

Beau cringed at his mother's peremptory manner. What sort of mother was she? The sort who was determined to have her own way. But as it produced the result he wanted, on this occasion, he could not complain.

"Very well," Eliza said, rising from the table to do as she was bid.

Beau waited for her at the foot of the stairs and a few minutes later she reappeared, wearing a chip bonnet decorated with a profusion of ribbons. It framed her face beautifully and for a moment he forgot she was hardly speaking to him, and was tempted to steal a kiss.

With this thought in mind, he moved toward her, only to be brought up short when he saw her forbidding expression. Chastising himself for his foolishness, he abruptly offered her his arm, as if this had been his intent all along.

They walked in silence down the garden path. Now that he had her alone, he was not sure how to start.

"Eliza, I must apologise for losing my temper with you. I was shocked—afraid that I wouldn't be able to save you. But I should not have shouted at you like that."

A flicker of something passed over her face, but then was gone.

"My behaviour was unpardonable," she said. "It is I who should beg your forgiveness for putting both of us at risk."

Her words took Beau by surprise, but the colourless tone of her voice concerned him. "There is nothing to forgive. You were angry with me, and I have no defence. But I have changed. However this started, I do care for you now."

Eliza gave him a weak smile. "That is kind of you to say so."

Kind? She thought he was being *kind* to tell her he cared for her?

"It's not like that," he said, walking away from her in frustration. He took a deep breath. "I've been trying to tell you. I love you."

There. He had told her—but the reaction was not what he hoped.

"Please don't say that. I expect your mother told you those were the words I wanted to hear, but I would rather you didn't pretend."

"But I'm not pretending."

Eliza peered deeply into his eyes. "If they were true, you would have said them before. You're only saying them because you were told to."

"But I'm not!"

"I'm sorry, but I don't believe you."

Beau's heart sank. Eliza had believed him before—believed in him. And now he had thrown it all away.

He gulped hard. "Do you want to break off our engagement?" he asked, dreading her answer.

"Cry off? How would that save your horses?"

"I won't hold you to it if you've changed your mind."

"I have not."

They stood in awkward silence. There seemed nothing else to say.

"I'm feeling a little warm," Eliza said after a few moments. "I'd like to go inside."

He nodded, and took her arm again, and they walked back to the house together without another word.

Beau thought he would be relieved she was still determined to marry him, but he wasn't. How could he be when she looked more as if she had agreed to a death sentence than a wedding? He could see the emptiness in her eyes, and he knew he had caused it—and it made him feel like the worst scoundrel alive.

It was his fault she didn't believe he loved her.

He had fought so strenuously against getting married that he had refused to admit his growing feelings for Eliza, and by the time Romeo was stolen, it was too late.

He should never have made that stupid bet. This wouldn't have happened if he'd realised sooner how much Eliza meant to him.

Would she ever believe anything he said again? She intended to go through with the wedding, but all hope of a shared intimacy was at an end.

Beau did not know if he could bear it, though he supposed, for the sake of his stables, he must.

He'd already lost Romeo. Now, he'd lost Eliza too.

He didn't want to be married to this iceberg. He would rather sell all his horses and live in retirement than see her over the breakfast table every morning, looking at him as if he were a stranger, remembering the laughter he had shut down by acting like a heartless cad.

# *Chapter 36*

ELIZA STARED OUT THE window of the travelling chariot as it trundled away from Holybourne House on its weary way to London. The carriage bore Beau's coat of arms, but he was not inside.

An hour earlier, she had watched him leave for Epsom. Although he no longer had a horse to race, she had encouraged him to go with Anthony. She wanted him to know from the start that she would not come between him and his horses. That was where his priorities lay, and she, as his future wife, must respect it.

Her heart ached for the love she would never have. If only he loved her as he loved his horses, then she could have a proper marriage like Georgiana.

The next time she saw Beau, it would be for their wedding. A day she should have been looking forward to with joyful anticipation, but she now dreaded.

The last week of her stay at Holybourne House had been a strain. It was more difficult to feign indifference toward her betrothed than she had expected, and his determination to pretend an affection he didn't feel made it even harder.

It was kind of him to try to make her think he wanted her. To try to restore her confidence in him. But it was an uphill struggle. It was her unwavering belief that his mother had put him up to it and the thought filled her with anxiety about the influence Lady Harting would have on their future life together.

Finch rode behind the carriage, leading Eliza's horse beside his own. It was a beautiful day, but as far as she was concerned, it might as well have been pouring with rain. The bright weather was at odds with her feelings, which were as dismal as she had ever known them to be.

By dinnertime, she would be back at the Castlefords' house in London, enjoying the balm of sisterly affection. It would not mend her broken heart, but it would soothe the pain of unrequited love. And maybe, though she thought it unlikely, she would tell her sisters how she felt. Despite her bitter disappointment at how strained her relationship with Beau had become, she was loath to confess the truth to anyone—even Georgiana.

She gave herself a shake. This was the path she had chosen. Her sister had warned her about him, but she had not listened, believing Beau could be something more than the downtrodden man his mother had made him.

But she had been wrong. He was as unreliable as Georgie had feared.

There was no point getting sentimental about what might have been. She sniffed in an unladylike manner, causing Sarah to clear her throat in disapproval. With an apologetic glance at her maid, she opened her reticule, found her handkerchief, and blew her nose.

Eliza wished it wasn't so hot in the carriage. Perhaps she could let in some air. She pulled down the window and a light gust of wind tickled her heated face, but it wasn't enough. If only she could get out of this stuffy atmosphere, she was certain she wouldn't feel so miserable.

Without hesitating, Eliza rapped on the roof, signalling her desire to stop, and a few minutes later, the coach driver drew up at a far from fashionable looking inn.

"What devilry are you up to now, Miss Eliza?" asked Finch, drawing his horse alongside. "Don't tell me you're travel sick, because if you are, it'll be for the first time in your life, and we've not travelled more than two or three miles."

"But I am," she said, glaring at her groom out of the window. "I am sick of travelling in this closed carriage already. I wish to ride. Have one of the men take down my trunk so Sarah can find my riding habit."

Finch muttered under his breath as she ordered him to make her horse ready, but she refused to listen. He would try to persuade her not to follow such a foolhardy course. Remind her that the roads were dirty. That it was not appropriate for a lady of quality to travel by horseback on the post road.

But his recriminations were pointless. She had to get outside. Now. Or she would suffocate. Besides, she didn't intend to ride along the turnpike road. They could take a route across country and meet up with the carriage at Farnham.

Not waiting to be released from her prison, Eliza opened the door and climbed down the steps. She breathed in the fresh air, allowing it to fill her lungs and calm her agitation. What a relief to be outside again.

There was no sign of an ostler, so one of the footmen jumped down from his perch and ran to hold the horses' reins whilst another retrieved her trunk.

Finch dismounted and looked around. "I don't think this is a suitable stopping place, Miss Eliza," he said in a stern voice.

She examined the dingy tavern. "It will do. All I require is a clean room where I can put on my habit and get out of this"—she waved her hand toward the carriage—"oven!"

Her groom opened his mouth as if he were going to argue, but she glared at him, and he closed it again. He had known her long enough to realise when she had made up her mind.

A scrawny lad stepped forward out of the yard, eyeing Whisper with patent admiration, and offering to hold the horses.

With a frown, Finch handed the reins to the boy and entered the hostelry to enquire whether there was anywhere that his mistress could change her clothes.

After a few minutes, a pleasant-looking woman bustled out of the inn door and invited her up to her best room. Eliza sighed with relief, and, with a smile of genuine gratitude, she stepped into the coolness of the building and followed the landlady upstairs.

Twenty minutes later, Eliza was riding through the fields on Whisper's back, the gentle breeze cooling her brow. As she observed the multitude of different-coloured wildflowers and inhaled the smell of grass, she felt the tension melting away. She always felt much closer to God when she was outside, enjoying the beautiful world He had created, and a blanket of peace settled over her heart.

The words her mother said to her—whenever she moaned about something not working out the way she wanted—popped into her mind. *Be thankful, Eliza Merry. That is God's will for you.*

She bit her lip, and the ends of her mouth edged upward as she thought of what she was grateful for. It was not that hard. She was thankful Beau loved horses. To wed a man who liked animals as much as she did was far from the worst fate she could contemplate. A bookish husband would be much worse.

And she loved him. That must be a plus, even though it hurt that he did not return her feelings. He had let her down, but it hadn't made her hate him. It had just made her angry—and sad.

She was also thankful for her family, and that she was on her way to London to see her sisters.

The pain in her heart did not go away, but she grew more content as she dwelt on what she had rather than on what she lacked.

When they had ridden for nearly an hour, they came to a wooded area where a stream cut across their path. Slowing their pace, they led their horses through the cool water.

Finch glanced up at the sun. "Reckon this is more or less in the right direction if you want to follow the river bed for a while. It's cooler under the trees."

She readily agreed, and they rode in the shade until Finch recommended altering their path.

"We can't be far from Farnham now, Miss Eliza. I suggest we cut across the field to our left and meet up with the road."

"You lead, I'll follow," she called back over her shoulder.

Finch pressed his horse past her and up the shallow bank and trotted in the direction he had indicated, but half-way across the field, he came to a halt and slid off his mount.

Eliza pulled up beside him. "Problem?"

He lifted his horse's rear hoof to inspect it and sighed. "I thought something didn't sound right. A shoe's come loose. Must have happened walking on the rough stream bed."

"We'll have to find a smithy in the next village. I won't risk him going lame because I insisted on riding cross country."

They headed for a group of cottages in the distance at a walking pace, hoping there would be a blacksmith nearby who could help them.

It wasn't much of a village—a few houses on a single street, with a tavern at the end—but beyond that, they discovered a smith who served the local farms. While Finch arranged for the horse's shoe to be replaced, Eliza tethered Whisper and looked about her.

An old man sat on a bench outside the inn, drinking a pint of ale. He cast an admiring glance at her mare. "That's a mighty pretty horse you have there, ma'am."

"Why, thank you," she said, unbothered at being addressed by a stranger, and always ready to hear Whisper's praises sung.

"A few weeks back, I would have said it was the prettiest horse I'd ever clapped my eyes on."

There was something about his words that pricked Eliza's interest. "Indeed? You've seen a prettier?"

He nodded. "Loveliest colt you ever saw. A handsome, rich bay with a white stocking on his rear right leg."

Eliza gasped and raised a hand to cover her mouth. How many bays with those markings could there be in Hampshire? The description matched Romeo exactly. There could be no doubt about it. He must have passed through this village after he'd been stolen. No wonder they had found no trace of him on the post road.

"How I wish I could see him," she said, letting out a long sigh.

The old man pointed into the tavern yard. "No trouble about that. He's in yonder stable."

"Are you sure?"

"I may be old, but I'm not an idiot, ma'am."

"I beg your pardon," Eliza said, hurrying to smooth the man's ruffled sensibilities. "It's just that a friend of mine—the man I'm going to marry, in fact—had a horse of that description stolen a few weeks back."

He stroked his chin. "Did he now? That explains a lot. Baxter won't like it. Gets mighty tetchy if there's any trouble."

Who was Baxter? The landlord? It seemed likely, but she wasn't sure she cared. Not if Romeo really was in the inn's stable. She gave the old man a dazzling smile. "Could you...would you show me where the horse is, please?"

He grunted and gave her a toothy grin. "For you, sweetheart, I'll risk Baxter's wrath." He picked up his walking stick and hobbled through the yard, with Eliza following behind. After casting a furtive glance about him, he led the way into the stables.

They walked down the line of stalls together, but her heart sank when they reached the end and there was still no sign of Romeo.

"Don't you be looking so glum," the elderly man said, shaking his head at her obvious disappointment as he walked to the end wall and turned right. There, in front of them, was another door, which was almost invisible in the gloom. It would be easy to overlook if you didn't know it was there.

"In here."

Eliza followed him through the doorway into a second stable.

Her mouth dropped open at the marvellous sight she beheld.

There, before her, was Romeo.

# Chapter 37

ELIZA ENTERED THE LOOSE box in front of her, and Romeo whickered in recognition. Her heart lurched at the sound she never thought to hear again.

"Hello, boy," she said, nuzzling her face into the colt's mane. "How good it is to see you."

The elderly man nodded. "I thought you was telling the truth, and now I'm sure. That horse recognises you, all right. You'd better get him out of here before those thieving rascals find out you've bubbled their plot."

Eliza jerked her head round toward him. "They're here?"

"Oh aye. Been putting up at The George for weeks. They think I don't see what goes on here, but old Stanton knows everyone's business."

"I must fetch my groom." She gave Romeo one last pat. "I'll be back for you."

They retraced their steps, as fast as Stanton could go, but as they reached the archway that led to the street, he raised his hand, directing her to stop.

Though puzzled, Eliza did as she was told. Two men walked past the yard entrance and entered the inn. To her surprise, one man looked vaguely familiar. How strange to see someone she recognised in such a remote location. Where had she seen him before?

When they had disappeared from sight, Stanton turned to her. "That was them."

"The thieves?"

He nodded.

Eliza's face hardened. If these were the crooks who had stolen Beau's horse and she recognised one of them, was it possible that some of Lord Harting's own men were responsible for the theft?

She walked across to the smithy with her new friend and found Finch peering about him anxiously, looking for her.

"Where have you been? We must be on our way."

Eliza ignored his grumbling. "Finch, this is Stanton."

The men nodded at each other.

"Miss Eliza—"

"I've found Romeo."

"What?"

"Stanton showed me where they were keeping him."

"Are you certain?"

She pulled a face. "I think you might trust me to recognise Romeo when I see him."

"Horse knows the lass," Stanton said. "Besides, I heard one of 'em when he was in his cups. Makes sense now. Said as how they'll never find him because they're looking in the wrong place. T'other one shut him up quick, but old Stanton heard him all right."

Eliza's forehead puckered. "What should we do? Fetch the constable?"

"Baxter wouldn't like that," the old man muttered. "Happen, I'll have a word with him." He shuffled away and disappeared into the inn.

"We can't leave Romeo here," she said. "We must tell his lordship. Perhaps there's still time for him to race."

"You know as well as I do that Lord Beaumont left this morning. By the time a message got to him, it would be too late. The contest is in three days."

Eliza felt the colour drain from her cheeks. "But Romeo must compete now we've found him. No one will believe he was ever stolen if he doesn't take part. Everyone would think Lord Beaumont had lied about the theft and forfeited the wager to save his horse, believing he couldn't win. He'd be a laughing-stock and the damage to his reputation on the racecourse could be disastrous."

She wrung her hands in distress. "Romeo must compete. He has to."

Finch shook his head. "Even if we took him to Epsom ourselves, you forget Jem was injured the night of the theft. Romeo has no jockey, and without a jockey, he cannot race."

Eliza chewed on her bottom lip as she thought it over. "You'll have to ride him."

Finch guffawed. "Aren't you overlooking something? I'm nigh on six feet tall and weigh far too much for that colt to have a chance of winning.

Though I'm flattered that you think I'd make a fine jockey, it just won't do. I'm too big. Now, if I were your size, I could give it a go, but..."

He stopped mid-sentence when he saw the gleam in her eyes. "Look here, Miss Eliza. There's no call for you to do anything mad."

"I'll ride him."

"No. Absolutely not. It would be too dangerous by far. I'll tell your father. He'll stop you."

"I'm sure he would, if he knew. But unfortunately—or rather fortunately—he's in West Meon, and your duty, Finch, is to me, not to my father."

He gave her a hard stare. "This is not like riding until you're fit to drop, to see where a balloon came down, or even dressing up as a lad to go out with the hunt. This is a public race we're talking about. If anyone saw through your masquerade, you'd be ruined. Not even his lordship could save you. Lady Harting wouldn't put up with the scandal. She'd stop your marriage, you can be sure of it."

Eliza mulled over Finch's words. Was she really risking her happiness? No. Her happiness was already gone, but if she rode Romeo in the race—if she could win for Beau—he'd be free. He would not have to go through with this sham of a marriage.

When he was ready, he would choose his own bride—and she'd be waiting.

And if he chose her then, she'd know she was his choice and not his mother's, and that he was marrying her because he wanted to, and not because he must.

In a matter of minutes, Eliza had formed the whole plan in her mind. After they secured Romeo's release, they would meet up with the chaise and she would inform Sarah they would join Lord Beaumont at Epsom rather than heading for London.

Finch would tell Beau Romeo had been discovered and that he'd found him a jockey. On the day of the race, she would leave town on Whisper, transform into her manly garb at a quiet inn, and then ride to the racecourse. With a little dissemblance, she hoped to keep everyone except her groom in the dark about what she was doing.

She dared not tell her maid. If Sarah learned what she was planning, she would try to stop her, and Eliza realised this was something she needed to do. Part of her said she was just trying to ensure Beau won his bet, but deep down, she knew it was a last cry for love.

It was a tremendous risk. If her behaviour became known, her reputation would be ruined and no one, least of all the Viscount, would ever want to marry her.

Stanton came out of the inn again with the landlord in tow.

Baxter bowed to her, a worried expression on his face. "Stanton said you wanted to talk to me, madam."

"We have good reason to believe you have a stolen horse in your stables."

The man looked aghast. "But I haven't got—"

Eliza raised her eyebrows in disbelief. Stanton agreed to stay with the horses while she led Finch and the landlord through the yard and stable to where Romeo was being kept.

Finch took one look at the colt and shook his head in disbelief. "Well I never. It's him."

"This horse isn't stolen," Baxter said. "It belongs to a man staying in my inn."

"I'm afraid you're wrong. This colt is the property of my betrothed, the Viscount Beaumont."

The man paled at the mention of his lordship's name. He muttered a string of disclaimers about how it wasn't his fault. "The men paid for their board fair and square. How was I to know the horse was stolen?"

"Provided you assist me to return the colt to his lordship, I will ensure you bear no blame."

"Yes, of course. Right away."

The landlord unhooked the horse's bridle and thrust it at Finch as if it were a poisonous snake. As soon as it was fastened, Baxter passed him the saddle, clearly eager for them to be gone as fast as possible.

When Romeo was ready, Eliza led him back to the front of the inn where the other horses were waiting with Stanton.

Baxter licked his lips nervously. "What am I to say to the man when he discovers the colt is gone?"

Finch glanced at Eliza before reaching inside his jacket and pulling out his purse. The innkeeper's eyes lit up as her groom dropped several guineas into his palm.

"Ah...yes...well. I'm certain I'll think of something," he said, pocketing the money before Finch could change his mind. "And now you've got his lordship's horse back, there's no need to call the...um...constable or...um...Runners, is there?"

Eliza wondered what other disreputable activity took place in the inn, that Baxter was so eager not to attract the law. It went against her principles to let the thieves walk away free. She wanted to bring them to justice, but if, as she feared, one of the men had been in Lord Harting's employ, she believed her uncle would rather deal with the matter in private. Her aunt would not thank her for making their household the subject of the latest scandal.

"No," said Eliza, "but I cannot vouch for such leniency in the future. I would be careful what you keep in your back stable. You wouldn't want any more thieves taking advantage of your good nature."

The landlord gave her a wary glance and muttered his thanks before disappearing into the inn.

Stanton held Romeo's lead rein while Finch fastened it to his bridle. When they were both mounted, the old man passed it to the groom and gave the colt a fond pat.

"Thank you for your help, Stanton," Eliza said, giving him a wide smile.

He beamed at her and touched his hat. "Glad to be of service, ma'am."

She urged Whisper forward, and they set off along the road at a steady pace, all the way to Farnham, where they met up with the chaise as arranged.

Eliza feared her maid would object to their change in plans, but Sarah could not stop exclaiming about the miracle of discovering his lordship's stolen racehorse and did not need to be convinced of the importance of taking it to him at Epsom without delay. If she did not fully understand why her mistress must take the horse in person, she was wise enough not to question it.

After sending word of their change of plans to Georgiana, they resumed their journey. Eliza was willing to ride again, so Finch was free to lead Romeo, but her groom had other ideas.

"If you're going to follow through with your mad idea," he said in an undertone, "then both you and Romeo need to rest as much as possible. I'll hire someone to lead Whisper. You will travel in the carriage."

Eliza knew he was right and conceded without an argument.

"We'd better stop overnight at Guildford and push on to Epsom tomorrow. By my reckoning, if we set off first thing, even at a walking pace, we should make it by early afternoon, and that still gives Romeo a day's rest before the race on Friday."

As the carriage trundled on its way, Eliza had plenty of time to reflect. Was her plan to act as Beau's jockey foolish? What if she raced and lost? She was not sure of the terms of the bet, as she had been too cross to ask. Would she make things worse for Beau if she failed?

It was a weary and less confident Eliza that arrived at the Red Lion the next day. But of one thing she was certain. It was worth the risk. Even if she had to retire to the parsonage in disgrace if she was discovered.

Because if she succeeded, she could give Beau what he wanted above anything else.

Freedom.

# Chapter 38

B EAU HAD NOT PLACED a bet all day. The racecourse had lost its thrill. Why had he bothered to come to Epsom at all? It was not as if he had a horse competing. Because Eliza had insisted. It would have been gratifying she had encouraged him to attend if she hadn't left him feeling she was eager to be rid of him. That she scorned the races. That she held him in contempt.

Beau would rather be somewhere—anywhere—else. He would have to face Cunningham eventually, and he still didn't know what he was going to say to him. He had delayed withdrawing from the contest until the last moment, dreading the older man's scorn, but he would have to do it tomorrow.

The shame of having to withdraw, even for a valid reason, would hang over him for months. Maybe years. Cunningham would make sure of that. He would drop subtle comments amongst their contemporaries, hinting how unfortunate it was that Beau's horse had been stolen, so Majesty could not prove his superiority.

Beau's hopes for his stud would be scuppered from the start, and his reputation would take years to recover.

Maybe it was just as well. If Eliza disapproved of the races, then perhaps he should give up his dream of breeding racehorses. Would that make her happy? Prove to her how important she was to him? It was a sacrifice, but it would be worth it if he won back her affection.

He woke from his reflections with a jolt when he heard himself addressed in a familiar voice.

"Finch?" he said, staring at the groom in surprise. "Why are you here?"

His thoughts flew to Eliza. A myriad of dreadful possibilities passed through his mind. "Miss Merry...is she well...has there been an accident...?"

"No, no. I bring good news, not bad. We've found Romeo."

Beau's jaw dropped open in amazement. "What? Where? How?"

"My mistress found him. She rode for the first stage of her journey to London and...um...to cut a long story short, we discovered him, quite by chance, stabled in a hamlet near Farnham."

Beau could hardly believe it. "Farnham? But that's only ten miles from my mother's home."

Finch shared Eliza's suspicion that one of Lord Harting's grooms might be responsible.

That made sense. Beau didn't know why he'd never thought of it.

"It's good of you to bring me this news in person, Finch. Thank you."

"I've done more than that, my lord. Romeo is stabled at the White Hart, not far from here."

"You mean he's in Epsom?"

"Miss Merry insisted."

His heart warmed to hear of Eliza's insistence. Maybe she still cared. Just a little.

Though with Jem's arm in a sling, he didn't see what good it would do him. With no jockey, Romeo still couldn't race.

"My mistress suggested I bring...um...young Robson with me. I can't promise he'll win for you, my lord, but I taught him to ride myself, and he's precious good with horses and willing to try, if you'll give him leave."

Beau considered his options. If he forfeited, he'd get to keep Romeo, but what use would his horse be then? His position would be untenable. He would be ridiculed—called a coward. It was unthinkable.

Should he let Robson ride his prized colt? If the lad rode as well as he had on the day of the hunt, he had a chance of beating the rest of the field, even if he couldn't outrun Majesty. Beau would probably lose his horse, but his reputation would be intact.

And what if by some miracle he won? He could prove to Eliza he wanted to marry her because he loved her and not to finance his stables. That possibility—slim though it was—made it worth the risk.

"Very well," he said. "Let me look Romeo over, and if I think he's in a race-worthy state, we'll see whether Robson can claim victory on Friday."

He followed Finch through the crowds, his head spinning, and his heart pounding with excitement. For the first time in days, he saw a glimmer of hope for the future.

When they arrived at the White Hart, the groom led him to a stall. Romeo whickered in welcome, and Beau hurried forward, burying his face in the colt's mane.

"How are you, boy? Did they look after you? I've missed you."

He inspected the bay colt and let out a sigh of relief. "All is well, Finch. He seems in fine health, and you've done an excellent job of getting him here without exhausting him in the heat. Now, where is young Robson? I'd like to thank him for stepping in at such short notice."

"I'm sorry, my lord. He's not here at the moment."

"Gone to watch the races, has he? Never mind. Make sure he's rested and spends as much time with Romeo as possible. The more the two are acquainted, the better they'll work together."

"I will. Till tomorrow, my lord."

Beau walked back to the racecourse alone, the glimmer of a smile on his lips. Romeo looked as strong as ever.

If Robson could create a bond with his horse, all was not lost.

There was a chance he could still win.

# Chapter 39

ELIZA LEFT THE RED Lion early on the morning of the race. A pang of guilt assailed her as she told her maid she was going for a ride and might be some time. That at least was true. She hated deceiving Sarah, but she had to do this. For Beau.

The staff of the inn were busy with their work and paid no heed as she slipped into the stable yard, where Finch was waiting with the two horses. He helped Eliza into the saddle, and they rode away from the hostelry in silence, heading for the place where Romeo was stabled.

When they arrived at the White Hart, she put the next phase of their plan into action, as Finch had insisted they act out a charade to protect her reputation.

After dismounting, Eliza raised a hand to her forehead, swayed dramatically, and collapsed into her groom's arms.

He called for help and, from under her lightly closed eyelids, she saw one of the stable boys run inside the inn. Her groom touched her arm, and she awoke from her false swoon as the landlady bustled into the yard.

"My mistress is unwell and needs to rest for a while. Please show her into the best bedchamber you have available."

The woman seemed overawed by Finch's demanding manner and hastened to do as he bid.

"Yes, of course. This way. Poor lady."

Eliza was shown into a simply furnished, but clean, bedchamber.

"I'm sorry I've nothing better to offer you. It's the races."

Eliza was relieved any room was available, otherwise their plan would have been hindered from the start.

The landlady summoned a lad to remove her boots and then banished him from the room before bustling forward to remove Eliza's gown and stays.

"Please send for my groom to bring my saddlebag," she said in a weak voice. "I need my vinaigrette."

By the time Finch arrived, the landlady had tucked her into bed. The woman would have searched the bag for her smelling salts, but Eliza stopped her.

"Please don't trouble yourself. I know where to find what I need. If I can lie down for a few hours, I'm certain to recover. It's only one of my headaches."

"Are you sure you wouldn't like me to summon the doctor?"

"No, thank you. I want to be left alone. Once I've rested, I'll be fine. Do not disturb me on any account. I will ring for your help when I need it."

"Well, if you're sure..."

Eliza thought she would never go. "I am. If I lie down quietly in a darkened room, I'll soon feel better."

Thankfully, this last plea, uttered as it was in a truly pitiful tone, convinced the well-meaning woman that to be left in peace was all she required. She drew the curtains and bobbed a curtsey before bustling out of the room.

Eliza heaved a sigh of relief, and once alone, she leapt from the bed and opened the saddlebag. She extracted the man's clothing and pulled on a shirt and a pair of breeches, transforming her—for what she hoped would be the last time—into Mr Robson.

The neckcloth proved more challenging. Her fingers fumbled as she tried to fold it neatly and wished William was there to fix it for her. She tied an imperfect knot and grimaced. There was not time for a second attempt. It would have to do.

She struggled into her boots, put on her waistcoat and jacket, and fixed her brown wig onto her head, with the pink and purple chequered cap already attached to it. Eliza examined her appearance in the mirror, and a slim youth, wearing Beau's colours, smiled back at her.

"You'll do," she said to herself.

She opened the door and confirmed no one was about before slipping from the chamber and down the stairs. The taproom was becoming busier, and the proprietors were so occupied they did not notice her sneaking outside and into the yard.

The faithful Finch waited with Romeo's reins in his hands. He looked her up and down, inspecting her appearance until heat rose to her cheeks. When he took a pace forward, panic seized her. For a moment, she feared he was going to take advantage of the bizarre circumstances they were in to steal a kiss.

Involuntarily, she stepped back, only for him to chide her stupidity.

"You've nought to fear from me, Miss Eliza," he said in a low tone only she could hear, "though you look mighty spry in those natty clothes. I need to straighten your neckcloth, or it will give the whole game away. Not even a groom would go about with such a shoddy excuse of a neck warmer!"

"Thank you," she whispered, holding up her chin to allow him to tidy her cravat.

He redid the folds before pausing and fixing her with a piercing stare. "Are you sure you want to do this? It's not too late to turn about."

"Are you fighting shy, Danny Finch?" she said, with a challenge in her eye.

"Nay, never say that, but now you're all grown up, there's so much at stake. If this came out—"

"If you wish to draw back, then do so. Never claim that I forced you into it."

"Huh! Lady Castleford would never forgive me if I let you go off alone, nor your mother for that matter, but why I allowed you to persuade me into it when nothing in the world could hide the fact that you're a girl—"

Eliza's head jerked round to face her groom. "Oh no. Surely not. I've fooled people before. Won't I succeed this time?"

Finch gave an embarrassed smile. "I expect it's just that I know you're no man that it makes it so hard for me to see you as anything else."

He cleared his throat rather loudly and turned back to the horse. "Well, if you're set on doing this, we'd better get going, or we'll miss his lordship's race altogether."

Finch hovered by Romeo, waiting to help her mount, but with the slightest shake of the head, Eliza indicated she meant to do it by herself. She wouldn't have his aid on the racecourse, so it would be as well to do without now.

She put her foot into the stirrup and swung herself into the saddle. It was quite simple when not impeded by skirts. Her groom tightened the girth and Eliza gave a big grin.

"I had forgotten how lovely it was to ride astride," she said, leaning forward over Romeo's mane, so only Finch could hear. "Come on. We'd better go before you suffer any more qualms of conscience."

As they drew near to the racecourse, she grew quiet. The roads were busy with horses and carriages making their way to the meeting, and she had to concentrate hard to make sure she didn't get separated from her groom.

Finch stabled his horse and led Romeo through the crowds toward the enclosure. Eliza's stomach churned. It was all so unfamiliar. People kept staring at her and her mount. A jockey attracted far more notice than she had expected.

Was she foolish to believe she could just turn up with the horse and win the race? Did they need papers or something? Had Beau dealt with all that? What if she fell off and was injured? She wouldn't be able to hide her sex. They would lose the contest, and she would have let Beau down.

Romeo would be lost forever—and so would she.

Pangs of guilt threatened to overwhelm her. Her family would be dismayed if her antics were discovered, but it couldn't be helped. She had to take that risk.

If she won, she would free Beau from the need to marry her.

That was the part she was dreading—breaking off her engagement. She gulped hard and tamped down the nausea caused by the sudden wave of pain. Perhaps she would stage a tremendous row.

A laugh caught in her throat. If her identity was discovered, she wouldn't have to manufacture a reason for the argument.

"Your lordship!" Finch cried out, waving to attract the attention of a gentleman standing near the enclosure. Eliza would have recognised that beloved profile anywhere. She bit back the emotion that welled up inside her and concentrated on the job in hand.

Though longing to look into his eyes, she didn't dare. Her groom had made excuses for her whenever Beau had come to see Romeo, so this was the first time they'd met since coming to Epsom.

As he turned his head, she lowered her own, suddenly shy at the thought of being seen by him, dressed like a man. Surely he would recognise her, even in this guise.

Eliza held her breath, fearing discovery, as Beau came right up to Romeo, but she need not have worried. He didn't so much as look at her. His eyes were only for his colt. A lump formed in Eliza's throat as she watched how tenderly he buried his face in Romeo's mane and patted his neck.

Perhaps she should have been a horse. Then he would have greeted her with that much affection.

At last, he raised his head and nodded at Eliza. She mumbled something incoherent and returned his nod, keeping her head down.

Fortunately, Beau did not seem to see anything amiss.

"I can't thank you enough for stepping in like this, Robson. Now, about the race. Your most serious rival in the field is Majesty," he said, pointing at a black horse a short distance away. "He belongs to Mr Cunningham, and that's the one you must beat above all others. He won at Newmarket and is favourite here. Follow him off the start and then, if Romeo has the speed, go for it down the last straight."

Eliza gulped rather heavily and gave a restrained nod to show she had understood.

"At least if Romeo runs, he has a chance."

She heard the doubt in his voice and realised he didn't hold out much hope of her riding to victory. It made her even more determined to succeed. Beau's uncertainty caused her own insecurities to vanish. She had to triumph for him.

Finch looked concerned that Beau was focusing too much attention on her and sought to distract him. "Fortunate thing, Miss Merry finding him like that, my lord."

At the mention of her name, his eyes clouded over, and he seemed to lose concentration.

Eliza felt a flicker of hope in her heart. Perhaps he cared for her. Just a little.

Finch coughed. "Isn't it time for the weigh-in, my lord?"

"Yes, of course," Beau said, coming out of his abstraction. He patted Romeo's neck. "Off you go. Good luck."

At last, he withdrew from the race enclosure and Eliza breathed a sigh of relief. She gazed after him, but looked away abruptly, her heart thumping in her chest, when she saw him join Anthony. Had Beau told him the name of his jockey? Would Ant stop her from racing?

But he didn't approach her, and when she dared to peek, a few moments later, the two friends had disappeared.

Finch guided her through the pre-race procedures, and when they were complete, he led her to the start. All around her, jockeys were brandishing their whips and looking more like men going into battle than into a race, their horses snorting with excitement.

Terror wrenched her gut as the start of the race drew nearer. What was she doing? She was seated on a horse, dressed in men's clothes, in a coarse masculine atmosphere.

What if her sex was discovered? What if she was jostled and unseated and fell to the ground? Would she be trampled on?

She prayed with all her might that God would keep her safe, though she had no right to ask. She'd put herself in this position, overruling her groom's advice to act in a way that would horrify her family.

Eliza grasped the whip that Finch held up to her, forcing her hand not to shake, and took her place.

She bent down low over her horse's neck and whispered to her mount. "Run like the wind, Romeo. For Beau."

<h1 align="center">Chapter 40</h1>

Beau and Anthony took their places. They had secured a spot on the incline above the circuit, giving them the best possible view of the course and, most importantly, the finish line.

"Do you think he's got a chance?" Ant asked.

Beau shrugged his shoulders. "A novice jockey on a strange, albeit fast, horse who has never raced before? Yes, there's a chance—but don't get your hopes up. It's only a slim possibility. There are too many unknowns."

He thrust his hands in his pockets and locked his gaze on the track. Although he'd warned Ant not to expect Romeo to win, he couldn't stop himself from hoping. The next three minutes could be the most important of his life.

When the signal was given, the two men fell silent. The race had begun.

Majesty was on form. The black had already pulled away from the rest of the field by the time he reached the first turn. Another horse was, maybe, a length behind. Could it be...?

Beau grabbed Ant's arm in his excitement as the horses cleared the next bend. Cunningham's black was in the lead, but his colt was keeping up.

"It's Romeo! Well, blow me down—Robson looks as if he was born to it."

"What? Who did you say was riding?"

"Robson—friend of Merry's who rode in the hunt with us," Beau said, without taking his eyes off the racetrack.

"Oh. I didn't realise," Ant said in a rather strange voice.

"I thought at the time he'd make a great jockey, but I never imagined he would be this good in his first race."

As they entered the final straight, the two horses were neck and neck.

"Do you see him—sat right on Majesty's back?"

"Is he fast enough to overtake him?"

"I think so," said Beau, hardly daring to hope. "We'll soon know. If Robson can stay on, he's in with a real chance."

"Pray to God that he stays on. Cunningham's jockey might get nasty if he feels threatened."

Beau was surprised at the earnestness in Ant's voice. "Don't worry. I'm praying!"

Half-way down the final straight, Majesty edged ahead again.

"Come on, boy," Beau yelled. "For Eliza," he added under his breath.

Robson crouched low over Romeo's neck and looked as if he was whispering in the horse's ear. With a sudden spurt of speed, the bay colt sailed past Majesty, winning the race by a clear length.

Beau clapped his friend on the back. "He won!"

Ant exhaled heavily, as though he had been holding his breath for a long time. "Yes. He won."

Almost skipping for joy at his victory, Beau headed for the paddock. He was free of his mother at last. Now he could prove to Eliza he wasn't marrying her to get his inheritance. He could make everything right again.

Cunningham walked over to him, shaking his head from side to side as if he could not believe what he had just witnessed.

He extended his arm toward him with obvious reluctance. "Congratulations. You have a real champion there. I take it you're in no hurry to part with him?"

Beau grasped his rival's hand and shook it. "Sorry, no—and I'm glad I don't have to."

The older gentleman gave a wry smile. "I shall be sad to see Majesty go, but I have other racers coming up behind him. I'll beat your Romeo yet."

Beau tilted his head to one side. "You're welcome to try."

Cunningham jerked his chin up, as if accepting the challenge, and strode off. Beau couldn't help thinking the man seemed more frustrated he'd been beaten than that he'd lost a vast sum of money and his prize racehorse.

When they reached the race enclosure, Ant held back, leaving him to approach Romeo on his own. The formalities had been completed, and Finch was leading him through the paddock where crowds of people were gathered round, eager to pat the winning horse and offer their congratulations.

"That was a tremendous run," Beau said, coming up behind them.

Robson jumped in the saddle as if his voice had startled him. He bent low over the horse's neck without meeting Beau's eyes. "Thank you, my lord."

"Take Romeo away, Finch. I'm staying at the King's Head, if you could deliver him to me there. And bring Robson too, of course. I want to arrange suitable remuneration for claiming such a splendid victory."

The groom nodded and continued on his way, but Beau stopped him, moving up to Romeo's head once more and rubbing noses with his horse. "Well done, my treasure."

To his surprise, Robson let out a whimper. Beau responded to the noise on instinct, staring up full into the jockey's face.

For what seemed like an eternity, their gazes locked. He struggled to breathe as he tried to fathom what he saw. It was the first time he'd scrutinised Robson's features. The man's pale blue eyes resembled Eliza's. The nose, the lips, the shape of his face were so similar to those of the woman he loved.

Too similar.

Beau's heart lurched as he came to a shocking realisation. Eliza was his jockey.

A myriad of emotions flooded his being as he processed his thoughts. Wonder, gratitude, hope, anger, but overcoming them all—horror.

What had Finch been playing at by allowing her to ride? It was only a stupid wager—a wager he shouldn't have accepted. What if her sex had been discovered? She would have been ruined. What if she had fallen? She could have been killed—and he would never have forgiven himself.

Beau felt his blood run cold as the colour drained from his face. He must have looked ghastly, because Eliza recoiled in her saddle, making Romeo shift uneasily beneath her. The movement broke the connection and, all at once, he came to his senses and plunged headlong into action.

"Make way!" he cried, grabbing the colt's reins. "Champion coming through!"

The crowds responded to the voice of authority and parted to allow them to pass.

Once they were clear of the masses, he returned control of the horse to Finch, struggling to keep his emotions in check.

He did not trust himself to be there when Eliza dismounted. He feared he wouldn't be able to restrain himself from scooping his darling girl into his arms, while she was still dressed as a man, causing a scandal they would all struggle to live down.

"Get out of here. Now."

He ground his teeth as he turned away from Eliza and walked off.

It was the hardest thing he'd ever done.

Finch needed no further encouragement. They left the racecourse without hindrance and were soon back at the White Hart. Eliza dismounted in a daze, hardly knowing what she was doing.

The entire hostelry stood empty, as the racegoers had not yet returned. Her groom tethered the horses in silence, and they made their way toward the inn door.

He motioned to her to wait whilst he entered, and as he did, he almost bumped into the barmaid, who seemed to be the only member of staff around. As he was a personable man, Finch had no difficulty engaging her in conversation, leaving Eliza free to slip inside and up the stairs.

The small chamber was as she had left it. She pushed the door closed behind her and leaned against it. If only it was as easy to shut out the expression on Beau's face.

What had caused that dreadful look? She would never forget it for as long as she lived.

He had recognised her—that was certain—and it had shocked him. That much she'd seen in his eyes. But the pallor of his skin, the scrunched-up eyebrows and the firm set of his mouth? Could shock alone explain those?

Was he angry with her? Ashamed of her reckless behaviour?

She had believed he was the one man who wouldn't care about propriety. The one man with whom she could be herself.

But maybe Georgie was right. Not even Beau wanted a wife who embarrassed him, and this time she had gone too far. That would explain his sending her away in disgust.

She had always intended to break off their engagement if she was victorious, but she had naively hoped that when he came to pick a bride in his own timing, he would select her.

And her heart broke all over again as she recognised the cost of what she had done.

She had won the race, but she had lost Beau.

A knock heralded Finch's arrival. He entered the room and sank to his knees to take off her boots, which she couldn't remove by herself. The tight expression on his face showed he wasn't comfortable being in a bedchamber with her with no one else around, but it was necessary for their plan. After what she'd done today, Eliza wasn't sure the proprieties mattered any more.

With a brief nod, her groom left, and she was alone again.

Tears welled up in her eyes and a few drops fell down her cheeks. She longed to indulge her misery, but she had a part to play if she was to have a shred of reputation remaining after this foolish adventure.

She ripped off the men's garments in disgust and stuffed them in her saddlebag. If there had been a fire lit in the grate, she would have burned them. With equal loathing, she tore the wig from her head and sent it to join her clothes before slipping between the bedcovers and ringing the bell.

The landlady came bustling in a few minutes later. She looked at Eliza and screwed up her face in concern. "Why, I don't think your headache can have gone one bit. You look as white as a sheet. Are you sure you won't rest a while longer?"

"No, thank you. I've stayed long enough already, and I must go before I'm missed."

After helping her dress and tidy her hair, the woman called a lad to help her on with the boots Finch had removed just moments before.

With her stylish shako pinned on her head, she was a lady again, and blinking back the tears that were not far away, she followed the landlady down the stairs.

"Ah, there you are Finch," she said in a loud voice. "I'm feeling a little better and am eager to be on my way. Please be so good as to ready my horse and settle our account."

"Yes, miss," he responded, smiling apologetically at the maid, who seemed sad to have him go.

Eliza mounted Whisper, appreciating the side-saddle for the first time in her life, and trotted toward the Red Lion with as much haste as she dared. Her only thought was to get away from Epsom before Beau found her. She could not bear to see that look on his face again.

Once back in the safety of her sister's house, she would write and break off their engagement.

Perhaps she would become a nun.

Eliza looked so unwell when she returned to the Red Lion that Sarah had no difficulty in believing she had been taken ill during her ride and had needed to rest until she felt better. She chided her for her thoughtlessness at sending no word to her, but when her charge burst into tears in response to her scolding, she became alarmed and hastened to exchange words of comfort for her reprimands.

"Never you mind," she said, fussing to make her mistress comfortable in the carriage. "We'll soon get you back to the care of Lady Castleford, and she'll know what's best for you."

Eliza smiled despite herself.

Not even Georgie could help her out of this one.

# Chapter 41

Beau walked away from the racecourse, not daring to look behind him at Eliza. His entire body shook with the effort.

When he reached the King's Head, he paced up and down his room, wondering what to do next. He didn't know where Eliza was staying. Romeo was stabled at the White Horse. Had she taken rooms there or somewhere else?

He wished he could go in search of her, but he didn't know where she would transform back into a lady, or how long it would take.

It was some consolation that Finch was with her. He was a reliable man, even though aiding his mistress in such an escapade was not the wisest thing he'd ever done. A wry grin crept onto Beau's lips. He had no doubt Eliza had persuaded him into it. He had seen her stubborn streak in action, and it was not easily cowed.

The stubbornness that had believed in his ability to succeed at Astley's, even when everyone else disagreed. That had almost got her killed, riding so wildly when she lost her temper. That had refused to forgive him.

But if she had risked so much by racing Romeo for him, did that imply she had forgiven him now?

The door burst open without ceremony.

"What did you say to her?"

Beau stared at Anthony. He'd never heard his friend so angry before. "What do you mean?"

"Don't play the idiot with me, Beau. I was standing next to you in the paddock—or perhaps you didn't notice as your eyes were so enamoured with your jockey."

"You know?"

"Yes. I've known for a long time. I saw through her disguise when she dressed as Robson to ride with the hunt. As soon as I heard the name of your jockey, I knew she was playing the same game again—except that this wasn't a game, and I was too late to stop her. I thank God he kept her safe. She could have been killed. But what's done is done. What's more important right now is what you said to her."

"Nothing," Beau said, a touch of annoyance in his voice.

"You said nothing to her?"

"No. I wanted to remove her from danger as fast as possible. As soon as I realised, I told Finch to get her out of there and left."

"Do you know what a precious thing it is you have there? She loves you. I would have tried to win her if she'd given me the slightest encouragement...but no matter. It's you she loves, not me. And you said nothing? No words of reassurance?"

Ant's words conjured up a variety of feelings, but Beau didn't stop to examine them, responding to his friend with growing irritation.

"I was afraid I'd give myself away. What did you expect me to do? Kiss her passionately while she was dressed as a man?"

Anthony shook his head in despair. "You don't get it, do you? You've no idea how that ghastly look on your face made her feel, and you've said nothing to soften it."

"I was shocked. Horrified at the danger she'd put herself in. Distraught at the thought she could have been killed—and it would have been my fault. Surely she realised that?"

"Not if you didn't tell her. I saw how you looked, and I observed her reaction to it. If I'm not mistaken, she's placed a different interpretation on your expression from the one you've given me. She thinks you're disgusted by her behaviour. By her."

Had he really made her think that? If he had...

"I need to see Eliza. Confess how much I love her and still want to marry her. Assure her I'm not disgusted with her—but with myself."

"Yes, you must. Where is she staying?"

"I don't know. Romeo was stabled at the White Horse, so she may be there. I'll ask Finch when he brings my colt over."

There seemed nothing else they could do but wait. Beau poured two glasses of wine and they sat down to discuss the race.

"It's a shame we can never boast to Cunningham that his jockey was beaten by a woman," said Beau.

"In her first race."

Beau glared at his friend. "In her first and *only* race."

"Of course. But I agree it's a pity we can't tell anyone. What will you do with Majesty?"

"Race him for another season or two and then add him to my stud. Romeo might be faster, but there's no doubt he's a fine beast with noble bloodlines. I feel rather sorry for him. Cunningham's affection for him seemed to dissipate with his defeat."

"It was arrogant of the man to bet so heavily in his favour. We all know the Good Book warns us that pride comes before a fall—"

Anthony was interrupted by a knock at the door.

"If you please, your lordship, there's a man below asking for you."

The two friends exchanged a glance, and with a nod, Beau followed the servant downstairs. The man pointed to the back door. "Out there, my lord."

Beau walked out into the yard, expecting to see Finch. Instead, he saw a harassed-looking Jem holding Romeo's bridle with his good arm.

"Sorry to trouble you, my lord, but I couldn't manage and—"

"Where's Finch?" he asked, cutting across Jem.

"Gone. He said he'd agreed with you about bringing Romeo here and, as he was mighty keen to go and Thompson was not about, I took him. Keep forgetting how little I can do with this dratted arm in a sling."

"Did he say...nothing else?"

"Just that he hoped all was in order, but if you needed anything further from him, to send word and he'd wait on you in London."

"Very good," Beau said in a wooden voice. He helped Jem see to the colt and then stomped back inside and up the stairs to his room. He slammed the door behind him and turned a woebegone face to Ant.

"It seems you're right. I've upset Eliza—again—and now she's gone."

"What are you going to do about it?"

"Go after her, of course. Are you coming?"

Anthony gave him a wry smile, accompanied by a brief nod, and he suspected his friend would have insisted on their immediate departure whether or not he wished it.

Beau barked orders at his valet. If Eliza had already left, there was no time to lose. He must see her and put things right.

His spirits rose at the thought of what she had risked for him, but a lingering doubt remained.

Would she still refuse to believe him when he told her he loved her?

·♥·♥·♥·♥·♥·

The miles flew by, and before Eliza had in any way recovered from the shock of being recognised by Beau, the carriage pulled up in front of Lord Castleford's townhouse. She was fortunate to find Georgiana at home and alone.

"How lovely to see you," her sister said, enfolding her in a warm embrace. "I thought you were going to Epsom."

Eliza didn't reply. She feared if she opened her mouth to speak, she would burst into tears, and she had no wish to disgrace herself in front of the servants. She shot her sister a pained look, and Georgie responded as she knew she would.

After ordering tea to be brought up to the drawing room, she put her arm around Eliza's shoulders and ushered her upstairs.

"I had no notion you planned to return today, but no matter. Your bedchamber is waiting for you. The journey must have been quite pleasant—not as warm as it has been—with a delightful breeze, though it is in danger of wrecking my hair every time I go out for a walk."

Georgiana chattered away comfortably, requiring no response from her until the door shut behind the maid who had brought in the tea.

After sitting down beside her on the sofa, her sister took both her hands and looked into her face. "What on earth has happened?"

"Nothing."

"Nothing? Two weeks ago, you wrote to tell me how happy you were because Beau had asked you to marry him. Two days ago, I get a scribbled note informing me you are going to Epsom and your return would be delayed. Today, you turn up, without your betrothed, looking like death. Don't you dare try to pretend nothing has happened."

Eliza knew Georgiana would not let her leave until she had an answer. She sat in stony silence, sipping her tea, seeking the courage to begin.

"I have made the worst mistake of my life."

"Have you broken off your betrothal?" her sister whispered, her face now as pale as her own.

"No, but I must."

"Why? Please don't tell me there is another woman. I warned you—"

Eliza scowled, rushing to Beau's defence on instinct. "He's not like that. He wouldn't dangle after anyone else while he was engaged to me."

"Then you're not breaking off your engagement because you're jealous?"

"No."

Eliza leapt to her feet and paced up and down the room before falling on her knees in front of her sister. "I've acted so foolishly. I must end our betrothal and release him from his promise."

She grasped Georgie's hands and gazed up into her face with pleading eyes. "You'll be so cross with me when you hear what I've done."

"I'm listening."

Little by little, the story came out.

"When I discovered Romeo, I became obsessed with the notion that I could win his bet for him, so he didn't have to marry me."

Georgiana raised her eyebrows. "What kind of warped logic was that? I thought you wanted to marry him."

"I do, but I wished to rescue him from being reliant on his mother, and believed if he was free, he would not wed anyone just yet. In a few years, when he was ready, I hoped he would choose me of his own volition."

"That sounds rather far-fetched, but I assume once you had the idea in your head, there was no stopping you. But how did you intend to win his bet for him? Didn't you say his jockey was injured when Romeo was stolen?"

Eliza said nothing, but fixed her eyes on the floor, waiting for Georgiana to put two and two together and realise what she'd done.

It did not take long. Her sister's mouth gaped open in a most unladylike way. "Never tell me you raced him at Epsom?"

She gave the tiniest of nods in reply.

"Oh, Eliza. How could you?" Georgie shook her head from side to side, a resigned smile on her lips. "Do you care so little about your safety and your reputation? Whatever would Father say?"

"Please do not lecture me. I'm miserable enough as it is. I thought no one would know."

"What a gamble, and all for nothing. You're not a seasoned jockey and it's no surprise you lost."

Eliza laughed hysterically. "Lost? No, I won."

"You won against all those men? Ha! How astonishing."

Georgie's eyes shone with admiration, but the sight did little to soothe Eliza's distress.

"Beau came to the paddock after the race and gazed into my face—and he knew. He kept staring for what seemed like an age and his expression—"

Her own face screwed up in pain at the memory. "I couldn't stand it. I wanted the ground to open up and swallow me. As for Beau, he could not escape fast enough. He gave Finch orders as if he were his servant, not mine. After that, my sole desire was to return here as soon as possible."

Eliza looked up into a pair of eyes full of sympathy and whimpered. "I had it all worked out, Georgie. I was so sure this was the answer, but I was wrong. My behaviour today embarrassed Beau, killing any affection he had for me. By winning the race, I've set him free, but I've ruined any chance of him ever choosing me as his bride. And I love him so much..."

She laid her head on her sister's lap and sobbed.

Georgiana let her cry. When she thought she had wept for long enough, she called for a fresh pot of tea and some cakes. She poured two cups and encouraged her sister to eat.

"Come on. Have a cake."

Eliza looked at her as if she had made a ridiculous request, but as Georgie continued to stare at her, holding out the plate, she obeyed and took one.

As it was impossible to eat and cry at the same time, Eliza alternately sniffed and nibbled at her food and soon became calm enough to raise her cup of tea to her mouth without spilling it.

"I shall break off our engagement as I planned. Set Beau free to follow his dreams."

"I think you should talk to him," Georgiana said tentatively.

"No! I can't. You would not suggest it if you'd been there. I cannot risk seeing that look of disgust again. No. I'll write him a note."

Her sister frowned. "You must see him in person. It's not something you should do by letter. You owe him that."

Eliza chewed on her bottom lip. Would she have the strength to release Beau if she saw him face to face? No. She didn't think so. Because she didn't *want* to break off her engagement—but she must. He deserved to have a choice about his future—even if that future didn't include her.

"No. I can't see him."

Nothing Georgiana said could change her mind and after a while, she gave up.

Eliza sat at her sister's writing desk and penned a brief letter to the Viscount Beaumont. Considering its length, it took a disproportionate amount of time to compose. It was no simple matter to find the words to break off her betrothal to the man she loved.

When her resolution wavered, she recalled his look of horror and reminded herself it was her duty to release him from what he must now deem an odious and unnecessary entanglement.

Once she had written the few lines that ruined all her hopes, she folded the paper carefully, sealed it with wax, and handed it to a footman to be delivered to Beau's London lodgings before she could change her mind.

There. It was done.

And she could spend the rest of her life regretting it.

# Chapter 42

IT WAS ALREADY LATE in the afternoon when Beau arrived back in London. He and Anthony had spoken little on the journey. For the first time in his life, he felt awkward in the company of his best friend.

Despite Ant's previous assurances that his feelings for Eliza were just brotherly, Beau now had reason to think otherwise. Ant had as good as admitted he was in love with her, but realised his case was hopeless.

Beau sympathised. Unrequited love was painful. He knew.

But now, after Eliza had risked so much for him, he dared to hope she still cared. Ant was unwavering in his conviction that she did—and while it scuppered his best friend's hopes, it strengthened his own.

With difficulty, Anthony persuaded him of the unwisdom of calling on Eliza as soon as they arrived, when she would be exhausted from the exertions of the race and the emotional scene that had followed.

After dining at White's, they returned to Beau's lodgings together. As they walked through the door, Carrick handed him a letter. "This arrived for you while you were at dinner, my lord."

He took the missive from his valet and tossed it aside without even looking at it. He was in no mood to read his mother's latest recriminations. They could wait until morning. He drank a single glass of whisky with Anthony, and then they both retired to bed.

When he awoke the next day, he felt refreshed, but his anxiety to see Eliza was growing by the hour. He sent his man in to wake Anthony, who was not an early riser, so they could breakfast together.

Beau was already dressed and seated at the table, pouring two cups of coffee, when his friend emerged from his bedchamber wearing an embroidered dressing gown.

"Morning," he mumbled. "I suppose it *is* morning? It feels as if it's only half-way through the night."

"It's past eight o'clock."

"Ah. As I expected—half-way through the night."

"Stop playing the dandy with me and come and have something to eat."

"Why the early start? We're in town—or had you forgotten? You can't go calling on Eliza at nine o'clock in the morning. It's not civilised."

"I thought we could ride."

Anthony wrinkled his brow in distaste. "Not at this hour."

After drinking a cup of coffee, Beau poured himself another and started on the toast.

His valet hovered by the table until he looked up. "Yes, Carrick. What is it?"

"Did you wish to send a reply to the note you received yesterday, my lord?"

Beau gave a bark of laughter. "That is not a very subtle way of reminding me I have an unopened letter."

He took the missive from his man. "What would I do without you, Carrick? Alas, my lamentable memory."

"I don't believe your powers of recollection are faulty at all," said Anthony. "You have a remarkable ability to recall the pleasant and forget what you would rather not remember."

Beau protested at his friend's accusation, but although he disclaimed, he admitted there was more than a little truth in them.

He fiddled with the letter in his hand. "Well, I suppose I should open it, as it might contain a happy announcement. I daresay if Frances has given birth to a boy, my mother will blast the news from the rooftops and somehow make it sound as though it is to her credit."

"Ouch," said Anthony. "Those are bitter words for breakfast time."

Beau ignored him and examined the address on the letter with a puzzled frown. "Hmm. This is not Mother's handwriting, but who else could it be from?"

"You are betrothed. Could Eliza have written to you?"

Could she? Beau turned the missive over and recognised Lord Castleford's arms stamped in the red wax.

He tore open the seal and devoured the contents, but as he read, the eagerness drained away, leaving him feeling numb.

"You're right," he said in a voice devoid of expression. "It's from Eliza."

His friend was buttering a slice of toast and did not look up. "Love letters at breakfast. How revolting."

"It is not a love letter. In fact, you might call it a poison letter. Eliza has ended our engagement."

Anthony's knife clattered onto his plate as his eyes shot up to meet Beau's. He didn't say a word. He didn't need to. His face said it all.

Beau stared at the letter, as if by staring he could somehow eliminate the hateful words from the page. "But I thought...I mean, I know I don't deserve her, but I thought...I hoped...that riding Romeo in the race meant something..."

"If she doesn't believe you care for her, she might suppose she's doing you a favour."

Beau looked at him blankly.

"Try to see it from Eliza's point of view. With the money from the wager, you have no immediate need for your inheritance. She overheard you say you were forced into marriage and thinks you had no intention of proposing until Romeo was stolen. If she believes you don't wish to be married, she may be giving you what she assumes you want."

"And what's that?"

"Freedom."

As Ant's words sunk in, Beau remembered all the times he had said as much to his friend and, worse still, to Georgiana. If she had relayed this to her sister, it was no wonder Eliza struggled to trust that he really wanted to marry her.

"She knows you could not cry off, so she's done it for you."

"My brave girl. How wrong she is. I must go to her, talk to her, make her understand."

Beau jumped up from the breakfast table and called for Carrick.

"I can't visit her dressed like this. Not that Eliza would mind," he said with a slight smile, "but it is not suitable for paying a morning call on a countess."

He disappeared into his bedchamber and exchanged his buckskins for a pair of buff pantaloons. Carrick passed him a cravat, and he attempted to tie it, but he botched the first attempt and had to discard it. His second fared no better, and after a third failure, he gave up and put himself in the hands of his valet. In his agitated state, he seemed incapable of tying his neckcloth in any style that would not proclaim him to have been drunk when he tied it.

"May I suggest your coat of blue superfine, my lord?"

Beau nodded and allowed Carrick to ease him into it, but after a moment, he changed his mind and asked for his dark green jacket of Bath coating instead. Five minutes later, he rejected that one, and tried on another, and in the end, he reverted to the blue superfine that his valet had suggested.

"You can't call on Lady Castleford at this hour, Beau," Anthony said. "They won't have finished breakfast."

"But I can't sit around doing nothing. I'll walk there."

"You'll still be too early."

"I can wait."

Not all Ant's warnings could deter him from setting out and it was not yet eleven when he arrived at Warren House and rang the bell.

As Lord Castleford's butler opened the door, Beau's heart thumped so loudly he thought the entire street could hear.

Would Eliza let him apologise, or had he lost her forever?

The uncertainty was agony.

# Chapter 43

Beau's heart sank as the butler informed him the ladies were not at home to visitors. He couldn't even leave his card to say he'd called, as he had left his card case in one of the coats he had discarded earlier.

He retreated from the door with all the dignity he could muster, balling his fists in his frustration. What was he going to do now? He couldn't stomach returning to his lodgings without seeing Eliza.

Hyde Park was nearby. He would go for a walk until he could call again.

It was not busy at that hour, and he was dismayed when a landau drew up beside him, emblazoned with the Earl of Harting's crest.

He gritted his teeth and turned to face the last person he wanted to see. "Good morning, Mother. How unexpected. I thought you were still in Alton."

"Come and sit with me, Beaumont," she said to him, as if he were a boy of six instead of a grown man. Accustomed to obeying his parent's wishes, it did not occur to him to refuse. He had nothing to do for the next hour anyway, so he might as well do what she asked.

He climbed into the carriage and sat down opposite her.

"You will be glad to know Frances gave birth to a healthy baby boy on Tuesday night."

"That's good news." He thought he meant it.

"After being assured of the safety of mother and child, we returned to London. There were pressing matters for Lord Harting to attend to, not least of which was obtaining a special licence for your wedding."

She held out the document to Beau, but he did not rush to take it. His future was unsure. He did not yet know whether Eliza would forgive him.

"It is no accident I have come upon you this morning. I knew your carriage returned to the mews yesterday, and I was en route to your lodgings when I saw you heading this way."

She paused and gave Beau a hard stare before pressing the licence into his hands. "Lord Harting and I are eager to set your wedding day. Caroline is to marry in July, and it is fitting that you, as her senior, should wed first. At the end of June, to be precise. The tenants will be gone, and we have enough time to prepare Langcroft Park for the ceremony. You will marry in the chapel there, like your father and I were, and your grandparents before that.

"The house is not ready for you. I have not inspected it fully, but work will be needed to make it fit to receive your bride. However, there is no call for you to delay your nuptials as you need not take up residence right away. After the ceremony, you will stay at Holybourne House while your staff prepares your home. Beaumont, are you listening to me?"

He jumped. He hadn't been able to get past his mother's opening words, for he too wanted to set his wedding day, but now it felt like a remote possibility instead of a certainty.

There was no point delaying the evil hour. He had to tell his mother how things stood.

"I regret to say that there may not *be* a wedding."

"What do you mean?" she asked, her tone so icy it chilled him to the bone. "Do not think that because you have won some horserace, you can jilt your betrothed."

Beau smarted at the mention of the race, but it didn't shock him that his mother knew. She knew everything.

"It's not me, but Eliza, who has broken off our engagement, and unless I can persuade her to change her mind, there will be no wedding."

Her ladyship did not reply, but sat digesting his words as the landau lumbered around the park.

"Do not despair, Beaumont," she said at length, in the same measured tone she had used to encourage him as a small boy not to cry, but to face his problems like a man. "You have everything a woman could desire: wealth, connections and a title, as well as a handsome countenance. I fear you have behaved very ill to frighten Elizabeth away. You must see her and make amends as soon as possible. She is a biddable girl and will wish to do what is right. I will remind her of the promise she made, and you need to apply yourself to being all that is charming—"

"I don't want a reluctant wife, or one who marries me out of duty. If Eliza has decided we do not suit, then I won't pressure her to marry me."

"Tut, tut. That shows how little experience you have of girls. You assume they know what is best for them, but nine times out of ten, they do not. Sometimes young people need a helping hand to ensure they make the wisest decisions."

Beau grunted in response.

His mother folded her hands in her lap, showing the conversation was over. She must have concluded she had said enough to persuade him to do what he was already planning on doing.

"Can I help you on your way?"

"By the entrance gate would be fine, thank you," he said, unwilling to expose his destination, as it would appear he was rushing to do her bidding.

The coachman drew the carriage to a halt, and Beau took leave of his mother and climbed down from the landau.

As he watched the conveyance move away, he mulled over her words. Her conversation had depressed rather than encouraged him. She was resolved to see him wed to the woman she had chosen for him, regardless how either of them felt.

Her determination wrapped around his neck like a scarf being pulled ever tighter, and Beau feared her interference would strangle any hope he had with Eliza.

His eyes glazed over as he stared at the special licence in his hands and then slipped it in his coat pocket.

He prayed he would have the chance to use it.

Eliza sat in the drawing room with her eldest sister, forcing herself to concentrate on the piece of embroidery in her lap. The stitches were even more ragged than usual, reflecting the state of her troubled heart, but she needed to occupy her hands.

Beau had come.

Georgiana had predicted he would call, and she'd been right, but what did it mean? Why would he seek her out when she had released him from his promise? Was it possible he'd been speaking the truth when he said he cared for her? That her behaviour hadn't appalled him as much as she had thought?

When the footman announced his name, and Beau strode into the room, looking as handsome as ever, an intense combination of pleasure and pain swept over Eliza, threatening to deprive her of breath.

After greeting Georgie, he turned to her and executed an exaggerated bow.

"How do you do, Miss Merry? I hope you have recovered from your recent exertions."

Eliza shuddered and lowered her eyes. Why was he speaking to her with such formality? Was it to remind her they were no longer engaged? Had he come only to mock her, making a sly reference to the race to emphasise his relief at being freed from his betrothal to such an unprincipled girl?

No. That wasn't like Beau, but the stiffness in his manner still bothered her.

Out of the corner of her eye, she saw him sit down beside her, but he didn't address her again.

As the silence continued, it seemed increasingly unlikely he was here to reiterate his declarations of love and persuade her to change her mind. So why *had* he come?

Her chest tightened as an unwelcome thought occurred to her. Perhaps he was only here at his mother's insistence.

Georgiana witnessed the constraint between them and attempted to draw Beau into conversation, avoiding the subject of the race.

"When did you return to London?"

"Yesterday."

"I understand Frances has given birth to a boy."

"Yes."

"What will they call him?"

"Charles, after his father."

His answers were brief, and as Eliza said nothing, the exchange was slow and stilted.

After fifteen minutes, Georgiana stood up, an exasperated expression on her countenance.

"You must excuse us. We have other engagements."

Eliza cringed at her words.

Yes, other engagements, whereas her own with Beau was over.

She had thought the look of horror she had seen on his face at the races had been dreadful, but this was more painful—to have him so close, and yet so distant.

Would they ever be more than strangers to each other again?

# Chapter 44

After Beau's visit, Eliza refused to leave the house. She would not walk in the park or go for a drive or attend a rout for fear she might meet Beau and be treated like a stranger again.

If he called, she locked herself away in her bedchamber and wouldn't see him. Yet perversely, she was glad he had come, and when his visits stopped, she sunk into a pit of despair from which she could see no escape.

She wished they could be friends as they'd been before love got in the way. Before she had put unrealistic expectations on him, which had ruined what they had.

For the first week, Georgiana let her wallow in her misery and grieve the loss of her love in peace, but then she started coaxing Eliza to go out with her.

"Charlotte and I are going shopping. Would you care to come?"

"No, thank you. I'll stay here."

"You're unlikely to bump into Beau in Bond Street."

Eliza scowled at her sister, ignoring the probable truth of her words. "I said no."

"You can't continue in this way," Georgiana said, a grim expression on her face. "It does you no good to mope because life has not worked out the way you wanted. If you don't come out of the doldrums, I'll send you home."

Although she feared meeting Beau, if she returned to Hampshire, she would lose all hope of seeing him. "You wouldn't?"

"I will, if you don't cheer up," Georgiana said, a touch of impatience in her voice.

"Easy for you to say."

"You act as if you're the only person in the world with heartache."

"What do you know of a broken heart?" Eliza said, her temper rising at the lack of sympathy in her sister's words, and sharpened because she knew they were true. "Everything has worked out all right for you."

Georgie leapt to her feet and raced over to the window, but not before Eliza had seen the tears streaming down her face.

She was immediately contrite. She walked over to her sister and put her arm around her shoulders. "I'm sorry. I didn't mean to make you cry."

Her sister hiccupped as she brought her emotions under control. "I'm not unsympathetic, Eliza. I know how blessed I am to be married to an honourable man who loves me. It's just that...I hoped...I might be in the family way by now. I assumed it would be part of God's will for my life that I would have children. It's too early to despair, but every month, it is like a kick in the stomach when I discover I am not with child, and when I heard Frances had given birth to a boy, I...cried."

Eliza took her sister's hands in her own and squeezed them. "Oh, Georgie, I'm sorry. I've been so taken up with my own problems that I've been oblivious to yours."

"And now I need to heed my own words and put them into practise," she said, drying her eyes. "I must not give up on life because it is not working out the way I wanted."

"Mother would tell us to be thankful for what we have."

"Yes, she would, and I'm glad to have you here with me."

"I'll fetch Charlotte. Let's go shopping."

As Eliza focused on being a more supportive sister, the pain in her heart faded to a dull but consistent ache, and when Georgiana suggested accompanying them to a ball at Almack's a few days later, she agreed.

It was not as if Beau would be there. Eliza knew how much he hated it. He had not even graced Almack's with his presence when he had needed to find a wife.

Her assumption was wrong. As soon as she walked through the door, she caught sight of him dancing with Horrible Harriet Whitlow. All the pain came flooding back with full force. What was he doing here, dancing with her? Was he still being forced to find a wife?

Eliza remembered her suspicion that Beau had only called on her at his mother's bidding. His presence here tonight seemed to confirm her fears. She had raced to set him free from his mother's power, but she had failed. He was being controlled by Lady Harting as much as ever. Had she given up everything for nothing?

What little colour she had in her cheeks faded away at the sight of him dancing with Harriet, but it was her own fault. She had released him, and she had no right to feel jealous anymore.

She sat down beside Georgiana and the other chaperons, watching the dance, picking at her gloves until she was sure she would make a hole in them. How she wished she hadn't come. Maybe going home to West Meon would be easier than seeing him fill her place at his side with Harriet, having barely paused for breath since she had called off their engagement.

An acquaintance of Georgiana's came across to talk to her. Eliza paid no attention to their conversation until she heard her name being mentioned.

"I understand your sister won't be Miss Merry for much longer. She is to be congratulated."

The woman paused, hoping for some encouragement to continue.

"Have I been a little premature, Lady Castleford? I know it hasn't been announced yet, but Lady Harting dropped a word in my mother's ear, and I thought..."

Her words petered out as Georgiana looked down her nose at her. She stared at the woman for some moments in silence and then said, in a measured tone of voice, "You thought...?"

Despite her annoyance at the woman's gossiping, Eliza struggled to bite back a laugh, seeing her sister give such a masterly set-down. She wondered who she had learned that from.

"Ah well. I did not mean to offend," the woman said, her cheeks growing red with embarrassment. "I see Lady Jersey, pray excuse me."

Georgiana pulled a face at her sister. "Our aunt has been eager to spread news of your engagement," she whispered, "and not that it has ended."

Eliza nodded. At least she was prepared now.

As the set finished, she thought with an inner sigh she would be obliged to dance the next. She glanced around, hoping to see Anthony. Instead, she spotted Beau making his way across the room toward her.

Eliza thought he looked ill. Perhaps his mother was giving him a hard time over the broken engagement.

He greeted Georgiana warmly before turning to her and executing a low bow.

"You look exquisite tonight, Miss Merry. May I have the pleasure of dancing the next with you?" He took her hand and led her onto the dance floor before she could refuse him.

Eliza was confused. Why was he behaving like this? Was he so disgusted with her he must treat her in this formal manner that was so unlike him? But if he felt like that, why ask her to dance at all? Beau's politeness was such a cold imitation of the friendship they had shared that it brought all her shyness to the forefront, leaving her as tongue-tied and awkward as she had been when the season had begun.

Was he punishing her for embarrassing him, paying her fulsome compliments that set her teeth on edge, because they were the same flirtatious words every other gentleman said?

She dismissed the thought as quickly as it came. Beau was not vengeful, but how else could she explain his behaviour? Unless his mother had a hold over him, and was still trying to persuade him it was his duty to marry her.

There was nothing Eliza could do but try to hide her feelings and enjoy the dance. He was an excellent partner, and as the lively reel precluded any but the briefest of conversations, she could forget, for a moment, that anything was amiss with the world. Almost.

As the set drew to a close, he gave her another formal bow.

"Would you care for some orgeat?"

Eliza nodded. He led her to a chair near her sisters and disappeared in the direction of the refreshments.

Georgiana was talking with Charlotte, leaving Eliza to her thoughts. She could not understand Beau's behaviour and was so lost in her reflections, she did not notice Lady Harting approaching.

"I am glad to see you and Beaumont have made up your differences," she said without preamble, sitting down next to her.

Eliza didn't know what to say. The words stuck in her throat.

"I felt sure you would both want to do your duty and keep your troth to each other."

She could not let this misunderstanding continue. "You are mistaken, aunt."

Lady Harting pursed her lips. "No. I believe it is *you* who are mistaken, Elizabeth. You are allowing a fleeting disagreement to cloud your judgement. A rector's daughter could not ask for more than what my son can offer in terms of wealth, title and connections and a splendid home in which to raise your children, besides his personal attractions."

Eliza's colour rose. Was her aunt suggesting she had agreed to marry Beau because of these things? And it was rather more than a fleeting disagreement. To judge by Beau's conduct toward her since she had been back in London, he had no wish to renew their engagement.

How could she convince Lady Harting they were not still betrothed without revealing what she had done? She must try.

"I do not wish to be a viscountess. I think...indeed, I fear...I am not suited to holding such an elevated position."

The tightness around Lady Harting's mouth faded and her lips spread to form a broad smile.

"It is natural you should feel overwhelmed with the honour of such a title and all that it entails. Such a large house to manage and so many duties you have not been raised to consider. But do not fret, my dear child. You will not be left to deal with your new responsibilities alone. I will be there, at your side, to help and support you as you grow into your position. It is not for you to decide whether you are worthy of the role. I have impressed upon Beaumont the importance of doing his duty, and I know you will wish to do yours."

Eliza felt nauseous as she envisioned spending her days in Lady Harting's suffocating company. To be married to Beau would be heaven, but to live with his cold politeness and his oppressive mother would be hell.

"I'm sorry, your ladyship, but I don't want Lord Beaumont to marry me out of duty. It grieves me to say it, but I do not think we suit."

Eliza rose from her chair, sunk into a deep curtsey, and moved away before Lady Harting could restrain her.

Her aunt's words cut her to the core as they made the motive for Beau's current behaviour all too clear.

He was pursuing her out of duty—nothing more.

Beau procured two glasses of orgeat and returned to where he'd left Eliza, only to find she had vanished. Instead, his mother was there to greet him.

"Elizabeth tells me you do not suit," she said, a fierce light in her eyes that did not match her emotionless tone.

A wave of protectiveness came over Beau, causing him to return her look with a furious one of his own. Eliza might never become his wife, but he would not let his mother upset her any more if he could help it.

"I don't believe that for a minute. Tell me what you said to her to make her flee."

She glared at him.

"What did you say to her?" His forceful tone mirrored his mother's so closely that it almost made him shudder.

"I reminded Elizabeth of the duty you both have to keep your troth to each other."

Beau closed his eyes in frustration and then opened them again. "That was not helpful."

"It was necessary."

He did not have the patience to stay and argue. He needed to talk to Eliza.

"Please excuse me," he said with a brief bow, turning on his heel to search for his missing partner without looking back.

After much manoeuvring past dancers and chaperons alike, he found her at the opposite end of the room, fanning herself to reduce the raised colour in her cheeks.

He handed her one of the glasses he still held in his hands. "You appear to need some refreshment, madam."

"Thank you." She took the glass and drank some orgeat.

"My mother has just informed me you have been telling her we do not suit," he said in a low voice, so that none but she could hear.

"It would appear you have been planning my future with her," she whispered back, her eyes blazing with anger.

Beau's nose twitched. It was impossible not to smile. Eliza was talking to him. Yes, she was angry, but at least they were having a conversation.

"Why are you still letting her dictate your life? You can make your own choices now, but you are so used to submitting to her wishes, you can't break free. She impresses upon you your duty to the bride she has chosen for you, ignoring the fact that I broke off our engagement. And she promises me her help—help that threatens what little confidence I have in myself.

"Do you intend to let her overwhelm your wife with advice and correct all the things she gets wrong? Will she even determine how many children you should have? For some unknown reason, she deems me suitable, though I have told her I am not fit for the role. Perhaps she does not know I ride racehorses in my spare time?"

Beau flinched at every accusation, but his smile refused to fade until she mentioned the race. His eyes clouded over as all his fears for Eliza's life flooded back to the forefront of his mind. Why had she risked herself for him? He was not worth it.

"If you ever do anything so foolhardy again, I will—"

All the colour drained from her face, and she recoiled as if he had hit her.

"You seem to have forgotten our engagement is over, my lord," she said, annunciating every word so he could not misinterpret her meaning, "and what I do has absolutely nothing to do with you. I don't wish to marry you. Please do not try to persuade me otherwise."

With this withering speech, she left him. Beau stared after her as she disappeared into the crowd.

It was too late to take back his angry words, but he must apologise for them. Why couldn't he control his temper? She thought he was angry with her, when, in reality, he was furious with himself.

For allowing her to believe riding Romeo to victory was what he wanted. That winning the race was more important to him than her reputation, her safety, her love.

He reflected on Eliza's complaints and agreed it might appear as though he was still under the maternal thumb.

But how could he convince her his choices were his own when they coincided with his mother's?

# Chapter 45

Beau turned Eliza's accusations over and over in his mind, knowing he deserved every one of them. He could not help wondering whether their conversation would have ended differently if he had not lost his temper.

Which was why he stood in the entrance hall of Warren House the next morning, waiting to discover if Eliza would see him, so he could apologise.

He was disappointed, but not surprised, when the footman returned with the message that the ladies were not at home to visitors, but it left him in a worse position than he had been before he'd talked with Eliza at Almack's.

How could he beg her forgiveness if she would not even speak to him?

He desperately needed wise advice, but who could supply it? His thoughts drifted back to his time with Eliza's family, and he wished he had parents like hers. His stepfather was distant, and his mother cared for no one but herself.

As he was about to leave the house, an idea popped into his mind.

"Is Lord Castleford in?"

Only by a flicker of his eyelids did the footman betray his surprise. Beau couldn't blame the man. He'd never made such a request before.

The servant took his card and disappeared down the corridor. A few moments later, he reappeared.

"His lordship will see you now. This way."

Beau was ushered into a small room lined with books. Castleford rose from his chair behind the imposing mahogany desk that dominated the space and extended his arm.

Beau clasped his hand and shook it firmly, and then both gentlemen sat down.

"To what do I owe this pleasure?" the Earl asked.

"I need advice—guidance."

"Go on."

"May I ask you a personal question? How did you...how did you persuade Georgie to marry you?"

"If you're looking for a magic formula to find the way to a woman's heart, I'm afraid I cannot help you."

He shot him a look laced with such sympathy that Beau felt encouraged, despite his words.

"But you must have done something to convince her."

Castleford's eyes glazed over, as if remembering. "I just kept loving her, and I thank God that, with a little aid from you and Ant, I was able to save her from the hands of a scoundrel. And when she would have given me up, to free me from her disreputable self, I showed her how much I loved her."

"But she won't believe my words."

"My brother once told me to find out what made Georgiana feel loved. Ask yourself the same question. What is it that makes Eliza feel cherished—for I assume it's my sister-in-law we're talking about and not some other woman?"

Beau grimaced. "Please don't tease me. I'm not in the mood. You know very well it's Eliza I adore."

He pondered over what Castleford had said. Had he shown her how much he loved her? He kept on telling her, but she didn't believe him. Not that words were her thing any more than they were his—and his words kept getting him into trouble.

What mattered to Eliza? He thought back to their time in Alton and remembered how she'd glowed when he'd rescued her from his mother's machinations. To judge by the accusations she had flung at him the previous evening, she believed he was still under her grip and falling in with her schemes yet again—but without the excuse of needing to save his horses.

"I must prove I'm no longer dancing to my mother's tune." He gritted his teeth as his hands gripped the arms of his chair. "I could make a complete break of it. Sever all ties with her—"

"Not a course I would recommend."

"It's not?"

"Apart from being overly dramatic, Beau, it's hardly a Christian response, and not one which Eliza would applaud."

"Oh. I see your point. But how—"

He broke off as a plan formed in his mind. "I think there's a better way to show Eliza I've taken control of my life, and I'm sure she'll approve of this. I'll take up the reins of my estate and learn to manage my property if it kills me. My mother doesn't believe I'm capable, but if I succeed…"

"I have every confidence you will."

"You do?"

"Don't sound so surprised. Not everyone thinks as poorly of you as her ladyship. You were born to this position. Your devotion to horses means you'll live in the country more than most of the nobility, and you'll soon learn to love the land. Though you're ignorant of how to run an estate, you inspire loyalty in your servants, and that is something money can't buy. With a competent manager at your side, I believe the role will be much more to your liking than you imagine. Do you have a capable steward at Langcroft?"

"My mother does not tolerate incompetence, so I'm sure Harris excels at his job—but he reports to her."

"He's paid out of your income, so he's your employee. If he won't give you the help you need, dismiss him. You can't afford to have a disloyal man at your side, however competent he is. If you come unstuck, send me word and I'll find a replacement."

"Thank you. It's a step in the right direction, but it will still be hard to convince Eliza I want to marry her because I love her, and not because my mother told me to."

"Have you declared your love for her?"

"She won't believe me."

"Ah, I see your problem. Have you kissed her?"

"I have given her several pecks on the cheek—"

"Such as you might give your sister. Have you *really* kissed her?"

Beau dipped his eyes as he answered. "Just once—but I did not trust myself to do so again."

Castleford shook his head in despair and took a few moments to choose his next words. "Eliza is not ignorant of the liaisons you've had—"

"That's all over. I regret my past behaviour, but I know God has forgiven me. Eliza taught me I don't have to carry the weight of old mistakes. I promise I'll be faithful to my wife. I've not thought of another lady since—"

"You're missing the point. Eliza knows she's not the first woman in your life, and if you did not kiss her again, you may have sent her the wrong message. That her kisses are deficient. Unless, of course, you had the sense to tell her why you would not kiss her again until you were married."

"You don't mince your words, do you?"

"I apologise. It is sometimes better to sacrifice subtlety for clarity, and tact has never been my strong point."

"Thank you for restraining yourself from telling me to my face what an idiot I've been. You need not. I already know. I'm ashamed to admit how much my horses meant to me, that I was willing to enter marriage so lightly in order to save them. Your brother was convinced she loved me. I pray she still does, and I can prove myself worthy of the faith she once had in me."

He rose to leave, and they shook hands.

"Don't give up," Castleford said, before releasing his hold. "You've come a long way since I've known you. God hasn't stopped believing in you, and I don't think Eliza has either."

Beau hoped he was right.

# Chapter 46

ETERMINED TO PUT HIS plan into action straightaway, Beau called on his mother as soon as he left Warren House. He was fortunate to find Lady Harting at home.

"Have the tenants vacated Langcroft Park as agreed?"

"Yes. Harris sent word yesterday."

"Good. I want to set things in order there."

"Then you have resolved your differences with Elizabeth? You wish to prepare the house for your bride? I am so pleased—"

"She likes to be called Eliza, Mother. And you can keep your congratulations. I've not been able to persuade *Eliza* to renew our engagement, and your interference hasn't helped."

She pinched in her cheeks, showing her displeasure, but Beau cut off the withering reply he felt sure she was about to utter. "I mean to travel post-haste to Langcroft tomorrow."

"Tomorrow? There's no need for that. Harris can do all that is necessary. Your place is here in London, fixing your interest with Elizab—"

He glared at her.

"...with Eliza."

"I want to see the estate for myself. Discuss with Harris what needs to be done."

His mother flared her nostrils and paused for a moment before answering. "Very well. Perhaps it is not such a bad idea after all."

Beau knew better than to revel in her capitulation. The pinched expression on her face disappeared, and her lips curled up at the edges. It might have passed for a smile on anyone else's visage, but that look made him wary.

He didn't trust her. He had expected more of a battle, and winning her over to his point of view with apparent ease set all his senses on the alert.

What was his mother up to now?

The next day, before Beau left town, he again tried to see Eliza. This time when he called at Warren House, he was shown straight upstairs to the drawing room.

Georgiana was alone.

"You must excuse my sisters. Charlotte has gone shopping for some new music to play, and Eliza"—she shot him an apologetic glance—"is not feeling up to visitors this morning."

"You need not pretend, Georgie. You mean she won't see me."

"I'm afraid so."

"Please, will you pass on to her my sincere apologies for upsetting her at Almack's? I don't know whether she told you what was said."

"Not this time."

"But you know...about Epsom?"

"Yes."

"I lost my temper at Almack's, just like I did after the race. Whenever I think of the danger she put herself in, for my sake, I feel so ashamed. She may have thought...in fact, I'm certain she believed...I was angry with her for what she did. But I wasn't. I was furious with myself, and I'm truly sorry for upsetting her—again. One day, I pray she'll be able to forgive me. I've made so many mistakes, Georgie, and I know it's hard to believe, but I love her."

"Oh, Beau. I wish I could help, but she is convinced you're only saying that because your mother has insisted you win her back by any means."

He winced at her words. It hurt that Eliza did not think him capable of any genuine feeling, but he didn't deserve her trust. He would have to earn it.

"I came to take my leave of you. I'm going down to Langcroft Park to learn how to manage my estate."

"When are you leaving?"

"Now. I had hoped to say goodbye, but..."

"I'm sorry."

Beau rose from his seat and headed for the door, where he paused.

"Pray for me, Georgie. Pray that Eliza will find it in her heart to forgive me for hurting her."

Eliza stood at her bedroom window, watching Beau walk away from the house to where his carriage was waiting. A footman opened the door of his travelling chaise—the same one she had returned to London in—and Beau climbed inside.

That was strange. Why wasn't he driving his curricle? When she examined it further, her agitation grew. Two pairs of bays were harnessed to the vehicle, which was laden with luggage. He must be leaving London—and she had refused to see him.

She rushed to the drawing room and flung open the door.

"Beau?"

"He's gone."

Eliza struggled to speak. "I know. I saw his carriage. Is he travelling out of town?"

"He had hoped to take his leave of you."

"But where's he going? If I'd known—"

"Would you?"

Georgiana's words hung in the air. Would she?

"He asked me to pass on his apologies for reacting so passionately to what you said at Almack's."

"Oh."

"Is that all you can say? I thought you loved him, but do you? True love keeps no record of wrongs, and yet you won't forgive him for hurting you. Your faith in him has dwindled because of assumptions you've made about his behaviour, and you've refused to let him defend himself. What more can he do? You're destroying your own happiness by your stubbornness. When are you going to talk to him and give him the opportunity to put things right?"

Eliza examined her feelings. Was she still angry, or had she forgiven him already? Part of her wanted to pardon his behaviour, but the rest of her was afraid—afraid that if she forgave him, she was laying her heart open to be broken all over again.

"Would it make any difference if you knew it was your last chance?"

Eliza twisted round to look her sister in the eye. What did Georgiana know? She felt her pulse quicken. "What do you mean?"

"Life is uncertain. How would you feel, letting him leave, unforgiven, if you never saw him again? You'll probably have another opportunity, but what if you didn't? None of us knows when we say goodbye to someone if we'll ever see them again on this earth. Unforgiveness is like an insatiable parasite, feeding on all that is good. Don't allow it to consume your love until there's nothing left."

Eliza felt a growing pain deep inside. Georgiana was right. She should have forgiven Beau.

"Where is he going? The next races at Newmarket are not for another fortnight."

"To Beddington, to Langcroft Park. He's taking possession of his estate and doesn't know when he'll return."

Eliza dropped onto the sofa. The flicker of hope his visit had occasioned fluttered and died. She'd missed her chance. He'd gone.

She jumped up again, stifling a sob, and ran back to her bedroom. After punching her pillow until her strength ran out, she collapsed on her bed in silent agony, hugging her arms to her chest, overcome by grief.

She was a fool to have let him go.

# Chapter 47

BEAU REFUSED TO DWELL on his disappointment at not seeing Eliza before he left town. Perhaps it was better this way. He would take control of his estate and prove he was not a puppet whose strings were being pulled by his mother. Then, maybe, she would believe his words of love.

When he arrived at Langcroft Park, his housekeeper, Mrs Allett, welcomed him as if he were the prodigal son come home. The woman was so overcome with emotion he feared for a moment she was going to take him in her arms and hug him.

"You look that like your father," she said, shaking her head from side to side in disbelief. "I can hardly credit you're not the Viscount himself. Except, of course, you are the Viscount now, my lord. I can speak for all your staff when I say we are mighty glad to have a Beaumont in charge again."

Beau thanked her, touched by her sincerity and grateful for her loyalty, though he had done nothing to earn it. That would make his task much easier.

Mrs Allett showed him into the breakfast parlour and bustled away to find refreshments. Beau examined the bright room, which seemed in good decorative order. He was drawn to the large windows along one side which overlooked the gardens.

He was still taking in the view when a gentleman interrupted him.

"My lord?"

The man was, he judged, in his mid-thirties and his face was creased with concern, as if he expected a reprimand. Beau hazarded a guess that this was his estate manager, whom he assumed Mrs Allett had summoned.

"Mr Harris?" he said, extending his arm.

The gentleman's face relaxed as he shook Beau's outstretched hand. "Forgive me, my lord, for not being here to greet your arrival. I did not realise—"

"How could you when I sent no word? I didn't decide to come until yesterday." He paused. Perhaps it was best to be frank. "Mr Harris, this is my house, my land, but I'm unfamiliar with my property and lack the experience to manage it. I am a stranger here, and put myself in your hands. Can you teach me what I need to know?"

The man's face lit up. As he talked, his enthusiasm for the task was palpable. He paused when Mrs Allett came in with refreshments, and she smiled at them both like a fond mother.

The tankard of ale was most welcome. Beau had not been prepared for his steward to launch right in, and his head swam with all the information being relayed to him.

The housekeeper must have observed the glazed expression in his eyes. "Might I suggest you take his lordship for a tour around the grounds before dinner? I'm sure he would appreciate a chance to stretch his legs after being cooped up in a chaise on his journey from town."

Mr Harris was quick to seize the suggestion, and Beau sent Mrs Allett a grateful smile as she left the room. It was interesting to see how much respect his estate manager and his housekeeper had for each other. It said a lot about the characters of his two most important members of staff.

For the next five days, Beau threw himself into learning about his estate. Mrs Allett gave him a tour of the house, and he could tell from the way she spoke how much she loved the place. It had been built by his father to impress his guests, with a magnificent, pillared entrance and ornate stucco panels on the walls, designed by the renowned architect Robert Adam himself.

Although he would not have chosen such an ostentatious design, Beau thought he could get used to it, and as the stables were built on the same grand scale as the house, he became reconciled to living at the Park permanently. He just hoped Eliza would be there to share it with him.

Mr Harris proved a patient teacher and was as devoted to the Beaumont family's interests as his housekeeper. He had taken over as steward from his father a few years earlier and knew the land well, having lived on the estate all his life and if, at times, he bombarded his pupil with too much information, the man never complained about being asked to say something again.

Whenever Beau felt overwhelmed and tempted to give up, he reminded himself he was doing it for Eliza, and kept going.

As he learned more about his estate and what it meant to be a good landlord, she was never far from his mind. When Harris introduced his tenants, Beau remembered the easy way she had spoken to the West Meon villagers and adopted a similar tone.

His mother would not have approved, but he felt sure Eliza would, and he was rewarded with a friendly deference that augured well for the future.

On the sixth day, Mr Harris had a meeting that would take the entire morning, leaving Beau at liberty to amuse himself. To his surprise, he felt at a loss. To do anything for pleasure seemed a waste of time. It would not move him toward his purpose, and he was growing impatient.

He wanted to return to London and visit Eliza. Without her, it was all rather pointless.

Beau drifted through the rooms of his house, trying not to think about the woman he loved, and failing. Anthony would be concerned to see him choosing to be inside instead of out riding.

The trouble was that, though Romeo was safely in his stables, and all set to be a champion, the old joy had gone. Looking at his colt caused too much pain. The horse was a constant reminder of what Eliza had risked for him, and of the love he had thrown away through his own stupidity.

A wave of despair passed over him. Had she given up on him? What if he was too slow to prove himself and she gave her heart to another—someone far worthier?

He found himself in the long gallery, where portraits of his ancestors hung in a narrow room that stretched the full width of the house. He stopped in front of the same picture that always drew his gaze—that of his parents.

It was hard to reconcile the bitter feelings he had for his father with the warmth his old housekeeper exhibited toward the man Beau had never known.

"Why did you do it?" he said, looking up at his father's face, as if by speaking the words aloud he would receive an answer. "Why did you serve me such a poor turn, making me wait for my inheritance? Did you mean to make my life a misery, subjecting me to my mother's will for so long? Why did you do it? Didn't you love me either?"

"He loved you."

Beau turned to see Mrs Allett standing behind him at a respectful distance, staring up at the same portrait. He had been so absorbed, he had not heard her enter the gallery and felt the heat rush to his cheeks that she had found him ranting at a picture.

"He loved you," the housekeeper repeated, undisturbed by his odd behaviour. "Your father was delighted to have a son. Much to your mother's annoyance, he would steal you away from the nursery and take you to visit his horses. The stables were full of magnificent animals back then, and he loved them more than anything—until you came along.

"He would sit with me in the kitchen and beg me to admire his fine lad. 'He has horses in his blood, Allie. You should see how the little man reaches out his hands to stroke their manes.' Aye. He loved you sure enough. You meant the world to him."

"Then why, Mrs Allett? Why did he draw up a will that forced me to depend on my mother until I was twenty-five, or be thrust into marriage before I was ready?"

"If I can be so bold, your lordship, I suspect he wanted to save you from making the same mistake he made. Your father kept putting off taking a wife, and when he married, he chose a beautiful woman of good birth who was young enough to be his daughter. It was a brilliant match for her—but it was not happy. Her ladyship resented living a secluded life in the country and came to hate what her husband loved—his horses. She projected her unhappiness onto him, causing him to withdraw from her even more. I believe he thought marrying young was your best chance for happiness."

Beau shook his head in wonder. His father had drawn up his will that way for his benefit? That had never occurred to him before.

"I know things haven't worked out for you like his lordship intended, but find it in your heart to forgive him. Your father would have been grieved you did not grow up here, where you belong."

"What happened to his horses?" Beau asked, though he knew the answer already.

"Your mother sold them. His lordship was out hunting when he died. He took a fall while jumping a hedge and she blamed the horse for his death. That is what she told everyone. It was her excuse for emptying his stables, but it wasn't true. The doctor said your father's heart gave out."

Beau let out a deep sigh. "So it wasn't the horse's fault, or his mistake?"

"No. But though she got rid of his lordship's animals, it appears she failed to wean her son from his influence, even after his death. From all I've observed, I suspect you love horses as much as he did."

"You're right, Mrs Allett. I believe horses are in my blood, and my mother has always hated me for it. At least now I understand why."

His housekeeper went about her work, leaving him staring up at the face so like his own, with less animosity than before. He sensed a new connection with his father, whom Mrs Allett said had loved him. A man who hadn't died in a hunting accident, as his mother had told him, but had been doing what he loved when his time had come.

"I forgive you, Father. I realise you never meant this to happen. You didn't intend me to be sent away from my home or to be under my mother's power. You wanted me to break free, but I didn't understand. One day, I'll restore your stables to their former glory and Langcroft Park will be full of horses again. And God willing, my wife will love them as much as we do."

His spirit felt lighter than it had for a long time. Perhaps he would go for a ride after all.

Mounted on his powerful black stallion, Jet, he rode out across the estate. How he wished he had known his father. His life might have turned out so differently. He would not have had to fight to keep his horses. He would not have been forced to consider marriage to save them.

But then, he might never have fallen in love with Eliza. And he could not regret that, even though it was torture.

Beau was riding through the woods on his return to the house when he heard the gentle thud of hoofbeats on the bridle path behind him. How strange. What would bring an estate worker out this way? He couldn't guess, but that was no surprise. There was so much he didn't know.

He thought nothing of it until the rider following him whistled, as if to gain his attention.

As Beau turned to see who hailed him, something slammed into the back of his head.

He slumped in the saddle as everything went black.

# Chapter 48

Beau had been gone for almost a week, and Eliza had heard nothing. She was so desperate for news of him she would have plucked up the courage to ask his mother if the opportunity had arisen, but her ladyship kept her distance, as if she had finally accepted it was all over between them. The realisation depressed Eliza's spirits even more.

While the family was still at breakfast, a footman brought in a note for Georgiana. She broke open the seal and read the contents with a growing frown. "It's from Lady Harting."

Eliza flinched at hearing Beau's mother's name. It was hard not to blame the woman for her current misery.

"She has invited Charlotte and me—nay, commanded us—to attend a meeting of the Hampshire Ladies' Charity this afternoon. They are planning a musical benefit, and she wants to consult our opinion on various matters. I think we should go. Our aunt is an influential woman, and it would damage the charity greatly if she withdrew her support. Would you mind very much if we went, Eliza?"

"Of course not," she said, relieved her attendance wasn't required.

After her sisters had left for Harting House, Eliza sat in the drawing room alone, flicking over the pages of the latest issue of *La Belle Assemblée*, trying to find something of interest to read.

Unable to concentrate on anything, she was not sorry when a footman disturbed her. "Please excuse me, madam, but there is someone to see you."

Eliza was not used to receiving visitors on her own, but she welcomed the interruption. "Did they send up a card?"

"No, madam. Lady Castleford rarely invites persons of her class into her drawing room, so I've shown the female into the book room. She claims to be Lady Harting's personal maid."

Eliza screwed up her forehead in bewilderment. Reed was here—to see her? An unwelcome thought flew into her mind. Georgiana had gone to visit their aunt. Had there been an accident?

"I'll come at once."

She hurried to the book room where the servant waited. The maid looked white in the face and was twisting a handkerchief around in her fingers, as if she couldn't keep her hands still.

Eliza's heart pounded. "What's happened? Tell me at once."

"If you please, miss," the woman said, bobbing a curtsey. "Lady Harting asks that you come with me immediately. Lord Beaumont has had an accident. No one knows if he'll survive, but he keeps asking for you, so that he might make his peace with you before it's too late."

Eliza sat down heavily in the nearest chair, not trusting her legs to support her.

"Lord Beaumont is injured? How? Where?"

"There is no time to explain. You must come with me. We don't know how long he's got."

Eliza's head was in a whirl. Beau could not be dying. He just could not. The thought was unbearable.

A sob slipped out, but she choked it away. What a fool she'd been, refusing to see him—to forgive him—but there was no point in ruing her mistakes now. She must concentrate on the present. As long as he lived, there was a chance to be reconciled. And if she was too late, she would regret it for the rest of her life.

Eliza prayed like never before, begging forgiveness for her stubbornness and pleading with God to let Beau live so she could tell him she forgave him. That she loved him.

Tears filled her eyes, but she blinked them away. "I'll fetch my pelisse and hat and come immediately."

She rushed upstairs to her bedroom, but there was no sign of her maid. Bother. Where was the woman? She rang the bell for her, but by the time Eliza had dashed off a brief note to her sister, explaining what had happened, Sarah had still not appeared.

She grabbed her things and hurried back to the book room.

Reed stood, twitching her hands, but gave a weak smile at her return. "Are you ready, miss?"

"I can't find my maid…"

"Then we'd better leave without her, or we might be too—"

"Yes, yes, of course. Let's go. I don't need her, anyway. There can be no impropriety in travelling without her if you're with me."

After leaving the letter for her sister with the butler, she hurried down the steps and into the carriage, which was waiting for them. The footman closed the door, and a moment later, they were on their way.

Eliza realised she didn't know where they were going. The need for speed had swept away all other considerations, fearing any delay might be disastrous.

"Tell me what happened, Reed."

"It was a riding accident, miss, just like his father. That great brute of a black horse of his threw him."

Eliza ignored the disparaging remarks about Beau's stallion and instead latched onto the unlikelihood of the event. She hoped foul play was not at work.

"Are you sure? Jet would never throw him without provocation. I cannot believe it."

"Sorry, miss. I know little about horses."

"And his injuries?"

"His head. He was unconscious when they took him back to the house."

"What house? Where did it happen?"

"In the woods, close to Langcroft Park."

Eliza inhaled sharply. Then Beau hadn't returned to town. He was still on his estate in Beddington, and it would take them an hour or more to get there, following the route that her poor love had taken several days before. She hoped they would be in time. She must be.

One thing puzzled her. If Lady Harting had been called to Beau's bedside, why hadn't she sent word to her sister to cancel their meeting?

"When did the accident happen?"

"I'm not sure. Some hours ago, I think."

"And his mother went straight to him?"

"Yes, miss."

"Is she with him now?"

The maid looked down at her hands, as if embarrassed to answer Eliza's question.

"Reed?"

"His lordship hit his head, so you mustn't blame him."

"For what?"

"Sending his mother away."

Eliza blinked hard as her eyes watered. Even on his deathbed, he was asserting himself. Dare she hope he was doing it to please her?

"The doctor said her staying might cause him more harm than good, so she did what he asked and left. We drove back to London, and her ladyship sent me to fetch you and take you to him, as the man believed that would calm him."

Eliza hoped he was right.

They lapsed into silence as the horses pulled the carriage along the turnpike road at a spanking pace. As they neared their destination, she found it increasingly hard to sit still. She fiddled with the strap of her reticule as she kept praying, asking God to spare him.

Her heart raced as if she were trying to escape from a wild beast, but the only beast she needed to run from was fear. Her dread of being too late. Of Beau dying.

The carriage turned off the turnpike road and followed several lanes before passing under a stone arch and up the driveway to Langcroft Park. She was vaguely aware of the massive columns that fronted the house, but she was in no mood to admire the architecture.

With difficulty, she restrained herself from jumping down from the carriage the moment it stopped. A footman helped her alight, and she ran up the steps and through the impressive portico to the front entrance. She rang the bell and stood back to wait.

"If you please, miss, we must hurry," said Reed, moving past Eliza and pushing the door open without waiting for a servant to answer.

The maid led her up the main staircase, along a corridor, and into a large chamber. On the left was a huge four-poster bed that dominated the room, and in the middle of it lay an inanimate figure.

"Oh, my poor love," Eliza said, pulling off her bonnet and pelisse and letting out a sob. As she rushed to his bedside and took Beau's hands in her own, she heard the door click shut. She glanced behind her to discover Reed had left them alone. How tactful of her—though not altogether proper.

Eliza leaned over his still body and lowered her face to just above his. She was so close, she could feel his breath on her skin. He was alive! The tiniest of smiles crept onto her lips. If there was life, there was hope.

"I'm sorry for not believing you. For not trusting you. We all make mistakes, and I should have given you the chance to put things right.

Forgive me for embarrassing you by riding Romeo. I thought you wanted your freedom—but I don't want to be free of you. Please do not die. I love you so much."

She stroked the hair on his poor bruised head, trailing her hand down the side of his face and over the hint of dark stubble on his chin. With the tip of her finger, she traced the outline of his mouth, and then she leaned over a little further until their lips met.

The tears fell, unheeded, down her cheeks and onto his skin as she kissed him with a feather-light touch, which made her lips tingle.

One kiss was not enough.

Again, she lowered her mouth until it touched his—but this time, he kissed her back.

A whimper of joy escaped her at this encouraging sign. Cupping his face with her hand, she stroked his cheek with her thumb.

"Oh, Beau. Please stay with me. Don't die."

Beau lifted one eyelid. "Am I likely to?"

Eliza blinked away a tear and brushed a lock of hair away from his brow. "You hit your head. They told me you might not survive. You asked for me, so I came."

He opened the other eye and stared at her. "I did? Not that I don't want to see you—I do. I thought I must be dreaming when I woke up to your kisses. And, in case I don't get another chance, will you please forgive me for messing up and marry me? I wasn't just saying it. I love you. But I warn you, this time it's for keeps. I won't let you go again."

"Don't say that."

"But I love you."

"Not that bit, silly. I meant about not having another chance. You will get better. I'll make you well."

"Am I missing something?"

"You're confused."

"That's an understatement. The last thing I remember is riding in the woods and then...?"

Beau screwed up his face as if plumbing the depths of his mind, trying to find an answer.

"Jet threw you."

"What? No, I don't think so…"

He touched the back of his skull. "Ouch!" The jolt of pain seemed to awaken his memory. "Now I recall—someone hit me."

"Are you sure? Reed informed me you'd been thrown."

"Yes. I've got a lump on the back of my head the size of an egg, but my brain is not so addled I can't tell the difference between being tossed from my horse and being struck from behind."

Eliza frowned. "It surprised me when Reed told me Jet had thrown you, but I couldn't think straight. She made me think you were dying."

Beau pulled her into his arms, crushing her against his ribs as he devoured her lips, kissing her as if his very life depended on it. He drew back slightly and looked at her. "Now, will you believe me?"

Eliza wasn't sure what she was supposed to be believing, but at that moment, she didn't care. The unbearable tension that had gripped her since Reed had told her of Beau's accident dissipated.

Beau was alive—and he loved her.

Eyes closed, she leaned toward him again, and he pressed a succession of tantalisingly sweet kisses onto her lips, before claiming her mouth in a deeper embrace that left her breathless.

"You're not about to die, are you?"

"Not that I know of. I hope you're not disappointed."

"No!"

"But you were brought here under false pretences."

"Yes, I was."

"Hmm. The question is—why?"

He sat up in bed and surveyed the room. "Where is your maid?"

"You didn't seem to mind her absence a moment ago," Eliza said, shooting Beau a provocative look.

"Are you being careless with your reputation again? You shouldn't be in a bedchamber with a man who is *not* about to die, even the one you're going to marry. You *will* marry me, won't you? It would be the height of cruelty not to, especially as you've told me how much you love me—"

"You heard?"

Beau smirked. "Every word. I thought it was a dream, and I didn't want it to stop. Well? Will you?"

"Yes," she said, grinning from ear to ear.

He leaned forward and kissed the dimple on her chin. "I've been wanting to do that for a long time. And this…and this…and this," he said, punctuating his words with kisses. He stroked the side of her face as she'd just done to him, and brushed his fingertips across her lips before once more pressing his mouth to hers.

At length he drew back. "Now, before I forget myself, you'd better go. As you went to such lengths to free me from marrying you out of duty, it would be a shame if we were forced to wed because I had compromised your reputation. I need you, Eliza Merry, to be certain I love you, and want you to be my wife because I can't live without you, and not because anyone is telling me I must marry you."

Eliza pouted. She had no wish to leave, but she supposed Beau had a point. With considerable reluctance, she walked across the room and turned the knob, but the door didn't budge. Thinking she had twisted it the wrong way, she moved it in the opposite direction, but it still refused to open.

"It's stuck."

Beau's eyes narrowed and a heavy frown creased his brow.

"What's the matter? Why are you glowering like that?"

He pursed his lips together, spitting out his next words in disgust. "Stuck or locked?"

# Chapter 49

BEAU ALREADY KNEW THE answer to his own question. The door was locked. All the pieces were falling into place in his mind. This was what his mother had been planning. Not content to leave him to work things out for himself, she had forced them together.

His glance fell on Eliza and his expression softened. He could not be sorry she'd come, but to have brought her here under false pretences—to have played on her emotions like that—was cruel, and it would be hard to forgive his mother for that.

He peeked under the bedclothes and was relieved to discover he was dressed, apart from his jacket and boots. After thrusting back the covers, he jumped out of bed and walked over to the door to try the knob for himself. It didn't budge.

"As I suspected. Locked."

"I don't understand. How can it be locked? We should call for Reed."

"She won't answer."

"Why not?"

"Because it was her who shut us in. Don't you see? This is all my mother's doing. She is so set on my marrying you she took the decision out of our hands. By the time we get out of this bedchamber, you'll be compromised in the eyes of the world and have no option but to become my wife or retire to a nunnery."

"I contemplated that," Eliza said with a wicked smile, "but I didn't suppose I'd be allowed to hunt if I became a nun."

Beau kissed the end of her nose. "Wretch." From her nose, it seemed natural to move to her lips, and it was a few minutes before he could resume his train of thought.

"Despite evidence to the contrary, I dislike having my hand forced. I don't want you or anyone else to doubt that I'm marrying you of my own free will. How can I prove you're my choice of bride if it's my inescapable duty to wed you?"

"How do you know I didn't plan all this to make you compromise me, so you'd have to marry me?"

"You have a point there. After all, a lady who rides astride in a public horserace must consider it a mere trifle to force a gentleman into compromising her reputation."

Eliza turned a deep shade of red. "That was uncalled for. You know I would never stoop so low as to plan something like this, though I doubt Horrible Harriet would have passed up the opportunity."

Beau chuckled. "Is that what you christened her? To marry The Honourable Harriet Whitlow was a fate I shuddered to contemplate. I never even thought of her except how to avoid her attentions. You are the only woman I've ever wanted to make my wife."

Eliza rewarded his words with another kiss. "What are we going to do?"

"I could keep kissing you until we're rescued."

"The prospect is enticing," said Eliza, pecking his forehead, and then his nose.

"Far too enticing," Beau said, putting some distance between them. He walked across the room to the windows, which looked out onto the formal gardens. "I think we'd better concentrate on getting out of here. Fortunately, I like to sleep with a window ajar, so unless our captors have secured it, this one should open."

As he spoke, he turned the handle of the left-hand casement, opened it wide and peered over the edge. "There's a portico along this side of the house, but it's too far below us to reach safely."

"I don't suppose you keep a rope in here?"

"No. We'll have to improvise. If we string the bedding together, that should give me enough length to reach the roof of the portico, and there is a sturdy wisteria beside it which I can climb down. Once I'm free, I'll slip into the house and unlock this door—"

"I'm coming with you."

"It's too dangerous."

Eliza raised her eyebrows. "More dangerous than riding in a horserace?"

"Huh! I can see I'm going to have my work cut out keeping you safe." He shot her a lopsided grin. "Very well. We'll go together."

They stripped the bed and Beau knotted the sheets together as tightly as he could.

"I'm impressed you know about the wisteria," Eliza said. "I wouldn't recognise one if I saw it."

He barked with laughter. "Neither would I, but the inspection of my property is paying off. The estate manager has proved most willing to teach me and is a very thorough gentleman. Harris pointed it out as a well-established plant we would not wish to uproot, and I assume he knew what he was talking about."

Beau tied one end of the sheet rope around the bed post nearest the window and pushed the rest through the opening.

"I'm afraid it's not quite long enough," he said, eyeing the other end, which was dangling several feet short of the surface below them. "I'll go first and catch you when you climb down. Can you clamber over the windowsill by yourself?"

Eliza shot him a saucy grin. "It's no different from sneaking out of my window at home to join the hunt—apart from these petticoats."

"Ah yes. The first time I met Mr Robson."

"Did you never guess?"

"I refused to believe a lady could control such a horse—but I was wrong."

"Anthony realised—and has teased me about it ever since."

"Do you appreciate how jealous you made me, laughing with him when you withheld your smiles from me?"

"Jealous of Anthony? How absurd. Why, he's like a brother to me."

Beau did not think it helpful to tell her just how unbrotherly his friend's feelings toward her had been. Anyway, that was a thing of the past. It must be. Eliza was going to marry him.

"I'll need to borrow a pair of...um...inexpressibles," she said, refusing to meet his eyes as the colour rushed to her face. "I don't think I can climb down in this dress."

Beau's mouth dropped open, and in silence, he retrieved some breeches from his dressing room and handed them to Eliza. She disappeared from view and, as she returned a few moments later without them, he assumed she had put them on underneath her petticoats. What a remarkable woman she was!

"You'll have to undo my dress," she whispered, turning away from him as another wave of colour flooded her cheeks.

Beau's fingers fumbled with the buttons as he tried to concentrate on the urgency of the situation, and not on what he was doing. If anyone discovered them now, they would have good reason to suppose he had compromised her. He needed to get her out of here. Fast.

As soon as he finished, he fled to the window, eased himself over the sill and climbed down the sheet rope. He dropped safely onto the roof of the portico and looked up just in time to avoid being hit by his boots, which came flying out of the window after him. Eliza continued to bombard him with pieces of clothing—his jacket followed by her shoes, hat and pelisse—and finally her dress, which spread out like a parachute over his head.

Beau was still struggling to disentangle himself when his intrepid bride landed beside him. Her cheeks blazing with colour, she grabbed her robe and threw it over the edge before scampering to the end of the portico's roof and climbing down the wisteria.

By the time he had thrown down the rest of the clothes and joined her, Eliza was standing with her back to him, waiting for him to button up her dress.

Unable to resist, he placed a kiss on the bare skin at the bottom of her neck, and she shivered delightfully under his touch.

"I think we should marry soon," he said in a voice husky with emotion as he refastened her dress.

"I agree."

They gathered their scattered garments and while they made themselves respectable, Beau contemplated what they should do. "I need some answers."

He took her hand and led her to a small clump of trees near the stables. "Stay here while I investigate."

Eliza opened her mouth to object, but he forestalled her, putting a finger over her lips as he stared down into her pale blue eyes. "Please don't argue. I love you and I'm trying to protect you."

He leaned toward her and let his lips brush hers in the tenderest of kisses. "I couldn't live with myself if something happened to you. I promise I'll come back for you when I see how the land lies."

She nodded to let him know she would do as he bid, and he headed for the stables.

Beau gazed around the yard and frowned. It was empty apart from a lad who was reclining on a hay bale, whistling. He recognised him as one of his mother's grooms.

"Where is everybody, Jensen?" he asked, making the young man jump.

He leapt to his feet, full of apologies. "I'm sorry, your lordship. I didn't know you was here. Reed said as how I could have the afternoon off…"

"Did she? And do you normally take orders from a maid?"

"No, my lord, but Lady Harting told me I was to do so today."

"You say you weren't aware I was here?"

"No, your lordship. There weren't anyone here when we arrived. Just Reed and the lady in the carriage who she said was going to be your missus. She told me to see to the horses and then I could have the rest of the day off, but I had nowhere to go, so I stayed here."

Beau rubbed his chin as he processed the lad's words. There was no one here? Where were his grooms? Had they suffered the same fate as he had and been hit over the head?

A brief inspection of the stables showed him Jet had incurred no injury from his supposed fall and Romeo was untouched, but his bays were missing and there was no sign of his staff.

Think. He must think. Servants talked. To preserve Eliza's reputation, he needed to choose his words carefully, and he wasn't skilled at that.

"I am delighted to learn that…um…Miss Merry is here, though I didn't expect her so soon. She has…um…come to look at her future home and give me her…opinions on some alterations I am considering, but it is a pity my mother could not accompany her. My betrothed can't stay in the house without a chaperon, and will have to return to London tonight. Please prepare my mother's carriage for the journey."

"Very good, my lord."

"And Jensen? Who drove here today?"

"I don't rightly know, your lordship. It weren't the normal coachman."

"Oh? And where is he now? Has he been given the afternoon off, too?"

"Nah. He's up at the house kissing her ladyship's maid. I saw them when I slipped into the kitchen to see if I could find something to eat."

"I hope Mrs Allett fed you."

"Weren't nobody there. Think they must all have the day off."

"Ah well. Harris probably thought they weren't needed. My plans changed at the last minute. How inconvenient. Could you fetch him if I told you where he lived?" Beau asked, holding out a coin.

Jensen required no more encouragement and sped off toward his steward's cottage.

Now for the troublesome duo up at the house.

For a moment he considered confronting them alone, but then he thought of his plucky bride and a lopsided grin crept onto his face.

His Eliza was equal to anything.

They would deal with this together.

# Chapter 50

ELIZA PLUCKED ANOTHER LEAF off the tree and pulled it to pieces. Why was Beau taking so long? Had someone else hit him over the head?

At last, she saw him coming out of the stable yard and had difficulty restraining herself from running to meet him.

He relayed the conversation he'd had with Jensen. "The only people in the house are Reed and the coachman."

"So no one was there to rescue us if we hollered?"

Beau tilted her chin up toward him and gazed down into her eyes. "No, my naïve little puss. To rescue *you*. No one would think twice about rescuing a gentleman from a compromising situation."

"Oh, I see. What are we going to do?"

"Get you out of here. I've ordered Jensen to prepare the carriage for the return journey, but first, let's find out what this pair of miscreants is up to."

They entered the house at the rear, crept along the passage past the housekeeper's room and kitchen, and up the back stairs. The building was swathed in eery silence.

"Quietly, now," Beau said. "I don't want them to come upon us unawares. Though I doubt they'd risk a direct attack, we must remember it's likely this man hit me over the head."

He pushed open a semi-hidden entrance in the wall in front of him and disappeared inside. Eliza followed him into a starkly decorated hallway.

"I'm surprised you found time to investigate the servants' passages when you've only been back for a few days," she whispered, closing the door behind her.

"I told you Harris was thorough."

They moved down the passage in silence, listening for any noise that might help locate Reed and the coachman. When they were level with the drawing room, Eliza heard voices.

Beau motioned to her to retrace her steps part way along the corridor. "If I've judged correctly, we should be outside the tapestry chamber."

They stood at the door and listened for the sound of any movement within.

He turned toward her. "Scared?"

"Of course not. I'm with you."

He gave a low chuckle. "Every other lady of my acquaintance would have a fit of the vapours, but not you. I believe you're enjoying this adventure."

They shared a grin as he squeezed her hand.

"Not a noise," he said, opening the door in front of them. As predicted, it was the tapestry chamber—and it was empty.

The entrance to the drawing room stood ajar and through it came the unmistakable sound of laughter. Beau manoeuvred his position so he could survey the area, and then moved away so Eliza could look.

Peeping through the gap, she spied Reed and a man snuggled up on a chaise longue, enjoying a bottle of port. *Beau's* port. As he turned, she saw his face, and stifled a gasp. She recognised him.

Eliza grabbed Beau's hand and hurried back down the passage, almost dragging him behind her. After putting some distance between them and the interlopers, she stopped.

"What is it?" he asked. "You look as if you've seen a ghost."

"That man. He helped steal Romeo."

Beau gaped in surprise.

"I saw him the day we found your colt and thought he seemed familiar, but I couldn't recall where I'd seen him before until now. It was when I was going to meet you for an early morning ride. I almost bumped into Reed on my way out of the house, and that man was hurrying away from what I supposed was a lovers' tryst. It seems I was right. But fancy her being entangled with a thief. Do you think she knows?"

For several moments, Beau did not answer, but his eyes took on a distant look, and his expression turned from one of surprise to something far less pleasant.

"Stop it. You're scaring me. Your eyes are so fierce they might burst into flames."

Eliza raised a palm to his cheek and held it there until he looked down at her. The ferocity disappeared as quickly as it had come.

"I'm sorry," he said, kissing her hand. "It's just that...this is the last piece of the puzzle, and I don't like the finished picture. That man is not a common thief—he's following orders. My mother's orders. She planned it all. She stole Romeo to force me to wed to fund my horses. When that didn't work, she arranged this ruse, tricking you into coming here, so you would be compromised, and I would be obliged to marry you.

"She knew I wouldn't ignore such an obligation, even though I no longer needed the money. To think of the humiliation she was prepared to put you through to get her own way. Our loss of dignity and the right to choose our own path. I'll never forgive her—"

"Don't speak like that, Beau. It was wrong—very wrong—of her, but you must forgive her, or it will destroy you."

"Hmm. If you say so."

"If you don't, it will be you who suffers for it, not her. My sister said if I held onto unforgiveness, it would eat me up inside, like a cankerous worm. If I had been quicker to forgive you for hurting me, this ruse would never have been necessary."

"But if she hadn't stolen Romeo, Jem would have ridden him to success, and you would not have risked so much for me. We would have been spared weeks of heartache—"

Eliza grasped his hands. "I know it's painful, but you must let it go."

"I expect you're right, but it will be so very hard to forgive my mother for what she's done."

"Now, what about Reed and her man? Isn't it time we dealt with them?"

"We? I'll deal with them. I don't want to risk you getting injured."

She pouted. "Please don't send me away."

"Is it always going to be this difficult to look after you?"

"Probably," she said with a mischievous smile.

"I'll go round to the gallery, and enter from there. You can watch from the tapestry chamber doorway, but don't come in. It could become unpleasant if Reed's accomplice gets handy with his fists. If either of them heads your way, slip back into the servants' corridor. Promise?"

Eliza nodded. It was a compromise, but at least she wasn't being banished. She positioned herself so she had a clear view of the action and waited.

A few minutes later, Beau flung open the opposite door of the drawing room. Reed and the man jumped to their feet. The two miscreants glanced at each other in horror before turning to face him.

"Your lordship," said her aunt's maid in a voice laced with alarm. "What are you doing up? You should still be in bed."

"Come now. Surely you didn't really believe I was on my deathbed. I admit my head is sore, but I assume I have your companion to thank for that."

She looked at the man standing beside her, who shot her a warning glance.

"There's no need for secrecy. I know my mother engineered this little charade."

"What do you—"

Beau held up his hand to forestall her. "I don't want to hear your excuses, nor any defence for this piece of cruelty—yes, cruelty. To force people into a course of action they have not chosen for themselves is both cruel and wicked."

"I was only following my orders—"

"What about your own sense of right and wrong? It was your lies, not my mother's, that brought Miss Merry to my side. As I am not on my deathbed, I wish to return her to her sister's house before she is distressed any further. Though I am grieved to admit it, I need your services to accompany her back to London—for propriety's sake. Wait out the front. I'll bring the carriage around shortly. And I suggest you pray Miss Merry is more merciful toward you than you deserve, or it will be a most uncomfortable trip."

"Yes, my lord," Reed said, hurrying out the door which Beau had entered.

Her accomplice remained, staring at the floor.

"Your services, however, I am happy to dispense with. I won't have a thief in my house."

The man jerked his eyes up, disturbed by Beau's accusation.

"I know you stole Romeo, as well as whacking me over the head, but I'm willing to offer you some leniency as you were acting under orders and my horse was returned to me unharmed. Now, get off my property before I change my mind and summon the constable to arrest you."

The man needed no second warning and fled after Reed.

As soon as he'd gone, Eliza rushed into the room and threw her arms around Beau. "You were magnificent."

He started to disclaim, but she put a finger to his lips. "No. Don't say anything. I'm proud of you, Lord Beaumont."

At her words, he raised his chin a little and, setting his shoulders back, he offered her his arm, and led her to the foot of the main staircase.

"We'd better see about returning you to London, to avert the wagging tongues. It would be a shame if your reputation was ruined when we've taken such pains to preserve it."

Eliza pouted. "Reputations are overrated. Why does it matter when we're planning to marry, anyway?"

"Because I don't wish for the slightest slur to fall upon my wife, and I won't have it said you forced me into marriage, or worse still, that my mother did. Please—it's important to me."

Eliza's shoulders slumped. "I know, but the thought of having to go back to that"—she waved her hands around, trying to find the words to encompass her negative thoughts about town—"closed-in-ness is depressing. I want to stay here. With you."

"I wish you could, but I don't see how you can until after we're married without my mother or some other respectable female here."

"Like Harriet?"

"No. Not like Harriet. I wouldn't trust her within a mile of me until we've tied the knot."

They both laughed.

"Why don't you join Reed outside while I remove the evidence of our escape?"

Eliza nodded and wandered out the front entrance and sat down on the steps leading up to the pillared courtyard to wait for Beau. She basked in the afternoon sunshine while her aunt's maid stood at a respectful distance, a tight expression on her face, and her hands in constant movement.

"I expect my mother will be surprised when you return tonight, won't she?" Beau said to Reed as he joined them. He paused. "When *was* she expecting to see you again?"

"Tomorrow, my lord."

"Where?"

The woman did not reply.

"Come on. Out with it."

"Her ladyship is coming here in the morning."

"Oh!" Eliza exclaimed, as realisation dawned. "My aunt planned to witness my humiliation. How...despicable."

"Quite so, my love—"

He broke off as a gentleman approached whom she guessed must be the estate manager. She jumped up from her somewhat undignified position on the steps and stood beside Beau.

"Thank you for coming so promptly, Mr Harris," he said.

"Fortunately, I was at home, but I confess I was not expecting to see you today. I was told"—he cast a sour glance at Reed—"you were riding to London, and sent your men to meet you there. I hope I did not get the wrong message."

"Not at all. I had a last-minute change of plans. This," he said, drawing Eliza forward, "is Miss Merry, who has done me the very great honour of agreeing to be my wife."

If the man was surprised, he did not show it, but bowed toward her, and hastened to offer his congratulations. "I am mortified I had no warning you were coming."

"Please do not blame yourself," she said, giving him a dazzling smile. "I was so impatient to see Lord Beaumont, I failed to inform anyone of my plans—not even him—and we almost missed each other. Now I find I've come a day too early, as her ladyship doesn't arrive until tomorrow, so I'll have to return to London tonight. How tedious! Beaumont has spoken so highly of you I'm sure we can rely on you to hire a full complement of staff and have everything in order by the time we return."

Mr Harris looked somewhat dazed, but accepted his dismissal without question, and disappeared into the house.

Beau sent Reed to the stables to wait for them in the carriage and turned to Eliza, drawing her so close she could feel his breath on her neck. "You were splendid."

"It would seem we bring out the best in each other."

"I would much prefer it if you could stay here with me, but if we're going to salvage your reputation, you must return to your sister's house tonight."

"I wish I hadn't got a reputation to save," said Eliza, pouting. "Are you sure I am respectable enough to be a viscountess?"

"You'll be a perfect viscountess—my viscountess."

He wrapped his arms around her and pulled her flush against him, dropping a feather-light kiss on her mouth. "Have you got the message yet, my darling? I adore you. I can't live without you. And I'm never, ever, going to let you go."

Eliza's eyes glowed with warmth as she curled her arm around his neck and brought his lips down on hers again, in a deeper, more satisfying embrace.

If only she didn't have to return to London, she would be perfectly happy.

# Chapter 51

LAUGHTER ERUPTED NEARBY. ELIZA broke away from Beau's embrace as heat flooded her face.

She recognised that laugh. Anthony.

Eliza had been so preoccupied she hadn't heard his carriage coming down the drive—except it wasn't his carriage, but Beau's, pulled by all four of his bays.

"What are you doing here?" her intended asked. "And why are you driving my horses?"

His friend handed the reins to the sheepish-looking man sat next to him, whom Eliza recognised as one of Beau's grooms, and jumped down from the box seat. Without waiting for orders, the man drove the vehicle toward the stables.

"I came to rescue you—but it doesn't look as though you need my help," Anthony said with a smirk. "Your valet pestered me to come down here, convinced you'd suffered an accident. Then I called at my brother's and found the household in complete disarray. Charlotte was in hysterics, and Georgie was beside herself, fearing Eliza had been lured away under false pretences by claims that you were dying. Everybody seemed to think you were in dire need of help—but it seems they were mistaken. I take it that congratulations are in order. If not, I shall have to knock you down."

Eliza glared at him. "Don't you dare. Of course we're going to be married, and it would be most unfair as he's already been injured once today."

"Then you *did* have an accident?"

"Yes. I got in the way of someone hitting me over the head."

"Ouch."

"Yes, and if we do not get Eliza back to her sister's house tonight, all my efforts at saving her reputation will be worthless."

Anthony raised his eyebrows in disbelief. "All your efforts? You looked as though—"

"My mother's carriage is waiting in the stable yard, with her maid inside. We were about to leave but we got…distracted."

"Quite understandable. If I'd won the hand of such a woman, I would be just as distracted."

A curious look passed between them that Eliza did not fully understand, but then Anthony nodded, and Beau's face relaxed into a smile.

"However, the delay is fortuitous," Ant said. "Georgie will arrive within the hour."

Eliza's eyes widened in surprise. "My sister's coming here?"

He chuckled. "She thought your reputation was in danger, and judging by the way the pair of you were behaving when I arrived, I quite see her point."

Another wave of heat rushed to Eliza's face, but Beau put his arm around her and gave her a comforting hug. "It seems you'll get your wish. You won't have to return to London after all."

They entered the house to discover the steward had been busy. Somehow, Mr Harris had recalled all the staff, and a footman was on duty in the hall, ready to receive Anthony's coat and hat.

"We should let the housekeeper know we have guests," said Eliza. "She will want to prepare the bedchambers. I hope she won't hand in her notice having to cater for so many people without warning."

Beau grinned. "Yes. We should inform her *we* have guests. Stepping up to your duties already, my love?"

"I thought—"

"I'm teasing you. And you need not fear her leaving. Mrs Allett belongs to the Park."

The housekeeper entered the room in time to hear Beau's words and nodded in agreement. "Very true, your lordship."

She bore a tray bearing two tankards of ale and a glass of lemonade, which she placed on a table. "Am I to understand you're expecting more guests, my lord?"

"Yes."

"And do you know how many bedchambers will be required?" she asked in a calm voice, without the slightest trace of irritation.

He shrugged and looked at Anthony for guidance. "How many of Eliza's family are coming?"

"I should expect the lot of them."

Beau shot Mrs Allett an apologetic grimace.

"Very good, my lord," she said, with the glimmer of a smile.

Eliza drank her lemonade, basking in the joy of knowing she no longer needed to return to town, while Beau explained to Anthony what had happened.

At the mention of Reed's name, she jumped to her feet. "Oh heavens. No one's told her of our change in plans. My aunt's maid must still be sitting in the carriage waiting for us."

"Let her! It went against the grain to show her as much leniency as we granted her."

Eliza pressed her lips together, a pleading look in her eyes. "We don't know what it's like working for your mother. Yes, Reed could have shown more compassion, but her employer didn't set a high standard for her to emulate. By showing grace to those who wish us harm, we may turn them from their evil ways."

Beau harrumphed. "I suppose."

Eliza rewarded him with a brilliant smile. "She's not the only one who's had a poor example to follow."

"You're right, of course," he said, letting out a reluctant laugh.

A footman disturbed them. "Are you at home to visitors, my lord?"

He responded in the affirmative and the man scurried away.

"Your sisters must have arrived."

She nodded, and with difficulty restrained herself from rushing to reassure Charlotte, whom she knew would have worked herself up into a frenzy of worry by now.

The door to the drawing room opened again. "Her Grace, the Duchess of Wessex, Mr—"

"Yes, yes. They know who we are," said the Duchess, batting the footman away with her fan. Eliza's grandmother glided into their midst, followed by her parents, her brother and her youngest sister.

Eliza leapt to her feet, staring at her relatives, unable to believe her eyes. Beau stood beside her, gaping, but whether in surprise or horror, she couldn't tell.

Anthony rose in a more leisurely manner and bowed.

"Grandmama," Eliza said, dipping into a deep curtsey.

"Oh tush." She wrapped her arms around her granddaughter and gave her an affectionate hug. "Now, where's this scamp you're supposed to be marrying?"

Eliza cast Beau a pleading look, and he stepped forward.

He took the regal old lady's hand and bowed low over it. "Your Grace."

The Duchess rapped his knuckles with her fan. "Yes, yes. I know you're a charmer, but does she want you?"

"Mother—" said Mrs Merry in a warning tone.

She ignored her daughter and kept her eyes fixed on Beau, as if examining him. Though he hadn't offered it, she took his arm and leaned heavily on it. "Help me to a chair, boy."

Eliza planted a kiss on her father's cheek. "I don't understand. What...why...how on earth do you come to be here?"

He drew his brows together and gave her a curious look. "Weren't you expecting us?"

"No."

Hetta crossed her arms in a self-satisfied manner. "I told you so."

Eliza shot Beau a questioning glance, but he merely shrugged his shoulders.

Her mother enveloped her in a warm embrace, and whispered in her ear, "Is all well?"

A smile crept over Eliza's face as she nodded. "Yes, Mother. All is very well."

"I am delighted to hear it, but somewhat confused. If you were not expecting us, you have no notion that Lady Harting invited us here to celebrate your nuptials. Tomorrow."

Eliza felt the colour drain out of her cheeks as she appreciated the full horror of her aunt's plans. Beau's mother had asked them to come. If they hadn't escaped from his bedroom, they would have been found in a compromising situation, not only by her parents, but also by her grandmother.

The embarrassment would have been...unthinkable.

"She what?" Beau said, sounding as outraged as Eliza felt.

William glared at Anthony. "You told me the match was off."

"It was," Ant replied with a chuckle.

Beau squeezed Eliza's hand. "But not anymore," he whispered in her ear, making her glow with pleasure.

"Hmm," said Hetta, staring at her. "You don't look as if you're being coerced into marriage."

"We're not, but..." Eliza shot Beau a pained glance and took a deep breath when he nodded. "...my aunt wanted to make sure of that."

"Lady Harting is as unprincipled as ever her mother-in-law was," the Duchess said, looking as if she had just sucked on a slice of lemon. "No heart. I'll not let her force my granddaughter into a marriage she does not desire—"

"But I do desire it, Grandmama. I think we'd better explain what happened today."

Before they could start, Georgiana swept into the room unannounced, followed by her husband and Charlotte. "Hold that thought. You may as well tell us all at once, and I insist on having a cup of tea to drink while I listen."

Everyone except the Duchess rose to their feet again to greet the newcomers. Once the bustle was over, and the party seated and served with tea, Beau took his place beside Eliza, and clasped her hand in his own. Between them, they told their story, each interrupting when the other was too hard on themselves.

"What madness," said Charlotte, when they reached the end of their tale, "to ride in a horserace. You might have been killed—"

"That's all I could think about," said Beau. "The trouble was, I couldn't convince your sister I was angry at myself for putting her in such danger. I never imagined—"

"I should have let you talk to me—" said Eliza, interrupting her betrothed and addressing him as if there was no one else in the room.

"But if I'd behaved more honourably and not tried to avoid getting married—"

"I should have been readier to forgive—"

"And I should have admitted how much I loved you instead of being afraid—"

Mr Merry held up his palm. "Enough. I am convinced you are deeply in love with each other. More than that, I see you are already working well as a team. I came here with deep misgivings, prepared to refuse to perform the ceremony, fearing you were being pushed into a marriage neither of you was ready for. But given what I have just observed, I no longer have any qualms. I will marry you tomorrow, if you desire it."

They glanced at each other and grinned.

"We'd like that. I believe Lord Harting and my mother arrive in the morning—"

"No."

All eyes turned to the Duchess.

Eliza's heart plummeted. Whilst she didn't need her grandmother's permission, it stung that she disapproved of her choice.

"I'm going to marry him, Grandmama, whether or not you approve," she said, a touch of ferocity in her voice.

"Yes, yes, of course, but I refuse to stay under the same roof as *that woman* after what she's done. I must be gone before she arrives. Huh! To think people called me conniving. If I remain, I might say something we'd all regret. No. There's nothing for it. The wedding will have to be tonight."

Her words were met by silence.

"Well? Is there a problem with that, Christopher? Can it be done?"

"Only with a special licence," Eliza's father said. "I assumed my brother would bring it."

"Fortunately, that's not the case." Beau retrieved a paper from his jacket pocket, where he had kept it close to his heart, and waved it in the air triumphantly. "I have it right here."

Mr Merry examined the document. "All is in order. I can marry you this evening, if you wish."

"Why wouldn't they wish it?" The Duchess stared at Eliza, her eyebrows raised. "You told me you were determined to wed him, whether or not I liked it. Why not marry him tonight? It's a shame he's only a viscount, but I daresay you'll rub along nicely together. I understand you've grown rather good at breeding horses, Beaumont. I expect a Derby winner or two from your stables."

Beau bowed his head. "I'll do my best."

"Hmm. Yes, I'm sure you'll do fine—despite your upbringing. Now that's sorted, perhaps someone will put their mind to such trivial details as dinner. I trust your household can cope with feeding all of us at such short notice?"

"Mrs Allett is equal to anything," said Beau. "We'll speak to her at once."

He grabbed Eliza by the hand, and they almost ran out of the room. Once in the corridor, he stopped and gazed down into her eyes with such warmth that it stole her breath away.

"Are you sure you want to get married tonight? If you'd prefer to wait and wed in your father's church, I'm prepared to cope with your grandmother's disapproval."

"I see no reason to delay, but what about you? Grandmama can be rather forceful, and if she is rushing you—"

Beau didn't let her finish her sentence, claiming her mouth with his own.

# Chapter 52

THE NEXT MORNING, BEAU awoke with a smile on his lips, and Eliza snuggled up beside him. For years, his mother had pushed and prodded, threatened and manipulated him, but in the end, he had reached this point of his own free will.

Eliza was his wife, and he was the happiest man alive.

As he kissed her cheek, she snaked her arm around his neck and drew him toward her. Their lips met in a caress filled with such promise that it almost turned him from his purpose.

He pulled away, his breathing ragged, as he uttered a single word: "Mother."

In an instant, his beloved's face was transformed, and she leapt out of bed with no further prompting, and dived into his dressing room.

A few minutes later, the now-familiar sight of a slim youth in breeches pranced in front of him.

Eliza's cheeks were tinted pink. "I hope you don't mind, but I've no habit with me and I desperately need to ride. The thought of facing your mother is—unnerving."

Beau chuckled. "I'd like to see her face if you met her like that. I can just hear her. *That's not suitable attire for a viscountess*," he said, mimicking her voice.

She attempted a smile, but he could tell his teasing had not reassured his wife. He put his arms around her waist and drew her close. "You've nothing to fear from her. I'll look after you."

"You'd better, or my grandmother will have something to say about it. You promised."

"However, I'm uncertain I approve of your attire."

Her face fell. "Oh? I thought...I hoped...too many uncomfortable memories?"

"On the contrary. It is most distracting, and I feel rather possessive. I'm not sure I want my wife displaying her legs for other men to see."

"Then you have no other objections?"

Beau shook his head. "It's part of who you are, my gorgeous, reckless wife—and I love you. All of you. Besides, I have a distinct advantage over other men. You're mine."

"Yes. I am."

With these words, a grin spread across Eliza's face, bringing out the dimple in her chin.

"I'll meet you in the stables as soon as this ordeal is over," he said, pressing his lips to hers one last time before she slipped out the room.

Once dressed for riding, Beau too left his bedroom, pocketing the key and shutting the door behind him. He stationed himself by a window overlooking the drive, so he knew the moment his mother arrived.

Even if he had not seen her carriage draw up, he would have known as soon as she entered the house. Beau cringed as her voice drifted up the stairs.

"Where is my son? I heard he had an accident. Take me to him."

"I'm not sure his lordship would—"

"Remember your place, Mrs Allett," his mother snapped, making Beau cringe with embarrassment. He would apologise to his loyal retainer later for subjecting her to his parent's poor manners.

He watched from a discreet distance as his housekeeper appeared at the top of the stairs, followed closely by Lady Harting. His temper bubbled up inside of him as he saw his mother enter his bedchamber without so much as a single knock.

He strode along the corridor and stopped at the threshold of his room. From the doorway, he could see her staring at the empty bed.

"I don't understand. Where is my son?"

"Right behind you, Mother," Beau said, strolling through the doorway. "I'm sorry if you travelled all the way from London to tend to me when it was no more than a bump on the head." He caught her eyes with a mocking stare. "I'm hardly dying, after all."

Lady Harting turned an alarming shade of red. "It would seem I've been misinformed."

He stepped forward and took her arm. "Come and sit down. You've suffered a shock and been in a needless worry about me. Mrs Allett will pour you a strong cup of coffee, and you'll soon be feeling more the thing."

His over-demanding parent did not make a habit of raking him down in front of an audience, and so Beau was able to lead her downstairs again to the breakfast room.

His housekeeper returned to her duties and left him alone with his mother.

"I trust you are fully recovered from your accident. When I received word that—"

"Don't," he said, interrupting her flow. "Don't lie to me anymore. It would have been ironic if your minion had hit me on the head a little too hard and killed me, don't you think?"

"I do not understand what you are talking about."

"There is no need for you to admit what you've done. It is enough that I know. Stealing Romeo. Arranging for me to have an 'accident'. Making Eliza believe I was dying, when all the while it was a ruse to trap her into marriage."

She opened her mouth, but he wouldn't allow her to speak. "No, Mother. Let me finish. What were you thinking of? I don't want a wife who has been tricked into marrying me. What kind of man do you think I am?"

Beau gazed into her eyes, looking for an iota of understanding, but there was none. Her expression was unyielding.

"If you will excuse me, I'm going riding with Eliza."

Her countenance lit up. "Elizabeth is here?"

"You know very well she is."

"I am glad to hear you have resolved your differences, but now is not the time to go riding. You should be preparing for the ceremony."

"There will be no wedding today."

His mother's expression hardened. "No wedding? Are you lost to all sense of propriety? Elizabeth's reputation will be ruined."

Her shock was obvious, but he did not rush to allay her fears. He allowed himself to relish just the smallest amount of revenge for all the heartache she had caused.

"Eliza's grandmother insisted she should not be forced into marriage against her will. The Duchess was adamant."

"The Duchess of Wessex is here?"

For the first time, Beau heard a note of uncertainty in his mother's voice.

"Was. Yesterday. She left after dinner, once affairs had been arranged to her liking."

"I see."

"I doubt it," said Beau, turning away to hide the half-smile that had crept onto his lips, and skipping down the stairs like a schoolboy at the end of lessons.

His mother did not give up. She followed him all the way to the stable yard, where Beau halted.

"Regardless of what the Duchess says, you'll have to marry Eliza. I won't advance you a penny out of your inheritance to fund your horses."

"That is no longer your decision. The trust will soon be drawn to a close and you need not concern yourself with my financial affairs ever again."

A small, hard smile appeared on his mother's lips. "So, you *are* going to marry Elizabeth—"

"Eliza. Recall, she likes to be called Eliza."

"Eliza will become an admirable viscountess in time. With me at her side to guide her—"

She stopped mid-flow as his wife walked into the stable yard, leading Romeo.

"What. Are. You. Wearing?"

Eliza cast him a wary look, but the wide grin on his face seemed to reassure her. "A pair of Beau's breeches."

Lady Harting clapped her hands over her ears as though offended by the word and he tried not to laugh. It was probably wrong of him, but he was enjoying his mother's discomfort.

"Now, where was I?" he asked. "Ah yes. You were offering your guidance to Eliza, but it won't be necessary. You have forfeited any right to interfere with our lives. Mrs Allett will teach her how things are done at the Park in the same way that Harris is teaching me about the estate. We'll make mistakes and laugh about them together. And there *will* be horses here again. Lots of horses."

"You will fail. Neither of you has any firmness of purpose…"

The rumble of laughter Beau had been trying to suppress worked its way up from his chest until he couldn't contain it. To suggest Eliza had no pluck was too ridiculous for words.

He burst out laughing, putting his mother out of countenance. Her self-assurance faded the longer he laughed.

"Horses will be the death of you, just like they were for your father."

"Another lie? Mrs Allett told me the truth. You knew the fall didn't kill him, and yet you still blamed his horse, and justified selling his entire stable. But he left me a greater legacy. His love of horses is in my blood."

Eliza raised her eyebrows at him. "You know what you must do."

Beau nodded. "I forgive you, Mother—"

"I don't need your forgiveness," she said, spitting out her words like poisoned arrows as if this rejection had the power to injure him.

"But I need to forgive you. Eliza told me I must. I learned from her that resentment eats you up like a cankerous worm and, if left unresolved, it can destroy you. I forgive you for stealing Romeo, for the hit on my head, even for playing on Eliza's emotions, making her think I was dying. That is the hardest thing to forgive, but for her sake, I will."

There. He had said it. And he meant it. And now he let it go.

A weight seemed to drop from his shoulders as the words of the Lord's prayer slipped into his mind—*forgive us our trespasses, as we forgive those who trespass against us.*

"I believe we could have been reconciled much more quickly if only we had talked to each other," said Eliza, glaring sideways at him.

He gave his bride a knowing look in return. "Absolutely. It is dangerous to make assumptions, isn't it, my dear?"

"Yes, it is. Especially when we're questioning the other's motivation," Eliza said, smirking in his direction.

Lady Harting cleared her throat. They turned away from each other with some reluctance and looked at her.

Beau had never seen her look so nonplussed. She was not used to being ignored.

Come to think of it, he was not sure he had ever dared ignore her before, but now, he was more concerned about Eliza's feelings than he was with what his parent thought.

With an inner sense of pride, he realised his own confidence had spilled over to Eliza, who no longer seemed afraid of her aunt.

Together, they were strong. A united front. Without taking his eyes off his mother's face, he grasped his wife's hand with his own and gave it a reassuring squeeze.

The effect on Lady Harting was ludicrous. Her mouth dropped open, and her eyes glazed over. "You are in love."

Beau gave her a sheepish grin. "Wonderful, isn't it? I realised the night Romeo was stolen—"

"You mean you were going to marry Eliza even if you won the wager?"

"Yes, and I wish you hadn't intervened, because she thought she was setting me free by risking her life for me riding my horse to victory—"

Lady Harting's face turned pale. "She what?"

"Oops! I forgot you didn't know she was my jockey."

"Dressed"—his mother waved her hand in Eliza's direction—"like that?"

Eliza nodded. "Yes—but don't boast about it. Beau wouldn't like it."

"This is most unexpected. I have been grossly mistaken about your character. A viscountess would never behave in such a manner." She locked eyes with her son. "Beaumont, you cannot marry this...hussy. I forbid it."

Beau's expression hardened and his tone turned icy. "Don't you *ever* talk to my wife that way again."

"Your *wife*?"

He put his arm around Eliza's shoulders. "Yes. We were married last night."

"But I forbid it."

"Apart from the fact that I'm of age and do not have to bow to your dictates, you're too late. You put the special licence into my hand yourself. Your eagerness to see us wed gave us the means and Eliza's father performed the ceremony late yesterday afternoon. And now, if you'll excuse us, my wife and I are going riding. Will you join us for breakfast?"

Lady Harting scowled. "I will not eat with you."

"As you wish. One more thing. Don't *ever* enter my bedchamber again without knocking."

A fiery blush suffused his mother's face as she hurried away.

"You were magnificent."

Eliza pulled his head toward her and fixed her lips on his. It was some time before they broke apart.

"Shall we ride?" he asked, glancing at their mounts.

Eliza tutted. "Anyone would think you were obsessed."

"I am," he said, kissing her again. "With you."

# Epilogue

## BEDDINGTON, SURREY, FOUR MONTHS LATER

"ARE YOU NEARLY FINISHED?" Beau asked. "Romeo is getting restless."

Eliza glanced past him to the racehorse, who tossed his head and snorted, but then became stock-still. The same could not be said of her fidgety husband, who stood sandwiched between them.

"Not just Romeo," she said.

William peered over his easel. "Ten more minutes should do it."

Eliza tried to calm the fluttering in her stomach. Time was running out, and she hadn't yet found the right words. The longer she delayed, the harder it became. If only she could predict how he would react.

There was only one way to find out. "I—"

"You didn't warn me how long I'd have to pose motionless for this portrait," Beau said, interrupting her.

"I thought you wouldn't mind, as we were together."

"You forget, I'm not supposed to do this." He leaned over and stole a kiss.

"It will take longer if you keep moving," her brother said in a matter-of-fact tone, peering over his easel at them.

Beau sighed and resumed his stance. "Sorry."

"At least I persuaded Will to paint us in front of the house this time."

"Ha! We couldn't very well include Romeo in the picture if we were in the drawing room, though I should have liked to see Mrs Allett's face if we had. I daresay she wouldn't have batted an eyelid. Anyway, what do you mean—*this time?* I'll be blowed if I'll let you talk me into having my portrait painted again."

Eliza pouted in a way she knew her husband couldn't resist. "What, never? I've set my heart on having a family portrait to hang in the gallery."

"Don't look at me like that if you want me to stand still. It's bad enough you're wearing that scarlet riding habit. I'll never forget the day you first wore it—"

"And how wet I got landing in the stream in a most indecorous way."

"I was remembering how plucky you were, and how comfortable your company was compared to Miss Whitlow's, but most of all, how tempted I was to kiss you after you'd fallen in the river."

"Perhaps I should have let you."

"Perhaps you should," he said, shooting her a look which sent the heat rushing to her face.

"See what you've done. William will have to paint me with bright red cheeks now."

"And your dimple," said Beau, kissing the small indent on her chin. "I insist he paints you with the dimple. Do you hear that, William?"

"I have painted Eliza once or twice before, Beau. I could draw her face from memory if I wanted. Do you know it that well?"

Her husband shot her a wicked look. "Better, as I've kissed every inch."

"Not a desire I share. I'd rather paint a pretty pair of lips than kiss them—particularly when they're my sister's."

"What? No lady love in your life?"

William paused, holding his paintbrush in the air. "No—but what's the rush? My grand passion is for my art, not for any woman, and I don't see that changing anytime soon. Too many pretty faces to paint."

"Well?" Eliza asked Beau, as her brother lowered his eyes to his canvas. "Will you agree to a family portrait?"

Her husband huffed. "Why would you want to do it again? Don't tell me you're enjoying this."

"No. I admit it's tedious. I've never enjoyed standing still for long, but I'd love to have a picture like the one of your parents, with your father balancing you on his knee. Please?"

"I suppose so, seeing as you asked me so nicely—though I daresay your brother will be in so much demand by then that you'll have difficulty securing him to paint it."

"Oh, I doubt that."

"What?" said Beau. "Don't you think he'll become a famous portrait painter?"

"Maybe—but not by next year."

"Next year?"

"Yes. Though I suppose we could wait—"

"You mean...?"

Eliza nodded. "Yes. Next spring."

Her heart stood still as his mouth fell open and all the colour drained out of her husband's cheeks. A wealth of emotions flitted over his countenance—disbelief, incredulity, fear, excitement.

As her words sunk in, his eyes grew wide, and the corners of his mouth turned upward until an enormous grin covered his face.

Beau let out a whoop, and as he took her in his arms and swung her around, all Eliza's fears about telling him her news vanished.

Just as suddenly, he put her back on her feet, a guilty look on his features.

"Sorry. I got carried away. I don't want to hurt the baby. There's so much I don't know, Eliza. It's...scary."

"I understand, but we'll learn together."

"Yes. We will."

"Are you two going to stand still so I can finish this portrait or not? I accept the commission in advance, though how any child of yours is going to be able to sit still for long enough to be painted beats me."

With a last squeeze of her hand, Beau resumed his pose and a wave of relief swept over Eliza as a new peace settled in her heart.

As soon as William looked down at his canvas again, Beau turned to the horse beside him.

"Do you hear that, Romeo? I'm going to be a father."

<h1 style="text-align:center">Author's Note</h1>

I hope you've enjoyed reading Beau and Eliza's story as much as I've enjoyed writing it.

Although a work of fiction, I've tried to make the historical detail and language as accurate as possible, based on my research at the time of writing. You'll find more information on the history behind the story in the glossary and historical notes.

The only fact I'm aware of changing is replacing the real rector of West Meon with my fictional Mr Merry.

A huge thank you to my editors, Abigail Flynn and my husband, Andrew, for all their feedback. My thanks also go to Helen Knowles and Philippa Jane Keyworth for their advice on how to get the horsey bits right—a major task for a non-horsey person. Any mistakes that remain are my own.

My thanks also go to you, my readers. I'm so glad you've found my books.

If you enjoyed reading this story, please leave a rating or review on Goodreads or wherever you bought this book. This encourages me and helps others find my stories. Thank you in advance.

# Glossary and Historical Notes

**Adam, Robert**: Robert Adam (1728–1792) was a Neoclassical architect and interior designer. He was one of the most influential Georgian architects.

**Admiral Nelson, The**: A public house in Whitechapel run by pugilist Daniel Mendoza.

**Almack's Assembly Rooms:** Almack's was situated in King Street, St James's. During the Regency era, the rooms were governed by lady patronesses who restricted entry to those members of the gentry and aristocracy who gained their approval, and it was necessary to have a voucher issued by one of these ladies to buy tickets to attend. Here, a young lady demonstrated her suitability as a marriage partner to prospective husbands, giving Almacks the nickname of the *Marriage Mart*.

**Assembly rooms**: A venue for balls and other social gatherings.

**Austen, Jane**: Jane Austen (1775–1817) was the author of six novels, including *Pride and Prejudice*. She grew up in Steventon, Hampshire, where her father was rector, and from 1809, she returned to the county to live in Chawton, near Alton. Eliza's father, Mr Merry, is the fictional rector of nearby West Meon, so I have imagined a relationship between the two families.

Miss Austen's words in Chapter 9 are inspired by her writing, especially *Emma*, and a line from a letter she wrote in 1808: "I consider everybody as having a right to marry *once* in their lives for love, if they can."

**Astley's Amphitheatre:** A popular arena for equestrian spectacles sited near Westminster Bridge. The *Times* on 27 April 1811 advertised that evening's show as *The Tyrant Saracen and the Noble Moor*.

**Backgammon**: A board game for two people.

**Balaam's donkey**: The story of Balaam's donkey can be found in Numbers 22 in the Bible. God enabled the donkey to speak to her foolish master, who had failed to see the angel blocking his way.

**Barouche**: A four-wheeled carriage which could accommodate four people on two seats facing each other and had a single, foldable hood which could be raised to protect those travelling in the forward-facing seat.

**Bath coating**: A type of fine woollen cloth.

**Beddington**: A village in Surrey, about 12 miles from Hyde Park, where Beau's fictional estate, Langcroft Park, is situated. Beddington is now part of the London Borough of Sutton.

**Beethoven**: Ludwig van Beethoven (1770–1827) was a German composer and pianist. He had composed more than 25 piano sonatas by 1811.

**Belcher, young**: Tom Belcher (1783–1854) was a noted pugilist. His elder, and more famous, brother Jem (1781–1811) was also a boxer.

**Benefit**: A benefit was a fundraising event for a particular cause, such as an actor, a boxer or a charity.

**Berkeley Square**: A residential garden square in Mayfair, in the West End of London. It was a fashionable address in the Regency.

**Bond Street**: A fashionable place to shop in Mayfair, in the West End of London.

**Bow Street Runner**: The Bow Street Runners were a professional police force established in Bow Street, London, by magistrate Henry Fielding in 1749. People outside London could request their help to track down offenders.

**Brace**: A protective arm guard used in archery. Made of stout leather, with a smooth surface, it is buckled around the bow arm, just above the wrist, to prevent the string from hurting it.

**Breakfast**: The first meal of the day, but not the first activity. Typically, people were up for an hour or two before gathering for breakfast. You can read more about a Regency breakfast on RegencyHistory.net.

**Breakneck**: Extremely hazardous; likely to end in a broken neck.

**British Gallery:** Also known as the British Institution for Promoting Fine Arts in the United Kingdom. It was set up to establish a school of British art and give British artists a place to display and sell their works. Jane Austen visited on 16 April 1811.

**Breeches**: A gentleman's garment like trousers that ended at the knees.

**Buckskin breeches**: A pair of soft leather breeches.

**Calling card**: A visiting or calling card was a small rectangular piece of card inscribed with a person's name and often, but not always, with their address.

**Cambridge**: Shorthand for Cambridge University. Oxford and Cambridge Universities were the only universities in England at the time of the Regency.

**Cap—to set one's cap at**: To set one's cap at someone meant trying to gain their affection. It often referred to a woman doing everything possible to obtain a marriage proposal from a particular gentleman.

**Chaise**: A carriage, typically with a single seat for two people.

**Chaise longue**: A low sofa, long enough for the sitter to stretch out their legs on. It has an arm at one end and usually a low back that becomes shallower toward the end without an arm.

**Chaperon**: A female companion for an unmarried lady.

**Cheshire cat**: The Cheshire cat and his proverbial grin dates back to 1770.

**Chicken-hearted**: Fearful, cowardly.

**Corinthian set**: A group of fashionable gentlemen who excelled in sport.

**Cloak bag**: A portmanteau; a bag in which clothes are carried.

**Curricle**: A light carriage with two wheels driven by its owner. The most fashionable curricles were pulled by a pair of carefully matched horses.

**Derby**: The Epsom Derby is a famous horse race, founded by the 12th Earl of Derby in 1780. It is a flat race for 3-year-old colts and fillies run over a distance of one and a half miles.

**Dowry**: The money, goods or estate settled on a woman which she brings to her husband on their marriage.

**Drawing room**: Short for withdrawing room. Ladies retired to the drawing room after dinner, leaving the gentlemen at the table to imbibe stronger drinks, such as port. It was the sitting room where the gentry received visitors.

**Enthusiast**: A disparaging term used of someone who took their religion seriously. In his *Dictionary* (1785), Samuel Johnson described an enthusiast as: "One who vainly imagines a private revelation; one who has a vain confidence in his intercourse with God."

**Epsom**: A village in Surrey. Epsom Downs is the site of the racecourse where the Epsom Derby is run.

**Euston, Lord**: Henry FitzRoy (1790-1863), later 5th Duke of Grafton, was styled Earl of Euston from 1811 to 1844. He was unmarried in 1811.

**Fighting shy**: Avoiding someone or something, like an army reluctant to face the enemy.

**Fives Court**: A popular venue for sparring matches between pugilists. It was located in St Martin's Street, Leicester Fields—the area around today's Leicester Square.

**Four Horse Club**: Also known as the Whip Club. It was a gentlemen's driving club. The club had an official costume which included a distinctive blue and yellow striped waistcoat.

**Gig**: A two-wheeled carriage, driven by its owner, and usually pulled by a single horse.

**Greatcoat**: A gentleman's overcoat. The most fashionable greatcoats in the Regency were full length and had several capes hanging from the shoulders.

**Guinea**: A gold coin worth 21 shillings or one pound and one shilling.

**Half-boots**: Flat, ankle-high boots that laced up at the front or the side.

**Hall's *Haemon and Antigone***: Listed in *The Literary Panorama* as one of the paintings on display at the British Gallery in 1811. William Merry's criticism of the picture is taken from the review.

**Hamlet**: A small village.

**Hampshire Ladies' Charity**: As far as I know, this is a fictional charity, but it is typical of the many charities set up to support charitable causes, such as lying-in hospitals, orphans, and schools.

**Hilton's *Entombing of Christ***: Listed in *The Literary Panorama* as one of the paintings on display at the British Gallery in 1811. Eliza Merry's criticism of the picture is taken from the review.

**Hyde Park**: A large park on the western edge of Mayfair. During the Regency, it was a popular place to promenade on foot, ride on horseback, or drive a carriage in the afternoon.

**Inexpressibles**: A euphemism used by ladies to refer to a gentleman's breeches or pantaloons.

**Jersey, Lady**: Sarah Child Villiers, Countess of Jersey (1785–1867) was a leading figure in Regency society, and one of the patronesses of Almack's Assembly Rooms.

**King's Theatre**: A theatre in Haymarket dedicated to Italian Opera. Also known as the Haymarket Opera House or the Italian Opera House.

***La Belle Assemblée***: *La Belle Assemblée, or Bell's Court and Fashionable Magazine addressed particularly to the ladies*, was a fashionable monthly ladies' periodical in the Regency. It was particularly popular for its fashion plates.

**Lady**: In the British peerage, the title of Lady is given to the wives of peers below the rank of duke, and to the daughters of dukes, marquesses and earls. The general rule is that wives use the designation Lady with their husband's title eg Lady Harting, and daughters use the designation Lady with their Christian name and surname eg Lady Caroline Merry.

However, when the daughter of a duke, marquess or earl marries a commoner, or a lesser peer who has not yet inherited his title, she retains her original designation of Lady with her Christian name and her husband's surname. When Lady Frances Merry married Mr Whitlow, the heir to a barony, she became known as Lady Frances Whitlow. When her husband inherits his title, she will be known as Lady Whitlow.

You can find further information about the use of titles on RegencyHistory.net.

**Landau**: A four-wheeled carriage which could accommodate four people on two seats facing each other. It had two foldable hoods, which could be closed or rolled down, depending on the weather. Something akin to a Georgian convertible!

**Leading-strings**: "Strings by which children, when they learn to walk, are held from falling." Samuel Johnson's *Dictionary* (1785).

**Lily-livered**: Cowardly. From Shakespeare's *Macbeth*.

**Lottery**: The State Lottery was run regularly, and people could buy tickets or shares for a chance to win a huge cash prize, or a share of it. The *Times* advertised a top prize in the February 1811 lottery of £20,000.

**Mail coach**: A fast, guarded coach which carried the post along post roads. Usually pulled by four horses, which were changed regularly to maintain a good speed. Mail coaches were not obliged to pay tolls, so turnpike keepers had to ensure the gate was open in readiness for them to speed through without stopping.

**Marriage licence**: There were two types of marriage licence—a common licence and a special licence. Usually issued by the local bishop, a common licence enabled a couple to be married immediately in the church of the parish where one of them had been resident for at least four weeks.

To marry in the chapel of Langcroft Park, Beau and Eliza needed a special licence. This was much rarer and more expensive and could only be issued by the Archbishop of Canterbury. It allowed a couple to marry anywhere and at any time.

**Mews**: A group of stables built around an open yard or along an alley, often with rooms above, situated behind or near to fashionable town residences.

**Midsummer's Day**: 24 June, the second quarter day of the year. The quarter days mark the beginning of each quarter of the year, and were regarded as days for settling debts, such as rent and wages. Contracts of employment, leases and the like typically began and ended on quarter days.

**Morning calls**: Short visits of ceremony paid to your acquaintances. Despite the name, they were normally made in the afternoon, between one and four o'clock.

**Newmarket**: Comprising two parishes, one either side of the Suffolk-Cambridgeshire border, Newmarket is home to the Newmarket Racecourse. The two race meetings that Beau attended were the Craven meeting from 15 April and the first spring meeting from 29 April.

**Neoclassical**: A style of architecture inspired by classical antiquity that developed from the Palladian style, applying the rules of symmetry more freely and incorporating more aspects of Ancient Greek art, such as cameos.

**Orgeat**: A refreshing drink made from barley or almonds and orange flower water.

**Ostler**: A man working in the stables of an inn.

**Pantaloons**: Long, close-fitting trousers worn by gentlemen of fashion in the Regency.

**Pelisse**: A long, fitted coat.

**Phaeton**: A light, four-wheeled carriage that was driven by its owner rather than by a coachman.

**Piquet**: A two-player card game.

**Post-haste**: As quickly as possible. Literally, with the speed of the post.

**Postilion**: A person who rode one of the horses pulling a carriage. A postilion-driven carriage had no coachman, but was guided by one or more postilions riding the nearside horses. A postilion could also work alongside a coachman, particularly if the coach were being pulled by three pairs of horses. A postilion was also known as a post-boy.

**Post road**: A road used by those delivering the post. There was a system of inns or post houses at stages along a post road where horses and postilions or post-boys could be hired and replaced. This enabled travel to take place at the highest possible speed by continually refreshing the horses.

**Purgatory**: A state of mental or emotional suffering.

**Regency**: The Regency period was the nine years from 1811 to 1820 when the Prince of Wales, the future George IV, ruled as Prince Regent during the last illness of his father, George III.

**Regent, Prince**: George, Prince of Wales, later George IV (1762–1830), was the eldest son of George III. He was recklessly extravagant and dissolute. He ruled as Prince Regent (1811–1820) during the last illness of his father.

**Reel**: A lively country dance.

**Reticule**: A lady's purse or small bag designed to carry around personal items that used to be kept in a pocket. Pockets became impractical when dresses became more streamlined, and so a reticule acted like a portable pocket.

**Robe pelisse**: A loose wrapping coat. *Ackermann's Repository* for March 1811 included a fashion plate for a robe pelisse.

**Rout**: An assembly or 'at home' on a large scale. The measure of success seemed to be that it was a squeeze rather than anything else. The guests did not sit, but moved from room to room, often with no entertainment provided. They usually began at 10pm or even later and lasted into the early hours of the morning.

**Scratch—to come up to scratch**: In boxing, the scratch was the line drawn between two fighters which they had to come up to at the start of each round, or they'd lose. Used figuratively, it means brought to the point of proposing.

**Season**: The season was the time of year when the upper classes went to London to socialise with each other. It was the best opportunity to meet a suitable marriage partner. During the Regency period, it typically ran from November or January through to June or July, roughly coinciding with the sitting of Parliament.

**Seat**: In horse-riding, this refers to the way a person positions their body while riding a horse.

**Set-down**: A snub, often by a person of some importance to someone of inferior social standing.

**Shako**: Inspired by headgear worn by the British Army, the shako was a tall, cylindrical, flat-topped hat, often with a peak and decorated with eg feathers and rosettes.

**Sloane Street**: Jane Austen's brother Henry lived in London with his wife Eliza. In 1811, their home was 64, Sloane Street, which is situated south of Hyde Park. In her letters, Jane Austen gives details of the party Eliza gave in April 1811, to which over 80 people were invited, and the excellence of the musical entertainment.

**Smallpox inoculation**: A way of preventing smallpox, by introducing the disease directly into the skin. Smallpox was a serious, contagious disease which was fatal in around a third of cases, where the patient had not been inoculated. Inoculation usually led to a less severe, more localised, infection, but could still be fatal.

**Smelling salts**: An aromatic substance used for treating headaches and reviving faintness.

**Steward**: A person appointed to manage another's affairs, such as their estate.

**Spillikins**: A children's game played with a pile of small wooden sticks. The object is to extract as many sticks as possible from the pile without moving the others.

**Spring—to spring your horses**: In relation to driving a carriage, to spring your horses is to drive them at high speed.

**Spunk**: Courage, pluck, mettle.

**St George's, Hanover Square**: The parish church of Mayfair, and hence the most fashionable church in London during the Regency.

**Stucco panels**: Fine plaster moulded into decorative panels.

**Superfine**: A type of fine woollen cloth.

**Swan, The**: A coaching inn in Alton, Hampshire.

**Sweetmeats**: Items of confectionery; fruits preserved with sugar.

**Tattersall's Repository:** Situated near Hyde Park Corner, it was the premier venue for the sale of horses and carriages by auction. There was also a subscribers' room where horse racing bets were settled.

**Tollgate**: A turnpike gate which blocked the way to travellers to make them stop and pay the toll for the stretch of road they were using.

**Travelling chariot**: A four-wheeled, postilion-driven carriage used for long journeys with a single forward-facing internal seat for two people. It was driven by one or more postilions rather than by a coachman sitting on a coach box which would obscure the travellers' view. Fresh horses could be hired at inns along the post road.

**Turnpike**: A tollgate or a road with a tollgate. Turnpike Trusts were set up by Acts of Parliament during the 18th and 19th centuries in order to improve the state of the roads. Trusts maintained individual stretches of road and had the right to levy tolls on road users to finance this. A turnpike gate blocked the way to travellers to make them stop and pay the toll for the stretch of road that they were using.

**Vent your spleen**: Freely express your ill-temper.

**Vinaigrette**: A small container holding an aromatic substance, such as smelling salts soaked in vinegar, used for treating headaches, reviving faintness and masking unpleasant smells.

**Wallflower**: A lady who sits by the wall at parties because she lacks partners.

**Waxy**: A racehorse owned by Sir Ferdinand Poole which won the Epsom Derby in 1793.

**Weymouth**: A fashionable seaside resort on the south coast of England which rose to importance through the repeated visits of King George III. Its sheltered bay makes it suitable for sea bathing all year around.

**Whicker**: The sound a horse makes when it recognises someone. I am told that it is the best sound a horsey person can hear.

**White's Club:** An exclusive club for gentlemen based in St James's Street, where gentlemen could discuss business or politics, meet with friends for conversation or cards, and have a meal. White's had a famous betting book that has been preserved. Members placed bets on all manner of things, from predicting the sex of a lady's baby to whether Napoleon would be successful.

# About the Author

Rachel Knowles loves happy endings. She first read Jane Austen's *Pride and Prejudice* at the age of thirteen and fell in love, not only with Mr Darcy, but with the entire Regency period.

She regularly gives talks on the Regency period, based on her extensive research, and is co-author of the popular Regency History blog.

Rachel lives in the beautiful Georgian seaside town of Weymouth, Dorset, on the south coast of England, with her husband, Andrew. They have four daughters and a growing number of grandchildren.

# Let's Keep in Touch

For book news, special offers and recommendations, sign up to Rachel's newsletter on her website regencyhistory.net/rachelknowles

# Follow Rachel on Social Media

amazon.com/author/rachelknowles

bookbub.com/authors/rachel-knowles

goodreads.com/rachelknowles

instagram.com/rachelknowlesauthor

facebook.com/rachelknowlesauthor

# Books by Rachel Knowles

**The Merry Romances**
*A Perfect Match* (Book 1)
*A Reason for Romance* (Book 2)
*A Single Obsession* (Book 3)
*A Misguided Devotion* (Book 4)

·♥·♥·♥·♥·♥·

**Women of Weymouth**
*Miss Harding's Hope: A Christmas Regency Romance*
*Miss Vincent's Vow* (Book 1)

·♥·♥·♥·♥·♥·

**Multi-author Series**
*Engaging Miss Shaw* (Hearts of the Hall)
*The Disappointed Daughter* (Cousins of Cavendish Square)

·♥·♥·♥·♥·♥·

**Historical Non-fiction**
*What Regency Women Did For Us*

Find out more about Rachel's books on her website:
RegencyHistory.net/RachelKnowles